THE OUTRAGEOUS EXPLOITS OF JERRELL LANDISH

WIZARDOM LEGENDS

JEFFREY L. KOHANEK

ALSO BY JEFFREY L. KOHANEK

Fate of Wizardoms

Eye of Obscurance

Balance of Magic

Temple of the Oracle

Objects of Power

Rise of a Wizard Queen

A Contest of Gods

* * *

Fate of Wizardoms Boxed Set: Books 1-3

Fate of Wizardoms Box Set: Books 4-6

Fall of Wizardoms

God King Rising

Legend of the Sky Sword

Curse of the Elf Queen

Shadow of a Dragon Priest

Advent of the Drow

A Sundered Realm

Fall of Wizardoms Boxed Set: Books 1-3

Runes of Issalia

The Buried Symbol

The Emblem Throne

An Empire in Runes

Rogue Legacy: Runes of Issalia Prequel

* * *

Runes of Issalia Bonus Box

Wardens of Issalia

A Warden's Purpose

The Arcane Ward:

An Imperial Gambit

A Kingdom Under Siege

* * *

Wardens of Issalia Boxed Set

THE SHOALS
Zakkan
Jinnaka
Ryxx
HASSAKAN
Nintaka
Sarmak
Antari
Pri
Prianza
THE FRACTURED LANDS
Anker
Nandalla
Cerulcos Sea
KYRANNI
Denalla
Straemor
Harken
Balmor
BALMORIA
Zialis
Dorban
GHEALDOR
Tiadd
Fastella
Westhold
Lamor
Tangor
Starmuth
Lionne
CORDIUM
Cor Cordium
Novecai Sea
Fralyn
ORENTH
THE GREAT PEAKS
THE MURLANDS
Eleighton
Yor's Point
Severan
FARROWEN
Shear
Marquithe
Horizial Ocean
Illustan
PALLANAR
Tiamalyn
Grakal
Souton
Norstan
Endover
Shurick's Bay
Rykestan
The Frost Forest
The Eight
Wizardoms
THE FROZEN WASTE

THIEF FOR HIRE

CHAPTER I
WAKE UP CALL

Heavy thumps against the door caused Jerrell to stir. He blinked and pressed his palm against his forehead. It pounded in time with the beat of his heart. His jaw was sore, his knuckles bruised with raw flesh visible.

"Landish!" a woman's voice called from beyond the door. "Get up! Now!"

"What does she want this time?" he muttered to himself before sitting up and peering around the room through bleary eyes.

A sliver of daylight shone through a narrow gap in the curtains. The sunbeam formed a bright stripe on the closed door. The room was a modest size with a table, chairs, a vanity, a chest, and a bed big enough for two. Clothing lay scattered across the floor—a black coat, a dark blue tunic with the collar torn, brown breeches, a pair of black boots, and pale small clothes. He lifted the covers from his lap and realized he was naked. Through a haze, he recalled the prior evening—a game of dice, tankards of ale, shots of swoon, a scuffle, an aggressive woman whose hands soon found their way inside his clothing...

With a yank, Jerrell pulled back the pile of blankets and found himself alone in the bed.

"When did she leave?" he frowned. "I don't think I even got her name."

Thump. Thump. Thump. The woman outside continued to pound on the door. "Landish!"

Sharri was unlikely to leave until she'd had her say. He sighed in resignation.

Holding a blanket to cover his midriff, Jerrell stood, and the room spun. He staggered to the door, his grip on the handle the only thing keeping him upright. After unlocking it, he eased the door open and peered around it.

The woman in the corridor shoved the door wider. It struck Jerrell in the head and sent him sprawling. The blanket lay beside him, leaving his naked body completely exposed.

A stoutly-built woman stood in the doorway, her fists on her broad hips and a hint of gray in her auburn hair.

She arched a brow while glaring down at him. "I see young women visit your room for reasons other than your sly tongue. While I can appreciate a pretty man as much as any woman, you may want to cover yourself."

Jerrell grabbed the blanket and pulled it over his groin before stumbling to his feet. He sat on the bed, touching his tender forehead. "Good morning, Sharri."

"Don't 'Good morning' me," she snapped. "I'll not allow you to charm me this time...even if you are naked."

"Whatever this is about..." he groaned.

"You know what this is about!" she shrieked and pointed down the corridor. "The fight you started last night will cost me far more than a few silvers. Two tables, six chairs, and a few bar stools are broken beyond repair. The front window is shattered, and the floorboards are bloodstained."

"The floorboards were already bloodstained."

"Not this badly." She crossed her arms, her plentiful chest bulging against them. "I want you out."

Jerrell sighed. "Listen. I am sorry for what happened, but it was not my fault. Some men are not made to play dice and do not deal well with losing. I even offered to buy those sailors a drink, but they would not have it. Instead, they demanded their coin back...a request I denied." He shrugged. "Those men started the fight. I merely defended myself."

"By knocking all four men unconscious?"

"It is much harder for them to stab me if they are asleep. Would you prefer I use my blades on them? I guarantee you would have had more than a few bloodspots to clean up."

"If you'd killed them, you likely would have found yourself in the city jail."

He shrugged again. "It wouldn't be the first time I visited a cell. Regardless, if you seek compensation for your damage, find the sailors. It was their fault, not mine."

"It is mid-morning, Jerrell. Those sailors are likely on a ship that has already set sail and is well beyond my reach. You, however, sit here, naked and hungover, in my inn." She held out her palm. "I want five gold pieces to cover the damages."

He nearly choked. "Five? The window and every piece of the furniture in your taproom wouldn't account for *three* gold pieces, let alone five."

"The amount is not negotiable, Jerrell. I want five gold pieces, and then, I want you out of here. As much as I like you, the trouble you cause is no longer worth your presence." She gestured toward the five throwing blades sticking out of the post in the middle of the room. "Your knives have drawn the last blood in my place."

"You didn't seem to think so little of my presence or my blades when I stopped those bandits from robbing you last spring."

"Times change, Jerrell, and when I look back on it, I cannot help but wonder if those men were here because of you. Until you showed, scoundrels like that rarely found my taproom."

Jerrell sighed. "Fine." He bent and picked up his coat. He reached into the inside pockets. His lockpicks and weighted dice were still there, but he couldn't feel the coins he had stored with them. He frowned. "Hold on."

Dropping to his knees, he turned around, slid his hand under the mattress, and located the hole he had cut. His hand felt inside but found only feathers. Alarmed, he dug around with similar results.

"I've been robbed." The realization hit him like a lump of lead to his gut.

Sharri guffawed. "*You* were robbed? I find that pleasantly ironic."

Jerrell stood and spun toward her, forgetting his blanket in his anger. "You don't understand! I had fifty gold in my possession!"

The woman gaped at him. "Fifty gold? I have run this inn for twelve years and have yet to collect fifty gold pieces. How could you possess that much wealth? Did you rob a wizard lord?"

Is she insane? Not even I *would steal from a wizard lord...I don't think.* He considered what to tell her and chose the truth, or, well, a fraction of it. "I sold an enchanted item to some old coot. Obtaining it nearly cost me my life. It was protected by a towering monster with the body of a man and the head of a bull."

She guffawed again. "Do you think me daft? I've heard plenty of wild tales from you, but that is ridiculous." The woman shook her head. "Who would ever believe such nonsense!"

"It is true."

Sharri held a palm up. "Save it, Jerrell. If you don't have the coin to repay me, I will be forced to call for the city guard and have you arrested for the destruction of my property."

He stepped toward her. "Please. I have been here for the better part of a year. You know me, Sharri. I will pay you back. I just need a few days."

She narrowed her eyes at him. "You promise to repay me?"

He could just flee the city, and he considered it, but he liked the inn keeper and felt responsible for her situation. "Give me five days, and I will get your gold."

The woman crossed her arms and considered his offer. "I will give you one week, but when it ends, you had best produce the coin or you will find yourself in the city jail." She glanced down and smiled. "In the meantime, try to keep that thing under control. The next time you wind up with a strange woman, you may wake up dead rather than broke."

She spun around and pulled the door closed. The room fell quiet.

Jerrell bent over, grabbed his smallclothes, and began to dress. Nearly a year had passed since he had used his skills for something other than drinking, gambling, and bedding eager women. It was time to seek out a mark and form a plan. *But first, I need water. Lots of water.*

THE MID-MORNING SUN shone down on Yor's Point, its heat causing Jerrell to walk down the shaded side of the street rather than remove his coat. He seldom took it off when he was awake.

While autumn had claimed the cooler, southern reaches of the Eight Wizardoms, the streets of Yor's Point were warm and thick with visitors. As a port city on the Novecai Sea, the year-long mild weather made it a popular destination for sailors and travelers alike, despite being off the well-tread paths that connected the Eight Wizardoms. The weather, the women, and the views were all reasons Jerrell had decided to settle there. But now, with all his coin stolen, his plan to retire young was in disarray. *I'll just have to find another way to regain my wealth.*

The street ended at a small square with a green-tiled fountain in the center. Carts lined the edges of the square, each selling foods or wares to hungry and needful buyers. Clusters of people stood before each cart while others crossed the square. The scent of spiced meat wafted over, reminding Jerrell he had yet to break his fast.

He altered his path toward a cart loaded with sausage links wrapped in canvas. Strings of exposed links dangled from a wooden rod over the cart, clearly intended to entice hungry shoppers. The rod rested in V-shaped cuts in the top of two posts rising from the cart. A pair of stray dogs sat near the cart, whining at the vendor who dutifully ignored them.

Jerrell approached the cart. "How much for a sausage?"

"One copper each," said the man.

Feigning to search for a coin, Jerrell looked down at his pockets while backing into the side of the cart. He looked up, intentionally hitting his head on the end of the rod and knocking it from its perch. The rod fell to the ground, taking the links of sausages with it. The dogs rushed in.

"No!" the vendor shrieked.

The man shoved one dog aside, but the eager pooch had already chomped down one sausage link. The surrounding crowd watched as the distraught vendor scrambled to reclaim his fallen sausages. With the others distracted, Jerrell casually grabbed a canvas wrap from the man's cart and slipped behind the baker's cart beside him. The woman who owned the cart was so focused on the sausage vendor's tug of war with two hungry dogs that Jerrell easily snuck a hard roll from her basket and continued through the crowd.

When Jerrell reached an uphill street, he unwrapped the bundle to reveal a trio of sausages inside. He bit into one and found it spiced to his liking. He continued eating as he considered his situation.

Almost a year had passed since he had stolen anything significant. His last adventure, a dangerous quest to a long-forgotten castle in the mountains, had been a windfall and had yielded, he had thought, enough coin to set him up for life. Such was not to be. The woman from the prior evening had targeted him. Did she know about his secret stash?

Did I mention something I shouldn't have? "I am fond of telling stories," he spoke aloud. "Perhaps while I was deep in my cups..." He frowned, unsure. "Regardless, she played me."

Despite a night of consumption, the woman remained firmly entrenched in his mind. His memory was among his greatest assets. Her image danced in his head—blonde, gorgeous, and possessing the lean yet shapely body of a goddess, it was impossible to imagine turning away her advances.

He could go after the woman and attempt to reclaim what she stole...if he knew her name. As it stood, he might never see her again and could not afford to wait in the hope he might stumble across her. A casual glance through an open shop door allowed Jerrell to note a pair of men in his peripheral vision. *Are they trailing me?*

The men slowed when he slowed. At an intersection, he turned, and they followed. Acting as if nothing was amiss, Jerrell continued down the street and turned into the nearest alley. There, he tossed the remainder of his breakfast into a refuse-filled crate, keeping his unhurried pace. When he was halfway to the next street, he stopped suddenly. The clap of footsteps behind him stopped as well.

He spun to find two men wearing bright tunics and puffy trousers tucked into their boots. One had a bandage across the bridge of his nose, his swollen eyes black and blue. The other man had a nasty-looking scab on one side of his bald head. Both were bigger than Jerrell. The one with the broken nose held a club in his hand. A scimitar rested on the other man's hip.

Some people are slow to learn. Jerrell addressed them in a glib tone. "As I told you last night, you men are not my type. Stalking me will not entice me into your bedchamber."

"You are a wise-arse little bastard," the bald sailor growled. "Your tongue has caused you trouble for the last time. It'll be a pleasure to cut it out and silence you for good."

"My, my." Jerrell shook his head. "You two are persistent. I would have expected you to learn a lesson last night. At least your shipmates had the good sense to avoid another confrontation." A rustle from behind caused Jerrell to turn as two more sailors appeared at the end of the alley. "Or not."

One of the newcomers stood tall and lean with long black hair tied in a tail. The other had shorn hair and stood no taller than Jerrell but had twice his brawn. The tall one wore a cream-colored tunic unbuttoned to his stomach and the hilt of a sword stuck up from the long scabbard on his hip. The short sailor wore no shirt at all, his thick muscles bulging as he pounded his fist into his palm. Both men had bruises and cuts on their faces.

"Welcome to the party," Jerrell said. "Now, it will be an even fight."

CHAPTER 2
THE TALES OF DEAD MEN

From both directions, angry sailors stalked down the alley toward Jerrell.

"Stop!" Jerrell demanded.

All four men ceased their advance.

"I am warning you now." Jerrell's tone lacked humor. "I will not hold back this time. If you don't turn and leave, I *will* kill you."

The bald man said, "We will take our chances."

Metal sang as he drew his scimitar. A second later, the tall one pulled a rapier from his scabbard. Their advance resumed.

Jerrell said, "I warned you, so don't come complaining to me when you are dead." He waited a few breaths as the men continued their advance. When each group was no more than five strides away, he burst into action.

Crossing his hands, Jerrell drew the blades hidden up his sleeves and loosed them in rapid succession. The first hit the tallest sailor in the eye. The man staggered backward, dropped his rapier, and clutched at his face, but it was too late. He collapsed in a heap.

The brawny sailor jumped to the side as the second throwing knife came at him, striking his shoulder rather than his chest as Jerrell had intended. The man twisted with the blow and stumbled against the wall.

When the other two sailors charged, the bald one with the sword winding back, Jerrell darted toward the wall and leapt. The scimitar swept beneath him and struck the wall with a clang. Just before gravity claimed him, Jerrell drew his dagger and flipped, slicing as he fell. The blade cut through the swordsman's forearm, causing him to release his grip. His sword clattered against the cobblestone street, and Jerrell kicked it away.

The man with the bandaged nose made a desperate swing, his club sweeping straight toward Jerrell's head. Jerrell ducked. The club sped past and struck the bald sailor in the throat. Eyes bulging, the man collapsed. Jerrell lunged at the club-wielder with an upward thrust. The dagger drove beneath the man's ribs and up into his heart. The man stumbled back against the wall, taking Jerrell's dagger with him. The sailor coughed and crimson spittle sprayed from his mouth. He slid down the wall and fell still.

A blow from behind struck Jerrell's lower back, causing him to stagger and driving the wind from his lungs. He turned as the brawny man, Jerrell's blade still in his shoulder, launched a fist at his face. With an urgent tilt of his head, Jerrell avoided the worst of the blow. The sailor's fist clipped the side of his head and then struck the wall.

The world tilted as spots danced before Jerrell's eyes. He fell to one knee and pressed a hand flat against the ground to stabilize himself while gasping for air. As the spots cleared, he looked up and found the sailor holding his wrist, his face twisted in pain. The man's face turned red. He scooped up the now-abandoned scimitar and spun back around. Raising the sword with fury in his eyes, the sailor chopped down, intent on slicing Jerrell in half.

Jerrell's free hand found the top of his boot and the metal handle inside the cuff. He yanked it free and dove sideways to avoid the falling blade. Before he landed, he tossed the knife with an underhand flick. The scimitar struck the paved alley with a mighty clatter. Jerrell's blade plunged into the attacker's chin.

The scimitar fell to the street as the sailor staggered backward. He tripped over a fallen comrade and crashed to the ground, his head striking the cobblestone with a sickening crack. Jerrell climbed to his feet and surveyed the scene.

The four sailors all lay still, two of them staring toward the blue sky, the other two at a brick wall. Nobody blinked. Nobody moved.

"I warned you," he said, rubbing his sore back. "That punch hurt, but at least it wasn't my face or groin. I'd hate to disappoint my admirers." He chuckled at his own joke.

With a sigh, he squatted, pulled his throwing blade from the tall sailor's eye, and wiped it clean on the man's tunic before sliding it back up his sleeve. He collected his other blades and rifled through the sailors' clothing for valuables.

After his search yielded only a silver nose ring and three coppers, Jerrell exited the alley and headed uphill, toward the wealthier district of the city.

THE STREET GREW STEEPER until it became stairs. Jerrell ascended the steps that led away from the harbor and well above the rooftops of the buildings close to the harbor. Still, he continued, passing various shops.

A tailor busily measured a man while three others waited their turn. The jewelry shop stood empty apart from a jeweler with an odd spectacle strapped to his face. He sat on a stool holding a small hammer and pick. Another shop was filled with nothing but rugs as big as Jerrell's room at the inn.

Finally, the street opened to a sprawling square with the Obelisk of Devotion in the center. Made of alabaster bricks, the obelisk's base was thirty feet across, and it stood one hundred fifty feet tall. A three-story wall bounded the far side of the square. Yor's Castle, home of the high wizard, looked down from a hilltop inside those walls.

A dozen Orenthian soldiers dressed in green and brown leather armor milled about the area near the castle gate. Some soldiers held crossbows, but most wore swords in scabbards on their hips. Apart from the soldiers, only a handful of people occupied the square. It appeared like just another quiet afternoon until a man in black and green robes stomped through the gate in the castle wall and marched across the square with deliberate strides.

A wizard.

With curly brown hair and a handsome visage, the wizard appeared to be in his late twenties. However, his face was red, and a fire burned in his amber eyes.

An angry wizard. Best to avoid him.

Four guards trailed the wizard, all surrounding a finely dressed man with black hair and a mustache, its tips waxed and curled. The man wore a green doublet and gold breeches tucked into boots folded over at the top. Tiny emeralds studded the sides of the man's boots.

What a fop. Jerrell turned his attention toward the castle, his thoughts churning.

While the estate surely held sufficient gold for his purposes, it was an immense building and would take time to scout and prepare a plan. He required a less daunting target, so his gaze shifted to the building across the square from the castle.

A series of red, clay-tiled roofs, each wider than the one above, marked a distinct and non-pragmatic design. Round, fluted columns bordered the dark entrance at the top of the stairs. A line of people slowly filed into the building.

The Temple of Oren. Jerrell grinned. Like all religious institutions, the temple relied on donations, some of which were significant.

He slid into line and followed the old woman at the rear. Just as he was about to enter the building, a ruckus broke out in the alley beside the temple, drawing his attention.

The noise came from the group who had just exited the castle grounds. However, the four guards now bracketed the wizard. Across from them stood the fop, who held his palms up in appeal.

The fop begged, "Please, Paloun, you must believe me. I did not tell Jakins, I..."

The hair on Jerrell's arms suddenly stood on end, warning him of impending magic. The wizard extended a hand toward the fop, who suddenly floated five feet off the ground. The man kicked and screamed, but to no avail.

"For your betrayal, you will die, Helwin," the wizard sneered and thrust his arm forward.

A bolt of lightning shot from his hand and struck the levitating man in the chest, blasting him backward. He crashed into the temple with a sickening crack. His body slid to the ground and remained still. The wizard turned and strode down the alley, away from the square, with two of his guards in tow.

Jerrell descended the stairs and approached the dead man. Blood oozed from his ears and eyes.

The two remaining guards stood at his side.

"What did this man do?" Jerrell asked.

One of the guards grunted. "He exposed one of our master's secrets to High Wizard Jakins."

"So, the wizard killed him?"

The other guard said, "You must understand, Jakins is our master's lifelong rival. The secret involved his business and caused Jakins to benefit while our master paid dearly."

"Who is your master?"

"His name is Paloun."

Jerrell had heard the name and knew the wizard to be among the wealthiest in the district.

The guards each grabbed one of the dead man's arms and lifted him off the ground. His toes dragged across the cobblestones, his head flopping with each movement of his body.

This man worked for the wizard?"

"Yes. He was the wizard's...master of trade." The two guards carried the man toward the alley, which was now empty.

Jerrell stroked his sore, scruff-covered jaw while turning the information over in his head, which also still ached from his fight with the sailors. He quickly reached a conclusion. One man's demise was another's opportunity.

He rushed to catch up to the guards. "I would like to speak with your master."

The guards stopped and shared a questioning glance before one asked. "And why would he wish to speak to a young pup like you?"

"It appears there is a job opening. I have skills the wizard may find useful."

UNCOMMON

Jerrell emerged from the wooded trail and waited as Paloun's guards dumped the dead man into the back of a wagon. The guards paid the driver and began a climb up the long run of stairs to Paloun's estate while the wagon started down a long, winding gravel road leading toward the sea, a thousand feet below. There, it met another road that ran parallel to the shore and headed back to the city. Turning toward the stairs, Jerrell began the climb while surveying the hilltop mansion.

Made of white marble with fluted columns, numerous terraces, and clay-tiled rooftops, it was a sight to behold. Green ivy climbed trellises to either side of the main entrance, and sculpted shrubs lined the hillside below the building. While not as excessive as the castle, the manor was big enough to house half a dozen families.

Upon reaching the double doors at the top, a guard posted there opened a door while the other two led Jerrell inside. He stepped into a circular entry hall with a tapestry on one side and a curved stairwell rising up the other. White marble tiles covered the floors, and a chandelier made of wooden beams hung from chains connected to the ceiling three stories above.

One of the guards gestured toward the hilt on Jerrell's hip. "I'll need your dagger."

"I happen to be fond of this dagger."

"If you want to meet with Wizard Paloun, you'll need to remove all weapons first."

Jerrell gestured. "You both wear swords."

"Wizard Paloun trusts us to protect him."

"Fine." In a flash, Jerrell drew the dagger, flipped it into the air, and snatched the blade between his finger and thumb. He held it toward the guard, hilt first. "Here."

The man accepted the dagger and eyed the jeweled hilt. "Where did you get this?"

"You wouldn't believe me if I told you. You want the others as well?"

"Others?"

Quick as a whip, Jerrell's hands crossed and came away with a throwing blade in each hand.

The guard blinked. "Where'd those come from?"

"Hidden in my sleeves."

After a glance toward his comrade, the man accepted the two knives. "Any others?"

Squatting, Jerrell drew the throwing blades hidden in his boots. "I suggest you always check a man's boots. You never know what he might be hiding there." He placed the two knives in the guard's palm. His last knife remained hidden in his coat, between his shoulder blades. *Best to keep one blade just in case...*

The guard squinted at Jerrell. "You mentioned having talents the wizard might appreciate. Tell me those talents include more than hiding weapons on your person."

Jerrell held his arms out. "Look at me. The two of you are both a half head taller than I am and outweigh me by a fair margin. Someone like me must take precautions. The visible dagger is meant to make others think twice before targeting me. The throwing blades, well, those are for anyone dumb enough to come after me anyway."

The lead guard grunted. "Wait here." He looked at his companion. "Watch him. If he moves, run your sword through him."

As the first guard walked off, Jerrell turned toward the other man. "Is this how you treat all of your guests?"

"You are not our guest. In fact, we are going to claim we caught you attempting to break in. The wizard will decide your fate."

Jerrell snorted. "It figures." People were forever twisting events to suit their needs. It was among the truths Jerrell had unearthed in his twenty-two years.

Moments passed before a robed figure emerged from the doorway with the guard a stride behind him.

The wizard stopped two strides away with his arms crossed. "Who are you and why were you trying to sneak into my manor?"

"I am a master of trade, but I find myself lacking the coin needed to invest in such activities."

Paloun eyed Jerrell from head to toe. "You look more like a common street ruffian than a businessman."

"I was recently robbed of fifty gold."

The wizard's brow rose toward his curly brown hair. "Fifty? How did you come by such a fortune?"

Jerrell smiled. "By making investments that paid handsomely. You may have heard about the worm infestation that destroyed the apple crop in Ghealdor two seasons past?"

"Of course."

"I caught wind of the disaster the day before the news reached Marquithe. Because of that knowledge, I purchased every Balmorian apple order I could, essentially cornering the market. The next day, the news reached Marquithe, and the other traders came after me, begging me to sell them my orders. Able to set my own price, I made a tidy profit." It was a lie. Not the story, just his involvement. However, Jerrell had met the man behind the trade in a Fastella tavern. After losing the love of his life, the man appeared to be doing his best to drink himself to death.

"That was you?" Paloun asked. "That story is famous among the shipping merchants."

"For good reason. You see, that was my first week as a trader. Over the next two years, I made numerous trades yielding significant profit for investors like you."

"So, what happened?"

"I came to Yor's Point on a holiday, hoping to enjoy the pleasant weather and beautiful women Orenth is known to possess." That much was true. "When I arrived, I was accosted. My belongings and the stash of gold were stolen." He touched his forehead, still red and tender. "This is evidence of the fight."

"And how did you come by the clothing you wear?"

Jerrell tugged on his coat. "This was my disguise. I had thought to dress in a manner that would help me blend in rather than appear like a wealthy merchant."

"Why not pay a bodyguard to protect you?"

"Alas, that was my downfall." Jerrell shook his head. The lies came easily. They were the core of his craft. "When I reached the docks below the city, my bodyguard beat me, stole my chest, and made off on the ship I had taken from Shear. No doubt he was in league with the ship's captain." Jerrell made a fist. "If I ever catch Grayden or Captain Turik, I swear I will see them dead." Of course, the names were made up. There were no such people...as far as Jerrell knew.

Paloun chuckled. "You have both a ruthless business sense and a penchant for vengeance. I admire both qualities. What did you say your name was?"

He smiled. "My name is Jerrell Landish, perhaps you have heard of me?"

The wizard shook his head. "Sorry, I cannot say I know the name. However, you appear to be an enterprising and resourceful young man in need of a job. I happen to have an opening. Are you interested?"

"Very much so. However, I desire to regain my previous wealth and wish to do it quickly, so if you have a particularly challenging task that pays well, I would like to hear it."

Paloun glanced at his guards and then stepped closer to Jerrell. He leaned close and whispered, "I have ten gold pieces to offer if you can remove Jakins and help me become high wizard of Yor's Point. Before that, I want to publicly humiliate the man. But before this discussion goes any further..."

The hair on Jerrell's arms stood and a shiver ran up his spine, warning him of the coming magic. Invisible ropes wrapped around his body, pinning his arms to his sides, and lifting him off his feet.

The wizard moved closer while glaring up at Jerrell. "You had best remember that I treat even the slightest betrayal with harsh measures. Helwin, my last advisor, paid with his life just an hour ago."

With a calm expression, Jerrell said, "I was in the square at the time and am aware of his slight against you. Despite knowing this, I am here. Since I have no intention of betraying you, I have nothing to fear...right?"

"Not from me. I cannot say how others may treat you for aligning with my interests."

The man turned away. The magic dispelled and Jerrell fell to his feet, landing with balanced ease. A few strides later, Paloun paused and glanced backward. "Well, come on. If we are going to talk, it will be over a meal. I barely ate any breakfast, and I'm starving."

Flashing the guards a grin, Jerrell said, "He likes me."

Jerrell sat on a third-story balcony overlooking Yor's Point. Paloun's hilltop estate stood just outside the city, which spread out along the hillside leading down to the sea. Far below, a ridge of black boulders ran along the spine of the point as it stretched out into the water. A white, sandy beach stretched along the shore north of the point. To the south lay the harbor, dominated by a pair of long piers and two dozen smaller docks. A ship sailed past, entering the mouth of the waterway that led to Shear. With its white sails bright in the mid-day sun, the ship was a striking contrast to the cerulean waters.

Paloun rested his fork on his plate, sat back, and used a white napkin to wipe his mouth clean. He set his napkin down and tented his fingers before his mouth while staring at Jerrell. While others might squirm under the scrutiny of a powerful and wealthy wizard, Jerrell leaned back and crossed his legs while his arm casually draped over the arm of his chair.

Finally, the wizard spoke. "Now that I've eaten, shall we get down to business?"

"Business before pleasure, I always say." In truth, Jerrell had never said that in his life. "If you have any ideas that can get me started, it will save us time and help you gain your vaunted position sooner."

"I am unsure if you are aware, but Orenthian tradition calls for another wizard to challenge the existing high wizard for his position."

"Challenge?" Jerrell asked.

"Yes. In a duel of magic...to the death."

"I see. I know little of magic and usually avoid such things. Why don't you just go off and challenge this Jakins character?"

Paloun scowled. "Jakins and I have known each other for fifteen years. Our two families were among the wealthiest in this district. Our relationship has been contentious, and he always perceived me as a rival, which often led to disagreements and even fights. When we were young, I often got the better of him, but when he came into his magic, it all changed. You see, Jakins and I attended the University together, and we, again, found ourselves pitted against one another but this time, in feats of magic. The tables had flipped. Although I was stronger physically, his ability with the Gift outstrips my own."

Jerrell nodded. "You are hesitant to duel with this wizard because you fear you might lose."

"Very good, Mister Landish."

"So, if I were able to help you tilt the odds in your favor..."

Paloun grinned. "It is encouraging to see how swiftly you grasp the situation."

"In addition, you wish to embarrass the high wizard before you slay him with your..." Jerrell waved his hand in a flourish. "Magic."

"I do."

Jerrell peered out over the blue water, noting an albatross circling above the bay with its wings extended. He considered the situation; reading people was his greatest skill.

From his posture to his clothing to the meticulous way he furnished his manor, Paloun was a proud man. He expected the same was true of Jakins. They both took their pride in their station and their wealth. While the second aspect of the plan was to assist Paloun into removing Jakins from his station, the first must tackle the high wizard's wealth.

"In order to embarrass him, I propose we find a means to cause him a significant financial loss."

Paloun grinned. "Agreed."

Jerrell thought back to a conversation from the prior evening. The sailors he diced with had just sailed from Lionne with a ship full of wine barrels and were to soon return for more. They claimed an early freeze was feared to have destroyed the grape crops, but the harvest had already taken place before the freeze—and what a harvest it was. The bountiful harvest had the ship's captain concerned that the price of wine would plummet once word got out from the Marquithe Bureau of Trade. That report was due soon, but until it was announced in Yor's Point, the price would remain stable.

Rubbing his jaw in thought, Jerrell decided he could use that information to his advantage but was unwilling to share it with Paloun until his plan was complete.

"While I need some time to consider how to make that happen, what about your challenge? Could we not also embarrass him just by your defeating him?"

Paloun stroked his jaw, covered in scruff like Jerrell's. "If done right, that would work, but it is not enough. A massive tear in his coin purse would set the stage before I land the final blow."

Jerrell considered all he had heard, and while he better understood the wizard's situation, he needed to meet Jakins to discover his weakness.

"I noted you and your guards leaving the castle this morning."

A cloud passed over Paloun's face. "That blowhard, Jakins, invited me to breakfast merely to gloat at my misfortune. I stormed out before finishing the meal."

"You said your man betrayed you in Jakins's favor?"

"Yes. Helwin. Jakins likely paid the man more than I had offered."

Jerrell said, "If he paid for betrayal once, he is likely to do so again. Can you get me in, so I may meet the high wizard?"

The wizard frowned in thought. "Well, the man is holding a ball in a few days."

"A ball, you say? I assume many guests will be in attendance?"

"Of course. Any wizard or merchant of means from here to Tiamalyn will be there. While Lord Horus will not join the event, his right-hand man, Kylar Mor, might even make an appearance."

"It sounds like an ideal audience for Jakins's public humiliation."

A smile stretched across the wizard's face. "That, it does."

"However, I must visit the castle first in order to properly prepare the dish of revenge you wish to serve."

Paloun considered the request. "Hmm. I suppose I can request an audience with Jakins for tomorrow. While I hate to give him the satisfaction, if I use the excuse that I wish to apologize for storming out this morning, I am sure he will accept."

Jerrell grinned. "Perfect. Make it happen, and bring me along."

"Very well. However, you will need a change of clothing. I cannot bring you there looking like a common thief."

Jerrell restrained from voicing his reply, the words ringing in his head, *Oh, but this thief is anything but common.* "If you can advance me the necessary funds, I will obtain suitable garb."

CHAPTER 4

THE DANGLING CARROT

Peering at the world through disorienting lenses, Jerrell waited at the foot of the stairs outside Paloun's estate.

The manor door opened. Four guards stepped outside and surveyed the area before the wizard emerged. With Paloun in the lead, the wizard and his guards descended the long staircase. When they reached the bottom, the men glanced at Jerrell and then walked past without comment.

"Wizard Paloun," Jerrell said in a nasal tone.

Paloun stopped and turned toward him. "May I help you?"

The glue holding the false mustache to Jerrell's upper lip tightened as he smiled. "If you would be so kind, I was hoping I might join you for breakfast."

With a furrowed brow, Paloun replied, "I am to meet with the high wizard, and I have no time for this."

Jerrell laughed, allowing his voice to return to normal as he removed the circular spectacles from his face. "So, you did not recognize me?"

The wizard's eyes narrowed. "Landish?"

Jerrell bowed. "At your service."

Paloun scanned Jerrell from the blond wig on his head to the polished black shoes on his feet. It felt odd to wear a stuffy doublet, tightly buttoned with ruffles puffing from beneath the collar line, but Jerrell had worn costumes in the past.

"Your clothing is certainly more appropriate, but why the disguise?"

"Jakins does not know me," Jerrell explained. "I have taken additional steps to create a persona to match his expectations. Besides, it will allow me certain liberties for future meetings."

"What does that mean?"

"Trust me." Jerrell slid the spectacles back in place and adjusted his voice. "Shall we head to the castle, Master Wizard?"

Paloun chuckled. "You sound like a sycophant."

"Precisely."

The six-man procession resumed their journey toward the castle, following the hillside path. The estates of wizards and wealthy merchants slid past while Jerrell explained his plan to Paloun. More than once, the man stopped to stare at Jerrell as he considered his own role. By the time they reached the castle gate, all actors were aware of what parts they must play.

Soldiers in green and brown bracketed the open castle gate while others stood on the wall above, gripping bows. A castle guard escorted them up a curved drive bordered by tall, narrow Cypress trees, appearing like dark green fingers pointing toward the sky. The drive leveled as they came to a paved courtyard occupied by an alabaster fountain. In the fountain stood the statue of a wizard lifting a polished metal sphere with sunlight reflecting off its surface.

Once across the courtyard, the escort led them to a set of double doors. A pair of guards bracketed the doors, one of them nodding to the sergeant as he opened the door.

Paloun paused and turned toward his guards. "Wait here for me. I should be about an hour, two at most." He then looked at Jerrell. "Master Pinkerton. Please join me inside."

Responding to the name Jerrell had given his persona, Jerrell nodded. "It would be my pleasure."

The two of them followed the sergeant into a grand foyer tiled in marble. An elegant stairwell ran along each wall, climbing to a loft above the entrance to a sprawling ballroom. Their footsteps echoed off the entrance hall walls as they climbed the stairs.

At the second floor, the sergeant led them to another stairwell. They emerged on the third floor and followed a long corridor illuminated only by the daylight that streamed through an arched window at the far end. Jerrell eyed the paintings and tapestries they passed, thinking that any one of them would be worth numerous gold pieces. Such lavish extravagance made him envy the privileges of the wizard class.

The sergeant stopped outside an open doorway. "His Grace is waiting on the balcony."

"Thank you, Sergeant." Paloun swept past the man.

Jerrell gave the sergeant a smile, pushed his spectacles up the bridge of his nose, and entered a chamber even more impressive than the initial ones.

A darkly stained table occupied the heart of the room. Eighteen chairs surrounded the table and a chandelier hung above it. A sitting area surrounded the stone fireplace on one wall. At the other end was a long serving table filled with trays covered by polished metal domes. Five servants dressed in black—two women in dresses and three men in long coats and trousers—stood beside the serving table. All clasped their hands behind their backs. A pair of open glass-paned doors and eight windows dominated the wall opposite the entrance, offering a spectacular view of the hillside city and the surrounding sea.

Paloun circled the table, passed the servants, and headed straight toward the open doors. Following him, Jerrell raised his spectacles for a better look at the younger of the two female servants. Her straw-colored hair was tied back in a bun, revealing a tan face with high cheekbones. He paused with an overt leer at the curves highlighted by her snug uniform.

"Very nice," he muttered, loud enough for her to hear.

Her brow arched, and the corner of her full lips turned up, but she said nothing.

Jerrell lowered his spectacles and stepped outside, giving a cursory glance toward the man standing at the door before taking in his surroundings.

A white marble railing surrounded a veranda ten strides deep and twice the length. A pergola covered the far end of the patio. Beneath the pergola sat a wizard dressed in silver robes with green trim. The wizard stood as Paloun and Jerrell approached him. His brown eyes appeared sharp; his dark hair waxed back without a single strand out of place. He stood a half a head taller than Paloun, who was half a head taller than Jerrell. His build was lean, lacking Paloun's broad shoulders. Jerrell suspected many women would deem him handsome.

Paloun said, "Thank you for the invitation, High Wizard."

Jakins smiled. "Welcome, Paloun. Who is your guest?"

Stopping, Paloun extended a hand toward Jerrell. "This is Ned Pinkerton, my new trade advisor."

The high wizard's stare measured Jerrell. "While the name seems familiar, I don't believe I have ever seen this man in Yor's Point."

Jerrell pushed his spectacles up and replied in his nasal tone. "Pleased to meet you, Your Grace. I see you have a keen sense of observation, for I only recently arrived at your fine city."

"Where did you come from?"

"From Marquithe via carriage and from Shear by ship to your harbor."

"Marquithe?" The man's brows rose. "The center of trade."

"Yes, sir. In fact, I spent the past two years at the Bureau of Trading."

"I see. Have you any trades of significance to your name?"

"Remember the apple shortage two years ago?"

"That was you?"

Jerrell tapped the side of his nose. "Enough about my past. I now work for Wizard Paloun and have focused my efforts on expanding his wealth."

Jakins gestured toward the shaded table. "Please. Sit." He then clapped his hands and took a chair.

The servants emerged from the dining room. Two men carrying trays set them on the table while the third set a plate with a fork, knife, and napkin before each person. The elder woman set a goblet before Jerrell and each of the wizards while the younger woman came by with two carafes—one filled with dark red liquid, the other with clear.

She leaned beside Jerrell. "Wine or water, sir?"

Jerrell grinned. "Wine, if you please."

The woman filled his glass and then filled Paloun's. When she reached Jakins, she poured water into his goblet.

Jerrell frowned. "No wine for you, sir?"

Paloun snorted. "Jakins never drinks."

The high wizard smirked. "I prefer to keep my mind sharp."

"Why, exactly?"

"The proper execution of wizard magic requires mental acuity."

Interesting, Jerrell thought. "What happens if you are drunk?"

"I might improperly cast the intended construct."

Paloun added, "Or, the construct could degrade before you finish executing the spell."

Jerrell asked, "Yet, you drink, Paloun?"

The wizard smirked. "Unlike others, it takes more than a few cups of wine to cloud my mind."

The domes were lifted from the trays, revealing steaming eggs, sausages, sweet cakes, and a pitcher of berries in a dark red sauce.

"Taster!" Jakins said in a loud voice.

The man standing beside the doorway walked over with a fork and spoon. He scooped a bit of egg and took a bite while narrowing his eyes. Once he had swallowed, he did the same with a bite of sausage. Finally, he put a sweet cake on a small plate and poured the berry sauce over it before digging in. After a couple bites, he nodded and stepped away.

Jerrell whispered, "What was that about?"

Paloun replied, "Jakins fears being drugged or poisoned."

Jakins waved the servants away, the taster left with them, and Jerrell was finally alone with the two wizards.

The high wizard spoke as he filled his plate with eggs and a pair of sausages. "If you were in my position, you would be wary as well. While I rule this district, I am not a wizard lord and cannot cure myself if poisoned." He slid a sweet cake on a small plate before pouring the berry sauce over it. "Conspiracies and whispers surround any court. Who knows when, if ever, the throne of Orenth will be open for a new wizard lord to rise? For all we know, Lord Horus may rule for centuries. Thus, high wizards are the primary targets of those who seek to secure a higher position for themselves."

Jerrell furrowed his brow. "I thought another wizard had to challenge you for your position."

"Another might, but few alive can hope to equal my magic."

The man appeared confident in his abilities, and when Jerrell glanced toward Paloun, he caught a brief grimace. The meeting had already yielded fruitful information.

As Jerrell filled his plate, he considered what he had seen and learned thus far. *When Paloun faces Jakins, he would have the advantage if the high wizard's faculties were impacted. Yet, Jakins avoids alcohol and has others taste his food for him, so I must find another way to addle his brains.*

Just as Jerrell began eating, a guard emerged from the dining room and stepped on the veranda.

The guard bowed. "Excuse me, Your Grace, but Wizard Paloun's steward just arrived and insists that the wizard urgently return to his estate."

Paloun rose to his feet. "Did he say why?"

"It has something to do with a courier who just arrived from Tiamalyn."

The wizard scowled. "That cannot be good."

Jakins stood. "If there is anything I can do to help..."

Paloun shook his head. "No. If the message is from Lord Horus, I must deal with it directly. I just pray he does not require me to visit our capital, not before your autumn ball." He bowed. "Please, excuse me, Jakins."

When Jerrell made to follow Paloun, Jakins interjected. "Master Pinkerton, there is no need for you to depart as well."

Jerrell said, "But I should..."

Paloun turned back toward him. "There is no reason to ruin your breakfast as well. Sit. Eat. Return to my estate when you are finished."

He stormed off with the guard in tow.

Jerrell sat. "That was unfortunate timing."

The high wizard took a drink of water and set his goblet down. "Perhaps or perhaps not."

Frowning at the statement, Jerrell said, "What do you mean, Your Grace?"

"One man's misfortune often becomes a boon for another." He tented his fingers before his lips. "What is Paloun paying you?"

Jerrell blinked. "I have been promised ten gold should our current venture turn out as we expect."

"Ten? A hefty sum. Your venture must hold promise."

"Oh, it does. You see, Wizard Paloun stands to double his own investment in just a few days."

The wizard's eyes narrowed. "A few days... A crop report from the Lionne wine district is expected in that time. What do you know?"

Jerrell shook his head. "I am sorry, but I cannot reveal that information."

A long, quiet moment passed with the wizard staring at Jerrell. "I will pay double what Paloun offered if you agree to turn this investment opportunity over to me."

Jerrell covered his smirk while he stared at his plate. *I have him.*

.

~

THE BREAKFAST with High Wizard Jakins was both a success and delicious. With a full stomach, Jerrell followed a pair of guards down the stairs, across the entrance hall, and outside. The men gestured toward the castle gate, where Paloun's guard waited.

"Thank you, sirs," Jerrell said in a nasal tone. "I bid you a good day."

He headed along the curved, downhill drive and was joined by Paloun's guard. The two of them passed through the castle gate. As they approached the temple across the square, Jerrell turned toward the guard, his voice returning to normal.

"Inform your master that the high wizard took the bait." He waved a rolled scroll. "This is a writ giving me full access to the high wizard's treasury."

"Why can't *you* tell him?"

Jerrell, still in costume, descended the stairs leading toward the harbor. Over his shoulder, he shouted, "I must head to the docks and place orders for wine. Lots and lots of wine."

CHAPTER 5

MASQUERADE

Jerrell eyed himself in the mirror, appreciating his work.

Intense, amber eyes stared back, framed by a chiseled, clean-shaven face. His often-disheveled brown hair was waxed back, mirroring the look Jakins favored. From Jerrell's perspective, it made him appear uptight and aloof, which was precisely his intent.

Draped over his body were dark green silken robes with silver trim down the seam and on the cuffs. He lifted the silver sash from the hook on the wall and secured it around his waist, cinching it below the sack tied to his midsection. The added layer made his stomach appear a far cry from the lean, muscled torso that hid underneath.

Movement in the corner of his eye drew his attention to the robed man standing in the doorway.

Spreading his hands out, Jerrell asked, "What do you think?"

Paloun frowned. "It is illegal to impersonate a wizard."

Jerrell rolled his eyes. "Which makes this the perfect disguise."

"Why do you say that?"

"As a member of the wizard class, what feelings are evoked when you consider an Ungifted pretending to be a wizard?"

The wizard rubbed his jaw. "In truth, I view it as despicable and almost unthinkable."

"Precisely. Others are unlikely to even question if I am Gifted, for who in their right mind would risk their life just to masquerade as a wizard"

Paloun grunted. "I see your point."

"Besides, if I am exposed and arrested, my incarceration will be short-lived, for when you are high wizard, you can pardon me, pay me my gold, and send me on my way."

Paloun's mouth turned up in a grin. "Me as high wizard. If you can make it so, I would pardon you of any offense. Even this."

While Paloun's statement sounded earnest, Jerrell doubted it. He knew wizards could lie and manipulate as well as anyone. "Do not tempt me." He spun around slowly. "Do I look the part?"

"You look just as arrogant as Jakins."

"Wonderful, but do I look like your cousin?"

"Parion has not been to Yor's Point in eight years. He was only fifteen when either Jakins or I last saw him, but you are the right height, and your appearance is close enough for others to believe the ruse...provided they have not visited our family estate in Grakal since his return from the University."

"It will be evening, and the lighting will be less than ideal, so close enough is all I need."

"We had better head outside," Paloun said. "Night is falling, and Devotion will soon begin. I would like to join the party once the vigil is complete."

The wizard walked off and Jerrell, dressed as a wizard, trailed his supposed cousin.

THE LAST OF the red sun slid into the sea on the distant horizon. Jerrell turned from it in expectation. Hundreds of people stood in the square outside the castle gate, waiting as the sky darkened. Most eyes were affixed on the upper reaches of the spire at the heart of the square.

The pink tinted clouds turned purple, and even that light soon faded. A beam of emerald light shot across the sky and shone upon the top of the obelisk. The gem in the apex came to life, glowing like a tiny green star. Everyone, even the wizards present, fell to their knees and began to chant in unison.

"Lord Horus, by the grace of our god, Oren, protect us from harm, and guide us forward..."

The chant droned on with every citizen in every city across Orenth joining in.

Each wizardom had its own god and its own wizard lord. While laws and customs varied from nation to nation, Devotion was universal and the price paid by any who chose to not participate was steep, sometimes resulting in execution. As he recited the prayer, Jerrell's mind wandered back to his teen years in Fastella, two wizardoms away.

As the capital city of Ghealdor, it was also the home of Lord Taladain, a harsh, ruthless wizard. Attuned to his god, Gheald, Taladain's magic carried a violet hue, and the words of his prayer differed from what Lord Horus required of his people.

Since his early teens, Jerrell had rarely participated in Devotion, instead taking advantage of the distraction to pilfer a kitchen or steal something of value he could later sell for coin. Growing up on the streets had taught him a great deal about life, and more importantly, honed his ability to read people.

When the beam of light faded, the gem in the obelisk fell dormant. Night held the city in its grip, the sky dark other than stars and the round moon. The people in the square ceased their chant and rose to their feet.

Paloun gestured toward the gate. "Time to join the party." He paused and eyed Jerrell. "Are you certain of your plan?"

Jerrell grinned. "I know my role and will play it well. Just be ready. Your opportunity will only last a short time."

Paloun clenched his fist. "Do not worry. You give the signal, and I will make the challenge."

They approached the gate where armored guards stood ready. The sergeant on duty, the same one who had escorted Jerrell and the wizard several days earlier, held out his hand. "Good evening, Wizard Paloun. I trust you have your invitation?"

Paloun removed a slip of paper from his robes and unfolded it. The interior glowed with a golden hue, the effect of enchanted ink. He handed the paper to the sergeant.

"Thank you, sir. I welcome you and your companion to Yor's Castle."

With a nod, Paloun walked past the man. Jerrell mirrored Paloun's actions. Together, they walked up a curved path illuminated by torches on poles. Other torches provided islands of light along the top of the castle wall. Music came from the building's interior, calling them toward it.

At the front step, they were met by servants holding trays of filled goblets. While the wizard chose to drink water and keep his mind clear, Jerrell was happy to accept a goblet of wine. He took a sip and swished it across his tongue before swallowing. It was a high quality Farrowen red. *How ironic*, he thought. *Jakins will soon own more wine than he can drink in a lifetime...assuming he survives the night.*

The pair climbed the stairs and stepped into the entrance hall where two couples stood clustered in conversation. The men wore fine doublets, the women form-fitting gowns with flared skirts. Men in robes and women in dresses stood in the loft at the top of the stairs, overlooking the crowded ballroom. The hum of conversation was loud, battling to rise above the strum of a harp coming from somewhere beyond Jerrell's view. Of the hundreds of guests in attendance, most occupied the ballroom, eating bite-sized morsels, drinking, chatting, and laughing. Among them were wizards and wealthy merchants, along with women in elegant dresses. *Many of those women are wizards as well*, Jerrell reminded himself.

Movement on the stairs drew Jerrell's attention. When he spied High Wizard Jakins descending, Jerrell nudged Paloun. "The target approaches."

Paloun turned a scowl toward Jakins as the high wizard reached the floor.

"Ah, Wizard Paloun," Jakins grinned. "I am glad you have decided to make an appearance."

"It is expected for anyone of means to be present. Never let it be said that I shirked the duty of my station." His tone of his voice clearly indicated Paloun was in a foul mood.

"Ahh. Duty. The lower class does not know how easy they have it, for duty can be a yoke that threatens to cripple those of us in power."

Jerrell covered his mouth to restrain his guffaw.

The high wizard's gaze turned on him. "Who is your guest?"

Paloun replied, "You remember my cousin, Parion?"

"Oh, yes. The lad from Grakal if I recall."

In his normal tone, Jerrell replied, "You've a good memory, Your Grace."

"You were a first-year student at the University when I last saw you."

"I completed my tenure and achieved master this past spring."

"Well done, my boy," Jakins patted Jerrell on the shoulder. "Perhaps you will one day rise to high wizard as I have."

"One can only hope, Your Grace."

The high wizard turned his attention back toward Paloun. "Have you seen Pinkerton?"

Growling in reply, Paloun said, "I have not."

Jakins feigned surprise. "You sound upset with him. What happened?"

"I paid him well to purchase trade rights on a certain commodity. Someone else apparently beat him to it and bought up every order in the district. The man promised to find out who was behind the purchases, but thus far he has given me no answers. If you see him, please send him my way."

"I will, indeed." Jakins stared toward the ballroom. "I hear the Farrowen minister of trade has already arrived. Rumor has it that he wishes to use this occasion to make a public announcement. I had better go and find him." Jakins clapped Paloun on the shoulder. "Enjoy yourself, my friend. My chef has prepared dishes to delight your tongue, and three barrels of Farrowen red have been tapped and are ready for your pleasure."

"I could hardly drink three barrels," Paloun said.

Jerrell added. "I am willing to try."

Jakins laughed. "I will see you two later."

The high wizard walked away, and Jerrell leaned close to Paloun. "He suspects nothing."

"Yet, he aches to rub my nose in his perceived victory. I cannot wait until the arrogant arse realizes the truth of it."

"Go on and mingle. I am going to get changed. It is time for Pinkerton to make an appearance."

Jerrell climbed the stairs, pausing at the loft. A pair of young women stood along the railing, both eying him. One was blonde with her hair arranged in a pile on top of her head. The other girl had brunette curls that clung to her face and tumbled down her shoulders. He flashed them a smile, his gaze flicking to the deep neckline of the brunette's red dress and its bountiful treasure.

He then recalled his objective, nodded to the ladies, and climbed the stairs to the third floor. The noise of the party subsided, since the corridor was empty. Jerrell tried the first door and found it opened to a study with an oak desk in the middle of the room and walls covered in bookshelves. With the door closed behind him, he tore his robes off, exposing the bundle secured to his stomach. Opening the sack, he pulled out a blond wig, mustache, and a blue doublet with silver trim.

CHAPTER 6

A CHALLENGE

Dressed as Pinkerton, Jerrell descended to the loft and slid past the same two young women who had smiled at him when he was dressed as a wizard. Both were attractive and the brunette's curves sent his pulse thumping. *Too bad I've no time to dally tonight.* Neither gave him more than a moment's glance, for despite his expensive doublet, he was not a wizard. That alone informed him that they possessed the Gift. *Best to avoid wizardesses anyway. Who knows what kind of spell an upset woman might place on a man?*

Amid the crowd on the loft, Jerrell stood at the railing overlooking the ballroom. His gaze swept the crowded room in search of a tall man with waxed hair and silver robes. Far across the room, he spied Paloun in conversation with a merchant wearing a long black coat. *There must be over two hundred people at this party.* He then spotted Jakins emerging from the kitchen with a pair of servants in tow.

Jerrell leaned against the rail and waved, hoping to catch the high wizard's attention. Jakins looked up at him and gestured for him to come down, but Jerrell shook his head and gestured back. While the high wizard was used to others bending to his whims, he had already displayed eagerness to meet with Pinkerton, and Jerrell knew he would bend to get answers rather than decline the offer. As expected, Jakins wove his way through the crowd and passed beneath the loft, into the foyer.

Jerrell turned from the railing and pushed his way through the guests clustered on the loft. He emerged from the crowd and peered down the stairs to find Jakins ascending. Without waiting, Jerrell climbed to the third floor with the wizard following.

The wizard exited the stairwell and furrowed a brow at Jerrell. "Why are we up here?"

Jerrell kneaded his hands while peering at the stairwell. He replied in Pinkerton's nasal tone, "Paloun is here. I wish to avoid him." Turning toward Jakins, he pushed his spectacles up. "Since I did not complete a single order for him, I fear he suspects betrayal. I saw what happened to the last man who betrayed him..." Jerrell convulsed with an exaggerated shiver. "I do not wish to die, Your Grace."

Jakins rubbed his jaw. "I believe you are correct. Paloun seemed irritated when I mentioned your name. Perhaps it *is* best for you to avoid him." He gestured toward the door beside Jerrell. "Let's step into my study."

Before Jerrell could reply, the man opened the door and entered the very same room Jerrell had recently vacated. Steeling himself in case things got ugly, Jerrell stepped inside and closed the door behind him.

The room was exactly as he left it, with his wizard robes, sash, and sack hidden on the seat of the chair pushed beneath the desk.

When Jakins headed toward the desk, Jerrell pulled a stack of papers from beneath his doublet and interjected.

"I have orders for two hundred thirty-six barrels of Farrowen red." He waved the orders, so the sheets of parchment fluttered against one another.

Jakins stopped and turned toward him with an arched brow. "Two hundred thirty-six? I did not expect you to be able to place so many orders in such a short span." He extended an open hand, in which Jerrell placed the orders.

"I had to work fast, sometimes actively outbidding others. I dare say, fewer than twenty orders against the coming harvest were placed by anyone other than yourself."

The wizard flipped through the papers, examining them in the light of the lantern. "Excellent. And, what did this endeavor cost me?"

Jerrell winced, for Pinkerton would have feared the wizard's reaction. "One hundred twenty-two gold pieces."

The wizard lifted his gaze to Jerrell, his eyes widening. "So much?"

"Yes, Your Grace. Like I said, I was forced to outbid others for numerous orders." As Pinkerton, Jerrell held his hands to his chest and kneaded them as if he were attempting to squash a bug caught in his palm. "With your writ in hand, I was able to place all but a handful of orders so payment was due upon delivery."

Jakins nodded. "Well, at least we have that. How much do I owe you?"

"Five gold are due tomorrow, before the ships set sail for Lionne."

"Five is a more reasonable number." The wizard walked up to the wall and pulled a tapestry aside. In a hidden alcove was a safe. Rather than using a combination or key to unlock it, the wizard held his palm against a metal panel. The hair on Jerrell's arm stood on end. The panel hummed, and the safe door popped open. The wizard reached inside and withdrew a small purse. Dozens of similar purses filled the safe. *Damn,* Jerrell thought. *Had I known the wizard had so much gold, I'd have given him a higher number.*

The man turned and tossed the purse to Jerrell, who snatched it out of the air with ease, forgetting his persona before purposely fumbling with the purse, making numerous attempts to catch it before it fell to the floor, the coins inside clinking noisily the entire time.

"Sorry," Jerrell pushed his spectacles up and then bent to retrieve the purse.

The wizard placed the orders inside the safe and then closed it. With the door sealed, he pressed his hand to the panel, using magic to lock it. He then walked to the door and stopped with his hand on the handle.

"You did well, Pinkerton. However, you should remain hidden in here until Paloun departs. The minister from the Marquithe Bureau of Trade has arrived and will soon be announcing the fall harvest. Once that happens, and Paloun realizes the opportunity he missed, he will be livid. If he catches you, I cannot protect you, and the situation could get ugly. I would not put it past that man to use torture while interrogating you, and I cannot have you exposing my role."

Jerrell, as Pinkerton, clutched the coin purse to his chest. "What about the gold you promised me?"

"You will receive your reward once my gambit comes to fruition. I will own just about every barrel of Farrowen wine in Orenth, which I will sell for a tidy profit."

The wizard opened the door, and Jerrell said, "Thank you, High Wizard."

"I will return soon. Until then, sit and relax." Jakins grinned. "Our scheme is almost at an end."

The door closed behind Jakins, leaving Jerrell alone. Rushing across the room, Jerrell pressed his ear against the door and listened to the wizard's footsteps as he descended the neighboring stairwell. He then turned from the door, squatted, and began rolling up the rug. He did not stop until the roll bumped into the desk legs. He removed the coin purse from his hip, opened it, and flipped it upside down. Dry, yellow leaves fell to the marble floor, forming a pile. Once the purse was empty, he tossed it aside and pulled a flint and striker from inside his doublet. He set the flint and striker down beside the pile.

He then went to the desk chair to grab the robe and sash hidden there. Returning to the room entrance, he hung both the sash and robe on a hook behind the door and then eased the door open. The corridor was empty, so he exited the room.

Upon returning to the second-story loft, Jerrell spied a male servant climbing the stairs from the first floor. Red liquid sloshed in the goblets upon the man's tray, reminding Jerrell of his thirst. He met the man at the top of the stairs, scooped a goblet from the tray, and sipped his wine as he made his way back to the loft railing.

Across the ballroom, he spotted Paloun speaking to an attractive woman with black hair and tawny skin. Her sleeveless yellow gown highlighted a slim figure. Jerrell watched Paloun closely. Paloun's gaze repeatedly shifted beyond the girl, toward Jakins, who stood just strides away. The high wizard was speaking to a balding middle-aged man wearing a midnight blue coat.

Jakins clapped the man on the shoulder and walked off, toward the harp player. Moments later, the music stopped, and Jakins turned to the crowd.

Arms raised, the high wizard shouted, "Guests! Welcome!"

The ballroom quieted.

"Friends, colleagues, subjects of my district, I welcome you to Yor's Castle." The high wizard lowered his arms. "Eat, drink, and enjoy yourselves. This event is my gift to you."

Applause echoed in the spacious chamber, the high wizard waiting until it calmed before he resumed.

"Today, we also have a special guest, a man who arrived in Yor's Point just this afternoon." Jakins held a hand toward the man in the blue coat. "Please welcome Master Loren Widor, a senior minister from the Marquithe Bureau of Trade." The high wizard paused while Widor raised his hand and waved. "The minister has come to share greatly anticipated information, and you will be the first in Orenth to hear it." He nodded toward the man. "Master Widor, the floor is yours."

The man dipped his head. "Thank you, Your Grace. I appreciate the opportunity to present directly to the wizards and merchants of your district. I arrived today, sailing directly from Lionne, the heart of Farrowen's wine supply to the world. Tomorrow, I will journey to Shear with this communication, and then I am on to Tiamalyn to share the report with Lord Horus himself." The man held up a ledger for all to see. "In these pages, I have the full harvest report from every vineyard in northern Farrowen.

"I am pleased to report that this harvest has been unlike any other. Despite a close call with an early freeze, the vineyards of the Lionne district have had a banner year. You can expect a steady and plentiful supply of wine unequaled in history."

The crowd clapped, some guests going as far as cheering. Paloun grinned and then laughed.

The high wizard, however, appeared ready to explode. With a red face, his arms stiff at his sides, his fists shook as though ready to commit violence.

"Argh!" Jakins shrieked in anger.

Everyone turned toward the high wizard as the room fell silent.

Jakins pressed his hand to his forehead. "I am ruined..." His gaze rose to the loft and sparks sizzled in his eyes when they met Jerrell's. "Pinkerton!" the wizard roared. "I am going to kill you!"

Jerrell spun around and ducked into the crowd. Rather than descending, he sprinted up the stairs and returned to the study. He raced in, closed the door, and slid on his knees across the marble floor. One hand gripped the flint, the other the striker. Repeatedly, he stroked them together, praying for a spark. The high wizard's voice carried through the closed door as he shouted orders to his soldiers and staff, spurring Jerrell's urgency.

Finally, an ember struck one of the dry leaves, causing smoke to rise. Jerrell blew on the leaf, nursing the spark to flames.

With the leaves smoldering, Jerrell pulled the gray-tinted handkerchief from the pocket of his doublet and tied it around his face to limit the fumes. He could not afford to have his faculties impacted by the sweet smoke.

He tore the wig off his head and placed it on the desk, beside a pyramid-shaped paperweight carved from black onyx. Gripping the paperweight, he backed into the corner and hid behind the door as the thuds of footsteps drew nearer.

The door opened and the high wizard stepped in, breathing heavily. "What the blazes?"

The wizard entered the smoke-filled room, his gaze shifting from the burning leaves on the floor to the wig on the desk. As the wizard approached the desk and lifted the wig, Jerrell crept up behind him with his arm cocked back. Jakins suddenly spun around, and Jerrell swung. The paperweight struck the wizard in the side of the head, felling him.

Jerrell then raced out of the room, closed the door, and stomped on the floor. His stomps were loud at first and rapidly grew quieter, hoping to sound as if he had raced down the stairs. He then crept down the corridor and slipped into the dining room. With his back to the wall, he lowered the cloth from his face and listened.

Moments later, the study door opened, and Jakins staggered out, coughing. Jerrell peered around the corner as yellow smoke seeped through the doorway and swirled around the wizard. Leaning against the wall, Jakins stumbled into the stairwell and faded from view.

Jerrell tore the fake mustache off and stuck it in his pocket with the spectacles. He then slipped the robes over his arms, used the sash to secure them, and walked out of the dining room while slicking his waxed hair back to ensure it was in place. Holding his breath, he hurried past the smoke-filled study and ducked into the stairwell.

Once again dressed as Paloun's cousin, Jerrell paused to watch Jakins grip the railing as he worked his way down to the main floor. Everyone in the loft watched the wizard and whispered to one another.

As Jerrell crossed the crowded loft, he heard numerous people whisper that the wizard was drunk. *They do not know that the man does not drink.* He grinned as he leaned against the railing over the ballroom and waited for the final act in his charade.

The middle of the ballroom stood empty, but the harpist had not resumed playing, so nobody danced. Instead, the room was surrounded by clusters of people speaking in hushed tones. The high wizard shouted at his guards, but nobody had seen a blond man in a blue doublet and spectacles.

When Jakins staggered into the ballroom, hand pressed against his head as he wobbled, Paloun strode toward the middle of the room and clapped his hands loudly. All eyes turned toward him.

"Jakins!" Paloun shouted. "By right of combat, I challenge you for the position of high wizard!"

CHAPTER 7

OUTCOMES

The challenge issued by Paloun stilled all conversation. It seemed as if every person in the castle held their breath. Wide eyes flicked from Paloun to Jakins and back, and then, the crowd began backing away from the two wizards.

"You challenge me, now?" Jakins lowered his hand to reveal blood on his palm. "Can you not see that I have been accosted?"

Paloun was not to be deterred. "I have made a public challenge. Per tradition, you must face me in a duel of magic. If you decline, you forfeit the seat of high wizard now and forever."

A handful of guests hurried into the entrance hall, away from the two wizards. Those who remained backed away until their backs were pinned to the walls.

Jakins growled. "I am searching for a conniving traitor. I'll not be goaded into doing something rash."

"Then you forfeit?" Paloun spread his arms. "I have many witnesses who will attest to your decision."

Jaw set and anger flaring in his eyes, Jakins said, "You know your magic cannot stand up to my might. I would never forfeit to the likes of you."

Paloun lowered his arms, his fingers bending to claws as he set his jaw and glared at his rival. "Then defend yourself."

More guests rushed from the room, some heading toward the front door, others disappearing into the kitchen. The few remaining stood as far from the two wizards as possible.

Suddenly, Jakins thrust his hands toward Paloun. Swirls of flames appeared and burst forth a few strides before fizzling out. Jakins frowned in confusion, but Jerrell grinned. *The drug worked. He cannot use his magic as expected.*

Paloun responded with his own attack.

Lightning shot from his fist and struck Jakins in the chest, blasting him fives strides backward. The wizard struck the marble tiles and slid across the room until colliding with the wall. He did not move.

With measured strides, Paloun approached the downed wizard. Tendrils of smoke rose from Jakins's still chest. A woman knelt beside the high wizard. She held her hand to his forehead and closed her eyes. Moments later, she opened them and shook her head.

"He is dead."

Paloun took a deep breath and turned to the room, speaking in a loud voice, "Jakins is dead. Per wizard right of battle, I, Randolph Paloun, declare myself high wizard of Yor's Point."

Jerrell shouted. "Long live High Wizard Paloun!"

The crowd repeated the call, again and again, the volume growing louder until everyone in the estate shouted in unison.

DRESSED AND PACKED, Jerrell cast one last glance back at his room at the Shoreline Inn. It had been his home for the better part of a year, yet, other than the gouges in the center post left by his blades, there was no evidence of his stay. *I will make my mark on the world,* Jerrell promised himself. *But my business in Yor's Point is finished.*

He had outgrown the seaside town and was ready for something bigger. His recent success with Jakins had proven that he was more than a mere pickpocket or burglar. The caper forced Jerrell to admit to himself how much he enjoyed the thrill of tempting fate and achieving what others might deem impossible. *How could I have ever considered retiring from such fun?* He headed down the stairs and stopped by the taproom.

Morning light filtered through a new window at the front, revealing dozens of empty tables, some of which were newly purchased. Only two tables were occupied, each by a pair of sailors eagerly eating a hot breakfast.

Sharri emerged from the kitchen and spied him as she brought a fresh plate of eggs to one of the tables. The barkeep then crossed the room and stopped before Jerrell.

With a fist on one hip, she looked him over. "I have to say I am surprised, Jerrell. I half expected you to disappear rather than repay your debt."

"I promised you would get your gold. Besides, I have grown to like you, Sharri. I also realize I have not always been an ideal guest, and I owe you for the trouble I have caused."

"Well, I thank you for it." She cocked her head. "You wouldn't have anything to do with what happened at Yor's Castle two nights ago?"

He grinned. "You heard about that?"

She snorted. "Everyone in Yor's Point is talking about how Jakins was fleeced by a bad investment and then killed in a duel of magic. All in all, it sounds as if the high wizard had a very bad night."

He chuckled. "Yes. That was my doing."

"Which part?"

He shrugged. "All of it other than the actual use of magic. That was Paloun's job. I prefer to keep my hands clean of such things."

She snorted. "Somehow, I doubt your hands ever remain clean for long."

Shrugging at the comment, he reached into his coat pocket and pulled out a gold piece. "This is for you."

"You already paid me."

"I know, but this is for any trouble that might come in the future. This last scheme attracted a lot of attention, and it is possible someone might come looking for me. If they do, just claim that I disappeared and stiffed you on the last week's rent. You have no idea where I am but wish you did, so you could wring the coin out of me yourself."

Sharri accepted the gold piece. "I appreciate it, Jerrell, but where are you going?"

"If you don't know, you won't have to lie about it."

"There is truth in that."

"Farewell, Sharri." He headed to the door.

"Be well, Jerrell. I wish you luck."

He flashed her one last grin. "Luck is the one thing I *can* count on."

THE SHIP SAILED out of the harbor and turned southeast. Standing at the port side rail, Jerrell watched the seaside city of Yor's Point grow smaller as the distance increased. He had ended up there on a whim and stayed longer than he had anticipated. The longer he lived there, the smaller the city felt, and Jerrell found himself seeking trouble as entertainment. Old habits are difficult to break.

"I should have left a season ago," he said to himself. "It is past time for something new."

The scheme he and Paloun had executed reminded Jerrell how much he enjoyed the thrill of testing his wits against others. Jakins had suffered in the end, but such was the struggle for those who desired power. If Paloun had not killed Jakins, another wizard would have come along and claimed his title. Jerrell's hand in the power exchange not only resulted in him being able to pay Sharri six gold, but he still had eight gold and a dozen silver pieces in his possession—enough to live off for a good stretch.

However, he was not about to sit back idly...not again.

He turned his gaze away from the city and toward his next destination.

The sails above Jerrell were fully puffed by the wind coming from behind the ship. Steep, rocky cliffs covered in patches of green bound both sides of the inland waterway. No more than ten miles wide at any point, the channel leading to Shear was a thing to behold.

The ship's captain strolled past, and Jerrell grabbed the sleeve of the man's red coat. "Excuse me, Captain. How long until we reach Shear?"

The captain stroked his thick black beard. "If the favorable wind holds, we should reach Shear at nightfall." The man passed Jerrell, climbing the stairs to the quarter deck before taking the wheel from his first mate.

Jerrell turned back toward the bow, ready to see the next sight and begin scheming about his next escapade.

~

A HINT of daylight remained in the western sky when the ship eased into Shear's harbor. It was a clear night, the round moon to the east painting the city in pale light. Above the city, a daunting cliff blotted out the western horizon. Here and there, warm light shone through windows of homes built on the wooded hillside. A series of enchanted lanterns lined the pier, guiding the ship toward an open slip.

Once the ship settled and the sailors had secured it to the pier, Jerrell hoisted his pack and crossed the deck. A pair of sailors slid a plank across the gap to the pier, dropping the far end with a thud. Jerrell bid them a good evening, crossed the plank, and headed toward the city.

He climbed the cobblestone incline toward a two-story wall made of rocks in a bed of mortar. Amber light from torches on the top of the wall revealed a host of guards standing upon it. The gate stood open and four armed soldiers in silver and blue stood ready, watching his approach.

"Greetings, gentlemen," Jerrell said with a casual smile.

One of the guards stepped before him. The man's hand rested on the hilt of the sword on his hip. "State your business in Shear."

Jerrell shrugged. "I am here for fun."

"Fun? What sort of fun?"

"Women. Drink. Dice. You know, the same as you soldiers seek when not on duty."

"Some do. Not me."

The comment earned the guard a snort. "Suit yourself."

"Don't go causing trouble in my city," the guard warned.

"Your city? I thought Gerald Wrenthal was high wizard here."

"High Wizard Wrenthal and his family occupy the castle on the bluff. He and the other wizards rarely bother with us down here."

"Down here?"

"The old city."

Jerrell patted the taller man on the shoulder. "Well, you can put your mind at ease. I don't plan to stay long." He walked away, not waiting for a reply.

A square with a bubbling fountain stood just inside the gate. The square stood empty other than a handful to people clustered around a pair of carts. One couple finished packing one of the carts and began pushing it across the square, the wheels creaking noisily.

Narrow cobblestone streets ran along the wall and led from the square in various directions, leaving five directions to choose from. Jerrell selected a street at random, strolling along it while surveying his surroundings.

The street was narrow, the buildings old but in good condition. Most shop doors were closed, their windows dark. A pair of guards approached, glaring at Jerrell until he walked past them. Jerrell paid them little heed. Like the sergeant at the gate, the men were wary but unlikely to start trouble. That would be Jerrell's job.

He came to another square with a familiar structure in the center.

The obelisk appeared identical to the one in Yor's Point. His gaze lifted to the cliff high above. Along the edge was a walled complex with a similar spire. *Two obelisks?*

A beam of blue light shot across the sky and struck the obelisk on the bluff above, which began to shimmer with bright blue light. Another azure light shone down on the lower obelisk, igniting it with the blue fire of Farrow.

The men and women in the square fell to their knees, raised their hands into the air, and began to chant. "Bless us, Farrow. Guide us in your wisdom, protect us from harm, and grant Lord Malvorian with your power so he might lead us to a better tomorrow."

A shove from behind caused Jerrell to stumble. He turned with a clenched fist to find two guards glaring at him.

"Kneel and worship Farrow and his chosen wizard lord, or you'll find yourself in a cell."

Jerrell narrowed his eyes and considered killing the two guards but thought better of it. Instead, he bit his tongue, knelt, and began to chant with the others. His mind drifted as he considered clever ways to locate his next mark. A plan solidified, one that would place his path in luck's hands.

Devotion finished and the square emptied. Jerrell followed a cluster of young men who joked and laughed as they headed along an uphill street. At the top, the men climbed a short flight of stairs and headed into a stone building. A sign depicting an unconscious man surrounded by stacks of coins was posted on the side of the stair railing. On the sign were the words the Lucky Lush.

"Perfect," Jerrell grinned and climbed the stairs.

CHAPTER 8
LUCK OF THE LUSH

The Lucky Lush's small interior consisted of a bar along the same wall as the door and six tables, half of which were occupied. Beyond the bar and tables, a pair of double doors stood open. Curious, Jerrell crossed the room, passed through the doors, and emerged on a rooftop patio. Tables, chairs, and benches, many of them occupied, filled much of the dark area, which was surrounded by a railing made of thick posts.

He strolled past the tables and leaned against the railing while peering out into the night.

The building was located a block from the outer wall of Shear's old city. With the added height from the climb, he found himself standing higher than the wall, which allowed him a clear view of the harbor.

A dark cliff a thousand feet tall stood on the opposite side of the water, no more than two miles to the northeast. In the sky above, the moon loomed, bright and round and ever-present. Jerrell had heard tales of days long past when the moon traveled across the sky, waxing and waning, sometimes full, other times hidden in shadow. He chuckled at the outlandish idea. Like legends of elves, dwarves, and dragons, the traveling moon was nothing but fodder for fireside tales. He then recalled his fight against the minotaur who guarded a legendary, abandoned castle. The monster had been all too real and the harrowing experience had nearly killed his companion, a warrior. *Perhaps there is some truth in those tales.* It was difficult to know what was myth and what was real when he had only visited a small portion of the Eight Wizardoms. Dismissing his musings, he gazed into the night.

To the northwest, the waterway grew to approximately ten miles in width, to the east, it narrowed to a river that began at Lake Grakal, many miles to the southeast, flowed past Tiamalyn, the capital of Orenth, and then continued until it reached Shear. That river and the waterway acted as the border between Farrowen and Orenth.

He turned from the railing and headed straight for the bar inside. With a gesture, he caught the attention of the massive barkeep. Standing at just over six feet, the man must have weighed three times as much as Jerrell; his heavy paunch hung over his belt. Graying curls clung to the man's face and the sides of his head, the top of which was barren and coated in sweat.

The man reached the end of the bar and asked, "What will it be?"

"Ale. A meal as well."

"Five coppers will get you two ales and a meat pie."

Jerrell slapped a silver on the bar. "Done."

"Find a seat." The man slid five coppers on the bar. "I'll be right back."

After collecting his change, Jerrell chose a table next to the one occupied by the four men he had followed inside. He sat with a sigh and set his pack down at his feet. The barkeep returned with two tankards and a steaming cast iron pot. Jerrell took a drink. The bubbles tickled his tongue and left a bitter aftertaste with a hint of fruitiness. As he sipped his ale, he sat back and listened. It was not long before he heard the information he sought.

FULL AND REFRESHED by the ale, Jerrell headed outside. He turned at the bottom of the stairwell, descending another set of stairs to a door below the street. He put his ear to the door and heard voices inside. When he opened the door, the raucous noise of a crowd filled the quiet street. Warm light beckoned him inside, so he followed it in.

Much like the dining room above, a long bar ran the length of the building, but this one was larger because it included the area beneath the rooftop patio. The tables downstairs were round rather than rectangular, and while five tables were occupied, Jerrell cared about only one of them.

A crowd of onlookers with mugs in their hands surrounded the table in the corner. Those seated watched one of their comrades shake a wooden cup, its contents rattling noisily. The man flipped the cup onto the table, and five dice tumbled out, rolling and bouncing before settling. It was a good roll, and when the others at the table reacted poorly, Jerrell knew it had been a winning toss. The man set the cup down and scooped up a pile of coins from the center of the table.

One of the players stood. "That's it. I am out. I can't afford to lose any more tonight, or I'll have nothing left to buy provisions for my trip to Marquithe."

The others waved and gave half-hearted goodbyes. As the man walked away from the table, Jerrell slid past him and headed straight for the empty chair.

He sat with a grin. "Good evening, boys. I hope you don't mind another player."

Jerrell surveyed the five men; three appeared to be sailors and the other two locals. The sailors appeared surly, two of them glaring, and the third sneering as if he was prepared to send Jerrell packing. *Best to lay down some honey.*

Jerrell slapped his hand on the table and pulled it back to reveal five silver pieces. "I just arrived in Shear. After paying for dinner and a room, this is all I've got left. I was hoping I might try playing a few games. I heard a man can turn five silver pieces into ten by playing a game of dice."

After his success in Yor's Point, Jerrell could afford to lose a bit.

One of the sailors arched a brow. "Have you played before?"

"No, sir," Jerrell lied.

"Well," he grinned, revealing a missing tooth. "I don't see why we can't show a lad like you the proper way to throw dice." The man glanced around the table. "What say you, men?"

Shrugs and nods revealed no naysayers.

Rather than starting at copper bids, as many players did, these men went straight to one silver piece per game. Although Jerrell often won even when not using his weighted dice, he did not wish to win this night. In fact, he sought to lose in epic fashion. Thus, he snuck his off-weighted die into the group each time he threw. When rolled, that die almost always came up as a one, tonight was no exception.

After three losing tosses, he doubled his bet, placing both of his last two silvers on the table. One of the men bowed out, but the other four, including all three sailors, matched his bet. Each took a turn throwing with Jerrell going last. When he rolled five ones, a disastrous roll, he feigned misery and dropped his face in his hands.

The man sitting beside him, the one who had opted out, patted his shoulder. "It'll be all right, son."

Jerrell lifted his head and looked into the man's eyes. "I've no coin left. After tonight, I'll be homeless and won't even be able to buy food. I had hoped Shear might offer me some opportunity, yet I have just arrived and am already in trouble."

A firm grip clamped onto his shoulder. Jerrell looked up to find a tall man wearing a black, brimmed hat standing over him. A brown leather vest over a cream-colored tunic covered the man's torso, his broad shoulders and narrow waist alluding to an athletic frame. The lines around his gray eyes bespoke of his years being somewhere north of thirty-five.

"I may be able to help." The man nodded to those seated at the table. "Thanks for the entertainment, boys. I would join you, but I've an early morning tomorrow." He looked back at Jerrell. "Follow me."

The man stepped away from the table. Jerrell grabbed his pack, rose, and followed the man to the door, far from the boisterous dice game.

The man extended his hand. "My name is Mond."

"Jerrell," he replied as he shook hands, wincing at Mond's firm grip.

Mond adjusted his hat and smirked as he looked Jerrell up and down.

Jerrell narrowed his eyes. *Why the smile?*

The man said, "I know what it is like to be in a bind. In fact, I am in a tight spot right now, and until tonight, I thought I had no way out."

"How so?"

"Have you heard the name, Gerald Wrenthal?"

"Of course. He is the high wizard of Shear."

"As high wizard, he lives in the castle on the bluff, where he is to have a party for his son the night after tomorrow. For the party, the man ordered three barrels of wine. Not just any wine, mind you, three barrels of Farrowen red." Mond tapped his own, muscular chest. "As an enterprising man who owns a wagon, I jumped at the chance to accept the order and promised to deliver it to Shear Castle a day before the event."

"Makes sense."

"However, something happened about a week ago. Someone eager to corner the market bought up every order of Farrowen wine from every ship passing through Yor's Channel. For days, I have been begging ship captains to accept an order or slide me an extra barrel but have been denied at every turn…until tonight, when a ship arrived just before Devotion. The captain agreed to sell me three barrels at a slightly inflated price. While I won't earn quite as much coin as I had hoped, at least the High Wizard won't be seeking my head on a pike."

Jerrell smiled inwardly, knowing that both the wine order shortage and subsequent availability were his doing. When Jakins died, his orders were all cancelled, leaving a sudden surplus.

With a straight face, he said, "I am glad you found a way out of the mess, but what does that have to do with me?"

"In my dire straits, I lost my apprentice. He saw his impending doom and left with a trader bound for Marquithe rather than remain and suffer the high wizard's wrath.

"Delivering wine barrels is a two-man job, and I am short a pair of hands. You appear fit enough for the task. I'll pay you two silver pieces if you help me load the barrels into my cart tomorrow and then unload them at the wizard's estate. It's not a lot, but it's the best I can do."

Jerrell considered the offer and the related opportunity. He had hoped his luck might lead to something interesting. In the past, he had avoided wizards because of the added risk, but he now perceived those risks as mere challenges. The wizard class possessed most of the fame and wealth, and the opportunity for him to advance by overcoming those challenges was enticing. A reason to visit the high wizard's castle would also give him the chance to see what lay inside. From there, anything was possible.

"I'll do it."

"Brilliant," Mond grinned. "Meet me at the docks in the morning. Arrive before the sun edges over the cliff."

CHAPTER 9
DELIVERY

Grunting from the weight, Jerrell and Mond hoisted the last wine barrel up into the wagon bed. The barrel rolled into the others before stopping. Jerrell leapt up into the wagon, gripped one end, and tipped the barrel up until it fell with a thud. Mond then pushed from the wagon's side and slid the barrel against the other two.

"There we go." Mond dusted his hands off. "Now it's up to Arnold and Penillis to get us to the top."

As the man climbed into the seat, Jerrell leaned over the wagon bed rail. "Did you say ornery penis?"

The man laughed. "Arnold and Penillis." He nodded. "Those are the names of my mules. However, ornery might be more appropriate."

With a snap of the reigns and a shout, the two mules reacted. The wagon lurched three times before matching the beat of the mules' strides. Rather than heading for the gate, the man guided the mules around the city walls and headed toward the uphill road.

Jerrell's gaze followed the road as it climbed the cliffside, performing dozens of switchbacks before fading from view. Houses lined the uphill side of each stretch. Trees defiantly clung to the hillside around those homes, creating an odd mixture of man and nature. A thousand feet above, the top of the cliff loomed, the upper reaches illuminated by the rising sun while the old city and the harbor remained draped in shadow.

"How long will it take to reach the top?"

"With this weight, I'd say an hour. Longer if the mules give me trouble."

"If that's the case"—Jerrell pulled his coat off and rolled it into a ball—"I am going to get some sleep. It's been a while since I was up before sunrise, and I could use the rest." Using his coat as a pillow, he lay down beside the three wine barrels.

THE SUN WOKE JERRELL. He opened his eyes and raised his hand to shade them as he sat up. The incline leveled as the wagon rounded a bend. Castle walls stood above the road, the pale stone brightly illuminated by the morning sun. The road curved along the wall as they entered the upper district of Shear.

Unlike the older buildings below, no wall surrounded the upper city, leaving the castle as the only defensible location. The streets were double or triple the width of those in the old city, which made it feel cleaner and more welcoming.

The wagon crossed a square, passed the open front gate, and then continued circling the castle until it reached a gate near the back. A quartet of guards blocked the entrance while others stood on the wall above it. As the wagon drew to a halt, one of the guards strode forward and addressed Mond.

"Good morning, Ca..."

Mond interrupted the guard. "How are you faring, Yeldin?"

Jerrell frowned, wondering what Yeldin had been about to say.

The guard's brow furrowed for an instant. "It has been quiet of late, and the weather has been pleasant, so things are as good as can be expected."

"What of tomorrow's event?"

Yeldin grimaced. "Wrenthal has invited just about every wizard in Farrowen and a few from Orenth, in addition to any official or merchant of note within a hundred miles."

"You are expecting a significant turnout?"

"Hundreds to be sure."

"Well, I have a wine delivery for the event, but I hope he has more than these three barrels, or he is going to run short."

"The high wizard keeps a few barrels in his cellar at all times. You'd think he'd roll a barrel out for his guards now and then, but I might as well wish for a gorgeous nymph to fall from the sky and ravish me until I cannot walk."

Mond laughed. "You've the right of it.'

Yeldin looked at Jerrell. "Who is this?"

"He is new to the city and short of coin. I hired him to complete the delivery."

"What happened to Hestin?"

Mond sighed. "He ran off with a trader bound for Marquithe when it appeared I had no chance of completing this order." He held out a sheet of paper to Yeldin. "I had considered going into hiding myself but a ship arrived in port last night with barrels of wine and no contract."

After a brief perusal of the order, Yeldin handed it back to Mond. "Go on. Head toward the cellar door. I'll send a man inside to find Steward Chalmers."

Mond tipped his hat to the guard. "I appreciate it."

Turning from the wagon, Yeldin began issuing orders. Several guards moved aside while one jogged off.

The reins snapped, the mules resumed their lazy walk, and the wagon rolled through the gate. They rode through a paved square inside the castle wall overlooking the river valley. In the square stood an obelisk like the one found in the old city.

The castle itself seemed to be a misnomer. Other than the wall, the complex lacked any of the features typical of a fortress. It was an extravagant four-story mansion with peaked clay-tiled roofs and diamond-shaped windowpanes surrounded by sculpted shrubs, green lawns, and paved patios. It appeared much newer than any structure at the foot of the bluff.

The wagon followed a curved drive past a courtyard, a bubbling fountain, and a pool filled with orange, black, and white fish. After rounding the back of the building, the downhill drive leveled. Mond pulled on the reins, and the wagon stopped outside of a set of dark blue doors.

A thump came behind the doors. One of them opened and a man wearing a blue coat and matching trousers emerged. Appearing somewhere north of fifty years old, he wore white gloves, and his graying hair was waxed in place without a single loose strand.

"Mister Mond," the man snapped, "is this the delivery that was due yesterday?"

Mond frowned. "The party is not until tomorrow, Chalmers, so I'd say this delivery is on time."

The uptight steward arched a brow. "Only one day to allow the wine to settle and cool?"

Climbing down from the wagon, Mond said, "It could not be helped. Last night was the first time in two weeks that a single barrel of wine rolled into port."

"Excuses will not get you paid."

Mond turned on the man and jabbed him in the chest with a finger. The wagon driver stood taller than the steward and carried twice the thin man's brawn. "Listen here. You will pay me and pay in full, or I will be driving off with these three barrels, and you can explain to the high wizard why you ran short during his son's party."

Chalmers scowled. "Bring the barrels into the cellar and place them beside the others. When you are done, take the stairs to the kitchens. I will meet you with your payment."

The steward climbed the stairs, propped the door open, and disappeared inside.

As Mond approached the wagon, Jerrell flashed him a grin. "You sure put that stuck up twit in his place."

Opening the wagon gate, Mond said, "Chalmers is so tight, I fear if I were to put my boot up his arse, it might lodge there permanently."

Laughing, Jerrell grabbed a barrel, tipped it, and eased it down until it lay on its side. With the barrel near the open tailgate, he jumped down, gripped one end, and lifted. Grunting at the weight, he followed Mond to the open door.

They stepped into a small dark room. A closed door stood on one side. Two flights of stairs waited on the other, one heading up and the other down.

Walking backward, Mond descended into darkness while Jerrell followed, doing his best not to lose his grip on the barrel. Finally reaching the bottom, he stepped onto a dirt floor and crossed a room dimly illuminated by daylight coming through a pair of narrow windows along one wall. Two barrels sat in the middle of the room while shelves filled with crates and sacks covered the walls.

Jerrell caught a glint of reflected light from an object resting on an otherwise empty shelf, and he moved closer for a better look. In the shadows, he spied a small statue of an armored man cast in gold. The sword in the warrior's hand was handcrafted of silver, and he stood on a circular dais encrusted with sapphires. The craftsmanship was stunning.

"What are you doing?" Mond asked.

"Look at this."

Mond moved to Jerrell's side and grunted. "That statue must be worth a fortune."

"Exactly. Why do you think it's down here?"

"When it comes to the wizard class, who can guess why they do anything?" Mond turned away. "For all I know, Wrenthal or someone in his family decided the statue was too ugly to keep out in the open."

"Ugly?" Jerrell followed Mond up the stairs. "I have seen few things that equal its beauty."

Mond walked through the doorway and stepped outside. "Not all of us see things the same way."

Following the man to the wagon, Jerrell asked, "What does that mean?"

The man spun toward him. "Take women for instance. What is the first thing you notice?"

After a brief consideration, Jerrell said, "Their eyes?"

"No. Don't tell me what a *woman* would want to hear. Be truthful, what do you look at first?"

Grinning, Jerrell said, "Their chest, same as any man."

"Not me. I look at their backside. Give me a nice round bottom any day."

Jerrell frowned. "Why?"

Mond shrugged. "It's just my thing." He walked to the back of the wagon with Jerrell following. "You could talk to ten men and get half a dozen different responses. Some like blondes, some prefer brunettes. Many are breast men, like you, while others desire shapely legs." He hopped up to the wagon bed.

"While I enjoy women as much as any warm-blooded man, why are we talking about them?"

"I am trying to make a point regarding beauty. It is subjective. While you might see one object as stunning, another may consider it boring or even ugly." Mond rolled the barrel to the tailgate and jumped down. "Grab that end. Let's get these delivered, so we can get paid."

The second barrel felt heavier than the first, and the third was even heavier. Once both were in the basement, Jerrell followed Mond up the stairs, casting one last glance at the statue of gold.

At the middle level, Mond closed the back door and dropped a heavy crossbeam in place.

"No lock?" Jerrell asked.

"This door is rarely used. The beam keeps others out, and that is all that matters."

They ascended another flight of stairs, the door at the top leading to another storage room filled with cookware, plates, cups, mugs, pots, pans, and sacks of food. The door across the room brought them to a kitchen where servants busily prepared a meal.

A bald man with a dark mustache and wearing a white apron looked up. "Ah. Mond. What brings you to my kitchen?"

"I just completed a delivery for His Grace." Mond led Jerrell past an oven large enough to live in. "I am to meet Chalmers for payment."

"The master of grouchiness passed through here a few minutes ago."

Mond reached the door on the far end of the kitchen and pushed it open. "I'll find him and be on my way. Have a good day, Pierre."

"You as well, Mond."

Jerrell followed the man through a dining room with a table that seated twenty and emerged in a room with a two-story ceiling and walls covered in windows. A massive chandelier hung above the room.

"Where is the furniture?" Jerrell asked.

"Likely in storage to clear space for the party." Mond led him across the marble floor and through a long rectangular hall with walls covered in tapestries. He stopped in the middle of the next room, standing in the center of a complex mosaic made of tiny colored tiles. "We will wait here."

Jerrell looked down and tried to make sense of the mosaic, but it was a complex symbol that held no meaning to him.

A door opened and Chalmers came through it. Before it closed, Jerrell spied a dark-haired young woman. She stood about his height and wore a striking yellow gown. A tailor knelt at her side with pins in her hand. When the woman in the dress spun to face Jerrell, her brown eyes met his, he smiled, appreciating her large, brown eyes and attractive appearance. Then, she smiled.

The door closed, obscuring the view while his pulse continued to thump in his ear.

Chalmers stopped before Mond. "I assume the delivery is complete."

Mond growled. "Don't insult me, Chalmers. I know my business, and everything went exactly as planned. High Wizard Wrenthal will be pleased, I am sure of it."

"Very well." The steward held out a leather pouch. "Take your coin and be gone. We've much to prepare before tomorrow evening's festivities."

The man sped down a branching corridor and headed up a staircase.

"You heard him. Let's go." Mond headed in the opposite direction from where they had entered.

"Where are you going?"

Over his shoulder, he said, "Out the front door. We will circle the building to get back to the wagon."

Jerrell crossed the entrance hall and slowed when he spied folded sheets of parchment on a narrow table along the wall. Golden light emitted from within the folds. With a quick but fluid movement, Jerrell snatched one and slid it into his coat.

Mond reached the door and turned toward him. "Before I forget, it is

best if you keep anything you saw or heard here to yourself. If certain information were to leak and cause Wrenthal or his family trouble...it would be
bad. Very bad."

Jerrell nodded. "Do not worry. I am not one to talk, especially where a
wizard is concerned."

"Good."

Jerrell followed Mond out the door, the stolen invitation hidden at his
side.

CHAPTER 10
PARTY CRASHER

Across the square from Shear Castle, Jerrell hid in the dark recess of a doorway. The jeweler who owned the shop had locked the doors and departed when the sun touched the horizon.

Devotion ended, and the people in the square outside of the castle's outer wall rose to their feet and went on their way. During the ritual, the sky had darkened until only the last memory of daylight faintly illuminated the western sky.

The square emptied. The night fell silent until the clopping of hooves interrupted the stillness. A horse-drawn carriage appeared from a street connected to the square and headed for the castle gate. The moment the carriage blocked the guards' view, Jerrell burst into motion.

With rushed steps, he crossed the open square, keeping the carriage between him and the gate.

The guards called for the carriage to halt. It stopped outside the gate while the men spoke to the driver. Jerrell closed the gap, crouched down, and slid beneath the carriage. He hooked his boots to the front axle and gripped the rear with his hands. When the guard stepped away and the carriage lurched into motion, Jerrell pulled himself up. With his stomach muscles tight, he held his body just inches above the cobblestone drive as the carriage entered the castle grounds.

The carriage followed a curved drive and rounded a fountain before stopping. Light from an open doorway shone on Jerrell's right, so he lowered himself to the ground and rolled to the left side of the carriage. Standing in its shadows, Jerrell pulled the folded robes from inside his coat, slid them on, and secured the sash. A castle guard approached the carriage, opened the door on the side facing the castle entrance, and a woman in a black gown stepped out.

Waiting a beat to allow the woman time to walk away from the carriage, Jerrell opened the door on his side, climbed through the carriage, and put his hand on the other door just before the castle guard closed it.

"Are you not going to let me out?" Jerrell asked

"What?" The guard stammered. "I apologize, Master Wizard. I could have sworn there was only one person inside."

Jerrell adjusted his lapel to ensure his coat was not showing. "I accept your apology. This time," he said, his tone edged with anger. "Now, please stand aside so I may climb out."

"I am sorry." The guard stood aside and held the door open.

As Jerrell climbed out, the woman who had occupied the carriage ascended the front stairs, handed a slip of paper to the servant at the door, and faded from view.

Jerrell began toward the entrance but stopped when the guard extended an arm to block the way. He looked at the guard with an arched brow.

"I cannot allow anyone in if they do not possess an invitation."

Reaching into his robes, Jerrell found the slip of paper he had stolen and handed it to the man. The guard opened it, and a golden glow shone on his face. After brief inspection, he handed it back.

"Have a good evening, sir."

Jerrell snatched the invite from the man and snapped, "I intend to, provided you are finished harassing me."

Although the armored guard wore a sword and stood a half head taller than Jerrell, he blinked and backed away. "Again, I apologize if I have offended you, Master Wizard."

Without a response, Jerrell stomped off, his robes swishing with each step. He climbed the front stairs and was met by a servant dressed in dark blue.

"Welcome to Shear Castle," the man said. "I will take your invitation."

Jerrell handed the slip to the man. "I had planned to arrive prior to Devotion but was delayed by an unexpected visitor. I hope I have not missed anything important."

The hum of conversation came from inside.

"The presentation of the high wizard's son is still pending." The man extended an arm toward the building's interior. "Please join the party. Food and drink are waiting inside."

Lifting his chin to bolster an aloof image, Jerrell swept past the man.

Flames in wall sconces illuminated the long entrance hall. Two pairs of servants stood along the side walls. Stopping in front of the man on his right, Jerrell lifted an empty goblet from a silver platter.

The woman beside the man gestured toward the long table behind her. "What is your drink of choice, Master Wizard? We have a fine Farrowen red, Pallanese brandy, and water for those who wish to avoid such indulgence."

Avoid indulgence? The mere idea of it rubbed Jerrell the wrong way, but after what he had discovered about wizard magic, he understood why some might avoid it. "Wine for me." He held his goblet toward her, and she filled it. Without thanking her, he walked away. After all, he was a member of the entitled wizard class.

As he reached the far end of the hall, the view expanded, and the noise of the crowd grew louder. The spacious, empty room he had visited the day before was now filled with guests.

Wealthy merchants in ruffled doublets and well-tailored coats stood among robed wizards and women in evening gowns. The scene reminded him of the ball in Yor's Point and had him wondering how often the ruling class held lavish parties. *Is this how the wizard class uses the taxes they demand of us Ungifted?* Granted, Jerrell had never paid a copper of tax, but he had heard others, ranging from farmers to business owners, complain about the tithes they were forced to endure.

His gaze then landed on a brunette having a conversation with a dark-haired wizard a few years Jerrell's elder. It was the woman he spotted during his delivery with Mond. Her yellow gown clung to her slim waist, accentuating the modest curves surrounding it.

Making his way across the room, Jerrell nodded to those who met his gaze and said things like *good to see you, you look well,* and *it has been too long.* Some guests nodded and replied as if they remembered Jerrell while others appeared confused. He ignored them and did not stop until he reached the side of the woman in yellow, which he timed to occur just as the man with her headed toward the dining room.

"I must say," Jerrell spoke in a friendly tone, causing the woman to turn toward him. "You appear ravishing tonight."

Her brow furrowed, her big eyes appearing like pools of amber. "Have we met?"

Jerrell took her hand and kissed it. "We have now."

"But you have not given me your name."

"Why would I give you my name? Do you not already have one for yourself?"

She laughed. "I do. You may call me Terissa."

"Terissa," Jerrell repeated it. "A beautiful name. How appropriate."

"And you are?"

"Wondering if you will continue to hold prisoner my captive heart."

She crossed her arms and narrowed her eyes. "Tell me your name or this conversation ends now."

Jerrell grinned. "You have spirit. Now, I am truly intrigued. You may call me Parion."

Her mouth twisted in thought. "I know that name from somewhere."

"My father is high wizard of Grakal."

"Oh, yes. I recall you from the University." Her eyes narrowed as she looked him over. "You appear to have filled out since I last saw you."

Stifling his worry, Jerrell asked, "When did you graduate?"

"Three years past."

"Ah. I only graduated this spring. Over the past two years, I must have matured."

"I can see that." She smiled. "I did not realize you were invited."

"Well, the invite came for my father, but he could not attend. I was already in the area for High Wizard Jakins's ball."

"You were there?"

He nodded.

"Was it like they say? Did Paloun truly split Jakins's body in two?"

Jerrell laughed. "Not quite. It basically came down to a lightning blast to the chest that killed Jakins." He found it interesting how stories became inflated so rapidly. *By the year's end, they may claim Jakins was blasted into a thousand bits.* Rubbing his jaw while narrowing his eyes, he asked, "I am curious. What else have you heard?"

She leaned close. "I heard Paloun was not working alone. He and his co-conspirator tricked Jakins into buying up hundreds of wine barrel orders due to a rumor that there would be a shortage. As we heard just a few days ago, it was actually a banner harvest for the Lionne district, which destroyed the value of those orders, leaving Jakins distraught and destitute. That is when Paloun issued his challenge."

That is frighteningly close to the truth. It was surprising that the information had reached Shear so quickly. "Did you get the name of the man working with Paloun?"

"Yes. It was Jerrell-something. Reportedly, he is some sort of a charlatan."

Jerrell grinned. His fame was growing. *Charlatan. I like that.* "I believe his last name was Landish."

"That's it." Her eyes lit up. "So...it is true?"

"As far as I can tell, yes."

She slid and arm into his. "Perhaps you would like to go somewhere more private, and you can tell me more."

When she held Jerrell's arm tight against her side, he had a difficult time focusing on the reason behind his visit. *What would be the harm in a little rendezvous with a beautiful girl?* His inner voice asked. Another voice answered, *She is a wizardess. Think of what she will do if she discovers your ruse.*

A bell rang, drawing his attention. A man in white silken robes with midnight blue trim and a sash to match stood in the opening leading to the entry hall. He stood six feet in height with broad shoulders and an athletic build despite the gray that peppered his dark hair and trimmed beard. A familiar face stood beside him.

Dressed in dark blue, the head steward, Chalmers, held a bell in one hand and shouted, "Attention! High Wizard Wrenthal would like a word with his guests."

"Welcome to Shear Castle," the high wizard said in a bold voice. "I hope you are enjoying yourselves."

As the man continued his speech, Jerrell groaned; he wasn't ready to abandon the girl at his side. However, the announcement was the distraction he was waiting for, and another opportunity of such caliber was unlikely to come again.

He leaned close to Terissa. "I must step off to the dining room. I've had nothing to eat all day."

"I can join you," she offered.

"No," he whispered while patting her hand in his. "You should remain, so you can witness the presentation. I will return momentarily."

"I suppose you are right. After all, Ferrol *is* my brother."

Jerrell nearly choked when he realized the girl was the high wizard's daughter. "Excuse me."

He slipped away and eased into the dining room to find four people adding food to their plates.

"The high wizard has begun his son's presentation." Jerrell stood beside the door and eyed the guests, waiting for a reaction.

"Oh. We should go out there," the woman said.

"Of course," replied the man with her.

The other two men followed, leaving Jerrell alone.

He crossed the room and pushed his way into the kitchen.

Six people were busy cooking – a man rolling beef into balls and placing them onto a pan, a woman stirring batter, another woman chopping vegetables, a man bent over and peering into a burning oven, another removing baked rolls from a pan and dropping them into a basket, and the head cook directing them. As Jerrell expected, the serving staff remained trapped in the ballroom and reluctant to move until the speech was finished.

"We ran out of wine and need another barrel," Jerrell announced.

"Already?" Pierre, the head cook asked. "We tapped two barrels less than two hours ago."

"What can I say? We wizards are a thirsty lot."

"Why are you in here rather than the porters?"

"I volunteered my services. Considering how much I intend to consume; it is the least I can do."

The man looked Jerrell up and down with an arched brow. "Pardon, but I do not think you can carry a barrel by yourself."

Wiggling his fingers, Jerrell said, "That is why I intend to use magic."

"Oh." The cook blinked and swallowed hard. "In that case, head down the staircase behind the kitchen. The barrels are in the cellar at the bottom."

Jerrell navigated past the long preparation table in the middle of the room and opened the rear door. When he was on the stairs, he closed the door behind him and descended to the landing. The double doors leading outside were closed with the crossbar securely in place. There was no getting in through those doors. *I am already inside.* He chuckled to himself as he hurried down to the cellar.

It was dark, too dark to see. Jerrell lifted his robes and drew his dagger. His thumb found the jewel on the hilt. Applying pressure, the jewel sunk in with a click. A soft blue light bloomed in the sapphire, illuminating his immediate surroundings. With the blade held up for light, he crossed the room and stopped before the shelf.

"Thank the gods," he muttered in relief. "It is still here."

He reached out and picked up the gold statue. It was heavier than he had anticipated, making him wonder just how much gold it contained. *I will be rich…again.*

Gripping his prize firmly, Jerrell climbed the stairs to the landing. He lifted the heavy crossbar and set it against the wall. Easing the door open, he peered through a narrow gap. There were no guards standing by the door or anywhere that he could see. He saw only the moonlit drive and the shadowy trees beyond it.

He opened the door and stepped out into the dark night.

A globe of light bloomed in the trees. A man in white silken robes stepped out with the light floating a foot above his open palm. The light illuminated a middle-aged face covered by a graying beard. Jerrell recognized the man instantly. *Oh, no. Wrenthal.*

The door behind him opened and another familiar face emerged from the shadows. *Mond?*

"He has the statue," Mond said. "I told you he would take the bait, Your Grace."

High Wizard Wrenthal appeared to be weighing Jerrell with his steel gaze. "You are in trouble, Master Landish."

"You know my name?"

"Oh, I know much about you." He raised his voice. "Guards!"

The rapid thuds of footsteps were joined by the clanking of armor. Two dozen soldiers rushed around the corner of the castle and down the drive. They surrounded Jerrell, forming a half-circle five strides away. Four of the men held loaded crossbows aimed at him. The others gripped swords.

"As you can see," Wrenthal said. "Fighting would be futile, and flight would be impossible."

"This was a trap."

The wizard grinned. "A trap set to capture a scoundrel."

I am in trouble.

CHAPTER 11

A PROPOSAL

Jerrell was ushered along a winding path, through the gardens beyond Shear Castle. The wizard and Mond led the way while the guards trailed behind him. Another man might have been frightened by such enforcements, but Jerrell was proud that they considered him such a significant threat. During the walk around the castle, he considered his situation and how he had fallen into such a predicament.

Mond appearing with the job offer just when Jerrell had played his hand of woe seemed fortuitous at the time, but looking back, he realized the man had followed him and was watching over his shoulder, waiting for an opportunity.

Finding the golden statue in the basement seemed odd at the start, but greed had clouded Jerrell's wits and caused him to ignore his instincts. In hindsight, he remembered that the other items were covered in dust, while the statue was pristine. It had been placed all alone so he could not miss it, and he was bound to survey any room he entered.

When he happened across the invitations with nobody looking, Jerrell had jumped at the chance. Now, he realized they had been left out for him to notice and Mond had led him past them intentionally, knowing the temptation would be unbearable. The wizard had counted on Jerrell finding a way into the party once he had an invitation. From there, it had been simple. The presentation of Ferrol would draw everyone's attention, creating the ideal moment for Jerrell to commit the theft. Lastly, the unguarded back door seemed innocent enough, but it made too obvious of a choice for his escape.

It had all been carefully planned. But why? Surely not to simply kill him or imprison him. *No, the high wizard wants something from me.* That certainty put Jerrell at ease as he followed the guards across an empty, moonlit plaza, toward the dormant obelisk.

The wizard stopped before a door in the base of the spire. Black iron bands ran across the door, secured by thick bolts that reinforced the dark wood. No handle was visible. A metal panel covered in symbols and scrawling script was mounted to the middle of the door. Wrenthal pressed his palm to the panel and a tingle crawled across Jerrell's skin, causing his hair to stand on end. A hum arose. A sound of scraping metal came from beyond the door, followed by a thud. The door swung open, and light bloomed from the room beyond it. The wizard strode into the room, followed by a pair of guards.

"Go on, Landish," Mond said.

Jerrell strode through the doorway, into a room that stirred his curiosity.

Glowing globes mounted to the brick wall provided light. The chamber was a dozen strides deep and just as wide. A circular dais stood in the middle. A column made of crystal ran from the center of the dais to the top of the chamber, a hundred fifty feet above. An altar stood at the far edge of the dais, two strides from the column.

Along the outer edge of the room, eight pedestals were arranged in a circle. White lines painted on the floor surrounded the dais, forming an eight-pointed star. Each of the eight pedestals rested on one of the star points. Complex runes marked the interior of the star.

A variety of strange objects rested on the pedestals, each a different design and color. A purple dog, a blue globe containing a silver lightning bolt, a diamond-shaped gem of pale blue, a yellow and black bee, a pyramid with a flat roof, a three-dimensional star of black onyx with silver edges, and a ruby-studded star-shaped blade. Yet, one pedestal remained empty.

The wizard climbed onto the dais and gestured toward the surrounding pedestals. "As you can see, I am a collector of the exotic."

Jerrell glanced at Mond, who stood a stride to his side. The man merely stared back, so Jerrell did his best to play along. "Very impressive, Your Grace."

Wrenthal cocked a brow. "You humor me."

"It seemed prudent."

"In your position, I suppose I would do the same."

"Yet, I know you have no intention of killing me or locking me in a cell."

The wizard smirked. "You think yourself clever, yet you fell into my trap."

"Perhaps I was curious as to why you set the trap."

His brows rose toward his hairline. "You knew?"

"The statue was all alone, too obvious for me to miss. Unlike the shelves, no dust covered it, so it was recently placed there. Similarly, the invitations were impossible not to notice, the opportunity to snag one too apparent. Then, there was the rear door, unguarded and easy to exit, nigh impossible to enter." All were things Jerrell had deduced after his capture, but the wizard did not know that, and Jerrell did not lie. He merely allowed Wrenthal to reach his own conclusion.

The wizard stroked his bearded chin. "What of Mond? Did you suspect him?"

Jerrell considered the question, weighing a boost to his own ego against the potential benefits of boosting Wrenthal's opinion of Mond. "Not until tonight. Even then, it was merely possible, for Mond could have been manipulated as well."

Wrenthal chuckled, his gaze shifting to Mond before he turned back to Jerrell. "You must wish to know why you are here."

"I will admit, I am itching with curiosity."

The wizard gestured toward the pedestals. "What do you see?"

Jerrell frowned. "Odd objects of questionable worth?"

"What do you not see?"

A grunt slipped out before Jerrell replied. "Whatever artifact should rest on the empty pedestal."

"Exactly." Wrenthal gestured toward the empty pedestal. "I wish it occupied."

With a shrug, Jerrell suggested, "I know a woman in Yor's Point who has a carving of an impressive, wooden penis. It might look fetching among your collection."

The guards chuckled, as did Mond. Wrenthal did not.

The wizard said, "A specific object belongs here. A gold owl with emerald eyes. It will be mine."

THE WIZARD and his guards escorted Jerrell back to the castle, taking him through a guarded side door and up a narrow stairwell to the third floor, where he was led to a dark, unoccupied room. The windows provided a moonlit view of the waterway and the old city far below. A sitting area surrounded a fireplace along one wall. A desk and credenza occupied the other side of the room.

Wrenthal walked to the window and stared out into the night. Jerrell stood a few strides behind the wizard, waiting while Mond and four guards lurked behind him. He was curious about why the room remained dark. Others might find the darkness unnerving. Jerrell embraced the darkness. It served as a cloak that any good thief wore to his own advantage. After a few minutes of staring out the window, the wizard broke the silence.

"I have held the position of high wizard for two decades." Wrenthal said. "Seven wizards have challenged me, desiring to take my place. Each found the price too steep and paid with their lives. Yet, time marches on and I age while Lord Malvorian does not. In the meantime, he sits on a crystal throne and gathers the prayers of his people, fueling magic unequaled by any except another wizard lord. The man has ruled Farrowen for eighty years, and another century may pass before death claims him. Without prayers to sustain me, I will be dead and forgotten long before he is gone."

The wizard spun from the window and looked Jerrell in the eyes. "Ambition led me to claiming the position of high wizard, yet that ambition now seeks another outlet. I am trapped with no way to increase my power without facing Malvorian, which would surely end me. Thus, I seek other ways to fulfill the need that drives me."

Jerrell replied, "I am with you thus far."

"Good, because I have a task suitable to someone of your skills."

"My skills?"

The wizard smirked. "Thieves are plentiful, but successful and resourceful ones are less common. To my knowledge, none are brazen enough to masquerade as wizards, something you have done successfully twice in a single week."

It was true.

"Besides," Wrenthal said, "the way you manipulated Jakins into purchasing all those orders for Farrowen wine impressed me. His publicly displayed financial disaster may have inflicted more damage than the lightning blast to the chest that killed him. To execute a ploy of that level reveals that you a more than a mere thief."

Jerrell felt his pride swell at the man's words. At the same time, he suspected it was the wizard's intention. "I am impressed as well. You are well informed."

The wizard smirked. "Power comes in many ways. Information can be as powerful as the strongest magic."

Jerrell laughed. "Spies. You have spies in your employ."

"As I said, you are an uncommon thief, but I also am an uncommon wizard."

"Now that you've done your best to flatter me, why am I here?"

"I see you can be direct as well as conniving. That is good, for knowing when to use either approach is a skill unto itself." Wrenthal strode over to the desk, leaned against it and activated the enchanted lantern beside him. "I need you to locate and steal the artifact missing from my collection."

Jerrell recalled the wizard's description—a gold owl with green eyes. "Where would I find this object?"

"It is in the possession of a longtime rival—a wizard named Kylar Mor."

The name sounded familiar. "I have heard his name, but I do not know this wizard."

"You will journey to Tiamalyn, locate the object, and acquire it. Before you return, you will find a means to publicly embarrass Mor, and I want it to be even more degrading than what you did to Jakins."

"Tiamalyn?"

"Oh, yes. You see, Kylar Mor is Lord Horus's right-hand man, making him the second most powerful wizard in all of Orenth."

Great. Another wizard to upset. It was likely he would also draw the attention of Lord Horus. "And what do I get for risking the wrath of this wizard?"

"You are an Ungifted caught dressed as a Gifted, while attempting to steal from the high wizard of Shear. Tell me why I should not kill you or lock you away for good?"

While the wizard had a point, he had also pursued Jerrell. "You need me, so neither will happen."

Wrenthal took a deep breath. "First, I am willing to pay you twenty gold pieces.

"First? What else are you willing to offer?"

"My, you are a brazen one, aren't you?"

"If I weren't, I'd be of little use to you."

"True." Wrenthal stepped closer. "I do have other plans for you, something that could benefit us both."

"I am interested."

"For now, the allure of twenty gold will have to suffice. Complete your quest, and we will discuss it. Until then, I will give you two things to assist you on your mission."

"Is one of them your daughter?" Jerrell asked with a grin.

Fire flickered in the wizard's stern gaze. "Stay away from Terissa." He scooped a leather pouch from his desk and tossed it to Mond. "Inside are five gold pieces, more than enough to pay for your journey and needs while in Tiamalyn. Use them wisely and in any way required to complete your assignment."

Why did he throw the coin purse to Mond? "You mentioned two things."

"The second is a partner to assist you in any way needed."

Jerrell frowned. "I work alone."

"You *used* to work alone. Not any longer. This is not negotiable."

"Fine. Who is this partner?"

"I believe you already know Mister Mond."

Jerrell turned to the armored man holding the coin purse. "I am stuck with you?"

Mond nodded. "It appears we are finished here. Return to your room at the Elder Inn and get a good night's rest. Meet me at the docks at sunup." He grinned. "Welcome to the team."

BEFORE THE SUN edged over the towering east bank of the waterway, Jerrell found himself on a barge. Dressed in his dark tunic, breeches, and coat, the breeze tossed his hair while twelve men rowed the craft from a small dock at the southeast edge of Shear. The city slowly faded into the distance as the barge entered the mouth of Grakal River and began its upstream journey.

The barge was an odd craft with a flat, rectangular deck wrapping around five flat-roofed cabins. At the stern of the craft was an observation deck, upon which the captain stood, allowing him to see over the cabins. The man pointed while issuing orders, his other hand on the tiller at his side.

Jerrell decided he wished to be freed of his pack and turned to Mond, who was dressed in a fresh tunic along with the same vest and brimmed hat as the prior day. "Which cabin is mine?"

"Ours," Mond corrected him.

"We are sharing a room?"

"The others are occupied by the crew, and we hired extra to allow us to travel at night."

"They work in shifts?"

"Aye. In fact, some crewmembers are sleeping now."

"So, I have to share with you." Jerrell groaned.

"Would you rather sleep on deck?"

"I'd rather sleep in a nice cozy inn with cold ale and hot food."

Mond grunted. "You'll find none of that here."

Jerrell looked behind them and caught one last glimpse of Shear. Ahead, the gorge narrowed, the river meandering through trees bordered by tall rocky cliffs.

"How many days to Tiamalyn?" he asked.

"The journey upriver takes longer than the return. Even rowing at night, it'll take four days."

"Four days? We could get there on foot faster than that."

"Would you rather walk a hundred miles?"

Grimacing, Jerrell shook his head. "No."

"If we traveled on foot, you'd have to carry your gear and sleep on the ground. It is autumn and the weather is bound to become less comfortable once we are farther from the sea." He patted Jerrell on the back. "Trust me. This is the preferred option. Besides, the barge has been secured by Wrenthal and will be waiting for us when we are ready to depart. If we need to leave urgently, you will be thankful for it."

Of all arguments the man had made, Jerrell found the last one the most compelling. He was embarking on a mission to steal a prized object from a vaunted wizard, after causing the man tremendous public embarrassment.

What could go wrong?

CHAPTER 12

TIAMALYN

Four days later, the barge rounded a bend in the river, and the roar of rushing water came from the most spectacular feature of a stunning view.

A quarter-mile of waterfalls covered the width of the river, the water spilling over the edge of a bluff hundreds of feet high. The city of Tiamalyn loomed beside the river, spanning the areas above and below the falls.

Ten-story walls obscured the lower portion of the city, but the palatial estates along the top of the bluff were impossible to miss. The biggest of them was Tiamalyn Palace, nestled at the western edge of the upper city, beside the waterfall. Tiers supported by fluted columns made it an impressive structure. Above it all stood the Tower of Devotion, the upper reaches burning with the emerald flame of Oren.

"So, this is Tiamalyn," Jerrell noted.

"It is a thing to behold," Mond said. "At least from the outside."

"What does that mean?"

"You will soon find out."

The men at the oars rowed with a fury, yet their progress was slow, since the current was noticeably stronger near the falls. The next twenty minutes passed slowly until, finally, the barge bumped into a dock. Ropes were thrown and tied, securing the craft. Mond spoke with the captain and then waved to Jerrell, who hoisted his pack and stepped off.

The two men followed a path along the docks before turning toward the city. The tall pale walls reminded Jerrell of Fastella, the only other great city he had visited. A raised portcullis at the gate allowed people, horses, and wagons to flow in and out of the city...provided they were not stopped for inspection, like the wagon now standing in the opening. After a few moments, guards dressed in green and brown leather backed away and waved the wagon forward. The guards then turned their attention on Jerrell and Mond.

One guard held his hand up to stop them. "State your reason for visiting Tiamalyn."

Mond said, "We come from Fray's Crossing, a village in north central Farrowen. My nephew has never been to the city. I thought to bring him for a week to expand his view of the world."

The man looked at Jerrell, his eyes going to the dagger on his hip before turning to the sword strapped to Mond's waist. "Why the weapons?"

"Would you travel without a weapon?"

"Probably not."

"They are for our protection, mostly to deter bandits and such, rather than let them believe we are easy targets."

"I saw you two coming from the docks."

"We traveled by foot to Shear and took a barge upriver."

The man looked at Jerrell. "Is this true?"

Jerrell nodded and replied, "Y-Y-Yes, s-s-sir."

When the guard narrowed his eyes at Jerrell, Mond interjected. "The lad has stuttered since he was kicked in the head by a horse. It affected his wits and destroyed his ability to communicate."

"Well, I hope you two enjoy your stay. Just don't go causing trouble."

Jerrell and Mond walked off. Once inside the gate, Jerrell looked up at Mond. "You lie easily."

"I've had a lot of practice."

Jerrell stared at Mond. "What, exactly, do you do for Wrenthal?"

"Right now, I am nursemaid to a mouthy thief who asks too many questions." He gave Jerrell a sidelong look. "What was with the stutter?"

"In my experience, most people lack the patience to deal with someone who stutters. I figured it was a quick way to cut the conversation short."

"Sad but true," Mond said before chuckling. "It worked, though."

They crossed the square and entered a street bordered by shops, some of which had boarded up windows. Potholes marred the otherwise paved street. When they crossed an alley, Jerrell noted crates filled with trash clogging the way. A beggar sat in a doorway with an empty cup beside him. Another lay sleeping beside the wall, his clothing in tatters. The people they passed often had dirty faces and stains on their apparel.

Jerrell leaned close to Mond. "This place reminds me of the Dregs, the worst district of Fastella."

Mond grunted. "Lower Tiamalyn receives little attention from the government. The upper city is impressive. If anything, the lower city is depressing."

"I assume the wizard we seek is in the upper city."

"Oh, yes."

"Is that where we are going?"

"No. Not yet." Mond looked up. "The sun will soon set. I thought you might enjoy a solid meal and a good night of sleep before we get swept up in our mission."

"And ale," Jerrell said. "Lots of ale."

Mond narrowed his eyes. "Ale softens your wits, slows your reactions, and leads to poor decisions."

Jerrell gave him a sidelong look. "Are you always such a bore?"

"You'll not call me a bore when my sword saves your life."

"I've run into plenty of trouble in the past and survived just fine without your sword."

"How often have you upset a skilled wizard with dozens of guards in his employ?"

Shrugging in response, "Other than Jakins...never."

"Jakins is a pale shadow compared to Kylar Mor. There is a reason Jakins settled for a position in Yor's Point rather than attempting to claim the throne in Tiamalyn, the center of power for Orenth. While ambitious, he could not stand up to Mor's magic or his intellect."

"You make him sound like a wizard lord."

"Close. As far as I can tell, he may be the most powerful wizard in the world other than the eight who sit on crystal thrones. As chancellor for Lord Horus, he runs the city. Horus trusts him and gives him full control over Tiamalyn while Horus deals with issues that affect the rest of his wizardom."

What have I gotten myself into? "I notice that you mentioned none of this before I agreed to Wrenthal's terms."

"It would have made little difference. Had you not agreed to do them, you would not have left the castle alive."

Jerrell narrowed his eyes. "I knew too much. You could not allow me to warn anyone of what Wrenthal had planned."

"I'm glad you see the truth."

"Yet, you are not worried I will betray Wrenthal now?"

"Why do you think I am here?"

Jerrell frowned. "What if I killed you and just went on my way?"

Mond grunted. "I find that unlikely. Even if you were successful and somehow got the better of me, Wrenthal is a persistent man. He would hunt you down. You'd never find peace."

"I am used to others holding a grudge."

"How many are high wizards?" Mond stopped and gestured toward a building to the right. A green leaf graced the sign over the door; the text carved into the sign read New Leaf Inn. "Here we are. I suspect you are hungry."

Just like that, the man transitioned from talk of killing me to ask if I was hungry. Jerrell found Mond's casual manner, in which he discussed everything from murder to eating, informative. *He clearly has a military background for killing to be so inconsequential. I will show him I cannot be shaken.*

Replying with a casual smile, Jerrell said, "Ravenous."

The man led him inside.

The floors were wood. A bar stood opposite a stairwell and a hallway extended beyond, leading toward the rear door. To Jerrell's right, rectangular tables with benches occupied the small eating area. All of the tables were occupied. The patrons ranged from an elderly couple to rough-looking men with scars and scowls marring their faces.

"Small taproom," Jerrell noted.

"I see two empty stools at the end of the bar."

To one side of the stools were a burly man whose tight coat appeared ready to burst and a man with a shaved head and thick black beard. Both appeared as rough as any in the place.

Jerrell made for the bar and slid onto an empty stool. He set his pack on the floor at his feet. A tall man leaned on the bar across from Jerrell. One eye was covered with a patch, the other ran over Jerrell and Mond suspiciously.

"What can I do for you two?"

Jerrell replied, "We'll need a room, food, and drink."

"I thought as much. I haven't seen you before, so you must be travelers."

"We are…"

Mond rested his hand on Jerrell's arm, stopping him in mid-sentence. "Minding our own business, which I am sure you can appreciate."

The bartender nodded. "Minding one's business is recommended unless you are seeking trouble."

"How much for a room and a meal?"

"A silver piece will get you that and a couple ales."

"Water for me," Mond replied.

"I'll take both ales," Jerrell offered as he slid a silver across the bar. "What's for dinner?"

"Mutton stew."

Jerrell sighed inwardly. Only gruel was worse than mutton stew. Both were served to soldiers and in the lowliest of taprooms, which informed him of the inn's clientele.

The man pulled a mug from a shelf, walked to a barrel, and opened the spigot. Dark, frothy liquid poured out. Once filled, he set the mug before Jerrell, who stared at it.

"I thought you were excited for ale," Mond said.

"I was, but I strongly suspect this mug was never washed."

The man chuckled. "You should see the things I've had to drink and eat. They make an unwashed mug seem awfully desirable."

Using his sleeve, Jerrell wiped the rim clean and then took a drink. The ale was heavy with a harsh bitterness.

A swipe of his sleeve wiped the foam from his lips. He looked at Mond and asked a question that had been irritating him like a pebble in his boot. "You mentioned Kylar Mor being the second most feared man in Orenth."

"So?"

"Wrenthal clearly has ambition. Why has he not found a way to claim a similar role in Farrowen?"

"Because Gerald Wrenthal cannot stand Lord Malvorian. Besides, not all wizardoms have the same political structure. Malvorian refuses to relinquish the governance of Marquithe, even though it would allow him to concentrate on more significant matters. In truth, I don't blame him. Marquithe is the center of trade for the southern wizardoms. All roads lead to it, and those roads are paved. No other wizardom can claim that."

"Why Shear?" Jerrell asked. "Lionne is the center of wine trade. Wouldn't high wizard of Lionne be a more desirable position than that of Shear?"

"Oh, there is no doubt Lionne draws more attention, which is the problem. In the time since Wrenthal assumed rule in Shear, Lionne Castle has changed hands four times."

"I see. Being high wizard puts a target on your back. To do so in Lionne adds three more targets just for fun."

"Exactly." Mond smirked. "Besides, Wrenthal is clever enough to know the power of information. From Shear, a nice enough place to rule, he can pull strings elsewhere without attracting attention."

The barkeep appeared from a door behind the bar carrying two bowls. He set them down in front of Jerrell and Mond.

"What about my water?" Mond asked.

The man rolled his eyes and walked back through the door. A moment later, he returned with a metal cup and set it in front of Mond. The water in the cup had a cloudy yellow tint.

Mond lifted the cup, sniffed it, and scrunched his face. "Sulphur."

"At least it's wet."

"Like I said, I've had worse." He took a drink and set the cup down.

Jerrell lifted his spoon and stared down at the bowl. "I vote we find another place to stay tomorrow night."

"We shall see."

"I just hope we don't get lice or some other unsavory infestation sleeping here."

Mond swallowed a spoonful of stew. "Again, I've had worse."

CHAPTER 13

THE BOWL OF OREN

The sun, hidden behind a puffy white cloud, approached its apex when Jerrell and Mond finally left the inn. Despite their late departure, Jerrell did not feel well rested. Between the physical discomfort of the barge's hard bunk and Mond's snoring, poor sleep plagued him during the journey to Tiamalyn. His hopes of better sleeping conditions upon reaching the city were crushed. The discovery of bugs in their mattresses forced them both to spend the night on the wooden floor, resulting in a fitful sleep and a sore neck.

As they approached the street corner, Jerrell glanced back at the inn. "Good riddance. I hope to never see that place again."

Mond arched a brow as they turned down a busy street, melding with the foot traffic. "I expected a thief like you to be at home in a place like that."

Jerrell had spent his teen years living on the streets, often enduring worse conditions than what he encountered at New Leaf Inn. "I guess I have grown used to edible food and clean accommodations."

"Like it or not, staying there for a night was the prudent choice."

Sighing, Jerrell said, "I get it. Had we come straight from the docks to the palace, we may have attracted attention. Spending a night there helps us blend in with the rest of the population."

"In this city, if you are neither Gifted nor wealthy, those in power treat you as something less than human." He gestured toward the citizens ahead of them, dressed in worn and stained clothing. "We now blend in with these people and they will provide us access to the upper city without anyone casting a second glance in our direction."

"The upper city? You mentioned an appointment at noon. I assume that is where we are heading?"

"Oh, yes." They exited a narrow street and crossed an open square. Hundreds of people flowed through the square, all bound for the uphill street on the far side. "Everyone here is heading toward the same place."

"Which is?"

"The Bowl of Oren."

Stories of the Bowl of Oren were not unfamiliar to Jerrell. They had even reached the streets of Fastella although it was hundreds of miles away.

The arena was purported to be massive in scale and to offer unequaled entertainment. While the only way to leave the arena was in a blood-soaked box or on the shoulders of victory, gladiators fought to escape the shackles of incarceration. Those duels to the death took place under harsh duress and sheer desperation, but they were the point upon which justice balanced.

They were halfway up the hill, following a road that ran beside the city's eastern wall, when Mond said, "You are quiet."

"I was considering what I knew about the gladiators."

"While I understand your interest, forget about those sorry souls. You'll not save them, and you certainly don't wish to join them. Instead, I suggest you focus on your objective."

Jerrell frowned. "I am surrounded by thousands of citizens eager to watch a fight. How is this supposed to help with..." People were too close to voice specifics, so he altered his sentence. "...my objective."

"Just remain alert. Do not worry. Everything we have done has been for a reason."

"Yet, you keep me in the dark and neglect to tell me anything until it is in my face. My help and skills were requested, and you refuse to allow me to make a single decision."

"That will soon change."

After a fifteen minute climb, they crested the hilltop and were greeted by a massive circular structure that towered six stories above the wide, brick street. Round fluted columns bordered arched entrances to the building, the ascending stairs inside coated in shadow. The Bowl of Oren. It could be nothing else.

Elegant carriages parked west of the building, behind a line of armed soldiers. No citizen from lower district attempted to break that line. Instead, the crowd split up and funneled through various entrances on the eastern face. Stopping beside Mond, Jerrell surveyed the view.

Impressive and pristine buildings surrounded the famous arena, each made of alabaster marble with clay tiled roofs. Red bricks paved the straight and broad streets of the upper city. On the bluff side of the main street were walled, palatial estates, each more impressive than the last until reaching the palace at the far end of the city.

Mond said, "The district on the bluff is called Highmount. The palace is up here, beside the falls. Wizards and wealthy merchants live in this part of the city. Those who don't, scheme to make it so. More than any place I know, Tiamalyn is a city of haves and have-nots."

"You seem to know a lot about this city."

"Not really. I have already shared most of what I know with you. The rest of what I can offer occurs soon. Let's head inside."

They joined the crowd funneling into the entrance nearest to the line of guards, entered the shadow cast by the stadium, passed between two thick columns, and climbed a staircase. At the top of the stairs, the crowd split apart, some ascending a stairwell to a higher level, others heading left or right to claim an open seat. Jerrell and Mond turned right and eased past dozens of eager spectators before sitting. Jerrell noticed that a wall divided their section from the one adjacent. Men wearing doublets or robes occupied the seats on the other side of the wall. At their sides sat elegant women in dresses of varying colors. It felt odd to be at an event attended by both the upper and lower class, who were simultaneously segregated.

In the center of the arena was a circular battlefield made of dirt and surrounded by fifteen foot walls. Iron bars blocked three open bays that were spaced along the western side. Racks filled with various weapons lurked in the shadows beyond the bars. Above the battlefield, spectators gathered on three levels, the noise of their eager conversations thick in the air. White puffy clouds dotted the otherwise blue sky as the sun reached its zenith. Soon, the only empty seats were those in the front and center of a section two sections down from Jerrell.

Horns echoed throughout the bowl. A wizard appeared amid a host of armored guards. He had angled eyes, a hooked nose, and a crown of golden leaves resting on his bald head. An emerald the size of a large grape graced the front of the crown. His robes were shimmery gold, his sash and lapel emerald green. Unlike most wizards, who appeared physically soft and weak, this man had thick shoulders and a bulging neck, belying the muscle hidden beneath the silk. The wizard was not alone, for a raven-haired beauty joined him. She wore a black and green sleeveless dress that exposed smooth tan skin and a plunging neckline. Plentiful mounds, which were impossible to miss, lurked beneath the dress, highlighted by a corset cinched around her slim waist.

"Who is that?" Jerrell muttered.

"The man is Lord Horus, ruler of Orenth. The woman is trouble personified."

"How so?"

"She is the wizard lord's wife, Grenda."

"Grenda." Jerrell repeated the name. "She looks a decade younger than him."

Mond laughed. "I venture everyone in the wizardom is decades younger than Horus. Just because he appears to be in his forties, more than eighty years have passed since he assumed rule, making him somewhere north of a hundred years of age."

Lord Horus stopped before the throne with Grenda beside him. The last guard took his place in the stands as another wizard appeared. He was tall with dark hair, tawny skin, and dark eyes. His silken green robes shimmered as he walked up to Horus and positioned himself at the wizard lord's side, opposite Grenda.

Again, horns blew. A section of the wall surrounding the battlefield was raised. A man dressed in a leather skirt, boots, and bracers emerged. On his head was a silver helm with a blue crest. While athletic, few would call him muscular and fewer would deem him tall.

Across the arena, another section lifted to reveal a man similarly dressed but with a red crest on his helmet. Muscles flexed as he strode out of the shadows into the center of the arena. The two men, neither of them armed, stopped before the throne and stared into the crowd.

The wizard lord raised his hands and clapped them together. Thunder shook the arena, causing Jerrell to jerk with a start. It left his ears ringing and the reverberation humming in his chest. The crowd fell silent.

"Welcome, citizens of Tiamalyn!" Horus's voice boomed, boosted by his magic. "Once again, we gather in the Bowl of Oren to witness those guilty of crimes fight for their lives. Per Orenthian tradition, innocence and redemption are proven or disproven on the field of battle. Should Oren will it, and either of these men survives the sentence they serve, he shall leave the Bowl a free man." The wizard lord raised his hand high. "When my arm falls, you shall begin."

Jerrell leaned toward Mond, his eyes on the two gladiators. "This fight appears uneven. Without weapons, the man with the red crest is bound to pound the one in the blue to a pulp."

"Perhaps," Mond said. "If he can last beyond the first phase of the duel, I believe the odds will flip in the thinner man's favor."

Lord Horus dropped his arm, and the wizard at his side flipped a giant hourglass over, the black sand inside pouring into the lower chamber. The two gladiators launched into battle. Fists, kicks, and grunts followed before the muscular warrior wrestled the other to the ground. The wiry man freed an arm and thrust his thumb into the bigger man's eye, freeing himself. The crowd cheered. The two men separated, the thinner man keeping a wary distance as the other wiped blood from his eye.

The sand in the upper chamber of the hourglass ran out, a horn blew, and the iron bars began to rise. The two men sprinted in opposite directions, each heading for a weapons rack.

The brawny man emerged with a great sword, five feet long and impossible to wield without excessive strength.

Jerrell shook his head. "Even if he is strong enough to lift it, that sword is too big and requires too much energy to swing."

The other man ran out with a spear.

Mond said, "Good choice when facing a great sword."

When the two warriors converged, the hulking gladiator swung his blade in a broad arc. The other man leapt back, just beyond the blade's reach, and then followed with a lunge. His spear plunged into the bigger man's stomach. The crowd roared.

The stunned gladiator dropped his sword and gripped the spear shaft jutting from his stomach. He staggered and fell to his knees as the crowd quieted. The thinner man looked up at Horus. There was a moment of complete silence. In the stillness, Jerrell sensed anticipation rise throughout the building. When Horus slid his finger across his throat, the cheers were deafening.

The standing warrior circled the kneeling man and drew a knife from the back of his skirts. With a swift stroke, the thin man sliced across the thick neck of the other. Blood spilled out. The man coughed and toppled over, dead. The crowd cheered. They seemed to thrive off blood and demanded more.

Jerrell leaned close to Mond. "Do you enjoy this?"

Mond grimaced. "In truth, I find it revolting."

"Then, why are we here?"

"You'll see."

While the victor circled the stadium floor and waved to the crowd, a quartet of guards raced out, lifted the dead from the bloodstained ground, and carried him away. The victor disappeared through a doorway that closed behind him. Horns blew again. Sections of the walls rose, and two new combatants emerged. Both were tall, their bodies covered in lean muscles. From their measured gait and calm demeanor, Jerrell knew in an instant that both were seasoned warriors.

Lord Horus stood, raised his fist to the sky, and dropped it. At the same moment, the wizard beside him flipped the hourglass, horns blew, and the fight began. This time, the battle was measured, the warriors trading, blocking, and dodging attacks until the hourglass expired and the weapon rack doors opened.

The gladiators quickly armed themselves, one with a sword and shield, the other gripping an odd weapon with a two foot blade at the end of a four foot wooden staff.

"What is that weapon?" Jerrell asked.

Sure enough, Mond knew the answer. "It is a naginata – a Kyranni weapon. For someone who is unschooled with it, it can be incredibly dangerous. I've seen soldiers lose fingers just attempting to wield one. On the other hand, those skilled with the weapon can be lethal killing machines."

The fight resumed, the man with the naginata spinning it faster than the eye could track. In return, the warrior with the sword and shield blocked strike after strike, occasionally countering with a lunge or swipe of his own weapon. The fight continued for several minutes and appeared evenly matched until one man made a mistake.

The warrior with the sword lunged forward when the other man's side was exposed. Rather than wait to be skewered, the other warrior spun out of the way, bringing his naginata blade around to strike his opponent's helmet with a clang. The soldier tumbled like a felled tree.

The victor stood over the downed man and looked up at Lord Horus, who slid his finger across his throat. *Another execution.*

In the stillness of the crowd's anticipation, a shout rang out. "No!" It was the gladiator. He threw his helmet aside to reveal a shorn head and a face covered in gray stubble. "Reagor is one of our best. I'll not murder him on the whim of the man who condemned him to fight. He deserves better."

The wizard beside Horus stood. "Your wizard lord has made his decision. You know the rules, Pohlar. Kill this man, or forfeit your life. The people of Tiamalyn will have blood."

The gladiator drove his naginata blade into the ground. "The people of Tiamalyn will be better served if Reagor continues to fight. He will give them what they wish in the blood of those who face him. And when he survives his sentence and earns his freedom, he will give them hope."

Lord Horus roared. "You have just condemned yourself, Pohlar!"

The other wizard thrust his hand toward Pohlar. The gladiator jerked, his arms pinned to his sides, and he rose thirty feet into the air.

"Any last words, Pohlar?" the wizard asked.

"I am Pallanese. Nothing is more important than honor. For too long, I forgot that. No longer. I would rather die with honor than live in this forsaken pit."

"Your wish is granted."

The wizard extended his other hand toward the weapon in the ground. It quivered and then tore free, spinning as it shot straight up. The blade end plunged into Pohlar's chin and emerged through the top of his head. The crowd gasped.

When the wizard lowered his hands, the dead warrior fell to the ground. His body lay in a grotesque position with extended arms and twisted legs. The other gladiator crawled to his hands and knees, shook his head, and stood to his feet. He stood over his dead opponent and lifted his gaze to the wizard lord.

"It appears your sentence does not end today, Reagor," Horus said. "We shall see if you can survive three more years in the Bowl. Perhaps you will earn your freedom. Perhaps you will end up like all the others."

Without a reply, the survivor picked up Pohlar's corpse, and carried it off, cradling the dead warrior like a child. The wizard glared at him while the men who had retrieved the previous corpse stood at the side of the stadium floor and watched Reagor depart.

Mond pointed toward the throne. "See the wizard standing beside Horus?"

"Do you mean the one who just murdered that man?"

"You are looking at Kylar Mor. Now, you have a sense of what you face."

Jerrell swallowed hard. The wizard's display was as telling as the ruthless nature of the gladiator's execution. Tall and handsome, the middle-aged man carried himself with blatant arrogance. *I must find a way to use his arrogance against him.* He also needed to do so without getting himself killed.

Mond said, "I have presented your target. The rest is up to you."

CHAPTER 14

THE GOLDEN GOOSE

In a shadowy doorway across from the Bowl of Oren, Jerrell and Mond waited as people poured out of the arena. While the bulk of the people were ushered toward the road leading to the lower district, the wizards climbed into waiting carriages. Among them, Jerrell spied Lord Horus, his stunning wife, and Chancellor Mor. A dozen armored guards escorted the trio into a garish carriage with green side panels and a white roof. The door handles, rails, and wheel spokes of the carriage were all plated in gold. Two guards climbed onto the carriage and sat on either side of the driver. The man snapped the reins, and the carriage began to turn around.

"Time to move." Jerrell stepped out from the shadows and headed down the broad street, straight toward the palace.

Mond kept pace with him but remained quiet. Rapid strides took them past gated entrances as they marched toward the palace. Clopping hooves came from behind them, growing louder as they approached. Moments later, a pair of workhorses trotted past, followed by the wizard lord's carriage. Five guards jogged along each side of the carriage. None gave Jerrell or Mond more than a glance.

The carriage and the escort of soldiers slowly grew more distant. Other carriages rode past, some turning to enter one of the massive estates along the top of the bluff. Jerrell ignored them. His focus remained affixed on the white, green, and gold carriage a quarter mile ahead of him. The carriage turned and faded into the palace gate. Guards on foot gathered at the gate, adding to the force already on duty.

Jerrell and Mond passed the palace gate at a quick pace and neared the wall at the edge of the city. All the while, Jerrell surveyed the home of Lord Horus.

Three-story walls surrounded the grounds. A gate tower stood beside the entrance. Armed soldiers patrolled the wall above the raised portcullis and on the ground below. He quickly counted twenty guards in total—too many for him and Mond to take in a fight, regardless of Mond's skill.

"I need to get inside," Jerrell said out loud. "Is there another entrance?"

Mond replied, "The palace wall connects to the city wall beside the river. The rear wall is on the edge of the bluff and overlooks the lower district. The side wall is adjacent to another estate. Because of this, the front gate is the only way in or out."

Jerrell stopped and turned toward Mond. "Yet, they must receive deliveries for food, wine, and other goods."

"Of course. However, I suspect such deliveries are inspected before they are taken inside."

"That won't be a problem." He gestured toward a building across the square from the palace. "That looks like an inn."

Mond turned toward it and nodded. "Ah. The Golden Goose. The most expensive in the city."

Jerrell grinned. "Which means clean rooms, soft beds, and good food."

"That place will cost us a gold piece per night."

While an outrageous price, it wasn't Jerrell's money. "Didn't Wrenthal give you coin for the mission?"

"He did."

"Well, let's spend it. Besides, the location gives us a perfect cover to watch for the next delivery."

Mond frowned. "You are crushing my hopes."

"Why is that?" Jerrell asked as he headed toward the inn.

"Wrenthal allows me to keep any leftover coin after a mission. He only gave me five gold pieces, so if we stay more than one night, I'll have nothing left for myself."

Jerrell laughed. "Now, *that* I can understand."

THE GOLDEN GOOSE was easily the most impressive inn Jerrell had ever visited. It was bright, airy, and clean. Those three things alone made it stand out. The rest made it a thing to behold.

Murals graced the dining room ceiling, three stories above. White cloth covered round tables. Each table was surrounded by chairs carved from wood so dark it seemed nearly black. The floors were covered in white marble tiles, and the veins in the marble glittered with silver specs. There was no bar; instead, two lofts overlooking the dining hall were furnished with upholstered sofas, loveseats, and cushioned chairs arranged into small sitting areas meant for groups of two to eight people. One could rent a room for one gold piece per night. Those rooms were in a building attached to the dining hall. Knowing the price of a room left Jerrell to imagine accommodations rivaling those in the palace.

Jerrell sat beside one of the towering windows along the front of the inn. Each window was twice the width of his arm span and stretched from the floor to the high ceiling. A field of wooden strips divided the window into square foot sections. Through one such pane, Jerrell watched a wagon roll up to the gate.

Two men sat on the wagon seat, the wagon bed filled with crates. After a brief discussion, the wagon rolled inside. Minutes passed with no activity while Jerrell sipped his ale. Then, the wagon reappeared and rolled out with the wagon bed filled with empty crates. Rather than heading toward the lower district, the wagon turned toward the city wall.

Jerrell hopped up from his chair.

"Where are you going?" Mond asked.

"I plan to tail that wagon. It is our ticket into the palace."

Mond rose to follow as Jerrell hurried out the front door. "What do you plan to do?" he asked.

Jerrell stopped and turned toward him. "I don't have time to explain. Either you follow and do whatever I say, or you can remain here." Not waiting for a reply, he turned and resumed his rapid pace with the wagon in his sights.

The wagon rolled through the city gates with Jerrell and Mond in pursuit. The wagon turned, and a wall obscured it from view. At a hurried walk, Jerrell strode through the gate in time to see the wagon enter a warehouse a quarter mile away. A cluster of similar buildings stood in a row beside it. He followed the road while surveying the area.

Down the hill beyond the warehouses was a river landing with a dozen docks. Moored there were barges, some plain and obviously used for cargo, others opulent and used to carry wizards along the river.

Jerrell continued toward the warehouse with Mond at his side, slowing as he neared it. He strolled inside as the two men climbed down from their wagon.

"Who are you?" the driver asked.

Jerrell smiled. "I am Samjin. This is Kenji." He thumbed toward Mond. "I was told to come see Perkins."

The driver frowned. "Who is Perkins?"

"I thought you were Perkins."

"No. My name is Gadwick."

"Isn't this warehouse thirteen?" Jerrell knew it was, for he had seen the number posted outside.

"It is."

"This is where we were told to go." Jerrell pointed at the other man. "Is he Perkins?"

"His name is Tern."

"Ahh," Jerrell nodded. "I am sorry."

The man waved his hands. "It's all right. You likely just have the wrong warehouse."

"No. I meant, I am sorry for this."

Jerrell drew a blade from each of his sleeves and released them in two quick flicks. The first took Gadwick in the throat, the second striking Tern in his open mouth as he attempted to cry for help. Gadwick staggered and fell against the wagon before sliding to the floor. His partner choked and stumbled backward, tripping over a crate. His head struck the wall with a loud thud. He did not move.

Mond grunted. "You killed them."

He had not wanted to. However, between Mond following him and the threat of death should he not succeed with the mission, Jerrell wanted to send a message back. *Jerrell Landish is not a dog who will cower in fright. No, this dog can and will bite back.*

"I was serious when I told them I was sorry, but I could not chance them shouting and alerting anyone in the neighboring warehouses. Killing them was the safest way to prevent them from foiling our mission. As they say, dead men tell no tales."

Mond grunted. "Why them?"

Circling to the front of the wagon, Jerrell lifted a sheet of paper from below the seat. "For this and for their wagon."

"What is that?"

"An order from the palace. We are to deliver a load of vegetables and fish before sunset."

"Fish? That won't smell too good."

"No, but it gives us a way into the palace." Jerrell walked over to Gadwick and pulled his blade free before cleaning it on the man's tunic. "Help me get these men into the wagon bed."

"Where are we taking them?"

Jerrell grunted as he and Mond lifted Gadwick and tossed him in the wagon. "Down to the river. We'll send them over the falls. Even if they are found, it will be far from here and they are unlikely to be identified before we are out of the city." After retrieving his other throwing blade and depositing Tern in the wagon, Jerrell climbed into the wagon seat. "When we are down there, we can ask about purchasing some fish." He lifted the reins and frowned. "Do you know how to drive a wagon?"

~

AFTER DUMPING the dead men in the river, Jerrell and Mond drove the wagon to the docks. By then, it was late afternoon and a cargo barge had appeared from upriver. The craft docked and workers began to unload crates of potatoes, squash, and other produce from Grakal. Mond purchased five crates of vegetables, along with a crate of freshly caught trout.

"This trip has become expensive," Mond grumbled as he and Jerrell loaded the crates into the wagon.

"Don't worry. I am sure the palace will cover this cost with a bit of profit for our efforts." Jerrell climbed into the wagon seat. "Let's see about a delivery."

Mond joined him, snapped the reins, and the wagon was away. As they rode the uphill drive and passed the warehouses, Mond asked, "What do you intend to do once we are inside?"

"I'll figure that out when we get there."

The wagon continued to the city gate, where the guards performed a brief search before waving them through. Jerrell hoped to receive similar treatment at the castle gate, but when the sergeant on duty looked over the order, his eyes narrowed, and a frown replaced his smile.

"Who are you?"

Jerrell thumbed himself. "I am Gadwick's cousin, Samjin."

"Where is Gadwick?"

Jerrell replied, "He came down with something nasty. Last I saw, he was throwing up blood."

The guard grunted. "Odd. He was just here this afternoon."

One of the guards said, "I thought Gadwick looked a bit peaked when he left."

Jerrell nodded eagerly. "Whatever he has, it must be bad. The man could not even stand when I left him."

"What of Tern?"

"His condition may be even worse. I doubt you will see him for a while."

"So, who is this guy?" The sergeant gestured toward Mond.

"This is my friend, Kenji. I hired him to drive Gadwick's wagon since I lack skills in that area. You see, I am a carpenter by trade and prefer to work with wood, shaping it into something useful and beautiful at the same time. For instance, I once made a..."

Jerrell decided to attempt to bore the man, diving into unnecessary details. By his fifth run-on sentence, the sergeant had heard enough.

"Go on in," the sergeant snapped. "Follow the drive to the stables. Someone will meet you there and tell you where to unload." He pointed toward a guard. "Corelli. Go inform Biscott that a delivery has arrived. Hurry. Devotion begins soon."

With a snap of the reins, the horses resumed their lazy walk and the wagon followed. As they passed the gate, Jerrell looked up. Archers lined the wall, watching them enter the domain of Lord Horus, one of the mightiest wizards in the world.

CHAPTER 15
CALL ME NESTOR

The brick drive rounded Tiamalyn Palace, leading the wagon past sprawling gardens, by a bubbling fountain, and through a grove of olive trees before ending at a courtyard. To the right stood the wall separating the palace from a neighboring estate. To the left, the palace loomed. Straight ahead, a building with a series of eight-foot-wide doors waited.

The wagon turned and slowed to a stop with the rear facing the palace. A tall man wearing a stained white tunic and dark green trousers emerged from the stables. "Another delivery?"

"Yes, sir." Jerrell hopped down and presented the order. "My cousin, Gadwick, wasn't feeling well, so my friend and I agreed to make the delivery."

The man gestured toward a door in the side of the palace. "You'll be going through there, but you had better wait for an escort. Did one of the guards alert the staff?"

"Yes."

"Good, because I don't have time for this." The man disappeared back into the dark stable.

Jerrell turned to Mond and shrugged. They climbed down and walked to the rear of the wagon. As they removed the rear wagon gate, the door to the palace opened. A man dressed in black trousers and a black coat with a silk green lapel stepped outside. He stood roughly Jerrell's height but with a slimmer frame.

The man clapped his white-gloved hands. "Hurry along, now. Get those crates inside. Devotion begins soon, and His Majesty requested fresh fish prepared for tonight's meal." His hair was waxed, his head tilted back as he looked down his nose. "You have the fish, don't you?"

"We do." Jerrell and Mond each gripped one side of the crate, lifted it, and walked toward the man. The stench of fish dominated Jerrell's senses and nearly made him gag. "Where do we put this?"

The man spun toward the building and opened the door for them. "Follow the corridor to the second door on your right."

With Jerrell walking backward, he and Mond carried the crate down the dark hallway. They reached the second door, which swung open when Jerrell leaned against it. They entered a food prep room, ten strides long and nearly as wide. Shelves lined the walls and a long, narrow table occupied the middle. Flour, a rolling pin, and a tub of lard sat on the table. The porter entered and walked past them to hold another door open across the room. They entered a sprawling kitchen where a dozen cooks worked feverishly.

A woman with graying hair tied back in a bun turned toward them. "What is this?"

"Good evening, Hilda," the porter said. "The delivery you were expecting has arrived."

"You've the fish?" Hilda dusted her hands on her apron as she rushed over.

"Fresh trout straight from the river," Jerrell replied. *Hilda. She appears to be in charge.*

"Wonderful. Set it here." The woman gestured toward a counter as she commanded, "Fisk. Tolford. Get these fish in the oven straight away."

After depositing the first crate, the porter, Jerrell, and Mond went to retrieve the crate of potatoes. This time, rather than heading down the corridor, the porter shooed them toward the stairwell and then slipped past them.

"Come along," he said as he descended into darkness.

Jerrell and Mond followed, and when they were halfway down, a door at the bottom creaked open. Soft blue light bloomed beyond the doorway. They passed through the door to find the porter holding an enchanted lantern. Long dark aisles waited beyond him, bordered by shelves stacked to the ceiling. Although the cellar was a big room, and the opposite end somewhere beyond the lantern's light, Jerrell could tell that they were alone.

He spoke softly to Mond, "Let's set this on the table beside the door." As they did, he kicked the door closed. "Make sure nobody comes in."

"What are you doing?" the porter asked. "That crate goes on a shelf in the third aisle.

"Sorry," Jerrell burst forward, closing the gap between him and the porter. He grasped the man's coat in one fist and pressed his dagger against the porter's throat. "Cry out and you die," Jerrell growled.

Round frightened eyes flicked from Jerrell to Mond and down at the dagger. "Take whatever you wish. Just don't kill me."

"I am glad we understand each other."

"What...what do you want?"

"Your name."

"Preston."

"Tell me, Preston, do you work for Biscott?"

"I do."

"And your room. Where is it?"

"Servant quarters, above the kitchen."

"Splendid. I am so glad you are complying. If you continue to do as I say, you will live."

"Anything. Just don't kill me."

"In that case, I will need to take your clothes."

"My clothes? Why?"

"Because, you appear to be about my size."

Jerrell planted his hand on Preston's face and shoved hard. The back of the porter's head struck the stone wall with a crack. His eyes rolled up and knees gave out. He slid to the floor, ending in a sitting position with his head flopped to the side.

"Help me undress him," Jerrell said as he sheathed his blade. "We have little time. Devotion begins soon."

~

JERRELL DUG into the pockets of his black coat, now worn by the unconscious porter, and removed his lockpicks. He then opened the door leading outside to find night had claimed all but a hint of light in the western sky.

"Put him in the back of the wagon and ride straight to the gate," Jerrell said to Mond. "Tell the guards I fell ill. In the dark, they will see my coat and think it is me. Hurry. You need to get outside the palace grounds before Devotion begins."

Mond lifted Preston over his shoulder. "I'll be watching the palace, so don't think you can leave without me noticing."

"I have no intention of sneaking away." It was true. He was focused on completing the mission. "Now, go!"

He closed the door and straightened the fancy coat he had taken from Preston. Like the tunic beneath it, the coat was tight around Jerrell's shoulders, chest, and arms, but otherwise fit well enough. Squatting, he lifted a trouser leg and slid his picks into his boot. Preston's shoes did not fit, so he was forced to keep his boots, but he didn't mind. It was unlikely anyone would look at his feet anyway.

Rising, he marched down the corridor and passed through the door leading to the kitchen prep room. The room was empty, and the tub of lard still sat on the counter. He scooped up a bit of lard, rubbed it on his fingers, and then mixed it in his hair. In moments, his wild mop was tamed and slicked back to match Preston's look. Nobody who knew Preston would mistake Jerrell for him, but he hoped to blend in with the other palace servants.

A woman's voice came from the kitchen. "Devotion begins!" It was Hilda, the head cook. "Everyone outside."

The door to the prep room opened. Jerrell spun around and walked through the door to the corridor, holding it open while the kitchen staff hurried past.

The head cook came through last. Her brow furrowed when she saw Jerrell. "Who are you?"

"Nestor. I just started here this morning."

"Damn, Biscott," she swore. "He said nothing to me during the staff meeting." She walked past Jerrell. "Come along. Devotion is starting and everyone must participate."

The head cook glanced back at Jerrell, who held the door and waved for her to keep moving. He followed her through another door and stepped outside to find the others on their knees, faces raised to the sky. High above the palace, the upper reaches of the Tower of Devotion were consumed by green flame. Beams of green light shot out from the tower, connecting to distant cities across Orenth. As one, they began to chant.

Now is my chance. While everyone had their backs to him, Jerrell cracked the door open and slid inside.

He rushed along the corridor until he reached a stairwell and began a quiet ascent. Turning at a landing, he came to the second level. Since Preston had said his room was above the kitchens, Jerrell suspected the second level held nothing of interest. He continued past the third level and came to the fourth and uppermost level, where he stopped and peered up and down the corridor. There was nobody in sight.

Jerrell stepped into the hallway, which was illuminated by enchanted lanterns on sconces every twenty strides. Tapestries and closed doors occupied the space between the islands of light. He walked up to the first door and tested the knob, which turned. He quietly eased the door open to reveal a dark room with a four-poster bed. Bright green light came through the curtains over the window. It seemed to be a simple bedchamber for guests, so he moved along.

He eased the door of the neighboring room open and found soft light coming from inside. A canopy bed stood across the room, and the light came from an enchanted lantern on the nightstand beside it. Yet, he saw nobody in the room, and an open door led to another room beside it.

On silent steps, he crept inside. As he passed the bed, he saw movement out of the corner of his eye and froze.

A girl no older than twelve sat up, her eyes wide. Ebony curls tumbled over the shoulders of her nightgown and she held a stuffed owl to her chest. "Who are you?"

Jerrell relaxed his posture. "I am a new porter, just hired today."

She frowned. "Why are you sneaking then?"

He smiled. "I did not wish to wake you."

"What is your name?"

"Nestor. And yours?"

She thrust her chin out. "Princess Irrika."

"A princess? I assume your father is Lord Horus."

"Of course."

"Why are you in bed at such an early hour?"

She stuck her lip out. "I was sent to bed early."

He gave her a sympathetic look. "Why would anyone do that to a sweet girl like you?"

"I refused to eat my dinner."

"Your dinner?"

"Yes." Her face twisted in disgust. "It was fish. I hate fish."

There were foods Jerrell avoided, so he understood. "I do not blame you. Why should you be forced to eat something you hate?"

She smiled. "You understand. I wish Hortencia was more like you."

"Hortencia?"

"Yes. My nursemaid."

"Would you like me to get you something else to eat?"

Her eyes lit up. "I certainly would."

He backed to the door. "I will head down to the kitchen and return soon."

Jerrell pulled the door closed and moved on.

The next door he tested was locked. Squatting, he removed his picks, slid one in the keyhole, and moved it until he found resistance. Applying pressure, he tripped the tumbler. The next pick soon found resistance as well and tripped the next tumbler. A third followed, Jerrell moving it carefully while holding the other two in place. When the third tumbler clicked, he twisted all three picks and the knob turned with his hand.

He eased the door open to a lavish room filled with soft light. A sofa, loveseat, and chair sat before a lit fireplace made of black marble, which was a striking contrast to the polished white floor tiles. A long dining table and a dozen chairs waited beyond the sitting area, the candles on the table flickering with amber light. On one end of the room was an open doorway, through which he spied books on a shelf, perhaps a study. *The golden owl may be hiding in there.* A set of double doors waited at the other end of the room, both closed. *They must lead to the bedroom.* After brief consideration, he entered the study first.

Crossing the room, he peered through the doorway. A massive desk occupied the middle of the room. Two walls were covered in books, a third wall by the door and an oil painting. A narrow glass shelf stood along the wall behind the desk. Light from the neighboring room glinted off strange objects resting on the shelf.

Jerrell circled the desk for a better look. The first was a statue of a gold dragon with blue and purple gems down its spine. The second appeared to be a simple pyramid made of crystal. Upon the third object was an obelisk with an emerald in the spire, reminding Jerrell of the one in the square outside of Yor's Palace. Moving to the end of the shelf, Jerrell eyed an object made of gold. It was the size of his fist, with emerald eyes, but it was not an owl. He frowned at the golden scarab in disappointment.

A quick search of both bookshelves and the desk yielded nothing matching the description of the owl, so Jerrell left the study and headed toward the closed doors across the room. Pressing his ear to the door, he heard nothing. He slowly turned the knob and eased the door open.

A silhouette of a person eclipsed the pale green light beyond the balcony doors. With a gasp, the person spun around and extended a hand toward him, causing a tingle to rush over his body. Invisible ropes wrapped around his torso and pulled him into the room.

Oh, no.

CHAPTER 16

SNAKE CHARMER

A globe of white light appeared in the dark bedroom, forcing Jerrell to squint. The light and the caster drew closer.

"Why are you not outside for Devotion?" a sultry voice asked.

A woman, Jerrell recognized her voice. "I came to attend to you...Your Highness."

The light dimmed, allowing him to see her.

Long black curls spilled over her shoulders. A silken bath robe clung to her significant curves. Large dark eyes highlighted a gorgeous face with full pouty lips. Those eyes narrowed as she examined Jerrell.

"I do not recognize you."

"I am new. Biscott hired me just this morning."

She gestured toward a tub between her canopy bed and the far wall. "I requested someone to come to run a bath after Devotion was finished. Rather than giving your prayers to my husband, you came to me instead?"

Jerrell turned the sentence over in his head and considered a dozen responses but there was something about her tone that sent him toward a risky choice. "I do not see why the queen must wait while her husband basks in the adulation of his people. Perhaps it is time the queen was perceived as an equal rather than an afterthought."

109

A smile bloomed on her face, and she crooned, "Oh, I *like* you."

The invisible bonds around Jerrell released, and he straightened his coat.

Queen Grenda crossed the room and stopped at the vanity beside the tub. A tiny cone of flame burst from her fingertips, lighting a pair of candles. She doused the globe of magic light, leaving the warm glow of the candles to illuminate the room.

"The chambermaid placed a pot of water on the fire before she left. Go and fetch it for me."

Jerrell passed through the doorway, crossed the sitting area, and found a heavy leather glove on the hearth. He used it to lift the steaming kettle from a grate in the fireplace and returned to the bedchamber.

"Very good," Grenda smirked. "Pour it in the tub. Stop when the cold water inside warms sufficiently."

He poured the water in the tub, steam rising as it sizzled. With his other hand, he stirred the water, wondering how he was going to escape. When the water felt hot to the touch, he stopped and set the kettle on the floor beside the wall before turning back toward Grenda.

"Anything else, my queen?"

She gestured. "Salts fill the cup on the vanity. Pour some into the water."

Jerrell did as asked, again stirring the water as it became cloudy and began to foam. He set the cup aside and turned toward Grenda. The queen coyly bit her lip and gave him a sidelong leer.

"You appear fit for a porter."

"I have not always been a porter."

She undid her sash and slid the robe off her shoulders. It fell to the floor. Candlelight flickered across her curvaceous, naked form. Her skin was smooth, her stomach flat, and her body completely hairless. The thump of Jerrell's pulse began to hammer in his ear.

"Do you find me beautiful?"

"I think you are stunning." It was not a lie. His nether region responded to the spectacular view, and his trousers suddenly felt too tight.

Grenda's gaze lowered, and she smiled. "As I can see." She stepped into the tub and slid down into water that reached her midriff. "Wash me."

Restraining his grin, Jerrell said, "As my queen wishes."

He picked up a washcloth and a bar of soap.

"No." She shook her head. "Remove your clothing and climb in the water first."

"I…"

"I command you to get in the tub."

"What about Lord Horus?"

She smirked. "Do not worry about my husband. He is consumed by Devotion. Afterward, he is to dine with Chancellor Mor. He will not return for hours."

Jerrell needed no further convincing. He began disrobing as his heart thumped in anticipation.

AN HOUR LATER, Jerrell and Grenda lay in her bed, both coated in sweat. She sat up, leaning on one elbow while her finger ran down his bare chest. "You never did tell me your name."

"Jerrell." In the numb afterglow of their lovemaking, he forgot his alter ego until after his name slipped out. He sighed inwardly, and said, "I joined the staff under the name, Nestor."

Grenda leaned closer and tapped his chin. "I knew you were not a servant."

His brow furrowed. "Why would you say that?"

"The apartment door was locked. Even with a key, no servant would enter without announcing themselves first. When I removed my bathrobe, a servant would have covered his eyes or turned away. You did none of those things. Instead, you gawked like an eager child being offered the toy they wished to play with."

Jerrell smirked. "Call me a child if you want. I did *really* want to play with you."

She kissed him and leaned back with a smile. "I noticed. You proved you know your way around a woman's body, which I enjoyed as well." Her smile faded. "Now, do you want to tell me why you were skulking around my apartment?"

"Skulking?"

"Do you prefer sneaking?"

"Actually, I do."

"Well?"

"I was looking for something rumored to be in Kylar Mor's possession."

"Why would it be in here?"

"I didn't know which chambers were his."

"Can you describe this item you seek? Perhaps I can help you find it."

Jerrell considered her possible motives, but she had thus far seemed earnest. "It is an owl made of gold with green emeralds for eyes."

"Hmm." She put a finger to her mouth. "I can't recall seeing anything like that in his office. Owls are the symbol of Oren, so I am unlikely to miss one made of gold."

"If not in his office, what of where he sleeps?"

"The man sometimes sleeps in his office, but most of the time he returns to his estate at night."

He lifted his head. "His estate?"

"Yes. Mor Manor is one of the estates overlooking the bluff. It is, perhaps, a quarter mile away."

Sighing, Jerrell's head dropped back down. "I suppose I had better head there next."

Grenda's hand tracked down his stomach. "Don't leave yet. I recently had a lover taken from me and have only just found you." Her hand moved lower, and his body reacted. "Oh, how fun. You appear ready for another go."

"I should..."

She clamped a hand over his mouth and gave him a level glare. "Don't make me use magic on you."

Although Jerrell wasn't sure if she was serious or bluffing, he relaxed. He could think of worse problems. *The search for the artifact can wait.*

When she removed her hand from his mouth, he said, "As Your Highness commands, we can give it one more go, then I must leave."

The sound of a door opening in a neighboring room caused Jerrell to sit up in alarm, which sent Grenda rolling off the bed and onto the floor.

"Ouch," she exclaimed.

He crawled over to the edge of the bed and looked down to find her sitting on the marble floor, stark naked. "Someone is here."

She grimaced, climbed to her feet, and rubbed her bare backside. "Yes. He always spoils my fun."

Dread crept up Jerrell's throat. "He?"

"My husband."

It would not be the first time Jerrell was caught by a jealous husband. However, the others were not wizards, and this man was more powerful than any wizard he had ever met.

He leapt out of the bed and scooped up his belongings. With his boots in one hand and clothing cradled in the other arm, he ran to the balcony door. The bedroom door opened, and Jerrell glanced over his shoulder to find a tall broad-shouldered silhouette in the doorway. An emerald glow surrounded the robed man.

Jerrell urgently tore the balcony door open and raced out. He only made it a step before an invisible force lifted him off the ground and yanked him backward.

CHAPTER 17

INCARCERATION

Pulled by an invisible force, Jerrell was hurtled back into the room. He landed on the bed, bounced, and rolled off to land on his hands and knees at Grenda's feet.

Jerrell looked up at the robed man standing over him. A grimace turned the wizard's mouth down as he lifted his gaze from Jerrell to Grenda. Tendrils of green mist swirled around the wizard.

Despite the gravity of the situation, Jerrell couldn't resist making a comment. He gathered his clothing and rose to his feet, using his boots to cover his groin. "I heard wizard flatulence was something to behold, but your gas actually glows."

Grenda guffawed and then covered her mouth while she continued to giggle.

The wizard's eyes flared as he shifted his gaze from Jerrell to Grenda. "Who is this?"

Her laughter calmed. "A new servant, or so I am told."

He grimaced at Jerrell. "I think not. No servant would speak to me so."

"If he is not a servant, why does he have a uniform?" She gestured toward the clothing in Jerrell's arm.

"Assuming he *is* a servant, why is he in here?"

"I wanted to bathe. Whitney was away at Devotion, so I had Jerrell take her place." She smirked. "His thorough efforts earned him my favor."

"I am sure they did."

"In fact, I was about to bestow my favor upon him again when you entered." The tone of her voice was an undisguised challenge.

Horus growled, "Why must you tempt my patience at every turn, woman?"

"It is your own fault since you ignore me and my needs, Horus."

"Again, you blame *me* for your transgressions."

"*You* rule Orenth and leave nothing for me. As wizard lord, victories and defeats, success and failure, are all to your credit, like it or not. Had you chosen to pay me more attention, Reagor would not be condemned to life as a gladiator."

Horus groaned and ran a hand down his face. "You know I loved Reagor like a son, yet you bewitched him and led him to your bed just to spite me. When I caught the two of you together, I had no choice but to send him to the bowl." His gaze swept from Jerrell's bare feet to his face. "This man, however, I do not know, so it will cause me no pain to watch him die."

Jerrell shook his head. "There must be another way. I had no intention bedding your wife, but she seduced me." Even angry, Grenda was stunning. "Who could resist her wiles?"

The wizard lord sighed. "I wish I had resisted them years ago. Instead, I am saddled with the trouble she causes me."

"In this, we are alike."

Horus pressed his lips together and took a long, slow breath before responding. "I sympathize with your plight. My wife thinks only of herself, willing to satisfy her own desires, regardless of the cost toward others."

Jerrell glanced toward Grenda, who glared at her husband with undisguised hatred. She stood naked with her arms crossed, causing her tremendous assets to bulge even further. *Stop looking, Jerrell.* His body had again begun to respond.

Turning back toward the wizard lord, Jerrell asked softly, "So, you will let me go?"

The wizard stood silent for a moment before replying, "Orenth is a pit of snakes, most of whom wear robes and hiss behind false smiles. Any perceived weakness will embolden them, and I will find myself fraught with schemes to kill me, so another might claim the crystal throne." He shook his head. "I cannot let you go. If word got out, it might be the end of me, even though I still wield the Gift of Oren."

"I won't tell anyone. I promise. In fact, you will never see me again."

The wizard rested a hand on Jerrell's shoulder. "I am sorry, son. It is not you I worry about spreading the rumor. It is my wife, the viper queen herself, who seeks to poison everything around me."

Jerrell's hopes fled and dread settled in his stomach like a lump of lead. He considered attacking Horus; the throwing blades in his boots were easily accessed. However, everyone knew wizard lords were able to heal any wound instantly. Reputedly, they could even burn poison from their own veins. *He is unkillable. To attack him would only incur his wrath. No. My best move is to buy time.*

"What is my sentence?" Jerrell asked.

"I have yet to decide. You will either fight in the bowl for a chance to earn your freedom, or endure public execution."

"Fight in the bowl?"

"For three years, if you can survive that long."

Jerrell sighed. "Those choices stink."

"It is our way, but I will not decide now. A night to dwell on it might give me clarity on your path. Until then, you will sit in a dungeon cell."

"Can I get dressed first?"

"Of course."

As the wizard and his wife watched, Jerrell set his boots down and began to dress, wishing he had his own clothing rather than the porter uniform. *At least I still have my own boots.*

When he was otherwise clothed, Jerrell knelt to pull his boots on. With subtle ease, he slid his lockpicks into his palm, taking care to keep them hidden from Horus as he stood.

Horus called out, "Guards!"

The apartment door opened, and a quartet of armed soldiers rushed into the room.

"Hold there for a moment." The wizard lord gripped Jerrell by the arm and pulled him toward the bedroom door. Jerrell caught the doorframe, stopping them both as he looked back at Grenda. "What are you doing?" Horus demanded.

"I am drinking in the view. Years may pass before I see anything her equal."

Grenda licked her lips and posed for him. "Thank you for the entertainment. Too bad the encore performance was spoiled before it began." She cocked her head. "I never got your last name."

"It is Landish. Jerrell Landish."

She smiled. "If you fight in the bowl, I will be there for luck."

"Luck is already with me. Goodbye, Grenda." He lifted his hand to his mouth, careful to hide the picks he slid into it, and kissed his fingers before blowing the kiss toward her.

Horus yanked Jerrell into the other room where four guards waited. They were not alone. Standing with the guards was a wizard in silver and green robes. *Kylar Mor.*

Lord Horus turned to the wizard. "Chancellor Mor, I leave Mister Landish in your charge. Shackle him and take him to the dungeon. I will visit him tomorrow to personally confirm his sentence."

Two guards stepped toward Jerrell, one spinning him around, the other clamping heavy shackles around his wrists. He was then rushed out the door with an armed escort.

In the hallway, he was met by a dark-haired girl hugging a stuffed owl. A woman wearing a stern expression stood behind the girl with her hand on the girl's shoulder.

Irrika's brow furrowed. "You said you were going to get me food from the kitchen."

"Sorry," Jerrell shrugged. "I lied."

She frowned. "You lied to a princess?"

He chuckled. "I lie to many people."

"You are not a porter, are you?"

"No."

The girl's eyes narrowed. "Is your name even Nestor?"

"Actually, it is Jerrell."

"Enough of this," Kylar Mor growled. "Let's get him to the dungeon, so I may be on my way."

The guards dragged Jerrell past the girl. "Be well, Princess," he said over his shoulder just before he was shoved toward a stairwell.

WHILE THE UPPER levels of the palace were bright with white walls, marble floors, and towering windows, the reaches beneath were far less inviting. The lead guard's torch illuminated the dank stairwell, its flickering light fighting the surrounding murk.

As was his habit, Jerrell counted fifteen stairs before the stairwell ended. The guards, one holding Jerrell's left arm, another his right, led him down a dark corridor, passing two closed doors before the hallway ended at a torchlit chamber.

The rectangular room was fifty feet long and half as wide. Dim moonlight seeped through a long barred window cut into the wall at the far end of the chamber. The walls were made of stone with eight wooden doors along each side. The doors were all closed and windowless.

Two jailors sat at a table near the door, playing cards beneath the light of a torch. The men's eyes widened when Jerrell and his escort entered the room. Both dropped their cards and scrambled to their feet upon seeing Kylar Mor.

"Chancellor Mor," one said, thumping his chest. "What brings you down here?"

"This prisoner requires a cell for the evening," Kylar Mor replied.

"Of course." The heavyset jailor gestured toward the lean one, who fumbled with the keys at his belt and rushed over to the furthest door on the right. "This cell is cleaned and ready."

"I did not say he needed a clean cell." The wizard crossed the room with Jerrell and the guards following.

The jailor paused. "Would you prefer a dirty one?"

Mor waved it off. "It does not matter. This man will only be staying one evening. Tomorrow, Lord Horus himself will come to issue his sentence."

The skinny jailor glanced at the heavier one, their silent exchange making it clear that they were ill prepared for the wizard lord's visit. "We will have the cells cleaned, so the smell is more...acceptable for His Majesty."

"Wonderful." The wizard gestured. "Open the door, so I may be rid of him and return to my estate."

After fumbling with the keys, the jailor inserted one into the lock, turned it, and pushed the door open. When the man pulled the key back, Jerrell got a good look at it, noting two teeth and a simple design.

The guards holding Jerrell's arms shoved him into the cell. Jerrell turned toward the open door. "Why are my wrists still bound? How am I going to eat or drink?"

"Who says you deserve such niceties?" asked Kylar Mor. "Enjoy your evening, Mister Landish. It may well be your last."

A guard pulled the door closed. The sound of metal on metal came from the door as the key was inserted. The lock clicked shut, and Jerrell was left alone in the dark.

THE SILENCE SCREAMED in Jerrell's ears. He sat on a pallet with his back against the wall, straining to hear beyond that silence. Occasionally, a noise would come through the solid door, alerting him to the movements of his two jailors.

He was tired, hungry, and most of all, thirsty. Sex could be physically draining, and it was late. While he fought his own exhaustion, he hoped sleep would claim the jailors, for he had been locked in the dark for hours... at least, he thought it was hours. Time seemed to trickle, and he may have dozed a time or two, so he wasn't sure.

Finally, many minutes, with Jerrell estimating at least half an hour, passed during which he had heard nothing but than his own breath exhaling. He turned, lay back on the pallet, and shimmied his shackled wrists below his backside, tucking his legs against his chest to allow the shackles past his feet.

Once again in a sitting position, he worked his jaw and slid the lockpicks from beneath his tongue. He pulled the picks from his mouth and then bit one. Holding the metal pick tightly between his teeth, he brought his shackles toward his face. The pick scraped along the iron as he moved the shackle back and forth, working blindly and wishing he had his dagger for light. Finally, the pick slid into a hole. Jerrell prodded, knowing the shackles were a simple design. *Press the release and pull them apart.* The pick found resistance, and he pushed down with his face. He heard a click and pulled his wrists apart as the first shackle came free. His fingers found the pick in his mouth and reclaimed it. The other wrist was freed moments later.

Jerrell moved to the door and ran his fingers across the metal plate until he located the lock opening. The first pick soon found a tumbler, the second following and tripping the other before he carefully turned the lock. The resulting click was far louder than he had expected.

"What was that?" one of the jailors asked.

"What was what?"

"I heard something from that cell."

"We locked a man in that cell just hours ago. He probably rolled over in his sleep."

Jerrell realized the guards had never searched him. *I still have two throwing blades in my boots.* He reached down and found the first, swapping the knife for his picks before grabbing the second blade. With both throwing blades in his grip, Jerrell pulled on the door. It swung inward, and torchlight seeped into the cell. He opened the door farther to allow himself room to pass. It emitted a squeak, but rather than freeze, Jerrell launched into action.

He burst out into the room as the thin jailor stood. A quick flick sent a throwing blade at the man, striking him in the eye. With less time to aim, he threw the other knife, targeting the bigger jailor's broad torso as the man stood, his belly causing the table to flip up. The table blocked the strike, and the blade stuck in its wooden surface with a thud.

Roaring, the massive jailor charged across the room, armed with a cudgel, while Jerrell stood trapped and weaponless.

CHAPTER 18
ESCAPE

The burly jailor rumbled across the room, huffing in wild fury. Rather than flee, Jerrell stood still with his eyes gaping and jaw dropped in feigned fear. The jailor closed the distance and wound back with his cudgel, prepared to inflict pain on his prisoner. The cudgel came around, and the jailor still did not slow. At the last moment, Jerrell dove to the dirt floor and kicked at his attacker's ankle, tripping him. The big man fell head-first in the dirt and slid into the wall. His head struck the stone with a crack.

Jerrell scrambled to his feet and stared down at the man, wary of a ruse. Other than the rise and fall of his back as he drew rasping breaths, the man did not move. A kick to the ribs caused the jailor to wobble, but he gave no other reaction.

Jerrell rushed across the room, gathered his two blades, wiped the bloody one off on the dead man's tunic, and hurried out into the corridor. A soft crunch of dirt sounded beneath his footsteps as he crept into the darkness. Fifty paces down, the corridor ended.

Surrounded by murk, he crept up the stairs with one hand on the damp cold stone walls. Fifteen stairs up, the passageway leveled and ended at a closed door. A sliver of light seeped through the gap under the door. He pressed his ear to the wooden surface and listened. Silence. His hand found the handle, and he eased the door open to a torchlit corridor. An open door waited at one end. In the light beyond the door, he spied guards sitting at a table while drinking ale, reminding Jerrell of his thirst. *No time for ale, now. I need to get out of here.*

The corridor was empty in the other direction, so Jerrell followed it, stepping as silently as possible. At the corner, he stopped abruptly. A guard strolled down the otherwise empty hallway, his back to Jerrell. The man paused to peer into an open doorway, then resumed his patrol.

Jerrell gripped one of his throwing knives and slunk down the corridor, taking long strides and timing his footsteps to match those of the guard. When the gap closed to just a few strides, he darted forward and leapt, driving his blade into the base of the guard's neck. Jerrell wrapped his other arm around the guard's head as the man staggered. His hand clasped over the guard's mouth, and he pulled him backward. The man stumbled a few steps and then slumped to the floor. Jerrell hurriedly dragged him back to the open door and into an empty sitting room.

With the door closed, Jerrell began to remove the guard's leather armor.

DRESSED AS AN ORENTHIAN SOLDIER, Jerrell emerged from the dark sitting room. Anyone who peered inside would find it empty. In the daylight, the lump behind the window curtain would be obvious, but at night, such subtleties were lost in the shadows.

A sword dangled from his hip, a metal helmet capped his head, and leather armor covered his body as he traversed the palace corridor with calm confidence. He came to an open hall surrounded by doors. A pair of guards stood at a door on one end while the doors on the other end were unguarded. *Those men must guard the throne room. That means one of the other doors will lead outside.* There, he would surely find other guards, but such encounters would not be easily avoided.

Jerrell sauntered into the room and when the two guards turned their heads toward him, he waved. "How are you faring?"

One of the guards snorted. "It's just another boring night in the palace."

Chuckling, Jerrell said, "A bored soldier is a live soldier. Those who find excitement are the ones who often end up dead."

The other guard replied, "That is what I keep telling him."

Again, Jerrell laughed. He then turned from them and lazily crossed the length of the hall, toward the unguarded doors at the far end. When he reached the doors, he opened one and stepped outside.

Four guards stood on the stairs outside the palace front entrance. He walked past them and descended the stairs without a word. Jerrell continued through an open plaza, which took him past the grove of olive trees and the fountain he remembered from earlier that day, and approached the gate, which was closed. Eight soldiers stood in a cluster just inside the gate, the hum of conversation growing louder as Jerrell drew nearer. One noticed him and nudged the man beside him. The second man stepped away from the group.

"What's wrong?"

"I was sent to replace one of the guards on patrol outside the palace walls."

The man frowned. "Do I know you?"

"My name is Landish. I just transferred here from Yor's Point. Arrived yesterday."

"Yor's Point? Who was your commander?"

"Captain Trevino."

"Jakins's man?"

"Yessir. However, when Jakins died and that bastard, Paloun, took his place, several us were told to find employment elsewhere."

"You were loyal to Jakins?"

"I am a soldier, so I am loyal to whoever pays me."

The guard grinned. "Well said, soldier. I am Sergeant Wheaton. I command the night watch at the palace. Who did you say you were to replace?"

Jerrell rubbed his jaw. "I can't recall the man's name. He was to be patrolling outside the wall..." When prompted, others often gave the answers they expected. Tonight was no different.

"Is it Corelli? His wife is due to give birth any day, now."

"Corelli! That's it!" Jerrell slapped his hands together.

The sergeant turned his face up toward the top of the gate tower. "Open the portcullis!"

The clanking of chains was joined by the creaking of a winch. The portcullis began to rise.

Jerrell thumped his fist to his chest, as he had seen soldiers often do. "Thank you, Sergeant."

"You'll find Corelli and Stoddem somewhere in the square or along the palace perimeter. When you reach them, send Corelli back here. I would like to speak with him before he is discharged for the evening."

"As you command, sir." Jerrell ducked beneath the portcullis and strolled out of the palace. He crossed the square and faded into the dark of night.

A SUNBEAM SHONE through the open curtains, illuminating the room Jerrell shared with Mond. Jerrell felt rested, and his spirits were high. His bed had felt like a warm cloud hugging him, a far cry from the cell he had escaped in the middle of the night.

He slipped his coat over his shoulders and twisted from side to side while peering at himself in the oval mirror above the vanity. His roguish appearance made him satisfied to be back in his own clothing. Leaning closer, he rubbed his stubble-covered jaw. It had been two days since he last shaved, and he had no desire to shave again anytime soon. *It makes me look older*. Others often underestimated him because of his youth and limited physical stature. Their underestimation worked to his advantage, but Jerrell could not help wishing for more respect...and fame.

The door opened, and Mond stepped into the room. "We need to leave before dinner, or I'll get charged for another night."

Jerrell turned toward him. "Didn't you enjoy the bed?"

"It was a bit soft for my taste."

"You must be too used to sleeping on the ground."

"The military will do that to a man."

Grinning, Jerrell said, "I knew you were a soldier."

Mond frowned. "That life is in the past."

"You aren't one for sharing feelings, are you?"

"Can't say I see any reason to do so."

"It might help you be less uptight." Jerrell nodded to the man in the corner. "Right, Preston?"

The man moaned. Or maybe he groaned. With the gag in his mouth, it was difficult to tell. Stripped down his smallclothes, Preston's petite frame shivered. Ropes bound his wrists to the chair arms and his ankles to the chair legs.

"Are you sure you don't just want to kill him?" Mond asked.

"I'd prefer to avoid it. I promised him that he would live if he cooperated. So far, he hasn't done anything to annoy me."

"Well, we must deal with him sooner or later. When we check out of this place, your time with him will be over."

"We can't release him, either. Not yet." Jerrell stood over the captive. "I am going to remove your gag. When I do, I suggest you behave. Cause any trouble, and your blood will stain this beautiful rug."

Jerrell was not lying. The rug was a thing of beauty and worth multiple gold pieces. If it weren't so unwieldy to carry, he'd steal it...assuming he wasn't occupied by more serious issues. He slid his fingers beneath the gag and pulled it under the man's chin.

Preston coughed, his body spasming with each hack.

Lifting a glass of water to his lips, Jerrell said, "Drink."

The servant complied. He drank heartily without stopping until the cup was empty.

After a gasping breath, Preston said, "More, please."

"In a moment. First, I have questions that need answering."

"Very well."

"Kylar Mor's estate. How do I find it?"

"It is on Tiam Lane, the street that runs from the palace to the Bowl of Oren. Look for the Mor family crest."

"Family crest? I am not familiar with it."

"Two dragons intertwined, one golden, the other emerald green."

Such a design would be distinctive and easy to identify. "What do you know of the man's schedule?"

"He holds court twice a week, but never on the days when fighting occurs in the bowl."

"What about today?"

"No. Today, he will visit the arena, sitting at the side of Lord Horus."

Jerrell peered toward the window. It was late morning, less than two hours from the first gladiator duel. He poured another glass of water and held it to Preston's lips. "You did well, Preston. Provided you've done nothing to misguide me, I see no reason why we should continue to gag you, but you must promise not to call for help."

When Jerrell lowered the glass, Preston nodded. "I will be quiet."

"Wonderful." Jerrell turned to Mond. "Since I am in a bit of trouble with the palace guards, it would be best if I had a hooded cloak to hide my face. Can you procure one for me?

Sighing, the man replied. "Fine."

"While you are out, get some food for our guest. When you return, I will head out."

Mond scowled. "You seem to enjoy spending my coin."

"It was not my idea to bring you along."

The man grumbled, "I am of half a mind to kill the both of you and be done with this farce."

"You injure me to the core, Mond. I thought we had become friends."

"If you think that, you have confused your little charades with reality." He opened the door and was gone.

Jerrell turned to Preston. "Mond will be gone a while, so how about I entertain you with a story? Would you like to hear how I got the better of High Wizard Jakins?"

A CARRIAGE RODE past as Jerrell stepped into the shadowed shop entrance. A bell on the door jingled when he opened it. Bells were a source of personal irritation to any thief, since they made it nigh impossible to slip in or out unnoticed.

He stopped and peered through the window at the front of the shop. Far across the broad street was a two-story wall, split in the middle by a gate crafted from wrought iron. Where the two gate sections met was a symbol depicting intertwined dragons, one of green, the other gold.

Footsteps approached from behind, and a female voice asked, "Can I help you?"

Jerrell turned to find a middle-aged brunette standing a stride away. She had green eyes, and her hair was tied up in a bun. Tiny glittering gems adorned the bodice of her black dress. Her slim figure lacked the curves Jerrell preferred, but she was attractive and had large blue eyes he might swim in if they were the sea.

Lowering the hood of his cloak, he smiled. "I was admiring the necklace in the window. Did you make it?"

"No. That would be my father's work. He is in the back, crafting jewelry as we speak." She looked Jerrell up and down. "Are you sure you are in the right store? Our clients tend to be wizards or wealthy merchants."

He huffed. "So, because I don't wear a pretentious doublet or silken robes, I cannot afford your goods?"

She pressed her lips together. "Is there something specific you wish to buy?"

Jerrell glanced toward the window, but the gates to Kylar Mor's estate remained closed. He strode past the woman, making his way deeper into the shop.

Diamond rings, pearl necklaces, gold bracelets, and other jewelry decorated shelves along one wall, the entire section separated from the rest of the room by iron bars that ran from floor to ceiling. On the other side were statues and figurines made of cast metal or glass, many of which contained embedded gems. Then, Jerrell spied something of interest.

A blue globe the size of his fist was mounted to a circular, silver base. Inside the globe, a lightning bolt of silver shimmered, reflecting the light of a nearby enchanted lantern.

He approached the object and pointed at it. "This is interesting."

"Yes. My father copied that from a drawing he found in an old book about mythical artifacts."

"How much does it cost?"

"It is one of a kind, made of polished crystal."

That is what you think. "Are you going to give me a price?"

The woman appeared to consider, but cast a glance toward the open door at the rear of the shop before responding. "Fifteen gold pieces."

The number was far too high. "I will give you three."

"Three?" she said, aghast. "I can accept no less than ten."

Jerrell glanced toward the window as a quartet of guards opened the gate across the street. A white carriage with gold and silver trim rolled out, pulled by a pair of white horses. The coach turned and rode northeast, toward the Bowl of Oren.

"Four. That is my final offer."

She frowned. "I told you, I cannot."

"Sorry. I changed my mind." He walked to the door and stepped outside.

A moment later, the bell jingled as the door opened behind him.

The woman called out, "I will sell it for six gold."

He paused and spoke over his shoulder. "I will think on it."

As he walked across the street, the guards closed the gates. A couple hundred feet down the wall, the gate to the neighboring estate opened, causing Jerrell to stop in the middle of the street. The guard pushing the gate worked alone and moved to grab ahold of the other side. An idea took hold.

Altering his direction, Jerrell resumed walking, straight toward the wall between the two gates. The rumble of horses and squeaking of wheels came from inside the walls. The guard holding the gate stood back, his head turned toward the estate interior.

Keeping a steady stride, Jerrell reached the wall and walked along it. Two horses emerged from the open gate, blocking the guard from view. As the carriage rolled through the open gate, Jerrell slipped between it and the wall. Once inside, he dove through a hedge and lay still.

CHAPTER 19

AN UNINVITED GUEST

From behind a hedge, Jerrell listened to the noise of the carriage growing more distant. One gate squeaked as it closed. The other gate followed, and the guard set the bar to lock the gate. He then whistled as he wandered along the drive toward the tiered white mansion at the rear of the estate.

Jerrell stood, dusted himself off, and followed the wall until he reached a corner. Turning, he walked along the wall dividing this estate from the one that belonged to Kylar Mor. As he drew even with the manor, he saw an olive tree with branches that extended beyond the wall. With a leap, he caught the lowest branch, pulled himself up, and continued climbing. Once above the wall, he glimpsed a mansion twice the size of the one beside him. Made of white marble with thick fluted columns at the fore, the building was impressive. A five-story tower loomed at the far end of the structure, capped by a cone-shaped roof of red clay tile. A brick drive ran from the stables behind the mansion to the closed gates at the fore, where a quartet of guards loitered.

Jerrell eased along the thick tree limb while holding to the branch above. As he drew closer to the wall, the branch beneath him thinned and began to bend and wobble beneath his weight. A crack resounded, and he leapt to grab the top of the wall as the broken branch fell to the ground. He pulled himself up to peer over the wall. The guards appeared oblivious, so he flipped his leg over, and lowered himself down the other side. Hanging with arms extended, he let go. His feet hit the ground, and he rolled backward, hoping to minimize the sound of the impact. Hidden behind a pair of shrubs, he waited. Nobody came to investigate. No alarm was sounded.

He stood, dusted himself off, and crept along the narrow gap between the hedge and the wall.

THE PUNGENT SCENT of horse manure tickled Jerrell's nose as he approached the stable behind Kylar Mor's mansion. Made of the same white marble as the manor, the stable was deeper than he had expected. He remained crouched as he snuck along the stable's outer wall. When he reached a window, he peered inside.

Daylight radiated through a large doorway illuminating the stable interior. Through the doorway, Jerrell spied the gravel drive that curved around the manor and led to the front gate. A closed wooden door in the wall opposite Jerrell connected the stable to the manor itself.

The door to one of the two stalls in the rear of the stable hung open. A man wearing brown trousers held up by suspenders was mucking out the stall. Manure filled the wheelbarrow beside the man.

Jerrell ducked down and rushed along the wall to the open doors at the front of the building. The manor blocked his view of the front gate, which also meant the guards could not see him. He leaned around the doorframe to peer inside. With his back facing Jerrell, the stable hand grunted as he shoveled another pile of manure into the cart. When the man bent over for another scoop, Jerrell slid inside, grabbed a shovel leaning against the wall, and crept across the dirt floor.

The stable hand lifted a shovel full of dung and dumped it in the wheelbarrow. His head turned toward Jerrell. "Who—"

A clang resounded as Jerrell's shovel struck the man. The stable hand collapsed in a heap, his forehead bloody and bruised.

Jerrell leaned his shovel against the wall, grabbed the stable hand by the wrists, and dragged him into the stall. He then closed the stall door, hiding the man from view. When he spun around, he nearly ran into the manure-filled wheelbarrow.

"That was close." He shivered when he thought of falling face first in a pile of horse dung. It was just about the grossest thing he could imagine.

He crossed the stable and opened the door leading to the manor. It led to a small room with cloaks hanging on wall hooks. Shoes, slippers, and boots lined the floor below the hooks. Across the room, he saw another door, which was closed. He glanced backward and spied a rope leading to the hay loft. The rope ran through a pulley secured to beams high above him. A lift dangled above the door, held in place by the rope. An idea struck, one that had Jerrell grinning at his own cleverness.

As soon as he had finished preparing his trap, Jerrell turned from the closed door leading to the stables and crossed the small room. He eased the other door open, slid inside, and closed it behind him.

A long open hallway ran from the rear of the building to a pair of double doors at the fore. White and gold veins marked the black marble floor. A closed door waited in the arched recess to Jerrell's left and another to the arched recess on his right. Soft humming came from somewhere ahead.

Moving with light strides, his footsteps nearly silent, he crept across the hall. Pinning his back against the wall on the right, he peered through the opening into a sprawling living room furnished with a pair of plush sofas, leather sitting chairs, end tables, and a massive marble fireplace. That room held the source of the noise.

A woman in a pale green dress and white apron hummed to herself as she dusted a long table beside the far wall. Carafes with pale brown and red liquids rested on the table, along with clean glasses. *Brandy and wine.* She bent over as she worked, her back to him.

Across from the living room was a dining room with a darkly-stained table surrounded by a dozen ornate chairs. A short flight of stairs waited beyond the dining room, beckoning him.

Careful to walk on the rug surrounding the dining room table, Jerrell crept to the stairs and ascended to a cavernous ballroom.

Murals graced the ballroom's arched ceiling, three stories above. The room was bereft of furniture and surrounded by tall windows covered by sheer curtains, allowing daylight in. Alternating black and white marble tiles covered the floor from wall to wall; the walls stood fifty feet apart in the shortest direction.

Another set of stairs took Jerrell to the second story. He followed a long corridor, toward a window at the far end of the manor. He passed a private sitting room and three empty bedrooms before coming to an opening in a rounded wall. To his left, a curved stairwell led down to the first level. To his right, the stairs climbed into darkness. Straight ahead was another sitting room with windows overlooking the gardens and gazebo behind the manor. Beyond the rear wall was a sprawling view of the lower district of Tiamalyn and the surrounding countryside.

Ascending, Jerrell climbed stairs that took him to the third floor. He opened the door to the room in the tower and found it to be empty other than some old, dusty furniture. Another corridor ran the length of the building. Jerrell followed it and found himself peering into a bedchamber fit for a wizard lord. A bed big enough for three and surrounded by sheer curtains sat in the middle of the room. Beyond the bed, a tub sunk into the marble floor. A trio of floor-to-ceiling windows surrounded the tub, again providing a spectacular view of the land below the bluff.

This must be Kylar Mor's bedchamber. Jerrell performed a quick inspection of the room, searching the wardrobe at the far end, the vanity, and the trunk at the foot of the bed. Finding nothing of interest, he moved on to the next room—the man's private study.

The desk held little of note, and the bookshelves held nothing but books, so Jerrell tried picturing the object of his search in his mind and wandered around the room, hoping luck might give him a clue as to its whereabouts. Nothing.

The only other room on the third floor was a bedchamber nearly as impressive as the first.

He then returned to the tower and ascended two stories, guided by light coming through a window near the top. Just beyond the window was a closed door made of ebony-colored wood.

Jerrell eased toward the door with his hand in front of him. A tingle ran across his skin, and the hair on his arms stood on end. *Magic.* Doubtless, it was a trap of some nefarious design.

He removed his dagger and tapped the hilt against the stone blocks near the door. A series of dull thuds informed him that each stone was solid... until one echoed with a deeper sound. Pressing his thumb against the jewel in the dagger activated its enchantment. The sapphire shone with blue light, which he held beside the stone block. Narrow cracks surrounded it.

Clever.

With his palm against the block, he pushed. A click sounded and the surface of the block swung open to reveal a metal panel.

Jerrell groaned. It required magic to activate. Something he did not possess.

His gaze went to the window, just a stride to the right of the false block.

Perhaps there is another way in.

Throwing the latch, he swung the window open and leaned out.

Five stories above the ground, the view was incredible. To the east and west, the estates of Tiamalyn's wealthiest citizens hugged the edge of the bluff with the palace at the far end, and the Tower of Devotion rising toward the heavens. Hundreds of feet below, the lower city stretched out into the distance.

A ledge protruded from the rounded tower wall, four feet down from the window. Jerrell stepped over the windowsill and slid down to the ledge. It was just deep enough for his boots to fit without his toes hanging off. Beyond his toes, a paved patio waited fifty feet below. Luckily, Jerrell held no fear of heights. There was no reason to fear them if he did not fall.

With his back to the wall, he shuffled along the ledge, slowly rounding the tower wall while leaning against the tower. Far below the bluff, people in the lower city streets stopped to point in his direction. Without the cover of night, it was impossible to hide.

As he rounded the tower, the wind buffeted him, tore at his cloak, and caused it to flap wildly. A pair of windows soon came into view. He eased toward the windows and drew his dagger. Not stopping until his back was to the first window, he fit his dagger in the gap between the windows and slid it up until it stopped. He strained against the latch, attempting to lift it. Suddenly, the latch yielded. His dagger flipped up and caused him to lose his balance. The opposite window popped open, and Jerrell grabbed hold of it to keep himself from falling. His boots slipped and the window swung him out, away from the tower as he held on with one hand, the other gripping his dagger.

Dangling five stories up and facing away from the tower, he flipped his dagger over his shoulder, and it sailed through the open window. Jerrell grabbed the window frame with both hands and kicked out. The window swung open wide and then took him back toward the tower. His knees slid onto the ledge, and he exhaled in relief as his heart hammered in his chest.

Still on his knees, he eased himself along the ledge until he was able to reach the window frame. When he had a firm grip on it, Jerrell climbed in.

CHAPTER 20
A TRAP

The uppermost floor of the tower in Kylar Mor's mansion instantly evoked Jerrell's curiosity.

Daylight streamed through four arched windows, which were equally spaced around the tower. The window Jerrell had used faced due west. The vaulted ceiling followed the lines of the cone-shaped roof, the interior revealing darkly-stained, exposed beams. Hanging from the center was a chandelier made of black iron covered by shining silver script. *Enchanted, of course.* Jerrell wondered how to activate it. The scrawling silver script of an enchantment also graced the inside of the closed door. The floor was tiled in black marble with white veins and gave Jerrell the impression of a massive, complex spider web.

A desk, a long table, and a single chair sat in the middle of the room. Three bookshelves made of ebony-colored wood lined the walls between the windows. The stairwell door and a small table occupied the fourth wall.

Jerrell approached the small table and found a black disk sitting upon it. Silver script ran along the edges of the disk. Curious, he picked up the disk. It was made of stone and felt cool to the touch. When he turned the disk over, so the silver surface faced up, the chandelier bloomed to life, illuminating the chamber with pale blue light.

"Neat." He set the disk down, silver side up. "I hope that damn owl is up here."

He moved to the nearest bookshelf and began inspecting it.

The upper shelves held books with black, dark red, or dark blue bindings. Silver runes appeared on some of the books, while other titles were embossed in gold. The smallest book was as thick as three of Jerrell's fingers. The largest would break toes if he dropped it on his foot.

The lower shelves featured interesting objects—a pewter cross, an amulet carved from stone, a golden chalice, a gold circlet with rubies mounted to it, and other oddities. However, the tingling across Jerrell's skin warned him to avoid touching anything, regardless of its worth.

He moved on to the next shelf and found it to be similar to the first. When he reached the third, he gasped.

"There it is."

A golden owl stood beside the shelf, resting in a small alcove built into the wall. With the shelf in the way, he was not able to see the recess until he stood near it.

Tentatively, Jerrell reached for the artifact, but felt no magic coming from it. He gripped the thing and lifted it off the alcove ledge. It was heavier than he had expected.

"For the gold alone, this is worth a fortune." He rotated the owl and the facets of its emerald eyes gleamed in the light.

Jerrell turned to the door and considered possible ways to leave the room. He did not know the nature of the enchantment, but regardless, it was likely to kill him should he trigger it.

"What if I am far enough from the door when it is triggered?"

He set the owl down on the desk and walked over to the table. The surface was clear other than a parchment with a complex symbol drawn on it. Notes were scribbled on the parchment's corner.

Gripping the table by the edge, he slid it backward until his backside collided with the bookshelf opposite from the door. He took a deep breath, eyed the door across the tower, and charged forward, pushing the table before him. Three quarters of the way across, when he was at full speed, he gave the table a shove. It continued across the floor, and he dove behind the desk. When the table reached the door, sparks of red energy erupted. The table exploded. A concussion shook the tower, its force lifting the desk off the floor and flipping it over. Jerrell ducked, but too late. The desktop struck the side of his head and the world went black.

In the Bowl of Oren, Kylar Mor sat in an ornate chair, suitable to his station as Chancellor of Tiamalyn. To his side, Lord Horus occupied a wooden throne padded by dark green cushions. The seat beside Horus, normally occupied by Queen Grenda, sat noticeably empty. Kylar suspected that was connected to the woman's indiscretion the prior evening. Privately, he wondered why Horus suffered such betrayal. The woman was attractive, but she did not respect her husband. *Does she respect me?* As he often did, Kylar imagined himself as a wizard lord. *If I possessed the power of a god, I would demand her respect.*

The repeated sounds of clashing weapons arose from the duel on the arena floor. Kylar expected it to end quickly, since one of the men was GaLang Reagor, and the other was a mere thug who had killed a man over a dice game.

After a brief flurry of strikes, one gladiator felled the other with a blow to the side of his head, the clang resounding throughout the bowl. The downed man held a hand to his helmet, but he did not rise.

When the victor peered up toward Horus in expectation, the wizard lord leaned over and asked, "What do you think, Chancellor?"

Kylar grunted. "You sentenced Reagor to the bowl for his betrayal."

Horus sighed. "Yes. I know."

"Make him pay by a thousand cuts."

"What does that mean?"

Kylar signed inwardly. "Honor means everything to Reagor. Forcing him to publicly murder a helpless opponent will injure him as much as any physical wound."

"I only wish Reagor had displayed such honor and spurned my wife's advances."

"Despite all else, he is only a man."

Horus shook his head. "If only I had a hundred more like him."

Rising to his feet, Horus faced the stadium floor and drew a finger across his throat. Reagor's head dropped to his chin, causing Kylar to grin. *He despises this.* Standing over the downed man, Reagor lifted his sword, tip down, and drove it through the man's throat. The downed gladiator stiffened, twitched, and fell still. The crowd roared.

A sense of satisfaction at Reagor's obvious discomfort filled Kylar's chest, causing him to sit back with a smile until one of his personal guards emerged from the stairwell and rushed toward him.

Kylar stood and scowled at the man. "What you doing here, Baskins? You are supposed to be guarding my estate."

Gasping for air, the man said, "It is an emergency, sir."

"What happened?"

"An explosion shook your tower."

"Did you investigate?"

The man shook his head. "It was magic, Chancellor. The men are afraid of what might happen if they go up there."

Kylar clenched his fist. "Run and make sure my carriage is ready." He then turned to Horus. "I have to leave, Your Majesty."

"Go on, Chancellor. We will meet again this afternoon, after I return to the palace."

Spinning around, Kylar stomped across the stands, his robes fluttering as he swept down the stairwell. He emerged at the carriage holding area, where a cluster of drivers stood in a circle, and their conversations stalled upon sighting him. Without giving them a glance, Kylar strode past numerous carriages and reached his own as the driver climbed up into the seat.

With a yank, he tore the carriage door open. "To my estate. Hurry." He paused before climbing in. "Baskins, you hang on the back."

The carriage leapt into motion, the guard scrambling to grab the rails and climb on the back. Estates rolled past as the horses ran the quarter mile back to his estate. With his head out the window, Kylar peered west. A trail of black smoke rose from his tower, causing him instant consternation. That chamber was where he kept his most prized possessions. The thought of losing even one book or seeing one item damaged... He clenched his fists tightly as anger seethed in his gut.

~

JERRELL STIRRED and opened his eyes. His head throbbed and his shoulder ached, but he was otherwise whole. He sat up and looked around and realized he was still in a room in Kylar Mor's tower.

The desk lay on its side just strides away. Sections of the destroyed table lay scattered across the floor, the pieces still burning. Black smoke filled the upper reaches of the room, some of which billowed through the open window. Worst of all, the door remained intact. After seeing what happened to the table, Jerrell did not even wish to imagine what it might do to him.

He scooped up the owl and stood. The room tilted, and he staggered. Clenching his eyes shut, he fought against his dizziness. Smoke invaded his next breath, causing him to cough. He stumbled across the room and opened another window to create a cross breeze.

The gate in front of the estate stood open with a trio of guards beside it, all facing toward the Bowl of Oren. Jerrell followed their gaze and spotted a carriage speeding down the street. He recognized the carriage immediately.

"Oh, crap."

He turned from the window and scurried across the room. The door was out of the question, so he went to the window he had used to enter the room and looked down. The drop was too far for him to jump without breaking a leg...or something worse. Although his head pounded and he didn't feel all that steady, he had no choice but to climb out and use the ledge.

With his back to the wall, he eased along the ledge. The wind tugged at him, as if taunting him into an attempt to spread his arms and take to the sky. He chuckled at the thought. Others had tried, but men weren't meant to fly. He suspected women weren't either, but he was wise enough not to say so to any of them.

Moving as quickly as he dared, he rounded the tower wall and approached the stairwell window. When he was able to reach out and grip the frame, he exhaled in relief. Moments later, he was back inside and racing down the stairwell.

~

When the carriage reached the entrance, Kylar found the gates already open. His other three guards stood to the side, watching as the carriage rolled up the long drive, circled the manor, and stopped just outside the stables.

Kylar opened the door and climbed out. "Baskins, tell the guards to watch the gate, and then guard the front door. Make sure nobody leaves except for me."

The man blinked. "You fear intruders?"

"I don't know what to think, but nobody is allowed in the tower, and I can't think of any way this could have happened unless there was an intruder."

He stepped into the shadows of the stables. "Lowell?" he called out. When he received no answer, he grumbled. "Where is that useless stable hand?"

Kylar went straight for the door connecting the stables to the rear of the manor, turned the handle, and pulled. The door was stuck. He then noticed a rope stuck between the door and the frame, just inches from the stable's dirt floor.

"What the blazes?"

Gripping the handle tightly, he yanked hard. The door popped open, causing Kylar to stagger backward. The rope zipped up, and the pulley above him squealed as it spun. He looked up just as a wheelbarrow in the hayloft tipped down toward him, dumping its load.

Manure pelted him in the face, head, and shoulders with bits going in his robes and wet chunks sliding down his arms, chest, and back.

Standing stiff, locked between shock and disgust, Kylar shook and wiped his eyes clean. Raw rage bubbled from his gut, to his chest, and finally entered his throat. He roared with anger as he stomped inside.

CHAPTER 21
OBJECTS OF INTEREST

Rushing to escape the mansion before incurring Kylar Mor's wrath, Jerrell raced down the stairs as fast as he dared, knowing a fall could be the difference between life and death.

He reached the ballroom, turned the corner, and descended the stairs to the dining room. He hurried across it, to the entrance hall, where he slid across the tiled floor and stopped. Across the living room stood the maid, her eyes wide as she stared in his direction.

The door leading to the stables opened, and a robed man stepped through, his head, face, and much of his body covered in horse manure. Jerrell grinned. *It worked.*

"Landish!" the wizard roared, the whites of his eyes creating a striking contrast to the brown dung coating his face. "I will kill you!"

The man thrust his hand toward Jerrell, who yipped and dove back into the dining room. A bolt of lightning arced past him and struck one of the white columns, sending a spray of shards in all directions.

Scrambling to his feet, Jerrell set the owl on a serving table beside the wall. He then picked up a wooden dining chair and moved toward the wall, pinning his back against it while holding the chair cocked to his side.

Angry grunts came from around the corner, drawing closer as the wizard stomped the length of the entrance hall. When the wizard's shadow came into view, Jerrell swung the chair around. The chair smashed into the wizard with a crack. A wooden chair leg broke and went spinning across the room while the wizard fell in a heap.

Jerrell snatched up the owl, raced to the front door, flung the door open, and sprinted outside.

A guard appeared on the porch with a sword in his hand. The man swung at Jerrell, who dropped to the ground. His momentum carried him across the marble tiles, allowing him to slide beneath the blade. Still on his back, he pulled a throwing blade from the opposite sleeve and flicked his arm up, releasing his grip. The knife stuck in the guard's back, causing him to cry out and stumble toward the open doorway. Realizing the blade was lost for good, Jerrell hurriedly leapt down the front stairs and ran along the path toward the estate gate where three guards were waiting.

The guards drew their weapons and spread out to intercept him. Jerrell shifted the owl to his other hand, drew the remaining blade in his sleeve, and threw it. The knife spun through the air and struck one of the guards in the chest. The man stumbled and fell against the wall beside the gate. Two armed men remained.

Slowing, Jerrell reached over his head, inside his coat, and drew the blade hidden in a pocket at the nape of his neck. Again, he threw. This time, the target moved. The man spun away, and the knife careened off the gate.

Just strides before reaching the guards, Jerrell came to a stop. The guards waved their swords and grinned.

Kylar Mor emerged from the manor, stepping onto the front porch and bellowed, "Now, you die!"

The wizard thrust his hands toward Jerrell. Expecting another lightning blast, Jerrell dove between the gate and the fallen guard. Sure enough, bright lightning burst from the wizard's hands and shot across the yard. The gate, made of iron, altered the lightning's path, causing the bolt to strike it. Sizzling electricity arced to the sword of the guard standing beside it. The man shook violently and collapsed as the electricity faded.

Jerrell drew a blade from his boot and threw. Still staring at his fallen comrade, the last guard didn't see it coming. With the knife buried in his ribs, he fell to one knee as Jerrell raced past him and into the street.

He ran as fast as he could, ducking behind a passing wagon to hide him from view should the wizard appear at the gate.

When he came to a cross street, he turned off Tiam Lane and was gone.

THE BEDS WERE UNMADE, and a man remained tied to a chair. Otherwise, the room Jerrell and Mond shared at the Golden Goose appeared as it had when they first entered.

"Again, I appreciate your cooperation," Jerrell said to his captive as he hefted his pack. "Do not worry. You will soon be freed." He walked up to Preston and set a gold piece on the chair seat. "This is for your trouble. When you return to the palace, do give Queen Grenda my regards. I found her...quite invigorating."

Preston's brows arched. "Invigorating? Half the staff despises her. The other half drools when she walks past."

"And how do you feel toward her?"

He grimaced. "The woman is a snake! And I'd sooner sleep with a snake than come within six feet of her!"

Jerrell smirked. "In truth, I can't disagree with any of those opinions. However, when a snake meets a snake charmer, such transgressions are equalized."

"What does that mean?"

The question earned the man a chuckle as Jerrell rested his hand on the door. "Just tell her that Jerrell Landish cherishes his memory of their meeting."

He opened the door, stepped out, and closed it behind him. Whistling, he walked casually down the broad corridor and took the stairs to the ground level, where a man in a white coat stood waiting.

"Good afternoon, Master Landish. I trust your stay met your expectations?"

"Hello, Jeebs. Our stay was splendid, but you should send someone to clean our room very soon. We left a bit of a mess."

"I will send the maid up immediately."

"Wonderful. This is for your efforts and impeccable service, but we must be going." Jerrell slipped the man a silver piece.

"You are leaving our city?"

"I am afraid so."

"Where to next?"

Jerrell knew but was not about to share that information. In fact, he preferred to mislead the man should anyone question him. "Oh, I am not sure. Perhaps I will head north. I am no fan of cold weather, and a winter in Balmor might be just what I need."

"Right you are, sir."

"Take care, Jeebs." Jerrell followed a corridor to a door at the rear of the building.

Once outside, he found Mond sitting on the wagon with the reins in his grip. "It is about time. I thought you were in a hurry to flee and avoid Mor's wrath."

"I thought to ensure I was not standing around waiting for you." Jerrell climbed into the wagon bed and lay down. "Let's get out of this city before somebody identifies me."

Mond snapped the reins and the carriage lurched into motion. He drove it down an alley that led to Tiam Lane. The wagon turned away from the palace and took them toward the Bowl of Oren.

Over his shoulder, Mond asked, "How many people have seen you?"

Jerrell considered the question. "There is a good chance some of Mor's guards survived. If you include them, Mor, Lord Horus, Grenda, Preston, the staff at the Golden Goose, and you, I'd say a dozen total. However, we are dealing with wizards, and they might have magic that would help them share my likeness with others. If so, any soldier in the city might be able to pick me out amid a crowd."

Mond grunted. "Great. I thought you were supposed to be talented."

"I retrieved the owl, didn't I?"

"I suppose."

Jerrell recalled something. "I have a favor to ask."

"What now?"

"Across the street from Mor's estate is a jewelry shop. Can you circle around to the alley behind it?"

"What the blazes for?"

"I asked for something special. It is a gift. I need to pick it up."

The man sighed. "Fine." He then muttered, "After one day in Highmount, the bloody thief thinks he is an entitled royal."

The wagon soon turned and turned again before the man drew it to a stop. Jerrell sat up. The alley was empty other than their wagon and a few barrels of trash. He hopped out. "I'll be right back."

Jerrell opened the rear door and stepped into a workshop where a man with a graying beard busily heated a crucible.

The man looked up at him. "What are you doing back here?"

"Sorry," Jerrell walked past. "My former betrothed was out front, and I chose to use the back door rather than listen to her shout at me."

The man grunted. "That, I can understand."

He entered the jewelry shop, and the woman he met earlier stood from her stool. "You are back."

Jerrell smiled. "I could not pass up another opportunity to gaze upon your face."

She placed her hands on her hips. "Oh, please. Why are you really here?"

He gestured. "The globe. I want to buy it."

"You'll not get it for four gold."

"I have six...five for the globe, one for your beauty."

She rolled her eyes and held out her palm. He dropped the gold pieces into it. She peered at them with a grunt, her brows arching. "Huh. I am surprised. The way you are dressed, I thought you intended to steal from us. I never expected you to have this much gold."

"I enjoy nothing more than surprising others." Stepping up to the shelf, Jerrell picked up the globe and frowned. "Can you wrap it to keep it safe?"

She produced a cloth sack, took the globe from him, and slid it inside before handing the sack to him. "Does this satisfy you?"

He smiled. "Oh, I am never satisfied and could always go for more."

"You are not referring to purchasing goods, are you?"

"I suspect you know what I mean."

She snorted. "Unless you intend to buy something else, please leave."

Jerrell gripped her chin, stared into her eyes, and smiled. "I love the feisty ones." He kissed her on the cheek, spun away, and passed through the workshop.

Back in the alley, he called out to Mond, "I am ready. Let's be off."

Whistles and the thunder of horses came from the street, causing him to stop. "Hold on," he said before creeping down the alley.

Dozens of guards rushed past, trailing behind a full cohort on horseback. He watched as soldiers headed toward the Bowl of Oren and then passed it. When it became clear they were heading down the road leading to the lower city, his fears were confirmed. Chancellor Mor had used his station to his advantage, and now, the entire city guard would be after Jerrell and the owl.

"Oh, crap."

CHAPTER 22

FLIGHT

Hidden beneath a tarp, Jerrell lay in the wagon bed while Mond held the reins and navigated the busy streets of Tiamalyn. Each bump caused his teeth to chatter and soon left his shoulder bruised. He ached to peer out at his surroundings but was disciplined enough keep his head down. Giving in to such urges could get a thief killed.

After twenty long minutes, the wagon slowed.

Mond's voice came from above him. "It doesn't look so bad."

"What do you see?"

"The soldiers at the gate are inspecting those who wish to enter the city."

"What of the ones leaving?"

"A wagon just drove through the gate. They ignored it."

Jerrell frowned. He was sure the soldiers he saw earlier were pursuing him. *If they aren't deployed to the gate, where are they?* The question bothered him like an itch he could not reach. He decided to chance it. "Go on through the gate. Perhaps we can escape the city after all."

Mond snapped the reins, and the wagon rolled forward. Jerrell gripped his dagger hilt, ready in case of trouble. Only one of his throwing blades remained, which irked him and left him feeling more than a bit naked. Tense and unable to see what transpired around him, he found himself holding his breath. A shadow passed over him, darkening the wagon through the tarp.

"We are beyond the wall," Mond said, sounding surprised. "I am heading toward the barge. Once we are on board and downstream, we should be safe."

Unable to stand it any longer, Jerrell pushed himself up and pulled the tarp back.

The city wall was already hundreds of feet away and growing more distant. At the gate, a handful of guards inspected incoming wagons and carts. Turning toward the fast-approaching river, Jerrell spied their barge, still secured to the dock farthest downriver, where the open field met the woods. There were no soldiers in sight.

"I don't get it," Jerrell said. "Where did those soldiers go?"

"Perhaps something else came up, something more important than you."

"I dumped a load of horse dung on the wizard," Jerrell said. "Even if I hadn't stolen from him and destroyed half of the items in his tower study, for that alone I would expect him to use everything in his power to catch me."

Mond shook his head as he chortled. "I wish I had seen Mor covered in manure. He is a boastful, arrogant arse. Such an embarrassment would be quite traumatic and something he is unlikely to ever forget...or forgive."

Jerrell frowned. Mor knew his name, had seen his face, and would likely carry a vendetta against him forever. "I may have to avoid Tiamalyn in the future."

"I would if I were you." Mond drew the wagon to a halt. They were only a few strides from the ramp leading to the docks. "Let's get out of here."

Jerrell threw the tarp back and hopped out of the wagon. "What about these crates?"

"Leave them. Someone will claim them when they find the wagon."

It felt odd leaving the items behind. The wagon, the horses, and the goods were worth good coin. *Someone will be finding a gift.*

The two of them headed down the ramp toward the barge and found the deck empty.

"Where is everyone?" Jerrell asked.

"Maybe they are napping. Regardless, they were warned to be ready for a quick departure."

Just as they reached the foot of the dock where the barge was moored, nine armored guards emerged from the trees along the riverbank. The two soldiers on the ends held loaded crossbows, which were leveled at Jerrell and Mond.

The soldier in the center commanded, "Hold! You are under arrest!"

They both froze. Under his breath, Jerrell asked, "How many can you take?"

Mond's hand hovered near the hilt of his sword. "Three or four. The narrowness of the dock would help."

With only one throwing blade, Jerrell would have to face four of five with only his dagger. That was too many to avoid serious injury or worse.

"Raise your hands, and feign surrender while backing away," Jerrell whispered. More loudly, he shouted, "We surrender."

They both held their hands up while backing down the dock.

The sergeant took a step toward them. "I told you to hold still!"

"We are." Jerrell and Mond continued to back down the dock.

The guard pointed at them. "Take one more step, and my men will loose their arrows!"

They both stopped, and the situation turned from serious to dire when a squad of soldiers on horseback emerged from the city gate and rode toward the docks.

"What now?" Mond whispered.

"Crossbows aren't all that accurate."

"We make for the barge?"

"Remain here for a beat. I'll draw their fire. You cut the front line. I'll cut the back."

Jerrell spun around and raced down the dock while weaving from one side to the other. Two rapid twangs came from behind. One bolt flew past and buried itself into a mooring post. The other tugged at his flared cloak briefly before tearing through it and sailing far out into the river. Drawing his dagger as he neared the end of the dock, he knelt beside a rope secured to the boat and urgently sawed at the rope while the soldiers raced down the bank. Now beside the bow, Mond sliced with his sword, severing the line. He then jumped onto the craft and turned to face the onrushing soldiers.

The rear line snapped, and Jerrell stepped quickly onto the barge, which began to float away. The lead soldier leapt across the widening gap but was met by Mond's blade. Three others followed, landing on the barge deck. Two turned toward Mond while the third came at Jerrell.

Gripping his dagger, Jerrell was ready for him. The man swung, and Jerrell leapt backward. A thrust of his longsword followed, but the soldier missed when Jerrell spun toward the cabin. The guard followed with a backhand swipe. Jerrell dropped to his knee, ducking beneath the blade. It struck the cabin with a solid thud. Jerrell lashed out and slashed across the man's front leg, causing him to stumble backward and raise his blade as he tried to catch his balance. Uncoiling his legs while lunging forward, Jerrell shoved the wounded soldier over the edge. The man disappeared with a splash.

At the front of the boat, Mond held the other two guards at bay, their backs to Jerrell, who snuck behind a soldier and thrust his blade into the man's kidney. The man cried out and fell to his knee as Mond drove his sword through the other guard. Seconds later, both were in the river.

The two bowmen standing on the dock finished reloading their crossbows and took aim.

"Get down!" Jerrell dropped to the deck as one bolt sailed past.

The other struck Mond in the arm, causing him to spin and stumble. The current caught the barge, and it began to pick up speed, just as the soldiers on horseback reached the docks.

Teeth clenched, Mond grunted as he pulled the bolt from his arm. Jerrell reached into his pack and pulled out a bundle of dried meat wrapped in leather. He unwound it the meat and dripped the leather into the river to clean it.

He knelt beside Mond. "Hold your arm out. I'll tie this around the wound."

Mond did as he was asked. Blood matted his tunic sleeve. Jerrell wrapped the strip around the man's right arm and tied it, making sure to apply pressure to the wound.

Glancing back toward the dock, he found the soldiers in a heated discussion. Finally, the five remaining on foot hopped into a boat and pushed off while the riders mounted their horses, turned, and faded from view.

"They are coming after us," Mond said.

"Your observational skills astound me once again."

The man climbed to his feet with a scowl. "Your sarcasm is going to get you in trouble one of these days."

"It wouldn't be the first time."

"Thanks for the bandage."

"I need you alive, so it seemed like a good idea. Can you still fight?"

He tapped the sword on his hip. "I am left-handed."

"At least we have that. If they catch us, we'll have to face five. In the meantime, grab an oar. Let's get this thing away from the Orenthian side of the river. Those horsemen are undoubtedly riding ahead, and I'd hate to be within easy bowshot."

SITTING ON A BENCH, Jerrell rowed on one side of the barge while Mond rowed on the other. Their efforts, combined with the flow of the river, kept the barge moving at a good pace, but not fast enough. *I wish we had more men rowing.* A brief search had proven the craft was empty, and while Jerrell was curious about the whereabouts of the captain and the crew, he had more pressing worries.

The soldiers in the fishing boat slowly closed the gap and had almost reached their barge. A guard in the bow raised a crossbow and took aim at Jerrell. Watching the man's hand, Jerrell gauged the right moment. When the trigger finger flexed, he lay backward. The bolt sailed over him and struck the cabin wall.

Jerrell sat up and abandoned his oar. One thing had become clear: He needed to deal with the other boat and swiftly. Scrambling around to the back of the barge, he reached into a trunk secured to the deck. A coil of rope rested inside the trunk. At the end of the rope was an anchor made of heavy iron.

Gripping the rope just a foot from the anchor, Jerrell hoisted it up and looked over his shoulder. The fishing boat had drawn even with the rear of the barge and was angled toward it, ready to board at any moment.

Jerrell extended his arms, spun in the opposite direction, and whipped the anchor around. When he again faced the fishing boat, he released it. The anchor hurtled toward the boat. A pair of soldiers cried out and dove to avoid the heavy object. The anchor landed right between the men and smashed through the hull with a mighty crack. The rope began to rapidly uncoil from the trunk beside Jerrell. He grabbed the other end of the rope and lashed it to an unused oar. When the rope grew taut, Jerrell leapt. The oar shot beneath him, flew past the edge of the barge, and crashed into the side of the fishing boat. The oar then flipped over the side, striking a soldier in the head, and knocking him out of the craft. The oar slammed down to the opposite rail so it spanned the width of the craft.

When a soldier near the bow stood, drew his sword, and prepared to cut the rope, the anchor line suddenly jerked tight, causing the boat to stop. The soldier stumbled backward and flipped over the rail, landing in the water with a splash.

Shouts arose as the gap between the fishing boat and the barge grew larger. The men in the water struggled to remain above the surface, splashing and coughing as they tried to float despite their leather armor. Meanwhile, the men in the craft cut at the anchor line. It broke free, and the boat began moving with the current; however, it was taking on water, and the distance between the two crafts continued to grow. There was little chance of the soldiers catching the barge again.

"That ends one threat." Jerrell rounded the cabins and stopped beside Mond, who rested with an oar across his knees. "Those riders are somewhere downriver. We need to act before we come across them."

Mond nodded. "Agreed."

"How's your arm."

"Not good. I can't even grip the oar with it."

Jerrell then spied a barge rounding a bend in the river. The men on board rowed hard, fighting the current as the barge headed upstream. Unlike their craft, this one had no cabins. In the center of the deck, a thick net covered a cluster of barrels and crates.

"It is a freighter," Mond said.

"I have an idea." Moving to the stern, Jerrell gripped the tiller.

"What are you up to, now?"

"We are going to board that other barge."

"Do you think those men will agree?"

He grinned. "Gold tends to make anyone agreeable."

CHAPTER 23
SURRENDER

Hidden amid the cluster of crates and barrels, Jerrell and Mond lay beneath the cover of heavy nets. Convincing the captain to turn the boat around and give them a ride downriver had cost them their remaining gold. One piece had gone to the freighter's captain and six more to his crew, who had sat with their oars on their laps, waiting. Through a gap between a crate and a barrel, Jerrell watched the abandoned barge float down the river, just ahead of them.

A landing with half a dozen docks came into view. A score of horses stood on shore above the docks. Soldiers with bows stood on the docks while others rowed out in a pair of fishing boats.

"All right, men," Willis, the freighter's captain said, "time to row."

One of the crew began to call out, "Stroke, stroke, stroke."

The oars dipped into the water with each command, and the freighter picked up speed.

Shouts came from the soldiers in the boats as they navigated their vessels to either side of the abandoned barge. As the boats met the barge, the freighter carrying Jerrell and Mond passed them. Jerrell shifted his position for a better view. *This is too good to miss.*

Soldiers climbed aboard the abandoned barge. Weapons drawn, they circled the cabins and began testing the doors, which were all locked, something Jerrell had done in hope of further slowing pursuit. It worked. The soldiers began kicking at the doors, intent on finding Jerrell and believing he and Mond hid on the craft. The first door broke open, and guards disappeared inside, searching for the two fugitives. All the while, the distance between the barge and the freighter steadily increased.

The freighter rounded a bend, and the soldiers faded from view.

"I would hate to be the captain in charge of those men," Mond said.

Jerrell chuckled. "Mor is out for blood, and he will extract it, with or without our capture."

Mond lay his head down and covered his eyes with the back of his arm.

"What are you doing?" Jerrell asked.

"Getting some sleep. The downriver trip is far faster than upriver, but we still won't reach Shear until tomorrow evening. Until then, I plan to sleep as much as possible."

Shear, Jerrell thought. *High Wizard Wrenthal is waiting for his prize. I just hope he does not betray me when I deliver it.*

JERRELL FINISHED his turn at an oar, rose from his bench, and relinquished his place to Eskin, a dark-skinned Kyranni with bulging arms. Stretching to work the soreness from his shoulders and arms, Jerrell found a new appreciation for the crew's work. *No wonder Eskin's arms are so big.* All eight men in Captain Willis's crew were muscular. Jerrell now understood why.

He sat on a crate in the middle of the freighter. On the crate beside him, Mond cradled his wounded arm. Like Jerrell, he had agreed to take turns at the oars to help reach Shear as soon as possible.

"That is exhausting." Jerrell's tunic clung to his body, his back and armpits damp with sweat.

"You weren't even at the oar for an hour."

"I know." Jerrell peered down the river. The bend ahead masked their view, only allowing them to see a short distance ahead. Rocky cliffs and thick woods bordered the river. The banks stood no more than two stories above the water, but by the time they reached Shear, those same banks would be hundreds of feet high. "I was already sore after sleeping on the hard deck last night. Taking turns at the oars is likely to make it worse."

"You heard Captain Willis. Our efforts can make the difference between reaching Shear tonight or sometime early tomorrow."

Jerrell understood, but he didn't have to like it. If the city was not in sight by the time darkness fell, the craft would moor to the side of the river until sunrise, which meant another night of sleeping on the hard deck. To avoid it, Jerrell was willing to endure a few hours of hard work.

"I am looking forward to a bath and a chance to wash my clothes," he said.

Mond nodded. "All of that, along with a hot meal and a soft bed, await our arrival."

The barge rounded the bend. A riverside village stood on the Orenthian side of the river. Empty docks lined the riverbank while a score of buildings stood higher up the bank, overlooking the water. At the far end of the village, a mill with a massive wooden wheel turned slowly, driven by the current. A line of fishing boats anchored in the water across from the docks blocked any route along the opposite shore.

"This is bad," Jerrell said.

Mond sat up and peered downriver. "A blockade. They mean to force us close to the Orenthian shore, where their bows can easily target us."

Soldiers in green and brown walked down the riverbank and onto the docks. More than one had a bow with an arrow nocked. Others appeared on the rock outcropping above the freighter. They also had their bows ready.

Jerrell hopped off the crate and walked to the stern, where Captain Willis stood with his hand on the tiller. "What do you think?"

Willis grimaced and rubbed his long black beard. "I think we are in trouble."

"Is there no way we can avoid them?"

"Other than rowing upstream, no. However, it is too late. We are exposed and their arrows are unlikely to miss all of us."

Jerrell sighed. Paying the man gold to reverse course and delay his delivery to Tiamalyn was one thing. Asking him and his crew to risk their lives was another.

"What is your opinion, Mond?"

The man held his wounded arm while staring at the blockade. "I agree with Willis. We have no choice but to surrender."

"Then, what?"

He shrugged. "I don't know."

Jerrell considered the situation and weighed his options. "I have an idea."

"What?"

"They are after me, not you, so I will use it to our advantage."

"Those men saw me fight their comrades to help you escape."

"True, but they will forget about you if I make a sufficient distraction."

Jerrell knelt between a crate and a barrel, reaching under the heavy netting for his pack. He dug around until his fingers felt the cool metal. He withdrew the owl and stood. His coat and cloak lay beside the pack, both discarded before his turn at the oar.

"Alright, Willis. Take us near the docks. I'll jump off as we pass by."

"Won't they make me stop?"

"No. They don't care about you. It is me Mor is after. You just sail on toward Shear unless they give you no other choice."

The captain's eyes narrowed. "I hope you know what you are doing."

Jerrell grinned. "I know people. The squad leader cannot return to Tiamalyn without me. Anyone else is irrelevant." Jerrell counted on the fact that Kylar Mor wanted him back, alive.

As the craft angled toward the docks, Jerrell stepped onto the edge of the vessel.

"Jerrell Landish," a soldier on the docks called out. "In the name of Chancellor Kylar Mor, I place you under arrest."

Jerrell held his arm up and waved the owl for all to see. "I know, I know. Mor is pissed because I stole his precious bauble. Please tell me the man has bathed. When I last saw him, he smelled like a horse's arse."

The guards on shore laughed, earning them a stern glare from their squad leader.

The craft drew near the dock and Jerrell prepared for the jump. He leapt across, his foot landing on the dock. The second foot missed...intentionally. Jerrell whirled his arms and rounded his eyes in feigned fear. The squad leader lunged out to grab him, but it was too late.

Jerrell fell off the side of the dock and was swept away by the current. The water was colder than he had anticipated, causing his chest muscles to tighten and making it difficult to breathe.

He passed beneath the second dock and resurfaced. His flailing arms splashed water, and he cried out, "Help! I can't swim!"

Shouts rang out, and soldiers ran along the riverbank while those on the dock dove into the water.

The river took Jerrell straight toward the mill's massive wheel. Just before he reached it, Jerrell took a deep breath and submerged. Under water, he gripped one of the wheel's fins with his free hand, while the other firmly clutched the owl.

The wheel pulled him deeper, taking him under the mill. As he came out the other side, Jerrell pushed off, and began to swim underwater toward the middle of the river. The bright sky provided light in the murky water, the ripples causing the sun to waver with each stroke. A shadow lay ahead. With powerful, sweeping breaststrokes, Jerrell swam toward it as quickly as possible. When he passed under the shadow, it blotted out the light and he swam upward. He surfaced beneath the barge, beside one of its two keels. A deep breath brought sweet air into his hungry lungs. With his free hand, his fingers numb from the cold water, he grabbed one of the ropes tied around the keel and held on, allowing the barge to pull him downriver.

Through the small shadowy gap between the barge deck and the water-line, Jerrell watched the village, the mill, and the frantic guards fade into the distance. Soldiers climbed along the steep shore, covered in trees and rocks, and peered into the water, while others dove under the surface again and again. Soon, the shouts faded. The freighter rounded a bend, and the shore obscured the village from view. Only then, did Jerrell release his grip.

The craft slowly passed over him, and when he reached the stern, he grabbed the tiller rod.

"What the blazes?" Willis looked down at him from his perch. "Where did you come from?"

"It is c-c-cold," Jerrell stuttered through chattering teeth. "Help m-m-me up."

~

THE SETTING SUN was masked by the high cliff to the west by the time the river widened to reveal the port city of Shear. Shadows blanketed the river valley and the lower city, the waterway empty of vessels other than a single ship that sailed toward the sea beyond Yor's Point.

Captain Willis turned the tiller, and the ship angled toward the docks. The crew rowed with renewed vigor upon sighting their destination, and the freighter quickly closed the distance, guided by enchanted lanterns mounted to the end of each dock. The craft slid into an open mooring and bumped into the dock. Lines were thrown around the mooring posts, and the barge settled into place.

Jerrell and Mond both stepped onto the dock before turning back to the craft.

"Thank you for your hospitality," Jerrell said.

"You don't owe me any thanks," Willis replied. "The gold we earned for this little trip was well worth the effort. In addition, we now have a story to tell over ales for years to come." He shook his head. "That little prank you pulled with the fake drowning... It was a thing of beauty."

Jerrell grinned. "If you think that was interesting, I have other tales to share with you if we meet again."

The captain tipped his hat. "If we do, I'll buy you an ale."

"It's a deal." Jerrell turned to find Mond waiting on shore. He walked the length of the dock and climbed up the ramp, stopping to peer up at the steep drive. "Please tell me we aren't going to climb that at night."

A beam of light shot across the sky, igniting the obelisk on the bluff with blue flame. Another beam shot down the cliffside and shone on the spire in the lower district.

"Too late." Mond gestured toward the obelisk as he led Jerrell toward the city gate. "Devotion has begun, so reaching the castle tonight will gain us nothing."

Jerrell frowned. *What does Devotion have to do with anything?* Despite his desire to voice the question, he focused on more pressing needs. "Let's find an inn, get a hot meal, and chase it down with some ale."

"For once, I am inclined to agree." He arched a brow toward Jerrell. "Do you have any coin left?"

"A pair of silvers."

"That is just enough to do the trick."

"What of the climb to the castle?"

"We'll have to do it by foot this time."

Jerrell sighed. "Great." One of the guards left the open gate and was striding toward them. Again, Jerrell sighed. "Here comes a guard. We had better kneel and get to chanting."

Mond dropped to his knees. "At least we are back in Farrowen and beyond Mor's clutches."

Kneeling, Jerrell joined in with the chant while his mind wandered.

As long as he was beyond Orenth's borders, he should be safe from Kylar Mor's thirst for vengeance. Still, the man was unlikely to ever forget, not until either he or Jerrell were dead. *It might be best to ensure we never cross paths again.*

Minutes passed. By the time Devotion ended, night had fully claimed the sky. Jerrell and Mond rose to their feet, passed through the gate, and went in search of an inn with a two spare beds. As they walked, Jerrell found his gaze repeatedly going to the building on the edge of the cliff above, where Shear Castle loomed like a sentinel, watching over the river valley. Even though he was back and about to complete his quest, a sense of dread roiled in Jerrell's stomach.

CHAPTER 24

COMPANIONSHIP

The next morning, fed and well rested, Jerrell and Mond began the long climb up the cliffside. The switchbacks soon began to pass in a blur; each seemed the same as the last and they had taken far too many to count. Jerrell's thighs and backside burned with each step. His boots grew heavier, and he wondered if someone had stuffed rocks in them just to test him. When they emerged from the shadow of the opposite cliff and the sun began to beat down on them, it only got worse.

"Good thing I didn't bother to bathe last night," Mond said.

Jerrell grunted. "Not good for me. If you can't tell, I'm avoiding standing downwind of you."

The man grunted. "Well, a hot bath will be waiting for both of us once we reach the castle."

"The last bath I had was my little swim in the river, which is anything but hot. However, right now, a cool dip sounds refreshing."

"Just keep climbing. We'll be there soon."

Two switchbacks later, the road leveled, and the castle walls came into view. Without pause, Mond led Jerrell through the front gate. The guards nodded at Mond but did not stop them or say a word.

They reached the castle, and Mond led Jerrell inside, where a man in a white coat appeared in the entrance hall.

"Welcome back, Master Mond."

"It is good to be back, Chalmers. Is the high wizard in? I didn't see his carriage outside."

"Sorry, sir. The high wizard was called to Marquithe a few days ago. He is expected back today or tomorrow."

"Good. When he arrives, let me know. We are delivering an item of interest, and he will wish to see it immediately."

"I will ensure you are notified," Chalmers said.

"Good. In the meantime, we each require a bath, a fresh tunic, and a mid-day meal."

"As you wish, Master Mond."

Jerrell frowned. *This servant defers to Mond. Clearly, he is something more than an ex-soldier.* The question continued to gnaw at Jerrell as he followed Chalmers up the stairs and to a bed chamber with a copper tub, a table and chairs, and a hot fireplace.

A coppery-skinned Hassakani woman stood near a fire, tending to a steaming kettle. Like the other staff, she wore a blue dress and a white apron. Unlike the others, her dress was unbuttoned just enough to give a hint of the enticement that hid underneath. Black locks spilled over her shoulders, and sadness lurked in her large dark eyes. The soft curves of her cheeks, chin, and nose spoke to her youth, and he figured she was somewhere around his own age. He found himself smiling, and she smiled back, the sadness fading.

"Prianna," Chalmers said. "Master Landish requires a hot bath. You are to see to his every need."

The man walked out the door with Mond, leaving Jerrell alone with the woman.

"Hello, Master Landish."

"Good morning, Prianna," he said in his most charming tone.

The corners of her lips turned up as she turned away. She bent over, her dress stretching tight against her nicely rounded backside as she picked up the steaming kettle. "Be a dear and close the door before you undress." She then poured the kettle into the tub, the water steaming.

Jerrell closed the door and took off his coat, hanging it and his cloak on a hook. He removed his tunic and smelled it. Even after the dip in the river, it needed a wash, so he tossed it in the tub.

"Prianna is a pretty name. It is a good match for your appearance." The comment earned him another smile. "So tell me. Shear is far from Hassakan. How did you end up here?" He sat and pulled off his boots.

"My parents fled my homeland when I was young. They settled just outside of Shear, where my father raised chickens. But...there was a fire, and...they are gone."

"I am sorry." He meant it. "I know what it is like to lose your parents."

Prianna nodded but said nothing more. Instead, she set another kettle on the fire and turned back toward him, watching as he stretched his toes. "Are your feet sore?"

"Yes. We climbed up from the lower city this morning."

"I could rub your feet if you like."

Jerrell arched his brow. "While that sounds enticing, my feet don't smell all that great right now."

"Perhaps..." The woman bit her lip, her gaze going to the floor. "I could do it while we are in the tub."

"We?"

Prianna shrugged shyly. "I thought you might like..."

"Oh, I would definitely appreciate your company."

She smiled and began to unbutton her dress.

Whistling happily, Jerrell slipped on a fresh tunic. The bath, and the other activities, left him in a good mood. When he was once again dressed, Prianna pulled the plug in the tub. The water ran down a narrow channel carved into the floor, flowing across the room and disappearing into a hole near the wall.

He slipped his boots on and stood as a knock sounded on the door.

Prianna crossed the room and opened the door. Chalmers stood outside with his hands clasped behind his back. Another man stood beside him, holding a metal tray with a shiny dome over it.

"Good afternoon, Master Landish. Since you missed lunch, I thought you might enjoy your meal delivered here."

Jerrell glanced toward the table, his gaze then shifting to the maid. "Can Prianna remain with me while I eat?"

"Of course, sir."

Claiming a seat at the table, Jerrell sat as the servant set the tray before him. The man lifted the dome to reveal steak with dark lines grilled into it, a baked potato with a slab of butter, and steamed broccoli. The servant departed as Prianna poured Jerrell a glass of water.

Jerrell asked, "Where is Mond, anyway?"

Chalmers replied, "He is meeting with His Grace."

"Wrenthal is back?"

"His carriage recently arrived."

"What about me?"

"He said he will send for you when it is time." Chalmers smiled. "Until then, enjoy Prianna's company."

The door closed and Prianna flashed Jerrell a smile. Despite the fine treatment, Jerrell's inner voice screamed at him. *Run.*

JERRELL OPENED the bedroom door and peered out. As he suspected, two guards stood beside the door. Two others waited at the end of the corridor. They might claim they were there for his protection, but he knew better. He closed it with a sigh.

From behind, Prianna slid her hands around his waist and leaned against his back. Her whisper tickled his ear. "Do you tire of my company?"

"Not at all." He turned toward her. "I simply do not enjoy being held prisoner."

She arched her brow, her hands running across his chest and then wrapping around his back. "Is this how you expect a prisoner to be treated?"

"We have been locked in this room for hours. What else would you call it?"

"A pleasant diversion?" Her hands slid lower, and she grabbed his backside.

While Jerrell had enjoyed her company and her eagerness, he began to suspect he was being used. Eyes narrowed, he asked, "Does the high wizard often ask you to entertain guests?"

She stopped. Her smile faded. "Do you think I am paid for this like some common whore?"

"I thought..."

Prianna stepped back and crossed her arms over her chest. "Perhaps, I am just lonely. Living in a castle is far better than being on the street, but the life of a serving maid isolates you from the world. The high wizard's guests either ignore the servants or treat us like dogs rather than human beings. The guards are cads who flee immediately after coupling; their own needs met, while I am left wanting. Where does that leave me? Am I doomed to find companionship only with the other servants? Chalmers is an old bore, Olin and Daggett prefer the company of men, and the rest are women.

"The moment you entered the room...the way you looked at me was different than the others. You saw me as a woman and made me feel attractive."

"You *are* attractive."

She gave him a sad smile. "You asked me questions and showed interest in my responses. I..." Her gaze dropped to the floor. "For the first time in years, I felt like neither a whore nor something less than human. You made me feel...desired."

Jerrell groaned. "Listen, I meant you no slight. This situation has me on edge. I do not trust Wrenthal, and being locked in here with you...I feared I was being manipulated."

"Not by me."

He wrapped his arms around her. She leaned into him with her head on his shoulder. Her hair smelled like flowers. "Well, as long as I am trapped in here, I don't see why we can't enjoy each other's company."

She leaned back and stared into his eyes. "There is something about you,

Jerrell, something different. Beneath your arrogance is a kindness. You are not quite as self-serving as you pretend to be." A smirk turned her lips up. "Your efforts to satisfy me during our love making proved as much."

He leveled a finger at her. "Don't you dare say that outside of this room. If the wrong people heard such a thing, they would use it against me. Kindness is often perceived as weakness. So long as I am alone and others believe I care only for myself, they cannot use threats of violence against others to coerce me."

She shook her head. "My, my. Now you are even worried about me?"

"I worry when innocents are hurt to advance the agendas of the greedy and the power-hungry."

She bit her lip and slid her hand into his breeches. "Turns out, I am not so innocent."

His pulse began to thump. He leaned in and kissed her. She responded eagerly, her lips soft, her firm body pressed against him. His fingers found the buttons on the front of her dress. He had undone three of them before a knock came from the door.

He turned toward it, panting for air. "Yes?"

"Master Landish," Chalmers called through the door. "The high wizard is ready to see you."

What poor timing. Jerrell turned toward Prianna. "I am sorry. I must go."

"I know." She nodded, stepped backward, and re-buttoned her dress. "I... am thankful we met."

"Perhaps I will visit again."

"If you do, please, ask for me."

He grabbed his coat from a hook, slid it on, and stuffed his cloak in his pack before scooping it off the bench and opening the door.

Chalmers stood in the corridor with a pair of guards. Four others waited near the stairwell.

"I trust you are rested, Master Landish."

"Yes. I feel quite well. Now, take me to Wrenthal. I am eager to be done with this whole thing."

Without a word, Chalmers headed toward the stairwell and began his descent. Jerrell trailed the man, and the four guards took up the rear. Having armed guards behind him made Jerrell's back itch, but it was not unexpected either.

Chalmers led him down a familiar corridor, and together, they stepped outside.

The sun's position above the western horizon informed Jerrell that he had spent most of the day locked in a room.

They headed across the square outside the castle. The obelisk loomed ahead, its long shadow darkening the wall that overlooked the river valley. Four more guards stood outside the door at the base of the tower. Chalmers knocked and stood back.

The door opened a few inches.

"Go on, Master Landish," Chalmers gestured toward the door. "They are waiting inside."

"They?" Jerrell asked.

When he received no response, he entered the room. The door closed behind him with an ominous click. Sunlight streaming from above refracted through the crystal column running down the building's core and illuminated the interior. Two people—Gerald Wrenthal, in silver and dark blue robes, and Mond, now wearing a dark blue captain's uniform—turned toward Jerrell.

Wrenthal gave an almost imperceptible nod. "Welcome back, Master Landish. From what Mond has told me, it appears you two had quite an adventure."

Jerrell played along, curious as to where the man was leading. "There were a few tense moments, but such is life for someone of my talents."

The wizard chuckled. "And what talents they are. I wonder which slight irritated Chancellor Mor the most—the theft of his precious artifact or his bath in horse manure."

"Mond told you about that?"

"Oh, yes. I know I asked you to embarrass Mor, but that went above and beyond anything I anticipated." Wrenthal's smile faded. "Now, I will accept the owl, if you please."

Jerrell approached Wrenthal. He slid his pack down his arm, dug past his cloak, and found the solid metal object. He withdrew it and held it out to

Wrenthal. The confident, aloof look in the wizard's eyes changed as he greedily eyed the owl.

"Give it to me," Wrenthal said as Jerrell placed it in his palm. He hastily spun away, climbed onto the dais in the center of the room, and placed it on the altar.

Jerrell eased backward Wrenthal's hands hovered above the owl and he muttered words of power. The tingle of magic rippled across Jerrell's skin. Glancing to the side, he found himself beside a white pedestal. Sitting on top was the blue crystal globe with the silver lightning bolt inside. Jerrell glanced back toward the altar, where the two men still focused on the owl. He reached inside his pack, found the globe he had purchased in Tiamalyn, and pulled it out. Moving swiftly, yet silently, he lifted the real globe and replaced it with the fake. The stolen object slid into his sack just before Mond glanced in his direction.

Wrenthal finished his chant. A hum filled the air, its vibrations rattling the chamber before it faded. The wizard broke into maniacal laughter that sent a chill up Jerrell's spine. "A resonance!" Wrenthal exclaimed. "It *is* real."

With his gaze fixed on the owl in his hand, the wizard stepped off the dais and approached the lone empty pillar. He carefully placed the object on the pedestal and turned toward Jerrell.

"You've done well, thief. Three others attempted to procure this item before you. None returned alive."

More information he chose not to share. "I told you I am the best," Jerrell said.

"No. You *were* the best."

"What do you mean?"

"I must apologize for breaking our agreement." Wrenthal thrust his arm toward Jerrell. Invisible ropes wrapped around his torso, pinned his arms to the side, and lifted him off the ground.

CHAPTER 25

THE PRICE OF AMBITION

Held captive by the wizard's spell—which suspended him three feet above the floor and rendered him immobile—Jerrell glared at Wrenthal while clenching his fists in anger. "We had an agreement, wizard."

"And I commend you on your success, but a price must be paid for ambition." The wizard pointed toward the door. "Mond, bring the others inside."

Scowling, Mond crossed the chamber and opened the door. "Come in. Tie him up."

Four guards entered, one holding a rope.

Mond drew his sword and held the tip against Jerrell's back as he was lowered to the floor. "Remove your dagger and give it to me."

Jerrell considered his options. During his flight from Tiamalyn, he had lost all but one throwing blade, which was currently hidden in his boot, leaving his dagger as his only other weapon. When weighed against a wizard and five armed guards, the scales tipped steeply against him—far too much to rely on luck.

Sighing in resignation, Jerrell drew his dagger and handed it to the man.

"Give me your pack."

He handed his pack over.

"Your coat as well."

The coat came off and was thrust at Mond.

"Take these. Put them in my office." Mond handed the coat, pack, and dagger to a guard before turning back to Jerrell. "Climb onto the dais. Press your back against the crystal column."

Jerrell did as Mond commanded. Two guards began to wind the rope around his torso, tying his arms to his sides and his back against the column. When they were finished, they backed to the edge of the room.

"What now?" Jerrell sneered at Wrenthal. "Are you going to make me sing for you? Perhaps you'd enjoy a ballad while you and Mond make sweet, sweet love."

"Ah. I expected you would remain defiant despite your hopeless situation. However, I will not be goaded by your irreverence. You see, tonight, you will witness a mere wizard rise to a wizard lord."

Jerrell narrowed his eyes. "Only a god may raise a wizard lord. Even then, a throne must be vacant, and it can only occur during a Darkening."

Wrenthal's brows rose. "You are more informed than I anticipated, particularly for an Ungifted. What you say is true, of course, and has been for millennia...until now." He turned slowly with his arms extended. "Never before has one man possessed all eight Avatars of the Gods. Owning them is but one requirement. The other requirements will soon come together and be brought to fruition once Devotion commences."

Jerrell did not like the sound of that. "Why am I tied to this column? I'll not attempt to stop you. As far as I am concerned, one wizard lord is as bad as the next, so whether it is you or Malvorian sitting on the throne makes no difference to me. You have your artifact. Let me go, and I'll be on my way."

The wizard shook his head. "That would do no good, for you are the guest of honor. I need you, Jerrell Landish. You see, a sacrifice is required. Your blood will allow me initiate the spell, and your life will enable me to seize the magic Malvorian wields and bestow it upon myself."

Jerrell swallowed hard and lifted his gaze at the towering chamber ceiling. Through the blue sapphire high above, came the dim light of waning daylight. Darkness would soon claim the sky, and when it did, Devotion would begin.

THE CHAMBER SLOWLY GREW DARKER. Night was falling over the city of Shear. As the shadows inside the obelisk thickened, Jerrell quietly strained at the ropes around him, but they were tied securely, and he could move little more than his wrists. Even if he were able to break free of his bonds, escaping the room was unlikely. Surrounded by Wrenthal, Mond, and three armed guards, Jerrell could hardly sneak away, not until it grew pitch black. So he waited and placed his faith in luck and his own cleverness to provide a path to safety.

Wrenthal circled Jerrell, eyeing him while holding a curved blade in his hand. The blade had a sharp point and a nasty appearance. Images of evisceration ran through Jerrell's head, pictures of the blade tearing across his abdomen and his entrails spilling onto the floor. *Stop it!* The quiet, along with the wizard's incessant circling had his nerves on edge.

"Mond," Wrenthal said. "Stand in a corner." He gestured toward the three guards. "Each of you, take a corner, so all four are occupied. Remain there throughout the ritual, regardless of what occurs, or your lives may be forfeit as well."

Each guard backed into a corner and was lost in the shadows. The wizard climbed onto the dais and stood at the altar glaring at Jerrell. Minutes passed. The tension rose as darkness consumed the last of the light. Lost in the thick murk, Jerrell strained at his bonds and tried to shimmy down the column. His progress was less than minimal; the rope barely moved.

The gem in the obelisk's apex suddenly bloomed to life, bathing the interior with azure light, which was brightest at the chamber's center. Surprisingly, Wrenthal had disrobed, and was now wearing only his smallclothes. The wizard lifted a metal tray from the altar and approached Jerrell.

"Hold out your palm," he demanded.

"And if I decline?"

"I will draw blood elsewhere."

Jerrell did not doubt it. He opened his left hand. Wrenthal gripped his wrist and raked the sharp blade across his palm. Searing pain filled him as a crimson line formed. The wizard tilted Jerrell's hand and blood dripped into the tray. He pressed a thumb against Jerrell's palm, eliciting a gasp at the pain. The blood flow increased, and the bottom of the tray was soon covered in blood.

Wrenthal turned and strode to the altar, setting the tray and knife on the stone surface. The man repeatedly dipped his finger in the blood and traced a complex symbol on his bare chest. When finished, he drew two more symbols on his face, one on each cheek. The wizard then began to chant in a strange language. The chant continued, increasing in vigor while Wrenthal raised his bloody palms toward the light above. The hair on Jerrell's arms stood on end as the tingle of magic ran across his skin.

Tendrils of white mist broke from the blue beam and flowed into the wizard, who shook with all the power raging through him. Streams of mist emerged from the objects on the pedestals—all but the blue globe Jerrell had swapped. *Would the globe have responded as well, if my bag had remained in the tower?* The streams swirled around the chamber and were joined by warm-tinted light coming from the chest of each the four men who stood in the corners of the chamber. The swirling light and mist spun faster and faster around Jerrell and the wizard, until they stood in the eye of a maelstrom of magic. All the while, the wizard kept his hands thrust toward the sky and chanted mystical, unknowable words.

The chamber floor began to quiver, and the column against Jerrell's back shook.

The wizard faltered in his chant and looked down with a worried expression on his face. "Something is wrong."

Wrenthal's eyes widened, as his body twitched and convulsed. An angry red light appeared in his eyes and smoke began to rise from them. The light grew brighter, and his body shook more violently. Tension rose, building toward something. Fearing what would happen, Jerrell squeezed his eyes closed and turned away, wishing he could run, but it was too late.

The wizard shrieked in agony. Similar screams came from the four guards in the chamber. The cries grew louder as the chamber and everything in it trembled. A concussion suddenly shook the room, reverberating in Jerrell's chest, followed by the chimes of shattered glass.

Everything fell silent.

Jerrell hesitantly blinked his eyes open and surveyed his surroundings.

Blue light from the sapphire above illuminated the room. The tendrils of magic were gone, the magic storm expended. Wrenthal twitched as he lay on the dais with his back against the altar. The guards were similarly incapacitated. Two were splayed out on the floor, while the other two slumped in opposite corners. Black empty sockets existed where their eyes had once been. None of the guards moved.

Peering closer at the wizard, Jerrell realized that the man's eyes and eyelids were also gone, yet his chest continued to rise and fall.

"What happened?" Jerrell asked.

"Help me," Wrenthal whimpered. "I...I cannot see."

"What about your magic?"

"My magic..." The wizard began to sob.

Jerrell brought the top of his boot to his right hand and slid his fingers inside to withdraw his last throwing blade. He used the blade to cut the rope. The ends of the rope came free, and Jerrell wiggled and strained against his bonds, causing the rope to unravel further. When his lower arms were freed, he raised his hand and cut again, breaking additional sections of rope lose until the last bit fell to the dais.

Jerrell squatted before the wizard. "Where is the gold I am owed?"

"My eyes..."

"The gold." Jerrell pressed the knife blade against the wizard's neck. "Tell me where it is, or I will end you."

"Search the desk in my study. There, you will find a pouch of ten gold pieces."

"Ten?" Jerrell lowered the knife and frowned. "I was promised twenty."

Wrenthal shook his head. "It is all I have." He blindly reached out, his fist finding Jerrell's tunic. The wizard pulled himself closer. "Please. You must help me."

The man had betrayed Jerrell. If the ritual had proceeded as planned, Jerrell would be dead. The thought angered him and left little room for pity.

"Your eyes are burned out. I doubt even wizard magic can fix that."

Wrenthal dropped his hand, and his body jerked as he sobbed, but no tears fell. *Can one cry without eyes?* Jerrell certainly did not wish to find that out for himself.

"I am ruined," Wrenthal said. "Another wizard will claim my position. My children and I will be cast out of the castle with no place to live."

"You can live on your family's estate."

Wrenthal shook his head. "I sold the estate to gain enough gold to procure the eight avatars. Now, even that is gone."

Jerrell sighed. "Listen to me well. You will not send soldiers or assassins after me. If you do, I will return to finish you...and your children. Is that clear?"

The man nodded numbly.

Rising to a stance, Jerrell said, "Remain where you are. I will send someone to help you while I retrieve my gold."

He turned, stepped off the dais, and crossed the room, tiptoeing through broken shards of blue crystal. The pedestal near the door stood empty, the false globe he had placed there destroyed. *Thank the gods I swapped that object, or I would not have left this chamber alive.* The realization made him wonder if his survival had been a result of luck or his own cleverness.

The blue flame snuffed out as Devotion ended, and the chamber fell dark. In the murk, Jerrell found the door and stepped out into the moonlight.

He crossed the empty square, pausing to slide the throwing blade back into his boot. As he neared the castle, he spied guards at the front door and ran toward it, stopping at the foot of the front stairs. "Help!" he cried.

"What is this?" a guard said.

"The wizard is injured."

"Injured? How?"

"He was performing magic, and something went wrong."

"What of Captain Mond?"

Jerrell pointed toward the tall shadowy spire across the square. "He is in the obelisk chamber with the high wizard, along with three other guards. All are in bad shape."

The two guards looked at each other and ran toward the obelisk. Jerrell casually climbed the stairs and stepped inside the castle.

The halls were empty, the corridors silent. For such an enormous building, it felt strikingly abandoned.

Jerrell visited Mond's office first to reclaim his coat, dagger, and pack. When he reached the wizard's study on the third level, he activated the enchanted lantern on the wall. He sat at the desk and began searching through the drawers. In the bottom right drawer, he located the pouch Wrenthal had mentioned.

A woman's voice came from the doorway. "What are you doing in my father's study?"

CHAPTER 26

TRUTH AND LIES

J errell looked up to find an attractive woman in a ruffled dress standing in the doorway to High Wizard Wrenthal's study. He recognized her immediately. "Hello, Terissa."

"You are no wizard, are you? Is your name even Parion?"

"No. It is Jerrell."

She frowned. "Why are you in my father's study?"

He stood and set the pouch on the desktop. "I am claiming the gold your father owes me."

"Owed for what? Where is my father?"

How do I explain what happened? She is a wizardess and might use her magic against me. He chose the sympathetic route.

Rounding the desk, he approached the wizardess. "What do you know of your father's plans?"

Her brow furrowed. "His plans?"

"Did you know he sought to use blood magic to help him acquire Lord Malvorian's powers?"

Her lips tightened. "Sorcery is illegal, an offense in the eyes of Farrow."

"Nonetheless, I assure you, he used such magic tonight." Jerrell held his left palm open, the cut across it raw and angry. His entire hand was covered in dried blood. "He tied me up, sliced my hand, and used my blood to paint symbols on his chest and face."

Terissa gasped, covered her mouth in horror, and shook her head. "He would never…"

"Power, Terissa. Your father hungers for it. You cannot deny it."

She remained silent, her hand dropping to her side as she lowered her gaze.

He continued, "His desire to become wizard lord drove him toward this end, but the ritual he performed did not go as planned. Rather than the magic consuming my body, as he intended, it claimed his eyes, along with the lives of Mond and three guards."

Again, she gasped and lifted her wide-eyed gaze to Jerrell. "Without his eyes…"

"His magic is useless."

She nodded as a tear tracked down her cheek. "What will we do?"

Jerrell's stern tone softened. "Listen. Your father retains his position as high wizard based on reputation. A decade has passed since anyone has challenged him, and if others are unaware of his malady, years may pass before another tries to claim his seat. I am prepared to help maintain that reputation so you and your family may continue to live here, provided you govern your district with justice and compassion. Can you do that?"

Terissa gazed into space while considering the idea. "I will send word to my younger sister. She may wish to return from the University early to help Ferrol and I run the household and to deal with the public in father's stead."

He gave a sad smile. "As I had hoped." Turning from her, he returned to the desk, reclaimed the pouch, and dropped it into his pack before slinging the pack over his shoulder. "All I ask is that you allow me to leave and live my life without worrying about your family coming after me."

"Why would we come after you?"

"I survived the ritual, while your father paid a steep price."

She shook her head. "It was not your doing. I know my father. He uses information and influence to manipulate others toward his own ends."

"That he does." Jerrell stopped before Terissa and cupped her cheek.

"Rule well and appreciate what you have. One slip, and all could be lost. It is rare for the wizard class to remember that."

He attempted to slip past her, but she gripped his wrist. "Wait."

"What is it?"

"Allow me to heal your hand."

He frowned. "I think I have had my fill of magic."

"Please. It is the least I can do."

Pushing beyond his reservations, Jerrell held his bloody palm out. She cupped his hand in hers and closed her eyes. The tingle of magic ran across his flesh. Before his eyes, the skin on his palm knitted back together, the cut sealing completely in seconds. The tingle faded and his stomach growled, suddenly eager for food.

She opened her eyes. "There. I suspect you are now hungry."

"I am."

Terissa gave him a knowing smile. "Your body provides much of the energy required for healing. The hunger you feel is a normal response."

"I rarely appreciate magic, but in this case, I thank you." He stepped into the corridor, intent on leaving.

From behind, he heard her say, "My handmaid told me of your time together today."

Jerrell stopped and turned back. "Prianna?"

"Yes. She said that...you made her feel special, made her feel as if she mattered."

"We all matter, Terissa, even if the wizard class sees us Ungifted as little more than beasts of burden."

"Perhaps...Perhaps I can help change that."

"If so, you would be the first wizard I actually respect."

He turned and walked away, eager to find a taproom with food and plenty of ale.

THE NEXT MORNING, Jerrell stopped by the kitchen of the Elder Inn, which was located just blocks west of Shear Castle. He purchased two sausages and set off with his pack over his shoulder. At the first intersection, he happened across a bakery, stepped inside, and purchased a loaf of bread before continuing.

The narrow street opened to the broad, paved road leading to the castle and lower district in one direction, and out of the city in the other. He turned and walked with the sun at his back, heading toward the outskirts of Shear. The shops and estates soon gave way to rolling hills covered in trees. Fields appeared amid the woods, some plowed, others occupied by cattle. After five miles of walking, he spied buildings through the trees and decided to pay a visit.

He followed a narrow gravel drive with grass growing between two wagon ruts. The trees parted to reveal a farmhouse, a shed, and a red barn, all built of wood. Split rail fencing ran from the barn, along the drive, and turned to surround open fields. Out in one field, a half a mile away, a farmer rode on a strange contraption pulled by a pair of horses. Long yellow grass covered the field ahead of him, but the contraption left piles of cut grass and sheared shoots in its wake.

Jerrell walked into the barn and paused to allow his eyes to adjust to the shadowy interior. Four stalls ran along one side of the barn, two empty and two with the stall doors closed. He walked up to one of the closed doors and peered over it. A piebald mare stood inside, eating hay. A saddle dangled from a hook on the wall beside the stall. A bridle and reins hung beside it.

"I've had enough of walking," he said to the horse. "How would you like to go for a ride?"

The horse continued eating.

He opened the stall and approached the horse. "What is your name?" No response. "I think I'll call you Freckles."

Holding the reins in his hand, Jerrell gripped the saddle horn, climbed up, and nudged Freckles into motion. The horse walked out of the barn, into the sunlight.

The farmhouse door opened, and a woman stepped out. Her brown hair was tied back in a tail, her hazel eyes bright and only a few years his elder. She wore a brown dress with a cream-colored bodice and was surprisingly attractive. Jerrell wondered how she ended up at a country farm.

"Who are you?" the woman demanded. "Why are you on my horse?"

He pulled the horse to a stop, flashed his best smile, and pressed a hand to his chest. "I am Jerrell Landish, the best thief in the Eight Wizardoms."

She pressed her hands against her hips. "If you are so talented, how come I just caught you stealing Betsy?"

Jerrell laughed. "Well said."

The farmhouse burst open, and a boy with tousled brown hair rushed to the woman's side. He wrapped his arms around her waist and stared up at Jerrell with big brown eyes. "Who is this, Mommy?"

"He is just passing through, Jack." She slid an arm around his shoulders and her gaze went to the field. "My husband works hard. We don't have much, but he keeps me warm at night, and we are mostly happy." She looked Jerrell in the eyes. "Please don't steal our horse. We can't afford to replace her."

Innocence reflected in the boy's eyes while his mother's gaze issued a plea for compassion. The boy reminded Jerrell of himself, and he recalled holding onto his mother's waist while the two of them stood in a cold street, begging for food. Days later, she found them a new home, a house occupied by seven other women. Young Jerrell understood that the house provided shelter and steady meals, and little else mattered at that point. By the time he realized what his mother did to earn such niceties, and why numerous men visited her every day, she was dying.

Sighing, Jerrell dug into his pack and removed two gold coins, eyeing them for a moment before looking back at the woman. "I'll buy her from you, so long as you tell others that I stole her."

"What?"

"Come up with an elaborate, shocking story. Make it something that would cause people to laugh and shake their heads in wonder."

The woman patted the boy and slid away from him as she walked up to the horse. "You want me to tell others that Jerrell—What was your last name?"

"Landish."

"—that Jerrell Landish robbed us and did so in a shocking, brazen manner?"

He handed her the two gold coins. "Yes, if you please."

She gaped at the gold in her palm. "This is too much."

"Perhaps too much for an old horse, but well worth the investment if you help to grow my fame. You see, I am out to make a legend of myself. A new, outrageous tale of my exploits told in the taprooms of Shear would be appreciated."

The woman smiled. "Next time my husband visits the city, he will have a story to tell. We will think up something good. You have my word."

"Wonderful." He turned his attention on the boy. "Take care of your mother. She is a woman to be cherished, and you never know when you might lose her."

The boy nodded with round eyes. "Yessir."

Jerrell nodded to the woman. "Be well. Thank your husband. Maybe we will meet again someday."

He rode down the drive and turned onto the road leading to Marquithe.

The action, intrigue, and hijinks continue in
Trickster for Hire
Book 2 of
The Outrageous Exploits of Jerrell Landish

TRICKSTER FOR HIRE

CHAPTER 1

NOT THE HERO YOU IMAGINE

Beneath the light of the full moon, Jerrell Landish strolled down the quiet streets of Marquithe, the capital city of Farrowen. His breath swirled before him with each exhale, and he held his wool cloak tight to fend off the chill. According to long-time citizens of the city, the end of winter weather was imminent. He hoped they were correct. While a bitter wind and light snow flurries were the worst weather the city had seen during the season, Jerrell was unused to such harsh conditions. Having lived his entire life on the coast, either Fastella or, more recently, Yor's Point, his only prior experience with inclement winter weather was during a quest in the mountains of northern Ghealdor.

He followed a narrow, shadow-filled street while his mind wandered. A full season had passed since his arrival in the city, and Jerrell had yet to find a purpose. His wealth had slowly dwindled, occasionally boosted by his use of weighted dice, but he took care to use them infrequently lest others discover his secret. He kept his eyes open and ears peeled, hoping to unearth some snippet that would give him guidance to a better future. Marquithe was known as a city of opportunity, and he was determined to find a means to capitalize on it.

The street opened to a moonlit square, hundreds of feet across. A foun-

185

tain sat in the heart of the square, and six streets branched from it, each entrance illuminated by the pale blue light of an enchanted lantern. Jerrell crossed the square and stopped to stare up at the Marquithe Bureau of Trading.

Five stories tall and spanning one entire side of the square, the Bureau was an impressive structure. More importantly, the premier merchants and officials in the southern wizardoms operated within her halls. Jerrell longed to take part in such prestige, but his inquiries into joining the institution had thus far only led to disappointment.

Sighing in resignation, he crossed the square and entered another quiet street.

A man and a woman passed the enchanted lantern at the next intersection as they headed toward him. The man held the woman close, and they both eyed Jerrell warily as they walked past. *I have no intention of robbing you. This thief has his sights set on more significant prizes.* Their footsteps soon faded behind him.

A woman's scream echoed in the night, the source coming from somewhere ahead of him. Jerrell burst into a run and turned at the next intersection, stopping when he spied a cluster of people a block away.

A pair of armored guards held swords ready, their backs facing a figure in a hooded cloak. Two still forms lay at their feet while four others on foot surrounded them.

Slipping to the shadowed side of the street, Jerrell crept forward.

A gravely male voice said, "Lower your weapons. Leave her to us, and you will live."

Twenty strides from the group, Jerrell hid in a dark doorway and drew his dagger.

One guard looked at the other, who said, "Begone, or you will end up like these two."

The first voice said, "Kill them."

Twangs rang out, crossbow bolts flying. One bolt struck a guard in the stomach, the other in the shoulder. The four shadowy figures rushed in, two with swords, one with a cudgel, the last with a dagger. Clangs resounded as swords flashed and collided. The wounded guards fought hard and managed to kill one of the enemy swordsmen before they were mowed down.

Another scream came from the cloaked figure as she ran down the street, straight toward Jerrell. The three remaining ruffians raced after her. Jerrell coiled himself as she raced past him. He then lunged out and swung his leg, hooking the ankle of her first pursuer. The man cried out and fell forward on his face. His sword slipped from his grip and clattered down the street before settling in place. The next man attempted to leap over his fallen companion, but caught his foot on an upraised leg, which sent him spinning and tumbling to the street. The third man, the one with the dagger, slowed and eyed Jerrell.

"Who are you?"

"Someone who disproves of crude men molesting innocent women."

The fallen men climbed to their feet, one gripping a cudgel while the other retrieved his sword.

The gravelly-voiced leader said, "Kill him. I'll go after her." He circled around his two companions as they focused on Jerrell.

Both men stood taller than Jerrell. The one holding the sword was lean with long limbs, the other man burly with a thick black beard. Holding their weapons before them, they blocked the street, which forced Jerrell to choose between fighting and fleeing in the other direction.

The man with the cudgel came at Jerrell with a bone crushing swing. Jerrell ducked, and the cudgel hit the brick wall beside him with a crack, sending shards raining down. He thrust with his dagger as he dove, raking the blade across the big man's exposed thigh. Landing on his hands, Jerrell rolled as the other enemy chopped down with his sword, the blade barely missing him.

Back on his feet, Jerrell retreated a few steps, drew a throwing blade, and loosed. The knife struck the swordsman in the chest with a thud. Stumbling backward, the man gasped and grabbed the hilt jutting from his ribs. His sword fell from his grip, and he collapsed.

The other man growled and limped toward Jerrell with the cudgel held tightly in his meaty fist. The man wound back and swung at Jerrell's midriff. Spinning away, Jerrell dropped to one knee, and drew another throwing blade. Keeping his rotational momentum, his arm swept out, rising as it came around. He released the blade. It sliced through the big man's beard before lodging in his throat. The cudgel dropped to the street. The man staggered and fell to his knees. A croaking sound emerged from his mouth, along with a spray of crimson spittle. He toppled over and fell still.

Jerrell rose and raced down the dark street, pausing at the first intersection to listen. A scream came from his right, and he sprinted into the darkness. Halfway down the street, he reached an alley with two shadowy figures at the far end...a dead end. In the moonlight, they appeared as little more than silhouettes.

"No, please," a woman pleaded. "I will pay you."

The man with the gravelly voice said, "I have already been paid. Now, it is time to earn that gold."

Jerrell sprinted down the alley. "Stop!"

The man spun toward him with a dagger in his hand. "You again?"

Slowing, Jerrell said, "Sorry your companions could not make it. They seem to have developed a fatal case of too many holes in their bodies."

The man's eyes narrowed, and he advanced toward Jerrell with his dagger ready. Jerrell reached behind his neck, drew the hidden blade from his coat, and threw. The enemy twisted, and the blade missed, sailing past him to hit the wall at the end of the alley. With a grin, the man came at Jerrell. Moonlight glinted off the blade in his hand, revealing a blackened edge. *Poison.* Alarmed, Jerrell realized even a graze could kill him.

The attacker thrust, just missing Jerrell's stomach when he twisted to the side. Jerrell slashed with his dagger, which the man dodged and then dodged again to avoid Jerrell's backslash. The enemy spun around and kicked, striking Jerrell in the shoulder and sending him stumbling backward.

The knife-wielder followed with a lunge and a swipe, forcing Jerrell to retreat until his back was pinned against the wall. Another slash. With nowhere to go, Jerrell grabbed the attacker's forearm, stopping the man's knife just short of his own throat. The man pressed hard, moving the poisoned blade closer with his superior size, which also brought his body a few inches closer to Jerrell. Desperate to keep the poisoned blade from piercing him, Jerrell thrust with his dagger, and the enemy jumped back, but Jerrell had him by the arm – his real target.

Jerrell's dagger plunged into the assassin's bicep, causing the man to cry out in pain. Yanking the man's arm while dropping to the ground, Jerrell pulled the man off balance, causing his head to collide with the brick wall. Jerrell twisted the man's wrist as he fell, which forced him to drop the poisoned dagger.

The assassin fell to his knees and wobbled while Jerrell snatched the poisoned dagger and stepped back.

"Who sent you?"

The assassin looked up at him. A streak of dark blood ran down his face. "I'll never betray my oath."

Jerrell grunted. "As I thought."

He thrust the poisoned blade at the man's face, piercing his eye, and drove it in to the hilt. The assassin toppled to the ground.

"Filthy murderer." Turning, Jerrell found the woman huddled in the corner with her cloak wrapped tight around her. In the shadows, she would be easy to miss. He approached her. "Are you all right?"

"Please, don't kill me," she whimpered.

His brow furrowed. "In case you missed what just happened, I saved your life. Why would I do that only to kill you?"

"If you let me go, I will pay you."

He sighed. "I will let you go, but before I do, you should be aware that you will not be safe."

"Why not?"

"Those were not street ruffians. They were paid to kill you."

"Assassins?"

"Yes." He pointed toward the man lying a few strides away. "The dagger he used had a blackened edge. There is only one reason to poison a blade. Who wants you dead?"

She stepped into the moonlight, allowing him to see her for the first time. Her red dress was of a fine cut, as was her coat. Brown curls sat piled on her head and held in place by a silver tiara. A silver necklace with a ruby pendant rested on her modest chest. In the shadows, it was difficult to discern her age or much else about her appearance.

Blinking as she stared at the dead man, she said, "I have no idea."

By the way she was dressed, the woman had access to wealth, which meant opportunity for Jerrell. "Until we figure out who is trying to kill you, your life is at risk."

"We?"

"I happen to specialize in this type of situation. If you hire me, I will help you remain alive and discover who was behind this vile act."

"How do I know I can trust you?"

"Your guards are dead. These assassins would have succeeded in their mission if not for me. I might be the only person you *can* trust."

She nodded. "Keep me alive, find out who is behind this, and I will reward you handsomely."

"Deal. What is your name?"

"Sorenna Souton."

His brow furrowed in recognition. "Souton? Like the silver mining town?"

"Yes. My family owned that land and founded the city centuries ago."

"Well met, Sorenna." He extended his hand. "My name is Jerrell Landish."

She accepted his hand and shook it. "Thank you for your heroism, Jerrell."

He grinned. "I may not be the hero you imagine, but I am certainly the hero you need. Let's start by getting you home. Where do you live?"

"My city manor is in Wizard Estates."

His brow arched. "Your city manor?"

"Yes. I have an estate in the country as well, a half-day's ride north of Marquithe."

Two estates. Jerrell took her arm, restraining a grin. "Lead the way but be ready to obey my commands should any trouble arise."

"Very well."

"But first, we need to return to the scene of the attack. I have some weapons to retrieve."

CHAPTER 2
MISTRESS SOUTON

An armed guard leaned against the wall beside the iron gates to Sorenna's estate. Inside the grounds stood an impressive mansion, three stories tall with peaked rooftops.

"Deshaun, open the gate," Sorenna commanded.

The guard spun around. Upon sighting the woman, he hurriedly unlocked and opened the gates.

As they squeaked open, the tall, bearded man said, "Mistress Souton, I expected you some time ago. Where are Davis and Wyatt?"

"We were attacked. Davis and Wyatt gave their lives protecting me."

The man eyed Jerrell while his hand gripped the sword hilt on his hip. At over six feet, he stood a head taller than Jerrell and likely outweighed him by a hundred pounds. "Who is this?"

"This man came to my rescue, dispatching the ruffians and saving my life."

Jerrell gave the man a nod. "My name is Jerrell."

"Hmm," the guard grunted. "How did you succeed when Davis and Wyatt failed?"

The man suspects the attack was a ruse and that I was part of it. Deciding to downplay his role, Jerrell replied, "Mistress Souton's guards did most of the damage. I simply finished the attackers off. Since they did not know I was there, I had surprise on my side."

The response earned Jerrell another grunt.

Sorenna led Jerrell through the gate. "Lock up and follow us to the manor. Derwin won't return until mid-day tomorrow."

"Yes, ma'am," Deshaun said, his tone still doubtful.

Sorenna led Jerrell down a drive bordered by sculpted hedges. The drive opened to a courtyard surrounded on three sides by the manor and connected stables. Rather than head to the main entrance, she made for the side door.

Once inside, she took an enchanted lantern from a table and activated it. Pale blue light bloomed, revealing a small room with coat hooks along one wall, most of which were occupied. She removed her cloak and claimed an open hook before turning to Jerrell.

In the light of the lamp, he was able to get his first good look at the woman.

Her face was plain, despite her makeup. She had a thin, frail build. Her age approached forty, and there was nothing about her he would consider attractive. Yet, she was a woman of means, and wealth held an allure of an entirely different sort.

Still holding the lamp, she turned toward the waiting corridor. "Come along. I could use some tea to calm my nerves after tonight's events."

He followed her while Deshaun stepped inside and caught up with them. The door at the end of the hallway led to a kitchen, where they were met by a middle-aged woman wearing a white apron over a black dress.

"Welcome back, mistress," the woman said.

"Elsa," Sorenna said. "I am glad you are awake. Could you please heat some tea for me?"

"Of course."

"When it is ready, bring it and two cups to the south sitting room." Sorenna crossed the kitchen, pushed the door open, and led Jerrell and Deshaun through a dark dining room. Beyond it waited a sitting room with a high ceiling. A stone fireplace stood along one wall while narrow curtained windows covered another. Spots of orange glowed amid the dark coals in the fireplace.

"Deshaun," Sorenna said. "Please add some wood to the fire."

The tall man stepped into a room adjacent to the fireplace and emerged with an armful of split logs. He knelt beside the hearth and fed the logs to the fire before leaning close and blowing on the hot coals. Flames came to life, licking the logs until they, too, burst into flames.

The woman claimed a padded chair covered in red velvet. "Please sit, Jerrell."

He sat on the sofa across from her, a low table between them.

With his arms empty, Deshaun stood. "Would you like me to stay here with you, mistress?"

"That is not necessary. Go and get some rest. I will require your assistance tomorrow. Two new guards must be hired before I am to return to the Bureau."

The mention of the Bureau drew Jerrell's attention, creating more questions, which he stifled...for now.

The man flashed one last distrustful glare at Jerrell. "If you need me, I will be in my room."

When the man's footsteps faded, Jerrell turned toward Sorenna. "Do you trust your staff?"

She blinked. "Deshaun and Elsa have both served me for years, as has our driver, Heath, and our porter, Jamison. I doubt any would be mixed up in something as nefarious as what occurred tonight."

"Our? You mentioned someone name Derp."

"Derwin. He is my husband."

"Where is he?"

"Staying at our country estate."

"He goes there often?"

"Yes. Once or twice a week. He usually stays overnight, sometimes for as long as three days."

"Why?"

"He meets with farmers and vineyard owners, negotiating prices for orders I trade at the Bureau."

Jerrell's brows arched. He had hoped the conversation might head this direction. "The Marquithe Bureau of Trading?"

"Yes. My family has held an office in the Bureau for many generations."

The information turned in Jerrell's head, leading to another question. "You kept the last name, Souton, after you wed?"

The woman huffed. "Sometimes men take their wife's surname."

His brows rose. "Your husband did this?"

She sat upright, her chest out and chin raised. "The Souton name has a long history in Farrowen. Our family is among the few Ungifted who own estates in this area and command respect among the wizard class."

He turned the information over and composed another question. "Do you have children?"

Her eyes softened, and her gaze dropped to her lap. "I am...unable."

Sensing her discomfort with the subject, Jerrell shifted gears. "If you operate an office at the Bureau, you must have enemies. Does anyone come to mind who might wish to see you dead?"

Her brow furrowed as she considered the question. "There have been a few recent transactions that directly affected others. In fact, one caused Palkan Forca to lose quite a bit of gold."

"Forca?" Jerrell had heard the name whispered in the streets and taverns of Marquithe. "Isn't he a wizard of some importance?"

"He is a powerful and wealthy wizard who is vying to take control of the local wizards' guild. The transaction I speak of set his plans back and left him with tons of iron ore and no place to sell it."

"Iron ore from Eleighton?"

She smiled. "Very good. You are well informed for a street rat."

Jerrell bristled. "I am more than I appear, I assure you."

"Well, for my own health, I hope that is true. Anyway, after the trade, Forca stormed into my office, screaming and threatening to do unthinkable things to me. He even used his magic to set a chair on fire before storming out."

"When did this occur?"

"Just last week."

Jerrell stood. "Take care when you interview applicants to replace your guards. Anyone might be in league with whoever is trying to kill you. More importantly, avoid traveling at night or anywhere other than busy public areas until you hear from me."

She rose to her feet. "What are you going to do?"

"First, I am going to get some sleep. Tomorrow, I will investigate Forca."

"How will I get in touch with you?"

"Don't worry. I will find you when we next need to talk. Until then, watch your back and take care not to eat or drink anything prepared by anyone you don't trust with your life."

Her eyes widened. "You fear poison?"

"Poison tainted the blade of tonight's assassin. There is no reason to believe it might not be used in other ways." He gave her a level stare. "Don't tell anyone about me. If the conspirator knows I am investigating, it will be much more difficult to catch him or her."

He headed out the door, his thoughts churning as he considered the situation and facts revealed thus far.

IN THE DEAD OF NIGHT, far across the city, Jerrell entered an empty, dead-end alley. A pile of refuse clogged much of the alley entrance. A rumble of snoring came from the inside of a large crate. *I see Urlan is back.* The homeless drunk seemed to spend half his nights in that crate; Jerrell wondered about the man's location on the other nights.

Continuing down the alley, Jace passed beneath clotheslines strung between the two buildings, the lines sagging with damp clothing. Two running steps and a leap allowed him to catch the end of a broken line hanging from his own building. Hand over hand, he climbed the line. Once he was high enough, he braced his feet against the wall and scrambled over to a second story window, hooking his feet on a ledge to keep from swinging outward. With one hand on the rope, he drew his knife and wedged it between the upper and lower pane, flipping the latch open before sheathing the blade again. He lifted the window and stuck a leg inside before releasing the rope.

His living room appeared as he had left it – clean, organized, and empty save for furniture. He slid in, careful to step to the side rather than on the open bear trap beneath the window. It was one of numerous surprises he had left for unwary intruders – one in his bedroom, one in the spare bedroom, and one connected to the apartment entrance. Should anyone attempt to enter through the front door, they would be met with a pair of crossbow bolts, and a bell warning Jerrell of their presence.

At the end of the corridor, he reached his room and activated the enchanted lantern resting on his nightstand. In its pale blue light, he sat on the bed, pulled his boots off, and flexed his toes. It had been a long day, but while it had begun much like any other since his arrival in Marquithe, it had led to a new opportunity.

Sorenna Souton possessed the wealth and connections Jerrell needed, but she could not help him if she were dead. *I need to figure out who is behind this.* Anyone desperate enough to pay for one assassination attempt would pay for another, but not until he or she realized the first was a failure. *I have at least a day or two before she is at risk. By then, I hope to have this conundrum resolved.* He threw his coat toward the door, and it caught on a hook. He lay down, doused the light, and closed his eyes.

CHAPTER 3
THE AVATAR OF FARROW

It was mid-morning when Jerrell slid out of his second story window and shimmied down to the alley. He walked past the pile of refuse where Urlan's snoring continued, stepped into the street, and paused as a wagon rolled past. Numerous people were visible in both directions. One couple turned and entered the first floor of his apartment building. A sign depicting a blue chicken graced the façade above the building entrance.

Following them, Jerrell entered the Blue Hen and found the dimly lit dining room quiet with three occupied tables and two patrons sitting at the bar. It was usually quiet during the day but would become far busier when evening approached. He found an open table near the door, sat in the chair facing the entrance, and waited for a server to appear.

A heavyset woman came through the kitchen door, her mouth turning down in a frown when she spied Jerrell. She delivered two steaming plates to the men at the bar and then headed over to his table.

Fists on her broad hips, she glared at him. "What did you do to my daughter?"

"Me? I did nothing to her, Frella. She is too young for me..."

"Not that. I mean, what misleading allusions have you planted in her head?"

"Well, I told her she has some potential as a thief..."

The woman slapped her hand on the table. "She is thirteen and impressionable. Worse, the girl gets all doe-eyed whenever you walk in the room. She dotes on you and the things you say are bound to impact her. I'll not have my sweet girl turned into a scoundrel like you."

"Listen, Frella..."

She shook her finger in his face. "No. You listen to me. You will fix this, or you will find a new place to live."

"But I have paid in advance, extending my lease to mid-summer."

"I don't care. I'd rather forego the gold than lose my daughter to a life that is bound to see her dead well before her time."

He sighed. "Fine. I will talk to her."

She nodded. "Good. Now, I suppose you are here to eat?"

"Yes. Make it quick, if you please. I have much to do today."

She snorted. "Besides lying, cheating, and attempting to bed women?"

With his hand pressed against his chest, Jerrell did his best to feign his affront. "You injure me. Is that who you think I am?"

"I think your tongue is a bit too slick, and you view yourself as more clever than you actually are."

"My tongue is merely friendly. As for my cleverness, I'll admit nothing... until I meet someone more clever than myself." He grinned broadly.

The woman rolled her eyes. "My point exactly."

"Regardless, I have found employment even you would deem worthy."

"How so?"

"I saved a woman's life last night, and she hired me to seek out who was behind the attempt."

She planted a hand on her hip and tilted her head. "Are you making this up?"

He shook his head. "While I might twist the facts now and then, the stories I tell of my exploits are nothing but truth, regardless of their outlandish nature."

"Very well. I will get your food. Just be sure to speak with my daughter next time you see her. If she ends up in a dungeon cell, I'll have your head."

The woman walked away, and Jerrell sat back with a sigh. "Why does nobody understand me?"

~

IN THE WARMTH of the afternoon sun, Jerrell followed a curved street past walled estates. Each gate barred the way to a long drive leading to a mansion. The manors varied in size and design, but any one of them was large enough to house numerous families. He came to a circular metal panel mounted beside a gate and paused to examine it. Embossed in the plate was the Forca insignia – the letter F pierced by a bolt of lightning.

"This is it," he said to himself.

Moving to the gate, he peered through. A long drive looped around a three-story manor with a five-story tower rising above one end. In many ways, the building reminded him of Kylar Mor's mansion in Tiamalyn. *Let's try not to anger this wizard. You are only here for information*, he reminded himself. He reached through the gate, lifted the bar, and let himself in.

A curved path past dormant shrubs brought him to a short rise of stairs bracketed by a pair of thick fluted columns. After climbing them to the front porch, he stood before the towering, arched doors, lifted the knocker, and gave it three solid thumps.

Moments passed before a man in a blue coat opened the door. He stood prim and tall, his dark hair parted down the middle, his mustache waxed and curled at the ends. "May I help you?"

Jerrell said, "I am here to speak with Palkan Forca."

"Your name?"

"Jerrell Landish."

"Do you have an appointment?"

"No, but I do have something he might find of interest." Jerrell lowered his pack and dug out a blue crystal globe with a silver lightning bolt inside it.

The servant's brow furrowed. "While it is certainly an interesting object, why do you believe Wizard Forca would care about such a bauble?"

"I believe this is called the Avatar of Farrow. Go and tell your master I have it in my possession. If he is not interested, I will be on my way."

The servant frowned, considering the request. "Wait here."

The door closed, and a click resounded as the bolt was thrown, locking him out.

"He doesn't trust me," Jerrell muttered to himself.

In truth, he couldn't blame the man. Although he had no intention of stealing anything today, he had done so many times in the past, and he looked more like a street thug than an entitled wizard or wealthy merchant, likely the typical guests to visit the Forca estate.

The sound of approaching male voices drew Jerrell's attention toward the drive. A pair of men appeared from behind the manor, strolling down the drive toward the gate. Both stood taller than Jerrell, and both were armed. When they reached the gate, they leaned against the wall beside it and continued chatting, neither looking in Jerrell's direction. *The guards must have been on break. Neither is very observant.*

He watched them for a moment before hearing a noise at the front door. The door swung wide to reveal the same servant, but this time, the man stood to one side. "Come in, Mister Landish. Wizard Forca has agreed to entertain your request to meet with him."

"As I had anticipated." Jerrell was sure to taint his tone with chagrin.

He stepped into a spacious receiving hall, the floor tiled in a dark green marble with gold and black striations. A circular fountain occupied the heart of the room, centered between two curved staircases rising to an open second-story loft, reminding Jerrell of Yor's Castle. Yet, this was a family estate while the other was the seat of a high wizard. *How wealthy is this man?*

"If you would, please follow me."

The servant climbed the stairs with Jerrell at his heels. A strip of midnight blue carpet ran up wooden stairs stained dark to match the lacquered railing. From the second-story loft, he peered over a ballroom, which again reminded him of Yor's Castle.

Continuing their ascent to the fourth floor, they emerged into a dimly lit corridor, quiet save for their footsteps. Extravagant tapestries and scenic paintings, all lush with color, covered the walls. They passed closed doors made of heavy wood, the house symbol of a lightning bolt piercing the letter F etched in gold on each.

Curious, Jerrell asked, "Where are we going?"

The servant opened the door at the end of the hallway and stood back. "Go on up. Wizard Forca is waiting for you in his study."

Jerrell moved past the man and paused for a beat. A circular stairwell went up to the right and down to the left. Dim light came from both directions illuminating the way.

When entering an unknown area where magic was undoubtedly involved, Jerrell preferred to walk behind someone familiar with the location. With his senses on high alert, he began an ascent up the curved incline. One story up, he reached a window, which provided light for the stairs. Another eighteen steps brought him to a closed door at the top. Reaching tentatively toward it and sensing no magic, Jerrell knocked.

A male voice called, "Come in."

Jerrell opened the door and stepped into a circular room with a raised, conical ceiling. The chamber was forty feet in diameter and illuminated by daylight emitting from six arched windows. The floor was tiled in black marble with an eight-pointed star full of strange symbols in the center. Books filled shelves between the windows. A massive table stood at the heart of the star, a pen, a capped inkwell, and a scattering of papers resting on its smooth ebony surface. A man in dark blue robes stood with his palms pressed against the table, his body leaning over it as he examined a complex symbol that reminded Jerrell of a flower gone mad, its twisting lines difficult to follow.

The man stood upright, his height easily exceeding six feet. Thinning brown hair capped a face Jerrell would consider neither handsome nor ugly. Intense green eyes stared back at him over a large nose while the wizard scrutinized him. Before Forca spoke a single word, Jerrell could affirm he was an intelligent, yet arrogant man.

"My steward tells me you possess an object you believe to be the Avatar of Farrow."

Jerrell walked into the room and reminded himself of his goal. With care, he explained, "A unique object has come into my possession." *Thank the gods*

I swapped this for a replica before High Wizard Wrenthal began his ritual. The serendipity of the simple act was not lost on Jerrell. It had saved his life while robbing the power-hungry wizard of his eyesight. "When seeking the ideal place to sell such an item, I spoke with an acquaintance who works at the Bureau of Trading. When I explained my belief that the object might have certain magical properties that would best suit a Farrowen wizard, he recommended you."

A smirk toyed with the corner of the man's mouth. "I see." He extended a long arm, exposing his open palm. "May I see this object?"

Removing it from his pack, Jerrell placed the globe in Forca's large palm. The wizard strolled over to a window and lifted the artifact to the light while peering closely at it.

With the wizard's mind focused elsewhere, Jerrell decided it was an ideal moment to measure the man's response. "My acquaintance tells me you recently had a patch of bad luck regarding the procurement of iron ore. He said you were quite upset, and some of the staff even feared you might tear the building down."

Forca snorted. "Hardly. While it was upsetting, I have had more significant setbacks. In this instance, it turned out to be a boon, for I was able to secure all shipments of chromium for the next few weeks." He glanced at Jerrell. "You cannot make steel without chromium, you know."

Jerrell nodded. "As I have heard. I am glad to know it all worked out."

Turning from the window, Forca strolled back to the table, cleared out an area, and set the globe down. "I need a moment to test this object."

"You aren't going to destroy it, are you?"

Forca chuckled and stood back. "No. I am ensuring it contains magical properties."

The wizard held an outstretched hand over the globe while staring at it intently.

The hair on Jerrell's arms stood on end, eliciting a shiver as magic flowed just strides away. A hum arose, the vibration causing the globe to hop across the table surface briefly before the sound subsided.

Forca picked up the globe and eyed it with undisguised lust. "I will give you ten gold for this."

Ten? For the man to offer so much so quickly, Jerrell knew it must be worth more than that. "While I appreciate the offer, I intend to show it to other wizards in the city first to ensure I receive the best offer."

The wizard spun toward Jerrell. "Which other wizards?"

Jerrell had only heard a few names since his arrival in Marquithe, but one had immediately stood out. "My next visit is with Wizard Orion Viskar. I believe he runs the local wizard guild."

Forca's eyes blazed. "You must *not* sell it to Viskar!"

"I..."

"I will give you twenty-five gold pieces, here and now."

CHAPTER 4

REWARDS OF THE BOLD

Wizard Forca more than doubled his original offer to purchase the globe, leaving Jerrell with a hefty sum of twenty-five gold – enough to live off for years. Jerrell had hoped for more, however, he needed more than wealth and had already discovered that a life of leisure was unsuitable to his personality. After briefly considering a counteroffer, he decided not to chance it. Should the wizard choose a less honorable path, he could incinerate Jerrell and keep his prize, and nobody would be the wiser.

Jerrell smiled. "Done."

"Wonderful."

The wizard set the globe on a table and knelt beside it, placing his hand on the floor tile in the center of the star. A glow arose from his palm and the tile shuddered. It rose a foot, exposing a metal safe. Forca traced his finger on the panel at the front of the safe and the door popped open. From inside, he withdrew a pouch before closing the door. When he touched the top tile, the safe lowered back into the floor and was hidden from view.

"That is an impressive place to store coin," Jerrell noted.

Rising, Forca said, "And should anyone attempt to access it without my magic signature, they would be met with a most unpleasant result."

"Has anyone tried it before?"

"One. A thief. He is dead. It turns out, a man does not live long when his blood boils at three times its normal temperature."

Perhaps it is best that I forget about this particular stash of gold.

Forca crossed the room and held out the pouch. Jerrell opened his palm. When the man dropped it, he found it to be quite heavy.

"You'll find twenty-five gold pieces inside." The wizard gave Jerrell a menacing stare. "I trust this payment comes with the utmost discretion."

"As far as I am concerned, I was never here. I know nothing of the globe, where it came from, or who owns it."

"Wonderful. I am glad we have an understanding." Forca stepped to the door. "You can show yourself out. Stop on the third floor and find my wife. Tell her she must accompany Godwin to his tutor's place. I am going to remain here for the rest of the day."

Jerrell stepped into the stairwell. "Who is Godwin?"

"My son." The man closed the door and slid the bolt.

VOICES ECHOED down the third-floor corridor, voices of a woman and a boy. As Jerrell drew closer, the conversation became clear.

The woman was speaking. "Your father will be down any minute now. You had better be ready when he arrives."

A sigh followed. "Yes, Mother."

Jerrell reached an open doorway and peered inside. An attractive blonde in her mid-thirties turned toward him. She had a voluptuous figure with a hint of added thickness to her mid-section. Her dress was tight across her chest and hips, both of which were ample.

The woman's blue eyes narrowed. "Who are you?"

"I am an acquaintance of Wizard Forca's. Are you his wife?"

"I am Portia Forca," she said in obvious apprehension.

"He instructed me to tell you to accompany your son to his tutor's."

Anger flared in her eyes. "He promised he would go today."

"It appears the situation has changed."

Arms straight down at her sides, her fists shook as a tear tracked down her cheek. "That blasted fool. He cares only about his ambition and ignores his family."

Jerrell struggled with a response before saying, "I am sorry."

Her expression softened. "It is his fault, not yours."

A boy around ten years of age emerged from the neighboring room. He resembled his mother, his hair the color of straw and eyes like the sea. He wore pale blue robes, his frame thin and lanky. "Who are you?"

Portia wiped her cheek dry and turned toward him. "Never mind that, Godwin. Are you ready to go?"

"Pa promised to take me."

"Your father is busy. He is an important man. It can't be helped."

His gaze dropped to the floor.

"Are you ready?"

"Yes, Mother."

"To the carriage, then," she gestured toward the door.

He walked past Jerrell, pausing briefly to eye him before moving along.

She followed, stopped at Jerrell's side, and gestured toward the heavy pouch in his hand. "Is that gold?"

"Yes. Your husband and I concluded a business transaction."

"Where do you live?"

"Across the city."

"Well, you had better ride with us then. Walking the streets with that much gold is bound to attract the wrong kind of attention." Without another word, she headed out of the room and down the corridor.

Jerrell sighed and followed. Based on her attitude, there was no way to avoid joining her.

A BLACK CARRIAGE waited in the stables. Jerrell climbed inside after Godwin while Portia spoke to the driver. A moment later, she climbed in. Rather than sit next to her son, she sat on the bench beside Jerrell. The carriage lurched into motion and rode down the drive, out the open gate.

"Tell me, Jerrell," Portia said as she gave him a sidelong look. "How long have you known Palkan?"

"In truth, we met only minutes ago."

"So, you know little of him?" She arched a brow in question.

"I only know him by reputation."

She turned and gazed out the window. "And what a reputation it is." The disdain in her tone conveyed more than words could.

The carriage took them along a downhill street, rounded a corner, and rode past the tall Enchanter's Tower.

Portia turned back to Jerrell. "After we drop Godwin off at his tutor's, the driver will bring you to your house."

"It is more of an apartment."

"Just as well." She patted his knee, her hand lingering there.

Jerrell looked at Godwin, who stared out the window with a pouting face, his arms crossed. *He resents this…or maybe, he resents his father.*

The carriage stopped outside a three-story building. The driver held the door open while Godwin and Portia stepped out. She said something to the driver and then escorted her son into the building. The door closed, and the driver climbed back into his seat, but the carriage remained in place.

Maybe the driver is waiting for me to tell him where I live? Jerrell frowned. He wondered if he should climb out and talk to the man. Before he reached the decision, the door to the building opened, and Portia emerged. She climbed back into the carriage and sat across from Jerrell. The driver yipped and snapped his reins, and the horses pulled the carriage down the street.

"I should tell the driver where I live," said Jerrell.

"Don't worry about that." Portia waved dismissingly. "It is mid-day, and I thought you might like to stop at an inn."

Truth to tell, he was hungry, although he sensed she had something else in mind.

"An inn sounds good," Jerrell replied, careful to keep his options open.

"This inn serves wonderful meals and delivers them right to your room" Portia gave him a long appraising look. "You appear strong and virile. I bet your stomach remains flat, other than the ripples of muscle."

My, she has tossed subtleties aside quickly. "I am…I suppose."

She leaned forward, her hand sliding from his knee to his thigh while giving him an unmistakable view of her significant cleavage. "I am a lonely woman, Jerrell. Can I convince you to spend the afternoon with me?"

His pulse began to race from her advances. For a beat, he considered the threat her husband presented should he get caught, but that was quickly discarded. A voice inside him whispered, *Just don't get caught, and all will be well.*

He flashed his best smile. "With a lady of your beauty? Of course."

The comment earned him a smile in return.

AFTERNOON SUNLIGHT FILTERED through the curtained window, dimly illuminating the room. Plates with the remnants of lunch sat on the table below the window. Beside the plates were an empty wine carafe and a half pitcher of water. An unused wardrobe stood along the wall beside the closed and locked door. While two beds completed the array of furniture in the chamber, only one bed was occupied.

Jerrell lay on the bed with his head propped up by a pillow. Portia's head rested on his chest, her arm around him, her soft skin warm against his. Upon their arrival, she had proven to be far more aggressive than Jerrell expected, tearing off his clothing and pushing him onto the bed before she disrobed.

Their coupling had been heated, frantic, and soon rose to a crescendo. Food had followed, along with small talk. The second round of bed play was slower, but tender and lengthy enough to leave them both exhausted. Their urges expended, they lay quietly enjoying each other's presence. Yet, questions burned in Jerrell's mind, bouncing around and seeking answers.

Finally, Jerrell decided he had shown sufficient patience and decided to voice them.

"Your husband is a powerful man. Do I have to fear him coming after me?"

She turned her head, so her chin rested on his chest. "Palkan only pays attention to his own ambitions. I have had other trysts, of which he remains unaware. This one will be no different."

"What of your driver?"

"Toddem is paid to maintain utmost discretion. He has worked as my personal driver for years, and I trust him."

That was a relief. "Have you heard of the Avatar of Farrow?"

"Of course."

"Your husband appeared awfully eager to obtain the object – eager enough to pay twenty-five gold pieces for it."

"So much?" She frowned. "While I understand why he desired the relic, I wish he had discussed it with me. That much gold will take time to recuperate."

"Why did he want it?"

"The Avatars are objects of power. With time and attunement, a wizard can use one to boost his own abilities."

"What if a single wizard owned all eight?"

She shrugged. "I don't think it does anything more than owning one of them."

"How so?"

"A wizard can only attune to a single object at a time, and such an object can only be used by a single wizard."

"Interesting." He rubbed his jaw. "I heard your husband lost a large sum recently in a trade dispute. How do you think he would react to something like that?"

"Palkan cares only about power. Gold is simply a means toward achieving it. A loss might be a setback, but one he would quickly move past." She climbed up his torso and brushed her lips against his, once, twice, and a third time before pulling way. "I wish I could spend more time with you, but Godwin's session will soon be finished."

Portia leaned over the edge of the bed and picked her shift off the floor before rising to her feet. He watched as she pulled it over her head and slid it down her body, her hips moving side to side to force the fit. The view caused his body to react, which was impossible for her to miss.

"As I had guessed," she said with a smile, "you are quite virile, indeed."

He leaned on one elbow. "Perhaps you could stay a bit longer?"

She picked up her dress and gave him a sad smile. "I am sorry, but I must return to the prison I have built around myself."

"Prison?"

"My lonely, loveless marriage." She stepped into the dress, pulled it up to her waist, and paused while staring into space. "There was a time when we were in love, but that man faded from my life years ago. By then, Godwin had been born and...well, I am simply trying to raise my son while Palkan pursues his own path and ignores us."

Once she finished dressing, she walked back over, leaned down, and kissed him. Cupping his cheek, she said, "Thank you for making me feel desired again. If you ever marry, do it for love and don't forget to remind her how you feel. If there is ever something I can help you with, I am in your debt." She turned, walked to the door, and opened it. "The room is paid for until tomorrow. You are welcome to remain here. If nothing else, you can enjoy another meal or two."

The door clicked closed, leaving Jerrell alone with his thoughts.

It had become clear that Palkan Forca was not behind Sorenna's assassination attempt, so he needed to investigate other suspects.

"I think it's time I met this woman's husband."

CHAPTER 5

DERWIN

It was a spring-like morning, the sun shining and the weather warm enough for Jerrell to carry his cloak over one arm. Despite the heat, he still wore his coat as he crossed the city; it was much more than a mere garment.

When he found nobody at the gate to the Souton Estate, he let himself inside and approached the main entrance. Three thumps of the knocker echoed in the courtyard. Then he waited impatiently while a pair of birds tweeted from the big tree in the front yard.

The door opened to reveal Deshaun, the guard he had met during his last visit.

The man grunted. "You're back."

"Sorenna must rely heavily on your keen ability for observation."

His brow furrowed. "Huh?"

"Never mind. Is Mistress Souton here?"

"Yes. She is having breakfast with Master Souton."

"Wonderful. I would like to join them."

The man glared at Jerrell for a beat before turning. "Follow me."

They crossed a long entry hall, climbed a short rise of stairs, and stepped into a dining room that jutted out into the backyard. Morning sunlight

211

streamed through six tall windows. While eight chairs surrounded the table, only two were occupied. Sorenna sat at the head of the table and a man with brown hair, green eyes, and a neatly trimmed beard occupied the seat beside her.

Upon sighting Jerrell, Sorenna set down her fork and wiped her mouth. "Jerrell." She stood. "You have returned."

The man looked from her to Jerrell. "This is the man who saved you?"

Jerrell sighed inwardly. *What else has she told him?*

Sorenna gave a firm nod. "Yes, Derwin. This is Jerrell Landish."

The man rose to his feet and rounded the table. He stood a head taller than Jerrell, with a handsome face, but a soft build – narrow shoulders, lanky arms, and a little extra weight around his midriff. He wore a navy-blue coat over a white ruffled doublet. The gilded buttons on the coat and cuffs reflected the morning sunlight.

Derwin extended his arm. "I am glad to meet you."

Jerrell took the man's hand, squeezing firmly as he shook.

The man winced and wrung his hand when Jerrell released his grip. With one hand cradled in the other, he looked Jerrell up and down. "Sorenna tells me you fought off numerous attackers."

"That is right."

"I...wouldn't have guessed you capable."

"I am often underestimated." If the man sought to spar with words, Jerrell was willing. Challenge flashed in his eyes as he glared up at Derwin, who grimaced back.

Sorenna placed a hand on Jerrell's shoulder, breaking the tension. "Please. Sit with us." She raised her voice and shouted. "Elsa! We have a guest."

"No need to feed me," Jerrell said. "I already broke my fast and could not eat another bite." Before departing the Good Tidings Inn, he had feasted on a wonderful meal of ham, eggs, and hot sweet rolls, all thanks to Portia Forca. "However, I will sit, so we might chat for a bit."

"Very well."

Sorenna reclaimed her chair while Jerrell sat in the chair opposite Derwin, allowing him to watch the man.

Elsa entered through a swinging door at the side of the room. "Yes, Mistress?"

"Would you please get Mister Landish a cup of tea?"

"As you wish." The woman walked out of the room.

"What have you found out?" Sorenna asked.

Jerrell considered his response carefully before speaking. "I have begun an investigation on Palkan Forca. There is no doubt he was greatly upset by your victory, but I have yet to find any proof that he was behind the attack."

Derwin interjected. "That wizard is known to be vindictive. I bet it *was* him."

Sitting back, Jerrell stared at Derwin for a moment, noting his eagerness to blame Forca. He decided to use Derwin's opinion to his advantage. "I find it concerning that the attack took place while you were out of the city. Is there any way he could have known you were away?"

The man blinked and glanced at his wife, who appeared about a decade older than him. "I leave the city every week, sometimes twice a week. While he may have had someone watching, it might also have been pure chance."

As Derwin spoke, he toyed with his utensils and never stopped moving. His gaze turned back on Jerrell. The moment their eyes met, he looked down at his plate. *He is hiding something.* The man's behavior piqued Jerrell's curiosity.

Elsa returned with a steaming cup of tea and set it before Jerrell.

"Thank you," Jerrell said as he lifted the cup to his nose, noting a distinct scent of lemon. He sipped it, burning his tongue, but acted as if nothing was amiss. "Very good." Setting the cup down, he leaned forward. "Derwin, Sorenna tells me you work hard securing deals while at the country estate. I have an interest in business. Can you tell me about it?"

The man appeared taken by surprise. "Well...I...sharing such information might be used against our business."

Jerrell had expected the man to resist. "Omit any details you wish. Surely, you must be able to share something. For instance, what took you away on this last trip?"

When Derwin glanced at Sorenna, she nodded. "Go ahead, dear. You can trust Jerrell."

The comment forced Jerrell to cover his mouth, lest they misconstrue his smile. It was not often he heard others standing up for him, and it felt good to have her trust.

With obvious hesitancy, the man began summarizing his latest trip and the dealings he had in the works. Jerrell asked questions and noted gaps in Derwin's reasoning, bringing him to his next question.

"When are you leaving next?"

Sorenna replied, "Derwin is leaving this afternoon."

"This afternoon?" Jerrell asked.

The man nodded. "Yes, my driver is to pick me up when the sun is halfway between its apex and the horizon."

Sorenna added, "He hopes to close an important deal and will be away for a night or two." She leaned close to her husband, placing her hand on his. "I will miss him while he is away."

Derwin smiled at her, but the smile did not touch his eyes.

Jerrell took a sip of his tea while considering what he had seen and heard, quickly coming to a conclusion. "I wish you success in your venture." *When he departs, I will be there to witness it.*

Just past mid-day, Jerrell approached the city jail and found the front door unlocked. He stepped inside a torchlit, windowless room with benches along one wall and a desk in the center. A guard occupied the chair behind the desk, his feet up and his arms behind his head.

The guard lowered his arms and feet as he sat forward. "Can I help you?"

"I hope so. Are you interested in earning a few silver pieces?"

The guard's eyes narrowed. "If you think I am going to release a prisoner for coin, you have another—"

"No. Nothing like that."

The man relaxed. "I am listening."

"I have always wondered what it would be like to walk the streets as a city guard."

"You want a job?"

"No. I just want the experience."

"I've been doing it for seven years. Trust me when I say it isn't that great."

"Still, it has long been a dream of mine." Jerrell rolled four silver pieces across the desk. The guard slapped his hands down on the coins, stopping them. "The silver is yours to keep if you allow me to dress in armor like yours for a couple hours."

The guard glanced down a dark corridor. "I could lose my job doing something like that."

In the other direction was another corridor, dimly lit by a barred window at the end. Barred cells lined the visible wall. A man in the nearest cell stood with his face between two bars, his hand gripping them as he listened to the conversation.

Jerrell slid two more silver pieces across the desktop. "Nobody needs to know. I just want the sensation of others respecting me when I walk the streets. As you may have noticed, I am not the biggest man, and others often shove me aside rather than stepping around me. I need the armor for a few hours, and that is all."

The guard eyed the coins in silence, so Jerrell upped the ante by setting two more silver pieces beside the others. "This is all the coin I have. What do you say? Will you help a man in need? Who knows? I may decide I like it so much that I sign up to join you."

With a swipe of his hand, the guard gathered the coins and slid them all off the desk and into his palm. He stood. "Follow me."

Jerrell followed the man down the dark corridor. A closed door waited at the end while another stood to his left. The guard opened the near door and stepped into a dimly lit storage room. Daylight poured through a narrow, barred window in the opposite wall. A weapon rack ran along the nearest wall while crates occupied the two rows of shelving down the middle of the room. On the other wall, armor dangled from hooks.

The guard gestured toward the armor. "Find something that fits. You can keep your belongings on one of the shelves below the armor. When you leave the room, take care not to talk to anyone. Just go on your way. My shift ends at sunset, so be back before then.

"Thank you, kind sir."

The guard closed the door, leaving Jerrell alone as he began to disrobe.

Minutes later, dressed like a city guard – a silver helmet on his head, leather armor with metal plates on his chest and shoulders, padded leather breeches, leather bracers with metal plates on his arms, and his own boots – Jerrell walked out of the jail and stood in the afternoon sun. A couple passing by gave him a familiar nod while stepping around him. *Odd how a uniform commands respect, although I might be inept with a sword and am as likely to break a law as anyone in the city.* Dismissing such musings, he turned and marched toward Wizard Estates beneath the gaze of the afternoon sun.

When Sorenna's estate came into view, Jerrell stopped and took a position outside a neighboring mansion. He crossed his arms, leaned against the wall, and settled in.

AN HOUR LATER, a dark red carriage pulled up and stopped outside the Souton estate gate. The driver was a big man. Armed with a sword, he looked more like a soldier than a simple carriage driver.

Sorenna's husband, Derwin, emerged from the gate, spoke to the driver, and climbed into the carriage. The driver snapped the reins, and the carriage lurched into motion toward Jerrell's location. Jerrell simultaneously began walking along the road in the same direction as the carriage. The carriage rolled past him as he reached the downhill slope. When it was a block ahead of him, Jerrell broke into a jog to keep pace.

Careful to never draw closer to the carriage, Jerrell ran in its wake while it navigated the busy streets of Marquithe. His breath came in gasps, the armor's weight wearing on him as his tunic grew damp with sweat.

They crossed the square outside the Bureau of Trading and entered a street heading due north. The city wall came into view, the gate beneath it open with the black teeth of the raised portcullis visible. The carriage rolled through the gate, passed a wagon undergoing inspection, and rolled out of sight.

Without slowing, Jerrell made for the tower beside the gate, tore the door open, and raced up the stairs. Light from a window at every other landing guided the way as he ascended ten stories. At the top, he came to the winch room where a pair of city guards lounged. With arched brows, they watched him run through and open the door across from the stairwell.

Jerrell stepped out into a stiff wind, which cut through the gaps in his armor. The wall itself was deeper than he had anticipated, the outer edge lined by a waist-high wall with merlons standing taller than Jerrell. An eight-foot-wide path ran in both directions, occupied by a handful of armored archers.

Leaning against the low wall between two merlons, Jerrell surveyed the area.

The city of Marquithe crowned a broad, rounded hilltop surrounded by rolling plains. Inside the walls, the highest point was at the center of the city, where the Tower of Devotion stood as the tallest structure. Marquithe Palace and the connected Temple of Farrow surrounded the tower. On three sides of the palace grounds stood Wizard Estates. On the fourth side, the merchant district lay nestled between the palace and the north gate, with the Bureau of Trading at the heart of the commerce center. The poorest districts butted against the city walls.

Long yellow grass dominated the hilltop outside the city. The nearest tree stood over a mile away, and farms covered the land from the hilltop to the north horizon. From his position, a hundred feet above the hilltop, Jerrell's view extended for thirty miles in all directions.

A half mile away, Derwin's carriage rolled along the north road, its distance steadily increasing.

Panting from the exertion of his run and subsequent climb, Jerrell leaned against the merlon and shook his head. "I don't understand. I thought for sure, I would catch him in a lie."

The carriage rolled on and approached another carriage waiting in the shadows of a copse of trees a mile outside the city. As Derwin's carriage drew near the other one, it slowed to a stop. The door opened. Derwin stepped out and climbed into the waiting carriage. Both carriages rolled into action, the black one carrying Derwin back to the city while the dark red one continued off into the distance.

Jerrell grinned. "Clever." Anyone watching from ground level would be none the wiser. The curve of the hilltop would have obscured the man's transfer from one carriage to the other. "Too bad for him, I specialize in cleverness."

Turning, Jerrell stepped back into the winch room and waved to the two men. "Everything looks good on the wall. Keep up the good work."

He descended the stairs and emerged in the square outside the gate just before the carriage reached it. A brief inspection took place, and the carriage rolled into the city with Jerrell, again, following. *Now, I will discover where that man spends his time away.*

CHAPTER 6
ASSASSIN

The black carriage stopped two blocks from Jerrell's apartment. Derwin stepped out and entered a shop with a lacquered map glued to the sign above it. In the map were three concentric circles with the letter C in the middle.

Still dressed as a city guard, Jerrell peered through the shop window as he strolled past. Three maps were displayed on easels at the front of the shop. Farther inside, he spied Derwin, waving his arms as he spoke with another man.

Three buildings down from the cartographer shop, Jerrell stopped and acted as if he were patrolling the intersection. A few minutes later, Derwin exited the building, climbed into the carriage, and continued down the street, right past Jerrell.

Again, Jerrell followed. Only a few minutes passed before the carriage stopped. Derwin climbed out and entered a three-story building. This time, the carriage pulled away without him.

"Interesting." Jerrell watched the building, waiting in case Derwin emerged.

The bottom floor appeared to be a cobbler's shop, but the shop itself had its own entrance, separate from the one Derwin had used. Minutes passed without sight of the man, so Jerrell approached the building. With his hand resting on his knife hilt, he opened the door and stepped into an empty stairwell. He heard nothing above him and considered the situation before heading back outside and ducking into the cobbler shop. The bell on the door rang, announcing his presence.

An older man with circular spectacles lowered to the tip of his nose emerged from the back room. Various sizes of shoes, slippers, and boots lined the shop's shelves.

"May I help you?" the shop owner asked.

Jerrell puffed himself up. "I am here on an investigation."

The man's eyes widened. "I paid my taxes, and I—"

"No. This is not about you."

The cobbler blinked. "What, then?"

"The apartments above your shop. Who owns them?"

"Well, I live on the second floor with my wife. However, just this past fall, I sold the top floor to a young couple."

"A couple you say? Can you describe the man?"

"Yes. His name is Darren. He is in his early thirties. Tall with brown hair, a brown beard, and green eyes."

"And the woman?"

"She is an attractive lass – blonde with dreamy blue eyes and a nice figure."

Jerrell grinned. "I thought you said you were married."

The man chuckled. "I've been married for forty years, but I'm still a man, and I'm not dead. It would be hard not to take note of that pretty thing."

Jerrell dug into his pocket and pulled out a silver piece, mostly because he liked the old man. "Thank you for your assistance."

The man arched a brow. "Thank you, sir." His brow then furrowed. "Has the couple in the third-floor apartment done anything wrong?"

"Oh, no." Jerrell didn't want to cause the cobbler alarm or give him any reason to warn them. "I was looking for someone else, but I must have the wrong address. I was told to visit a cobbler shop on Sizemore Street."

"Sizemore? That is two streets over. You must be looking for Yousef's Footwear."

"Oh, yes. That sounds right!" Jerrell turned to the door. "Have a good day."

He stepped outside, noted the building's location, and headed back the way he came.

~

WHEN JERRELL REACHED the cartographer's shop, he was met by a closed sign, so he peered inside the window. Nobody was inside the shop, but the door to the back room stood open, revealing movement.

Thump, thump, thump, he pounded on the door. Nobody answered, so he knocked again.

A burly, middle-aged man emerged from the back room, striding toward the door with purpose, his face a thundercloud. He unlocked the door, threw it open, and snarled. "Can't you read? We are closed!"

Jerrell narrowed his eyes. "Can't you see? This uniform gives me privilege."

The man's expression softened. "Sorry. I've had a long day and have much to do."

"Really? You draw maps. Is there some sudden demand for a map you don't have in stock?"

"I..." The man frowned. "What is this about?"

"Let's step inside, and I will explain."

The man appeared reluctant but nodded and stepped in anyway.

Jerrell followed him and scooped up a board near the entrance with a map of Farrowen burned into it. As the man turned toward him, Jerrell swung. The board struck the side of the man's head with a crack, splitting the board in half and causing the man to stumble. Jerrell wrapped one arm around the man's neck and another around the top of his head as he positioned himself behind the cartographer. Squeezing with all his might, Jerrell held tight while the man stumbled around the shop, knocking over two easels before turning and backing rapidly, using his weight to drive Jerrell into the wall. The impact drove the wind from Jerrell's lungs, but he held on tight. The man staggered forward, appearing ready to fall. Feebly, the man tried to fight, his fingers raking at Jerrell's armored forearms. Then, he dropped to his knees and went limp.

~

JERRELL SPLASHED water on the cartographer's face. The man woke, spluttering and gasping.

"There you are."

The back room of the cartography shop made it clear – this man was no ordinary map maker. Weapons ranging from darts to crossbows to knives covered one wall. The adjacent wall held vials with various dubious substances while the shelf above held a long glass aquarium with three black scorpions inside.

"I am Jerrell. What is your name?"

The man grimaced. "Philo."

"So, master of maps," Jerrell said to the man tied to the chair in front of him. "I have a question about a recent client visit."

Philo strained against his bonds, but to no avail. "If I get my hands on you..."

In a flash, Jerrell's dagger was in his hand with the tip pressed against the man's neck. "You live only because I allow it. Assassins often die young. You have exceeded the average age, so you must be wise enough to know when to yield."

The man inhaled, his nostrils flaring while his eyes sparked with anger. By his third breath, the anger cooled, and the tension eased from his body. "You are no city guard."

"No. Unlike someone pledged to uphold the law, I bend such rules to suit my needs without hesitation."

"What do you want to know?"

"A man visited you shortly before you closed the shop. I need details behind that visit."

"And if I tell you?"

Jerrell pulled his blade back and smiled. "I will let you live. Any other benefits depend on whether or not I believe what you say."

"All right. The man paid me ten gold pieces to kill a woman."

"Her name?"

"Souton. Sorenna Souton."

"Did you receive payment?"

"He gave me half. The rest comes when she is dead."

Jerrell dug into his uniform and pulled out a small purse, dangling it in front of the man's eyes. "Five gold lie nestled in this purse, along with a few silver pieces. How about I let you have it, and you forget about your objective?"

"You want to pay me to let her live?"

"Very good." Jerrell crooned. "I was hoping you were smart enough to see what was in front of your face."

"What about my client?"

"Testify in writing that he paid you to kill her."

"But if I do that, it will destroy my cover."

"In Marquithe, yes." Jerrell spread his arms out. "This is a big world, Philo. You are free to resume your business anywhere else. I suspect after selling the shop, in addition to your recent windfall of ten gold pieces, you will do just fine."

"And if I decline?"

Eyeing his blade as he twisted it, Jerrell said, "Then, I will have no further use for you."

Philo frowned. "You promised you wouldn't kill me."

"I always honor a promise and would refrain from personally harming you." Jerrell tapped the aquarium, causing the creatures inside to shuffle. "However, your pet scorpions might feel otherwise, especially after I shake them up before dumping them on you."

The man glared at Jerrell for a long, quiet moment before chuckling.

"What is so funny?"

"You have a knack for this. Have you considered becoming an assassin?"

"While not completely off my resume, it is a role I avoid unless I know the target deserves it."

His brow arched. "An assassin with a conscience? That is poor business."

"And that is why I usually apply my talents elsewhere." Jerrell spun the man's chair around. A table with a quill and an inkwell sat before him. "Start writing. I left your wrists free enough for that. Once I have your signed confession, I will free you and be on my way."

The man drafted the note as Jerrell requested. Once he had signed it, he arched a brow while looking up at Jerrell. "How do you know I won't come after you?"

Jerrell flashed him a devilish smile. "Oh, I would enjoy that. Just don't come crying to me when you end up dead."

Philo snorted. "Sorry. I only kill for gold. If nobody is paying me, I may as well be on my way."

"As I thought." Jerrell sliced the rope tied to the chair arm, freeing one of the man's arms. "It might take you some time, but you can now free your-self." *By then, I will be away from here.*

He opened the front door, stepped into the street, and headed back toward the city jail. *Time to change back into my own clothes and pay Mistress Souton a visit.* He didn't know how she would take the information he had to share, but it was time for her to take steps to protect herself.

CHAPTER 7
COMEUPPANCE

A thick bank of clouds blotted out the night sky, masking the moon and leaving the city of Marquithe cloaked in darkness. Nestled in the sleepiest hours between midnight and dawn, the streets were empty and silent save for the rustle of the wind. While spring was imminent, the cold nights remained as a reminder of winter's last grasp on the city.

In the darkness, Jerrell crept silently along the second-story rooftops. Noise came from below, alerting him. He moved to the eaves and peered past the white mist of his swirling breath. A pair of men in dark cloaks strolled down the street, passed the enchanted lantern at the corner, and faded into the night.

Resuming his advance, Jerrell approached a three-story building that rose above the others. Soft warm light flickered through a third-story window. Smoke rising from the brick chimney beside the window hinted that the light came from a fireplace.

Moving on silent footsteps, Jerrell approached the building. He ran his fingers, numb from the cold, across the uneven stones of the fireplace and found a grip. A short climb brought his head even with the window, allowing him to peer inside.

The lumps beneath a thick quilt indicated someone sleeping in the bed across the room. The clothing strewn across the floor – a pair of breeches, a doublet, smallclothes, a dress, and a shift – informed Jerrell that two people occupied the bed.

He let go with one hand, drew his dagger, and reached over to the window. With care, he slid his dagger blade between the two windowpanes and wiggled the hilt while applying pressure. The latch moved and the window popped open. Slowly, Jerrell pulled on one side, stopping the window just shy of the chimney. He released his hold on the chimney and twisted quickly, so both hands gripped the windowsill. Pulling himself up, he lifted a knee onto the ledge and climbed inside.

The warmth in the room was a welcome contrast to the chilly night. To his right, a fireplace burned, the logs transformed to mere black and gray skeletons, surrounded by flickering flame and glowing coals. Beside one wall stood a nightstand and a queen bed. A canopy with white lace trim covered the bedframe. Against the wall opposite the bed stood an ivory colored vanity with an oval mirror, brushes, makeup, and other feminine items.

Jerrell turned his attention to the bed and spied a pewter pitcher filled with water on the nightstand. The bed's occupants, a middle-aged man with brown hair and a neatly trimmed brown beard and a blonde in her twenties, both lay on their sides, facing each other. A flowered quilt covered their bodies, one of his arms exposed as it lay draped over her hip.

Time to wake up.

Jerrell grabbed the pitcher and turned it upside down over the bed. Water drenched the head of the sleeping male, sending droplets splattering in all directions. Both gasped and bolted upright, their eyes wide in shock; the quilt fell to their laps exposing bare torsos. The man was out of shape, his hair covered stomach bulging with a softness that bespoke large meals and little physical activity. The woman possessed a far more attractive figure, her perky breasts and modest midriff belying her comparative youth.

As they turned toward Jerrell, he snatched the man's hair with one hand, leaned in with a sneer, and twisted his dagger in front of the man's face. "I suggest you remain quiet unless you wish to die."

The man whined, "Please, don't hurt me."

"You are in trouble, Derwin."

Derwin blinked in recognition. "Landish? How did you find me?"

Jerrell gauged the man's demeanor and decided he was unlikely to pose a physical threat. He pulled his blade back and allowed the man to look at him.

"I know your type. Greedy, self-centered, and lacking integrity. You told your wife you were visiting your country estate, but instead you traveled across the city to the apartment of your mistress."

Derwin's eyes flicked from side to side, as if he were seeking a means to escape.

"Your wife?" the woman exclaimed. She scooped up the quilt and shot out of bed, using it to cover herself while leaving him completely naked. "You told me your wife was dead."

The man turned toward her and rose to his knees. "To me, she is all but dead. I love you, Leah. I can think of nobody else."

Her face clouded over in anger. "You told me we were to marry. But you are still married to *her*?"

"And we will marry...once I am free to do so."

She grabbed a jewelry box from the vanity and threw it. He raised his arm to protect his face. The hurtling object struck his elbow, bounced off, and spilled out on the bed. Gold, silver, and gems of various colors glittered in the firelight.

"Ouch!" Derwin winced. He lowered his arm and crawled to the edge of the bed. "Listen, Leah. Soon, we will marry and be together forever."

The woman glared at him with fire in her eyes. "I have heard that before."

"This time, Sorenna will be dead. In fact, it may have already happened."

Jerrell laughed, and they both turned toward him.

Derwin asked, "What is so funny?"

"I paid Philo a visit today. He is thankful for your down payment, but when offered the rest of his fee in exchange for leaving town rather than paying Sorenna a visit, he decided it was a good time to close down his shop in Marquithe."

The man's jaw dropped. "I...I don't know who you are talking about."

In a flash, Jerrell lunged for Derwin, driving him back on the bed and pressing his dagger against the man's throat. "You paid to have your wife murdered. Twice. Give me a reason why I should not kill you now, you swine."

Derwin's eyes bulged as Jerrell's dagger tip bit into his neck. "Please. I beg of you. Do not kill me."

"You will survive, but only if you listen and do what I say."

"I'll do anything."

"Your wife is dissolving your marriage. Her estate and the money that comes with it will revert solely to her."

"But what about me?"

Jerrell smirked. "You purchased this apartment, didn't you?" It was a guess, but an educated one.

"I...well, yes, but I bought it for Leah."

"In that case, you can live here with her...if she still wants you. You see, Derwin, your wife has moved her wealth to new accounts, hired new guards, and changed the locks on her family manor as well as her country estate. If you show up at either location, you are to be killed on sight."

Derwin's face blanched. "She cannot..."

"Oh, yes," Jerrell grinned, "she can and she did."

The man began to shake, his cheeks turning red as a fire burned in his eyes. "That damn woman...I will kill her."

Jerrell's fist smashed into Derwin's nose, knocking the man backward. He rolled off the bed and landed on the floor at Leah's feet. She frowned down at him.

Circling the bed, Jerrell stopped before Derwin as he sat up. Blood ran from his nose, past his lips, and dripped off his chin.

Leveling his dagger in front of Derwin's face, Jerrell growled. "If you ever attempt to harm Sorenna again, I will find you, and I will end you. Regardless of how much coin you spend, should you ever again come into wealth, no number of paid guards can protect you."

Derwin began to sob. "I am ruined."

Jerrell lowered his blade. "You should have considered that before you tried to murder your wife." He moved to the open bedroom door and gently ran the back of his fingers down Leah's cheek. In a softer tone, he said, "If I were you, I'd reconsider your relationship. Derwin is destitute and without a job, so his lavish gifts have come to an end. Besides, if he is willing to kill one wife, who says he won't also try to kill the next one?"

Her eyes widened in realization. "That is...horrible."

"Aye."

Exiting the bedroom, Jerrell crossed the dark sitting area and made for the apartment door. Once in the stairwell, he descended two flights and stepped outside as a quartet of city guards approached the building.

"Good evening, gentlemen," Jerrell said with a smile.

One of the guards eyed Jerrell with a furrowed brow. "What is this about? A message left at the city jail requested a squad come to this address, but it did not say why."

"The why is upstairs in the third-floor apartment. His name is Derwin Gray, the now ex-husband to Sorenna Souton. He is also the man identified in the assassin's confession you received this afternoon."

The guard gestured toward the door. "You heard him. Let's arrest Mister Gray."

The squad poured into the building, leaving Jerrell alone in the dark, quiet street. Humming happily, he strode off into the night.

CHAPTER 8
A SIP OF BRANDY

Beneath gray skies, Jerrell approached the Marquithe Bureau of Trading. As he drew near the door, two guards blocked his path.

"No weapons allowed," one said in a gruff voice.

With a shrug, Jerrell handed over the dagger on his hip. "Don't go playing with it," he said as the man applied a tag to the hilt. "It's sharp, and you're likely to lose something if you aren't careful."

The other guard wrote the tag number on a slip of paper and handed it to Jerrell. "Funny."

Before Jerrell could enter the building, a hand pressed against his chest. "Hold on," the guard said. "We need to pat you down."

The guard began to pat Jerrell's body, starting at his shoulders and working his way down, the man's hands sliding across his chest, back, and down his legs. If he noticed the knives hidden in his boot, he said nothing. The guard didn't even bother to check his sleeves, where two more blades remained hidden.

"All right." The guard moved aside. "You're free to enter."

Jerrell grunted. It felt as if the man had merely gone through the motions of a search without applying any real effort. The five blades still hidden on his body were proof of that.

He passed through the double doors and stepped inside. Above him, the view was open all the way to the high ceiling, five stories above. A long desk with half a dozen workers sitting behind it waited straight ahead. Beyond it, people sat on benches, apparently waiting for an appointment.

To his left and right, four levels of railed lofts overlooked the atrium-like interior. Walls broke each loft into five separate lounges, most of which were occupied. Windows at the front and rear of the building provided light. The hum of many conversations echoed throughout the spacious building.

Jerrell leaned against the desk and waited while a clerk dressed in a black coat and beret recorded numbers into a ledger, the feather on his quill flicking furiously. He appeared around Jerrell's age, but with a long lanky build.

After a moment, the clerk peered up at Jerrell through round spectacles. He frowned in annoyance.

"Yes?"

"I have an appointment with Mistress Souton."

The man's brow furrowed. "If you have an appointment, your name would be in this ledger." His hands covered the open ledger as though the world's greatest secrets were hidden within its pages.

"Why don't you take a look for yourself?"

"And your name would be?"

"Landish. Jerrell Landish."

The clerk lifted the ledger so the black cover faced Jerrell. After a moment, he lowered it. "Huh. I actually do see that name. It says I am to bring you to her straight away."

Jerrell smirked. "Let's go visit her, you pompous arse."

The comment earned him a sneer. "I don't know why a woman of her renown would honor an appointment with a street rat like you."

"Which is why you sit at the reception desk rather than holding an office at the Bureau. If you learn to judge others by their abilities and character rather than their appearances, you might improve your lot."

The clerk blinked, huffed, and stood. "Follow me."

He spun around and led Jerrell to a stairwell. They climbed to the fourth level and followed a hallway with closed doors to one side and open offices to the other. After passing three offices separated by five-foot walls, the clerk stopped at the fourth office.

Bowing, the clerk said, "Pardon me, Mistress Souton, this man claims to have an appointment with you this morning."

Sorenna sat in a cushioned chair. An elderly man sat on a sofa across from her. "Ah. Welcome, Jerrell. Come in. Have a drink, and take a seat. Master Vanderkash and I are almost finished."

Jerrell flashed the clerk one last smirk before entering Sorenna's office. Surrounded on three sides by a solid wall and the loft railing on the fourth, the space was six strides deep and just as wide. Capped carafes of wine, brandy, and water rested on a wooden credenza along one wall while a sitting area of three cushioned chairs and a sofa occupied the majority of the space.

After pouring himself a glass of brandy, Jerrell claimed the chair opposite Sorenna.

The old man examined Jerrell through rectangular spectacles. His gray eyebrows flared out past the wire rims and the sparse hair on his head appeared disheveled. "So, you are the one who sniffed out the plot to murder Sorenna?"

"I am."

"Well done, Master Landish. I've long said we could use more men like you. Too often, others manipulate situations from behind a curtain of anonymity and leave those of us who play by the rules underequipped to deal with the issue."

Sorenna said, "Which brings us to the reason for this meeting. I was informed this morning that Derwin has been taken into custody and is being held in the city jail."

Jerrell nodded. "As I expected. Again, I am sorry you were betrayed by your own hus—"

Sorenna held up a hand, stopping him. "The truth might be harsh, but it does not change because you wish it were otherwise. I now see it was Derwin's own ambition that led him to my arms in the first place. He never truly loved me, but instead, sought to assume my wealth. While his betrayal stings, I no longer grieve for our marriage. It is time for him to pay for what he has done. Speaking of which, the city guards informed me that Derwin paid another assassin yesterday, one whom you convinced to confess and forgo completing his contract."

Jerrell nodded. "That is right."

She sat back with a smile. "See, Orville. I told you this man is resourceful."

"That he is, Sorenna." The old man nodded approvingly.

"Do you agree to co-sponsor him?"

"I do."

Jerrell frowned. "What is this?"

"The Bureau consists of offices that address nearly every need of trade, save for one. We merchants have nowhere to go should we require special services, such as the one you provided to me these past few days. I wish to rectify that if you are amiable to the idea."

While he had an inclination as to what she meant, he wanted to hear her say it. "Please explain."

"Orville and I wish to sponsor you for an office here at the Bureau. The sponsorship would last for one year, after which you must pay an annual fee to maintain ownership, provided you prove the value of your services during the trial period."

His heart fluttered, and a smile tugged at Jerrell's lips. "I would get my own office?"

"Of course. It would start on the second floor, but in time, you might rise to an upper level. Few Ungifted ever reach the top floor."

"And what is the annual fee?" Jerrell took a sip of his drink.

"Twenty-five gold pieces."

The number caused Jerrell to choke. Once his windpipe was clear, he repeated their words. "Twenty-five gold?"

"It is a hefty sum, but you will find an office here will provide you with opportunities you won't find elsewhere. Those opportunities will also lead to increased wealth."

The old man added, "Stars rise here at the Bureau. With such an auspicious start, surely your path will lead to greatness."

Jerrell suspected the man was attempting to convince him by feeding his ego, but he did not care. After all, they were giving him exactly what he desired. A chance to increase his fame and attain fortune greater than any thief before him.

"All right. I accept. What do you need from me?"

"There is a catch."

Jerrell groaned. "I suspected as much."

"Our sponsorship is an investment, and as businesspeople, we would like to see a return on that investment."

"You require a portion of my earnings."

She smiled. "You are a bright one, Master Landish. Yes. Orville and I will each earn a twenty percent royalty on your gross income for the first year. It will still leave you sixty percent, and without the overhead of paying for your office, it should be of little consequence."

While Jerrell disliked the idea of being beholden to anyone, he knew he could not secure an office at the Bureau without her support. "Very well. Is there anything else?"

"How, exactly, would you describe the services you offer?"

He rubbed the stubble on his jaw. "Um...thief for hire?"

Orville snorted. "You can't very well advertise yourself as a thief."

Jerrell paused and considered alternatives. "How about trickster for hire?"

"Trickster?"

"Yeah. If nothing else, it will arouse curiosity."

Sorenna laughed. "That it will."

Jerrell sat back with a grin. "I thank you, Mistress Souton. This is exactly what I have been seeking."

"If not for you, I would be dead. This is the least I can do." A sparkle glinted in her eye. "Now, how about we all have a glass of brandy to celebrate?"

Jerrell emptied his glass and held it out for Sorenna to refill it. He could not restrain his grin. After a wasted winter, he had achieved his goal. *My name will soon be known across the southern wizardoms. I wonder what new adventures will come my way.*

CHAPTER 9
WAITING IS THE HARDEST PART

Jerrell arrived at his office at the Bureau in mid-morning as he had for the previous forty days. He settled into his office on the second level, which faced the open atrium interior of the building. While all the offices on the top level might be the highest aim, the private, enclosed rooms along the outer wall of the second level were also in higher demand, giving him a more immediate goal to strive toward.

Mere minutes passed before he grew bored, so he got up and walked three offices over. Inside was a man in his late twenties, bent over a table while he logged notes in a ledger. His straw-colored bangs swayed as his quill moved back and forth. He wore a dark purple coat over a white tunic. The buttons on the front of the coat and the cuffs were made of shining brass.

"Good morning, Kolbert."

The man looked up at Jerrell and pushed his bangs aside. "Hi, Jerrell. How is business?"

Entering the office, Jerrell sat with a sigh. "I am going crazy waiting for something to happen."

Kolbert nodded. "It was like that for me at first. But word slowly spreads, and soon, you will have a client. One becomes two and two become four. By the time a year passes, you will have more business than time."

"You buy and sell bolts of cloth – a traditional business that has existed for millennia. Mine, however, is a bit more...specialized."

Rubbing his jaw, Kolbert nodded. "You might be right, but based on the stories you have told me, there are people willing to pay for someone with your unique skills. It just might take more time."

Jerrell sighed. "I know. However, sitting in this building doing nothing while coin exchanges hands all around me...well, it is driving me nuts."

"If it helps, twice in the past week, I heard your name mentioned while I was dining at local inns. Word travels. Sooner or later, someone will come seeking you."

Rising to his feet, Jerrell said, "I just hope it's not someone seeking to put a knife in my back."

The other man chuckled. "You do have a way of causing others trouble. Sycamore is still pissed about the dead fish you put in his desk."

Jerrell grinned, recalling how the old man had shrieked in disgust. "You can attribute that to boredom as well." He stood. "I will let you get back to work. Do you want to meet for ales later?"

"Are you paying?"

"I will buy two rounds, but that's it for tonight. I will run out of coin by mid-summer if I don't get business soon."

"In that case, I will buy tonight."

Grinning wider, Jerrell nodded. "Even better."

When Jerrell turned toward his office, he spied Eggert, one of the Bureau clerks, heading in his direction. Eggert was Jerrell's age and had a tall, thin frame and a sharp face. He was not alone.

The clerk escorted a man dressed in a dark blue doublet and black breeches tucked into brown boots folded over at the top, giving him the appearance of a bureaucrat. He appeared to be in his thirties and had shoul-der-length brown hair with a matching goatee. He stood a few inches taller than Jerrell. His frame lacked muscle but each step exuded arrogance.

The clerk stopped outside of Jerrell's office. "Master Landish?"

"Yes?"

The clerk gestured toward the man at his side. "This is Master Tarin. He has requested a meeting. Since he doesn't have an appointment, he agreed to meet your appointment minimum." The clerk held a gold piece out to Jerrell.

"Thank you, Eggert." Accepting the coin, Jerrell stepped back into his office, moved past the sofa, and sat in the chair at the back.

The man gave the clerk a questioning look. "This is him?"

Eggert nodded. "Yes, sir." He then walked off, leaving Tarin alone at the entrance.

Jerrell gestured toward his sofa. "What are you waiting for, Tarin? Come in and have a seat."

The man entered the office and settled across from Jerrell, his gaze fixed on him the entire time. "From the tales I have heard, I expected a more imposing figure."

"I can stand on the tips of my toes if that would make you feel better."

Tarin chuckled. "No need for that." He sat back and crossed his legs. A quiet moment followed while Tarin tented his fingers before his mouth. Finally, he spoke in a quiet tone. "I represent a wizard of some import."

Jerrell's brow furrowed. "Did you travel from Eleighton?"

The man blinked. "Why would you ask that?"

"The mud crusted on your boots has a red tint. You can't find soil that color here. Eleighton is the ore center of the southern wizardoms and well known for its red soil."

Tarin smiled. "Well observed. While a simple thing, not one person in a hundred would have come to that conclusion so quickly."

"I doubt you have met anyone quite like me."

"Ah." The man nodded knowingly. "I had heard you were arrogant."

Jerrell was not surprised. While he preferred to consider himself confident, others had called him arrogant before. "What else have you heard?"

"Rumor says that you had a hand in placing Paloun in the position of high wizard at Yor's Point."

"I'd say I had more than two hands in making that possible."

"Good. Finding someone who is willing to deal with wizards, especially those in positions of influence, can be quite difficult."

Jerrell's eyes narrowed. "Not even wizards are infallible. However, they present certain risks that require additional compensation."

"My employer is willing to pay you fifty gold pieces if you can procure an item for him."

Sitting forward, Jerrell's interest fully piqued, he asked, "What item could be worth such a sum?"

"That is the question." Tarin frowned. "I can't say for sure."

"I don't find that information very useful. How am I to get the item if you don't know what it is?"

"Let me explain." The man rubbed his jaw. "What do you know of High Wizard Montague?"

"He rose to the position of high wizard of Lionne about a year ago."

"Exactly. Yet, the question is how did he do it?"

"I presume he challenged the High Wizard Garue."

"Oh, he did, but by all accounts, Garue should have bested Montague with little effort. Not only did the former high wizard possess natural abilities Montague could never achieve, but he had studied and perfected his craft. You see, Garue was in his mid-forties while Montague, a weaker challenger, was only twenty-eight. Other than the recently departed Wizard Jakins and the new high wizard of Yor's Point, Paloun, not a single high wizard across the eight wizardoms is younger than thirty-five. Most don't reach the exalted position until their forties."

Jerrell frowned in thought. "Are you suggesting Montague had assistance as Paloun did?"

"No. Those who witnessed the duel have stated that Garue was ready for the battle, unlike the situation with Jakins. There is no way another wizard was involved, for that would not have escaped the notice of the Gifted witnesses. Somehow, Montague defeated Garue on his own."

"All right. So, what does that have to do with me and the object I am to retrieve?"

"My employer believes Montague possesses an item of power, something that enhances his abilities. Not only did he crush Garue, but he destroyed numerous challengers since rising to his station. Now, nobody is willing to challenge him despite the allure of ruling the wealthiest Farrowen district outside of Marquithe."

"So, you wish me to steal this object, whatever it is, and hand it to your master in exchange for the fifty gold pieces?"

"Very good, Mister Landish." Tarin smirked and gave a slow nod. "You have concluded your objective all on your own."

Jerrell considered the situation and everything that had not been said. It sounded too much like his deal with High Wizard Wrenthal, a deal that had ended in betrayal. "I want to see the gold, first."

"As I suspected," Tarin replied, "which is why I have already placed fifty gold pieces in the control of the Bureau." He reached into his doublet and pulled out a sheet of paper. "This is your contract. Sign it and hand it to one of the clerks. "When you procure the item and deliver it to Eleighton, my employer will give you his signed copy and you will receive your gold."

Jerrell looked over the document. All appeared as it should, so he reached for the quill on the table, dipped it in the inkwell, and applied his signature. His scrawl was a mess. His writing was atrocious, but at least he knew how to read and write. Many with his background did not have a literate parent to instruct them on such things, and while Jerrell's mother had died when he was ten, by then he could read as well as most adults.

"Done," Jerrell handed the signed contract over to Tarin, who rose to his feet.

"It has been a pleasure, Mister Landish. Good luck, and may the gods watch over you."

"Luck I have. As for the gods...I will worry about them when they prove they care about me."

Tarin shook his head. "You have a bitter perspective for one so young."

"My experience belies my age."

"Which gives me confidence in your quest. If you need me, I will be staying at the Sunny Skies Inn here in Marquithe."

"I'll be back in a week or two. Until then, send my best wishes to High Wizard Gurgan."

Tarin stared at Jerrell for a long beat and then grinned. "You continue to impress, Mister Landish. Perhaps you will not end up dead after all."

The man walked off, leaving Jerrell alone with his thoughts. While the contract sounded risky, the danger provided additional intrigue and quickly made him forget his earlier boredom. In addition, spring in Lionne promised fair weather, and it was a city he had only visited once. Eager to return, he capped his inkwell and stood.

When I get to Lionne, I need to conduct some research on this Montague character. He stepped out of his office and paused. *But first, I had better tell Kolbert I can't meet him for drinks tonight.*

CHAPTER 10

LIONNE

Rather than draw the attention that would come with a carriage, Jerrell chose to hitch a ride with a trader driving his wagon to Lionne. The ride would take longer than if he had stolen a horse, but he was in no rush, and four days in a wagon provided more comfort than three days in the saddle.

The driver, a man named Dean, was a nice enough fellow but lacked the mental acuity to maintain an engaging conversation. To avoid the pain of listening to the man's dull thoughts, Jerrell slept through much of the journey, until, at last, the city came into view.

Beyond the dark walls of Lionne, ships sailed in and out of the bay, the white sheets on their masts full and taut. Puffy white clouds dotted the blue sky to the west as the sun reached its apex. Across the river from the city, scaffolding bordered the partially constructed frame of a fortress. Dozens of men, wagons, carts, and oxen moved about the construction site while piles of hewn stone blocks covered the hillside, waiting to be mortared into place.

"What are they building?" he asked.

Dean grunted. "I hear it's a fort for the Thundercorps."

"Another garrison?" Jerrell recalled the fort on the waterway between Yor's Point and Shear.

"Yep. That's what they called it."

"More Thundercorps soldiers? Is Malvorian planning a war or something?"

The man shrugged. "So long as I don't have to do no soldierin', it don't matter to me."

The road turned, taking the wagon toward the city walls, which were three stories tall with a tower standing directly over the entrance. The guards posted outside the gate watched as clusters of people on foot and a man driving an empty wagon entered the city.

When the wagon drew close, a guard with a blue cape stepped out and held his hand up.

"Hold."

Dean tipped his hat to the man, "Hello, good sir."

"What's in the wagon?"

"Nothin' but empty barrels. I'll be stopping by some vineyards in the morning to swap 'em for full ones."

The guard turned to Jerrell. "What about you? What is your business in Lionne?"

"I came to view the sea," Jerrell said with wide eyes, his tone filled with wonder. "I ain't never left Marquithe before, and when Dean said I could ride with him, I knew this was my chance to visit the sea."

The guard snorted and turned to his companion. "I wish something as simple as the sea excited me that much."

The other guard laughed. "The only thing I've seen you excited about is the ladies down on Velvet Street."

The first guard grinned. "And that's where I'll be heading when my shift is over."

They both laughed while waving the wagon forward.

As the wagon rolled past the gate, Dean looked at Jerrell with a frown. "How come you were suddenly talkin' all different?"

Restraining himself from an overt eye roll, Jerrell explained. "I spoke and acted the way the guards expected me to. It's easier than answering questions."

"Huh," Dean grunted. "If you say so."

"You can let me out here." Jerrell had endured the man long enough and preferred to avoid another frustrating dinner conversation.

Before the wagon entered a shadowy street, the driver pulled back on the reins, drawing the wagon to a halt, and Jerrell hopped out.

"Best of luck to you," Jerrell waved as he walked away.

People crowded the main street, most dressed as commoners and a few as servants for local businessmen or wizards. Everyone seemed to be going about their daily business – selling, purchasing, or bartering for food or goods. Jerrell came to an alley alongside an inn, the sign at the front depicting a hat with a plume and the words Feathered Cap Inn written below it. Hungry, Jerrell decided it was time for a hot meal.

Inside, the scent of roasted poultry greeted him, and he immediately felt satisfied with his choice. He followed a corridor past the kitchen and into a taproom where a vaulted ceiling was supported by heavy wooden posts and beams stained a dark brown. A brief scan of the room had him tally twenty-three people, fifteen of whom were men. Of the eight women, three appeared to work at the inn, two serving tables. Six men sat at the bar, a large woman working behind it. Nobody seemed to pay him much attention, nor did anyone appear threatening. However, Jace knew threats often arose where one might not expect them.

Selecting an open stool at the bar, he sighed as he sat and set his pack on the floor by his feet. He slapped his hand on the bar, and the big brunette behind it shot him a glance. Between two fingers, he held a half-silver. The woman came over and arched a brow.

"What'll it be?"

"Ale, a meal, and a room."

She held out her hand, palm up. When he dropped the coin into it, she spun around, grabbing a fresh mug. After filling it, she slid the mug in front of him as foam spilled down the side.

Jace lifted it, took a sip, and grinned. "My lips thank you."

The woman snorted and headed toward the kitchen. Mug in hand, Jace spun around and took a read of the room.

Four men sat at a table, leaning forward in hushed conversation. Their mugs sat untouched as the men focused on other things. *Whatever they are up to, it is most likely illegal*, he thought.

His gaze shifted to a group three tables down, below an open window. Two men and two women sat there, all eating, talking, and laughing. Deciding that the table was boring, Jerrell turned as the barkeep reappeared with a steaming plate of potatoes and half a chicken.

She set the plate in front of him. "When you are finished, I'll have one of the girls show you to your room."

Without a reply, Jerrell began eating. The food tasted better than anything he had eaten in days.

WITH HIS PACK stored safely in his room, Jerrell stepped out into the late afternoon sun. The street brought him to a square near the harbor gate. People surrounded the carts and wagons parked along the wall, purchasing goods that ranged from freshly caught fish to produce to meat pies. In the center of the square, the local Obelisk of Devotion loomed above the crowd.

To the east, Lionne Castle stood on a bluff overlooking the city, the pale ramparts bright in the light of the late afternoon sun. Much of the building was visible above the wall, with terraces and two towers easily sighted from anywhere within the city. Montague undoubtedly lived in the castle, but Jerrell needed to form a plan before paying the man a visit. *I need to know more about him.* The best way to do that, he decided, was to catch the ear of other local wizards.

A woman walked past with a wicker basket of fish. Jerrell caught her arm and turned her toward him as he flashed his most charming smile. "Pardon me, pretty lady."

The woman wore her brown hair up in a bun. Her appearance was rather plain, and she was clearly older than him, but she smoothed her dress with her free hand and smiled in return. "Can I help you?"

"I just arrived in the city and am seeking a buyer for a unique and expensive piece of jewelry. Can you tell me where I might find such a person?"

She pointed toward the coastline. "The largest estates lie in that direction, along the sea. Most are wizards, though."

"And where would these individuals dine?"

"I suggest you visit the Coastal Kitchen. With the prices they charge, only those with coin to burn eat there. You'll find it on the hillside just outside the eastern wall."

"Thank you." He touched her arm. "It is rare to find a pretty woman who is also kind."

She gave him a gracious smile. "My, you are sweet."

"Have a good evening, miss."

Jerrell walked away before the conversation went any further. It was one thing to use a touch of honey to obtain information; it was another to encourage her into believing he sought more than that.

He followed the street along the wall and came to a set of stairs. Climbing it, he passed through an arched opening in the wall and followed a hillside path overlooking the bay. Forty feet below, the surf crashed into rocks jutting above the water. Beyond it, aqua blue blanketed much of the bay before giving way to darker waters. A ship with full sails sped toward the harbor while gulls circled overhead.

The path continued uphill and brought him to a bluff where a curved road headed toward the castle in one direction and large hillside estates in the other. The nearest building had a red, clay-tiled roof with a rooftop veranda. Above the eaves of its covered porch was a white stone placard with the word Coastal carved in it.

Jerrell climbed onto the porch and stepped inside.

Round tables covered in white cloth filled the spacious dining room. The entire wall facing the sea was made of tall windows divided into diamond-shaped panes. Five of the tables were occupied, three by couples, the other two by quartets.

A man in a white coat approached Jerrell. "May I help you, sir?"

In a haughty tone, Jerrell said, "I have just arrived after a long voyage. I was told this establishment offered the finest food in Farrowen."

"We offer the finest dining, I assure you."

"First, I would like a brandy. Do you have a bar where I can relax?"

"Yes." The man gestured toward a stairwell, the steps covered in dark red carpet. "Head upstairs to our rooftop bar. The view, the drink, and the company are the best you will find in Lionne and beyond."

"Thank you, good sir." Jerrell held a silver to the man. "This is for your assistance."

The man bowed his head and pocketed the coin while Jerrell headed for the stairs, wondering what awaited him.

CHAPTER II
SEEK A WEAKNESS

The stairs took Jerrell up to a second story lounge where a couple in quiet conversation sat on a sofa sipping wine. The lounge was otherwise empty. A small, unoccupied bar stood to the other side while the corridor led to a pair of open doors.

Jerrell headed through the doors and stepped outside to a flat rooftop veranda surrounded by marble railings. The bar beside the door was shaded by an awning that extended from the roof. Beyond the bar, the round tables on the rooftop, and the railing, the sea sparkled over a hundred feet below.

Three people sat at the bar, two of them men in robes, the third a woman in a yellow dress. She laughed at something the man beside her said, her hand on his arm, giving Jerrell the impression that she was either in love or sought to ensnare the wizard.

He claimed a stool between the couple and the wizard at the far end of the bar.

A barkeep in a white coat walked up while drying a wine glass. "May I help you?"

"Yes. Farrowen red, please."

"A goblet or carafe?"

Jerrell glanced at the goblet of the man beside him, noting it was a quarter full of the red wine. "A carafe will do."

"That will be two silver pieces."

Despite the cost being twice what Jerrell expected, he reached into his pocket, withdrew a pair of silvers, and slid the coins across the bar. The man scooped them up and turned to the barrel on the counter behind him.

He filled a carafe, setting it and a goblet before Jerrell. "Enjoy."

Jerrell filled his cup and tapped on the shoulder of the man beside him. The wizard appeared roughly his own age. The man turned and arched a brow in question. "Yes?"

"I notice your drink is nearly empty. I have an entire carafe here and thought you might like a refill."

The man grinned. "Why, thank you."

Jerrell filled the man's cup and set the carafe between them on the bar. "My name is Jerrell. I just arrived in Lionne."

"Mine is Cannady."

"I assume you live here?"

"Yes." He gestured farther down the coast. "My family's estate is half a mile away, near the end of Shoreline Road." His brow furrowed. "What brings you to Lionne?"

"I have an office at the Marquithe Bureau of Trading and was hoping to broker a deal with High Wizard Montague."

"Montague?" Cannady sneered. "I can't stand that arrogant arse."

"Truly?" Jerrell sipped his wine to cover his grin. He set the goblet down. "It seems you know him."

"Yes. He and I grew up together and even attended the University at the same time. However, we never got on well. Like most people, I am put off by his self-entitled attitude."

"And this was before he rose to high wizard?"

"Oh, yes." The man paused to take a gulp of wine. "That is the most puzzling part."

"What is?"

"Like I said, we trained together at the University. More than once, he and I were paired up for duels of magic. Never once did he defeat me, and I am not particularly powerful with the Gift. Yet, he suddenly had the ability to destroy High Wizard Garue?" Resting his hand on his forehead, he said, "I don't understand how it is possible."

"I heard Montague has already had to defend his position numerous times."

"That's because, like me, most of the wizards in Lionne were certain Montague was a farce of a ruler. We discounted his victory over Garue as pure luck. First, my uncle, Lassiter, challenged him and was soundly destroyed. Then, my friend, Luis, took his chances and ended up dead, as did his older brother who sought vengeance, believing Montague had somehow cheated. The last was a wizard from Shear who thought Montague was an easier target than Gerald Wrenthal. They hauled his body out in pieces."

The story matched what Tarin had told him. "So this wizard somehow became more powerful?"

Cannady stared into his glass and nodded. "Much more powerful."

"And you don't like him."

"I hate him."

"In that case, perhaps you can help me."

The wizard looked up at Jerrell with glassy eyes. The sun had not yet set, but he was clearly already drunk. *His tongue wags freely, lubricated by wine.*

"While I intend to deal with the high wizard, I prefer to do so from a position of advantage. Perhaps he has a weakness I can exploit?"

"Hmm," Cannady rubbed his jaw. "Beside his arrogance, his biggest weakness is women."

"Women?"

"Montague perceives himself as some sort of idol and expects women to throw themselves at him. In the year since his rise, I'd say he has bedded three times as many women as he had in the prior fifteen years."

Jerrell smiled. The information had cost him only a few silver pieces, yet it offered distinct possibilities. "These women, do they have anything in common?"

The man emptied his wine goblet and set it down on the bar. "Well, I'd say they have poor taste in men."

The comment caused Jerrell to chuckle as he refilled the man's goblet. "I mean from a physical perspective. The ones you have seen, did they look similar in any way?"

Staring into space, Cannady frowned before nodding. "Breasts."

"I would certainly hope so."

"No." The wizard cupped his hands before his chest. "They were busty women. Every one of them."

"And their hair color?"

Cannady shrugged. "Brown, black, blonde...even a redhead or two."

Clapping the wizard on the back, Jerrell said, "Thank you. To show my appreciation, you can have the rest of my wine."

"Where are you going?"

"I need to plan my meeting and figure out how to get an audience with him."

"Hold on." The wizard slid his hand into his robes and fumbled around. He withdrew a folded parchment and held it toward Jerrell.

"What is this?"

"Montague is holding a party at the castle tomorrow evening. This will get you in."

Jerrell accepted the paper. "Thank you, but how will you get in if I have your invite?"

Cannady shook his head. "I'd rather drink piss than watch that arse gloat while women fawn over him."

Jerrell chuckled. "Enjoy your evening, Cannady. Perhaps we will meet again one day."

Beneath darkening skies, Jerrell rushed across the harbor-side square and stopped by a woman stacking empty baskets on a cart. In one basket was a lonely loaf of bread and crumbs indicating those that had already been sold.

"Excuse me, miss."

She turned toward him. "I've one loaf left if you've a copper."

"Tell you what, I'll take it for a silver if you can answer a question."

The woman wiped her brow and nodded. "I'll do my best."

"Can you direct me to a local wig maker?"

She gave him a level glare. "Do I look like I need a wig?"

"No. Not at all. I simply seek the information."

"All right, then." She pointed. "Take that street toward the inland gate. Turn left at the second intersection, and you'll find a shop on your right."

Jerrell held out a coin. "As promised."

She took it and passed him the loaf. "Come back tomorrow morning if you'd like a fresh, warm loaf."

He tore off a chunk and took a bite while heading down the street. Shadows surrounded him, the darkening sky highlighted by long, wispy, pink clouds.

When he reached the shop, the door was closed and locked, as he had feared. He pressed his face against the window and peered past a dozen wooden heads covered in hair – black, blonde, and brown, some with curls, others straight. Further back, he spied movement, spurring hope.

He pounded on the window. A shadow emerged from the back of the store. In the dim light, he spied a heavyset, middle-aged woman with a full head of blonde curls. She drew near the door and shouted, "The shop is closed! Come back tomorrow!"

The trip to Lionne had already cost Jerrell plenty, but his reward would be well worth it should he succeed.

He pulled out two gold coins and pressed them against the window. "I want to buy a wig. Tonight."

The woman frowned. "For two gold pieces?"

"Sell me a wig now, and they are yours."

She moved to the door, threw the bolt, and eased it open with her palm showing. "Put them in my hand."

"You aren't trying to rob me, are you?"

"I am taking care that you don't rob me. Give me the gold, tell me what you seek, and I will be back with your wig."

Jerrell dropped the coins in her hand. "I need a woman's wig. It must look elegant, as if she were dressed for a ball."

"What color?"

"Doesn't matter."

"It matters to me. What color is her skin. What about her eyes?"

"Her eyes are brown, and her skin is…like mine."

"Face shape?"

"Again, much like mine."

The shop owner appeared to examine him before closing the door. Moments later, the door opened, and she held out a black wig with piped curls. "This will do. I can't say why anyone would have a wig emergency, but I will take your gold if you will begone."

Jerrell accepted the wig and said, "Thank you."

The door closed, and he turned away, walking down the street. He examined the wig. It was the first step in his plan, but he would need more help to execute it.

He came to an intersection where a man in a sweaty tunic fumbled with a lantern on a post. A blue light flickered to life inside the lantern, and the man ran off toward the next intersection.

A door two buildings down opened, and a pair of men exited, both smiling, both dressed in bright tunics, tight breeches, and tall boots that marked them as sailors.

As they headed toward Jerrell, one man patted the other on the back. "She was a siren, that one. I expect she will haunt my dreams for years to come."

The other sailor replied, "Mine was pretty, but she appeared to lack interest, as if she was bored of my company."

Jerrell nodded to the sailors as they walked past him.

The first sailor said, "Perhaps you should have paid her more attention."

The other one snorted. "I already paid her in silver. That should earn her attention."

"Even when paid, a woman wants to feel like a woman, Bart."

The men's voices faded as their forms blended with the thickening shadows.

Jerrell turned from them and approached the house they had exited. A red sign beside the door displayed Mariam's Place.

"Perfect," Jerrell said to himself.

He dug into his pocket and counted out his remaining coin, finding two gold pieces, eleven silvers, and six coppers remaining. With a gold piece in hand, he climbed the steps and knocked on the door.

It opened to reveal a young woman in a form-fitting red dress. Tall and thin with long blonde hair and blue eyes, most would call her attractive. "Hello," she said in a sultry voice. "Come in, sweetie."

Jerrell followed her into a sitting room. Four women occupied the room, along with one man. He was tall with a brimmed hat in his hands, which he was kneading nervously. Judging by his clothing, Jerrell assumed he was a farmer.

"Do you see something you like?" his escort asked.

Jerrell examined the women. Two were significantly older than him, the others lacked the curves he preferred. "Hello, ladies. While I consider you all attractive, I am seeking someone special. She should be..." He stopped in mid-sentence when another woman walked into the lounge.

She stood his own height with brown hair and blue eyes that matched the blue in her dress. Her olive skin had the smoothness of youth, but the intensity in her gaze spoke of someone intelligent and experienced. Most notably, her slim waist accentuated significant curves that stirred his blood.

"Oh, I like you," he said. "What is your name?"

She examined him from head to toe while sliding her hand down her hip. "I am Hedra."

"Hello, Hedra. Are you free for the evening...and most of tomorrow?"

She arched a brow. "That will cost you."

He sidled up to her and opened his palm, displaying two gold coins that glittered in the light of the lantern. "Will this do?"

Hedra snatched the coins and smiled. "You have me to yourself until dinner tomorrow."

"Good," he grinned back. "You will earn that gold, but not in the way you think."

CHAPTER 12
A USE FOR GRAPEFRUIT

"Pucker your lips," Hedra said, pursing her own. "Like this."

Jerrell did as instructed, sticking his lips out so the woman could rub a glossy substance on them.

She stood back and tilted her head, her eyes narrowed in thought. "You make a surprisingly pretty girl, Jerrell. Perhaps I could get you a job here. We sometimes get patrons asking for pretty boys."

"No, thank you. I really wouldn't enjoy that type of thing." He held his hands up in apology. "No offense."

The woman shrugged. Dressed in a thin shift, the simple motion oozed sensuality and heated his blood. "I am not offended. I have a job I do well, and it earns me a good living. Sometimes, I even enjoy it."

He shifted closer and placed his hand on her hip. "You seemed to enjoy yourself last night."

She raised an eyebrow. "All my partners believe the same. Sometimes it is a performance. Sometimes it is the truth. How do you know which applied to you?"

He chuckled. "Fair enough. Just to prevent any unnecessary wounds to my pride, I'll believe your affection was earned."

Hedra turned and pulled a dress from the wardrobe, then handed it to him. "Put this on. It will be a bit snug at the waist, but it should fit." While the dress would not be returned, the gold Jerrell had given her more than covered its replacement.

Jerrell ran his hands down the corset he wore, his chest filled out with a pair of grapefruit. "Are you calling me fat?" he said in a high-pitched voice as he held his hand to his cheek in dramatic fashion.

She laughed. "Not at all. In fact, you are one of the fittest men who has ever visited my room. However, even a thin young man such as yourself has a wider waist than a fit woman."

He slid his legs into the dress and was reminded of the smooth skin on his shins. It felt odd to have his arms and legs shaved, but Hedra had insisted and had proven skilled at doing it for him. It was among numerous activities he had enjoyed during their morning bath.

When he pulled the dress up and slid his arms through, he found the half-sleeves tight on his biceps. The dress design left his shoulders and upper chest exposed. That had been shaved as well.

He spun around. "Will you button me up?"

"Can't do it yourself?" Her hands worked the buttons as she spoke. "Perhaps all men should do this once or twice, just to gain a better appreciation for the pains we women go through to look beautiful."

The comment earned her a snort. "I saw how you looked this morning, without makeup, jewelry, or fancy garments. I doubt you ever look anything less than gorgeous."

She finished and turned him around, running her hand from his shoulder across his upper chest, before leaning in and kissing him. "Your words are smooth, Jerrell. I'll give you that."

He smiled. "You kissed a girl. How did it feel?"

With an arched brow, she gave him a sideways look. "You think that was the first time?"

"Oh, *now* I am curious."

Hedra shook her head. "A story for another time. You hired me to help you, and we are finished. Take a look in the mirror."

He crossed the room and stared into the oval-shaped mirror. The person staring back at him was unfamiliar, save for the eyes.

His mess of dark brown hair was hidden beneath a black wig, piled at the top with curls hanging down his upper back. The rouge applied to his clean-shaven cheeks made his face appear narrow. His eyes looked bolder, a result of the dark lines of kohl. The red gloss brightened his lips while making them appear fuller. Between his fruit-stuffed corset and the padding strapped to his hips, he filled out the striking red dress in an impressive fashion.

Hedra appeared behind him and reached around, holding the mask before his face so he could see through the eyeholes.

"This is what they wear?" he asked.

"Yes. Masquerade balls are a current trend among the wizards, adding an air of mystery to the event. You must admit, it will be difficult for anyone to guess you are a man by appearance alone." She frowned. "You do know how to walk, right?"

Hedra sashayed across the room with one hand on her hip, her backside shifting from side to side in a fluid, sensual motion. Jerrell had to force himself to pay attention to how she walked rather than merely enjoying the view.

He followed at the same slow pace, doing his best to emulate her.

She laughed. "That was a bit much, but it will do. Just be sure to keep an easy pace, as if you own the moment and wish to draw everyone's atten-tion." She handed him white gloves and a pair of slippers. "These are Daniella's. She has the largest hands and feet among the girls here. I hope they fit."

Since Jerrell's height was modest for a man and average for a woman, finding a dress that fit was not difficult. The size of his feet was another matter altogether. He sat on her bed and pulled the first slipper on. His foot barely fit, and his toes cramped. Sighing in resignation, he forced his foot into the other and glanced toward the window.

The sunlight had faded as dusk claimed the streets of Lionne.

"It's growing dark. I had best be going."

Hedra walked him to the door, opening it for him. "I wish you well."

"Thanks, Hedra." He took her hand. "I know I can trust your discretion."

She smiled and held a black shawl toward him. "Discretion is the soul of my job. Loose lips shorten a whore's career. If I shared stories of the men who have come through this door, I would surely be dead by now."

Jerrell accepted the shawl and draped it across his shoulders as he descended the stairs. He passed through the lounge while slipping his hands into the gloves. Five women sat in the room, two of whom were occupying male customers. Both men eyed Jerrell as he strolled past and tested his womanly walk. Glancing over his shoulder, he saw the men staring at his backside, which gave him an odd mixture of discomfort and satisfaction.

Stepping outside the brothel, Jerrell climbed into the waiting carriage. He had paid the driver to pick up a brunette at dusk and given him directions to take her to the castle. The man was to ask no questions and had been paid extra for his troubles.

The carriage lurched into motion and eased down the dark streets of Lionne. Jerrell pulled the curtain back and stared out the window, watching the city slide past.

The foot traffic had thinned, and enchanted lanterns illuminated each street corner with soft blue light. At the second intersection, the carriage turned and passed through the eastern gate. The wagon soon began climbing upward, navigating the switchbacks to the high wizard's castle. Situated at the top of the bluff, warm light in the windows made the building appear like a giant overlooking the city. The man currently holding the castle undoubtedly believed that was the case. Jerrell dropped the curtain and sat back, considering what he knew of the high wizard as he tied the mask to his head.

Stories of Montague had helped Jerrell devise his plan. While the wizard might be skilled with magic, the power had gone to his head. His own pride and lustful nature were his weaknesses, and Jerrell sought to capitalize on them to get what he needed.

The carriage reached the gate outside the castle and stopped with a lurch.

The driver handed Jerrell's invitation to the waiting guards, who read it and peered inside the window before waving the driver along. Moments later, the carriage stopped again, and the door opened.

A man dressed in a dark blue coat over a white doublet bowed. "Good evening, Wizardess." He held his hand toward Jerrell, who took it gently before climbing out. The man gestured toward the open castle doors. "The party is inside."

"Thank you," Jerrell said in a high voice as he handed the man his invitation.

Swaying his hips, Jerrell climbed the stairs and entered the castle. He paused inside the doorway to scan the crowd.

A vaulted, mural-covered ceiling capped an entrance hall three stories tall.

The massive chandelier hanging over the room held dozens of lit candles. Wizards and wizardesses mingled in the space – the men dressed in robes of various colors, the women in gowns. Masks, decorated with sequins that sparkled when they moved, covered the upper half of the guests' faces.

Numerous men in the room turned to Jerrell, their gazes sweeping the length of his body. He ignored them. He only sought one man. As though his head were on a swivel, Jerrell scanned the room, stopping when a man with dark hair descended the stairs at the far end of the hall. Dressed in a silvery robe with shimmering stitching and a dark blue sash, the man was difficult to miss. His squinty eyes and narrow lips detracted from his appearance, but Jerrell was aware of the man's ego.

Montague reached the floor and shook a wizard's hand, nodding as he greeted him and the wizardess on the man's arm. Jerrell began walking across the floor, focused on Montague, drawing the high wizard's gaze. The man drank in the view as Jerrell advanced with slow, easy steps and swaying hips.

When he reached Montague, he touched the man's hand as Hedra had taught him. "High Wizard, I thank you for inviting me." His finger ran up Montague's arm, as if he could not resist doing so. "Your home is exquisite, nearly holding up to the image of the master of the castle," Jerrell said in his best sultry voice.

Montague smiled. "Welcome to Castle Montague." He tilted his head and narrowed his already squinty eyes. "I didn't get your name."

"Oh, sorry," Jace held his gloved hand to his chest, purposely drawing his attention there. "I am Terissa Wrenthal, from Shear. I have come in my father's stead."

Wrenthal still hides in his castle for fear of others discovering his malady. Jerrell prayed Montague did not know Terissa well enough to note the differences between his appearance and hers – darker hair, broader shoulders, a fuller bust and hips.

The smile returned to the wizard's face as he took her hand, bent over, and kissed it. "Ah. The eldest of the legendary Wrenthal girls. I am graced by your presence. While it is disappointing your father could not join me, I believe I have come out ahead in the exchange."

Jerrell smiled coyly, knowing he had the man on the hook. A few drinks, a bit of dancing, and just enough physical contact would reel him in.

MONTAGUE OPENED a pair of oak doors with a flourish, revealing his sprawling bedchamber. "Here we are, as promised." He waved his hand while rubbing his fingers together. Jerrell sensed the tingle of magic as flame bloomed from candles on both nightstands and the table in the sitting area. "This is where the magic happens." He laughed while escorting Jerrell in, the pair walking arm in arm.

Jerrell giggled in his high voice while playfully hitting the man. "Oh, you nasty man."

"I can do nasty." Montague waved his arm, and the door slammed closed.

He gripped Jerrell by the hips and leaned in for an unexpected kiss. Jerrell had no choice but to comply or risk exposing himself. Montague's lips were surprisingly soft, and Jerrell had to admit, the man was adept at kissing. Finally, Jerrell pushed him away and flashed a coy smile.

"Do you mind if I wash up?" Jerrell asked. "A woman must properly prepare herself."

"Of course, my dear." Montague gestured past her. "The washroom is through those doors."

Jerrell walked toward the room, forcing himself not to rush. The remaining hair on his arms stood on end as the candles in the room ahead of him lit up in another display of Montague's casual use of magic.

As soon as he was safely in the washroom, Jerrell closed the door and moved to the vanity, where a bowl waited beside a pitcher of clean water and a towel. From between the two grapefruit on his chest, he pulled out a vial and slid it into his left glove, uncapping it with the vial facing upward when his hand was at his side. The mirror in front of him reflected a woman who was more nervous than she appeared. Montague's repeated use of magic had reminded Jerrell of the risk involved. Any wizard was dangerous, but the man outside the door was a high wizard – one who had killed his predecessor and four would-be challengers in the past year.

He took a deep breath, gathered his courage, and shifted to the door. When he opened it, he was caught unprepared for what awaited him.

Montague had shed his robes and stood completely naked, save for a gold bracelet secured around one ankle. The man was even thinner than Jerrell had suspected. Judging by the sight before him, Jerrell wondered what exactly had fed the man's ego, because he was not impressed.

"My, you are quick," Jerrell said.

"Come, join me." Montague gestured toward the bed. "I will prove I am far from quick."

Jerrell observed a decanter filled with brandy and a pair of glasses on a table beside the wall. "Yes, of course." He walked to the table. "But first, a drink."

Jerrell pulled the stopper from the decanter and poured two glasses. He dropped the stopper on the table and fumbled to pick it up with one gloved hand while the other hovered over one of the glasses and tipped up, allowing the liquid in the vial to pour into the brandy. Montague's hands gripped Jerrell's hips, and the man began kissing his neck. After hurriedly capping the decanter, Jerrell turned and handed Montague the tainted glass of brandy.

"A toast," Jerrell said in his sultry voice. "To High Wizard Montague. May you someday take over for Lord Malvorian."

Montague smiled. "I can drink to that." He then slammed back the half-filled glass as if it were water.

Jerrell took a sip and tried to back away, but the man was too aggressive. He pulled Jerrell close with one hand pressed against his lower back, the other groping Jerrell's chest as his mouth went to his neck.

The man stopped and pulled back, his face twisting into a frown. With both hands, he squeezed the fake breasts, and Jerrell knew trouble had found him. Before he could react, weaves of magic wrapped about his wrists and ankles, lifting him into the air. His dress suddenly tore open down the front, followed by his corset. Both grapefruit fell to the floor, along with Jerrell's clothing, leaving him in only his wig, smallclothes, slippers, and white gloves.

"I don't suppose you find this funny?" Jerrell asked in his normal voice.

CHAPTER 13

A STOLEN PRIZE

Held immobile, Jerrell found himself facing a furious and naked high wizard.

"You!" Montague roared in outrage. "How dare you!"

The wizard flung his hand open, and invisible ropes of magic launched Jerrell upward. He slammed against the ten-foot ceiling, banging the back of his head and back. The wig fell to the floor. He blinked at the pain in his head and stars in his eyes while wheezing for air.

Suspended, his vision cleared, and he found the wizard holding his own head.

"What..." Montague wobbled and fell to one knee. "What did you do to me?"

The wizard fell face-first to the floor, and his magic faltered. Jerrell plummeted. He landed on the man's back, the impact driving the wind from Jerrell's lungs. Gasping for air, he rolled off the naked man and held his stomach. As his breath returned, he crawled forward and lifted the man's foot. He squinted at the ring of gold around Montague's ankle, recalling it from memory.

After stealing the bracelet from an ancient castle over a year earlier,

Jerrell had sold it for ten gold coins while passing through Lionne. Soon afterward, Montague had risen in power.

The bracelet must, somehow, augment his abilities. No wonder Gurgan wants it so badly. Jerrell chuckled at the realization that he was about to yield a second solid profit from the same artifact, one he had first obtained while seeking a different artifact. The irony made him smile while he searched for the bracelet's release. It took him a moment to locate it, and when the bracelet unclasped, he slid it off Montague's ankle. On the inside, he spotted the scrawling silver of the enchantment.

Bracelet in hand, Jerrell ran to Montague's closet and found an unassuming dark blue robe. It was too long, so he hiked it up the best he could and used a yellow sash to tie it at the waist. He then went to the washroom, washed the makeup from his face, and rubbed the remainder away with a towel.

Once back in the bedroom, he stopped to consider what to do with the man lying face down on the rug. Inspired, he hoisted Montague onto the bed and propped him up against the headboard. He used strips of the ruined dress to tie the man's wrists to the bedposts and another to gag him. The entire time, Montague remained unconscious. Jerrell wondered how long the sleeping drug would last.

When he had finished, Jerrell collected the two grapefruit and approached the doors, peering out before stepping through the doorway and closing the doors behind him. The third floor was empty. The ruckus of the party continued from downstairs. He descended past the second story and stopped a few steps above the crowd.

"The high wizard!" Jerrell shouted. "He has fallen ill. You must hurry!"

Servants and guests rushed up the stairs, pushing past him.

Whistling, Jerrell walked through the crowd and out the door, juggling the two grapefruit while the enchanted bracelet remained hidden safely inside his robes. From inside came cries of surprise followed by laughter. *They have found the high wizard.* A grin split his face as he nodded to the confused carriage driver and climbed inside, knocking four times to signal their departure.

With a snap of the reins, the carriage began the trek back to the city.

Jerrell would be gone early the next morning and on his way to Eleighton with his prize. Wizard Gurgan would reward him as agreed, and the legend of Jerrell Landish would grow to become even more impressive.

"What a wonderful evening," Jerrell said as he stared out a window overlooking the moonlit harbor.

IT WAS A DECIDEDLY SPRING-LIKE DAY. The air smelled sweet, the sun felt warm, and the birds chirped in excitement. Riding a horse he had purchased with the last of his coin, Jerrell left Lionne at daybreak with a full pack of provisions secured to the saddle.

Rolling hillsides, some covered by vineyards, others by trees, moved past while Jerrell rode south. As the miles passed and he traveled farther from both Lionne and the coast, his surroundings evolved. Open fields of yellow grass covered big stretches, bound by thick tree lines and occasional farms.

The day passed slowly, paced by the trot of his steed, and by the time he reached the fork that led toward Eleighton, it was mid-afternoon. Turning southwest, he guided his horse along the paved, uphill road. Mountains loomed in the distance. While he had never visited Eleighton, the map he carried showed the city nestled within that mountain range. It was a shorter ride than the one from Marquithe to Lionne, but it was clear he would not reach those mountains until sometime the next day. Thus, with the sun licking the mountains on the western horizon, he pulled his horse off the road and into a small clearing surrounded by trees and bordering a trickling brook. It seemed a good enough place to sleep, especially with the brook providing fresh water for his mount to drink and for him to refill his water skins.

He decided to forgo a fire since the weather was mild. Instead, he wrapped his cloak around himself and leaned against the trunk of an oak. Stars emerged while the waning light gave way to night. Exhaustion claimed him, and he slipped into the world of dreams.

THE CRUNCH of a footstep startled Jerrell. His eyes opened to find a bearded man standing over him. With his head still thick with the fog of sleep, Jerrell's reactions proved a beat too slow to avoid the man's kick. The toe of a hard boot slammed into his ribs, cracking them, and driving the wind from his lungs.

On instinct, Jerrell reached for his dagger, but the man stepped on his forearm, pinning it to the ground and eliciting a groan of pain.

The man squatted and held a dagger of his own to Jerrell's neck. "Remain still or I'll slice you from ear to ear."

The stench of his breath caused Jerrell to gag, which was difficult since he was still trying to reclaim his air. "What do you want?"

"My friends and I own this road and require a tithe from anyone passing through."

Other men dressed in dark clothing emerged from the shadows. Two held crossbows locked, loaded, and aimed at Jerrell. Four others wore swords at their hips. An eighth man gripped a quarterstaff, leaning on it while he approached, stopped at Jerrell's side, and stared down at him with the staff ready.

The bracelet is in the saddlebag, Jerrell thought in alarm. "I have no gold coins," he snapped.

The bandit holding a blade against Jerrell's neck flashed a humorless smile. "We accept silver and even copper, along with items of value." The man reached down and drew Jerrell's dagger, eyeing it as he lifted it into the moonlight. "This, for instance, will fetch a pretty coin on its own."

If you knew of its enchantment, you would realize it is worth far more than you expect. Still, it did not carry the value of the bracelet. "Take it. Just let me live."

"Perry," the man squatting before Jerrell said, "bring the rope."

"Got it, Jax." One of the swordsmen approached, uncoiling a rope. He handed one end to the leader and rounded the tree. After four revolutions, he stopped and tied the ends together, binding Jerrell to the trunk with his arms at his sides. Only then did Jax rise and step back.

He pointed toward Jerrell's horse. "Check his pack and the saddlebags."

Two of the men approached the horse. One removed Jerrell's pack and began digging through it. The other opened the flaps on the saddle for inspection.

"The pack only holds food and supplies, Jax," said the man with the pack.

"There are only two water skins in this one," the man checking the horse added. He circled the horse and dug into the other saddlebag. "What's this?" He removed a bundle wrapped in a black wig, held it up in the moonlight, and laughed. "It looks like we've got us a man who enjoys dressing as a woman."

The other bandits laughed while the man pulled a dress out from the pack. "Look at the gown he has as well." The comment spurred another round of laughter.

An object fell from the dress, briefly reflecting moonlight before it disappeared in the long grass.

"What was that?" Jax asked.

The other bandit tossed the red dress and wig aside before squatting. He dug in the grass and stood, holding a circular metal object in the moonlight. "It's a bracelet."

Jax stalked over to the man. "Give me that." He tore it away and examined it in the moonlight. "I will take this myself." The man walked over to Jerrell, glowering down at him. "You told us you were broke."

"I said I had no gold coins. It was not a lie."

"But you said nothing about the bracelet."

Jerrell considered the response and dropped his gaze in feigned shame. "You saw the wig and the dress. Would you have said anything about it?"

The weight of the bandit's glare was palpable; Jerrell worried that the man might kill him anyway. Instead, the man laughed. "No, I suppose I'd do anything to hide that bit of information."

"Untie his horse. We will take it with us." Turning from Jerrell, the man waved to his companions. "Let's be off. Should this sissy somehow free himself, we've little to fear from a man who prances around in a dress and a wig."

The bandits laughed as they and the trailing horse walked off into the night.

Jerrell struggled against his bonds, bending his wrist and stretching his fingers while attempting to reach the hilt hidden just below the cuff of his sleeve.

A shout echoed in the darkness, followed by the sound of hooves that slowly faded into the night. "Horses. They had horses, and I didn't hear them approach." This was unlike Jerrell; he was usually a light sleeper. His adventures in Lionne and day in the saddle had exhausted him more than he had realized.

Grunting, he tried harder to reach the hilt, his fingers grazing its edge. When that did not work, he twisted and shimmied until he was able to move his arms around his hips and into his lap. Wrists crossed, his right hand was able to draw the blade hidden in his left sleeve. He held the knife edge up and began to saw at the rope. It separated with a snap, and he cut at the next bond. Moments later, he had freed himself. He stood with one hand pressed against his side. The bruised ribs hurt. His food, water, and belongings had been stolen, but a coal of anger simmered in his gut. He squatted beside the river, scooped a few handfuls of water into his mouth, and then set off after the bandits.

IN THE MOONLIGHT, the road looked like a pale ribbon winding through the thick shadows of the surrounding woods. When moving downhill, Jerrell ran, allowing gravity to push him along until he reached an upslope, where he would slow to a walk. Again and again, he repeated this cycle, constantly searching for signs and listening for sounds that might tell him where the bandits were camped.

He came to a rise far more extensive than the others. His legs grew weary as he continued to climb. The road wound back and forth, forcing Jerrell along switchbacks, before it leveled and began a descent into a wooded valley. To his right, a gray outcropping of rock stuck up from the hillside and jutted out toward the valley. Upon spying the pale rock, Jerrell waded through the underbrush and scrambled up the boulder. He walked to the edge, which overlooked a drop of eighty feet and then met a downslope. From his perch, he surveyed the vista before him.

Wooded hillsides bordered the valley on all sides, making it approximately five miles across. Here and there were gaps that ran north and south along the valley floor. The distant rush of water, along with the dark gaps, informed him that a river flowed below. He spied the pale strip of the road approaching the dark stripe of water, where the road came to a bridge. To the north side of the road, not far from the river was a small clearing with a flickering, amber light.

"A fire. At last." He exhaled in relief, happy to know he had not passed the bandits in the night.

Hope gave him renewed energy. He climbed down from the rock and walked down the road, knowing stealth would serve him better than speed now that his target was in sight.

CHAPTER 14

AMBUSH

Having grown up in the city, Jerrell was no woodsman. Although he lacked knowledge of how to deal with elements unique to a forest, such as avoiding the crunch of fallen leaves beneath his feet, he knew stealth required patience. Thus, he made a broad circle around the bandit camp, looking for the best angle to approach. In the thick shadows of the woods, the loop took time and required care to avoid alerting the men to his presence.

On the side of the camp opposite from the road, he found a dirt path that ran along the top of the riverbank parallel to the water. Wearing his dark cloak and hood, he crept along the shadowy path, careful to avoid surrounding branches and brush. The steady rush of the river helped to disguise his footsteps.

Through a gap in the forest, the camp came into view.

Knee-high grass covered much of a clearing a hundred feet across. The horses were tethered to a fallen tree on one side of the clearing while a bank leading down to the river bordered the other. In the middle of the area, a fire pit smoldered, the flames close to dying out. The dark shapes of men sleeping on the ground surrounded the fire. A low rumble of snoring came from one of the men; it was the only sound apart from the water. Remaining silent and still, Jerrell watched the scene for a few minutes to ensure everyone was asleep.

As he was about to approach the camp, a shadow moved in the trees between the clearing and the road. The shadow approached the camp and stepped into the moonlight. The man was tall and lean with a scabbard on his hip. He slowly rounded the camp, briefly looking down at the sleeping men before staring into the shadowy forest. *A sentry. They must rotate watch.* Jerrell considered sneaking over to the horses to search the saddlebags for his dagger and bracelet, but if anything went awry, he'd have eight armed men after him. *No, better to eliminate them.* It would be tricky, but the element of surprise would be on his side if he could quietly deal with the sentry.

Jerrell waited until the man passed his location and continued along the edge of the clearing. With the man's back to him, Jerrell eased himself backward, down the trail, until he came to the thick trunk of a towering pine. He squatted and felt around, his fingers finding a rock that fit in his fist and another twice that size. Rising, he purposely stepped into the shrub beside him, ensuring the small branches cracked beneath his boot.

The man circling the clearing spun around at the sound and stared in Jerrell's direction. He crossed the clearing and peered into the forest. Sensing the man's hesitancy, Jerrell cracked another branch under his foot. The man drew his sword and held it before him while creeping down the trail.

Hiding with his back pinned to the tree trunk, Jerrell listened in tense silence. The sound of footsteps slowly drew closer. Just when he expected the man to pass the tree, Jerrell tossed the smaller rock back toward the camp. It passed through some leaves and then landed with a thud, causing the bandit to spin around in alarm. Jerrell stepped out from behind the tree and leapt. As he came down, he smashed the bigger rock into the back of the man's head. The bandit stumbled as Jerrell wrapped his arm beneath the taller man's armpit and around his chest. The bandit's body went limp, and his blade fell to the dirt. Jerrell slowly lowered the dead bandit to the ground.

Standing over the man, Jerrell stood still until his breath calmed. Still gripping the big rock, he crept toward the camp, where the snoring continued. Hood raised, he stepped into the moonlight. Seven silhouettes lay around the hot coals. Nobody moved. Just like the sentry, Jerrell circled the camp while surveying the area.

Beside two of the men were crossbows, bolts loaded, launch arms locked back. Taking careful steps, he approached a snoring man, squatted, and retrieved the crossbow lying beside him. He then stepped over the man and stopped beside another bandit, who cradled his crossbow as he slept. Gathering his courage, Jerrell prepared himself. He would have little time once the chaos began.

Closing his eyes briefly, he thought, *Luck, don't fail me now*. Opening his eyes, he took aim with the crossbow and pulled the trigger. The bolt shot through the man's thigh, pinning it to the ground. The man's eyes flashed open while his mouth gaped in pain. The man reacted by pulling the trigger on his crossbow, and the bolt shot into the back of a bandit lying ten feet away. Jerrell raised the crossbow and flipped it around before thrusting it into the wounded man's forehead, knocking him out.

A bandit lying just a stride from Jerrell bolted up into a sitting position, spied Jerrell, and shouted, "Wake up! We are under—"

The startled bandit's sentence was cut short when Jerrell rammed the butt of the crossbow into his face, snapping his head back.

The others woke from the noise. When the man with the broken nose stumbled to his feet, Jerrell threw the crossbow at him and then burst into a run, following the bow as the man dodged it. The distraction allowed Jerrell to land a kick, his heel striking the bandit in the chest. The bandit fell back, tripped over the rocks ringing the fire, and fell into the hot coals. His clothing burst on fire and he screamed. He burst into a run past Jerrell and headed straight toward the riverbank. Orange flames streaked behind him as he launched himself into the river. By then, the remaining four men were in motion.

Jerrell threw the rock and struck a man in the side of his head as he tried to rise. The man fell to his side with a hand to his bloodied scalp. With his hands now empty, Jerrell backed away hastily while the four bandits spread out.

"Look here. It appears our little girly man has a spine after all," Jax said as he held a longsword before him. "Let's sever that spine."

Jerrell squatted and waited, his hands gripping the tops of his boots, his thumbs resting on the hilts hidden inside them.

One of the bandits appeared worried. "I think he killed Koen, Gray, and Forrester."

The one with the bloodied head added, "And where is Hollis? He was supposed to be on watch."

Jax snarled. "Will you two stop your whining and just kill this bastard?"

"Bastard? That is hurtful." Jerrell watched them closely. "I never asked you to tie me to a tree and steal my belongings. However, I can be a reasonable man. Give me back what you stole, and I will let you live."

The bandit with the quarterstaff snarled and came at Jerrell, the staff spinning in his hands as he twisted from side to side. When the bandit drew close, he shifted his weight to the right and his staff rose for a downward strike. Jerrell leapt sideways, barely avoiding the blow as he released a throwing blade. The knife buried in the attacker's sternum as the staff slammed down on the ground. Staggering, the attacker stumbled to his knees with one hand around the hilt jutting from his torso. The man toppled over as Jerrell stood with another knife ready.

"He killed Puck!" one bandit exclaimed.

Another said, "And where'd the knives come from?"

"Shut up, you two." Jax waved his sword toward Jerrell. "Puck was stupid to go rushing in like that. We outnumber him, so let's spread out and attack at the same time."

The three men parted, each holding a sword and eyeing Jerrell who backed away until his heel found air. He stopped and glanced backward to find himself on the precipice of the steep downslope. Fifteen feet below, white foam bubbled around the river rapids.

Jax snickered. "We've got him now, boys."

Jerrell eyed each of the men, one circling to his right and another to the left while Jax blocked the route straight ahead. They were only five strides away. "This is your last chance. Return my belongings or suffer like the others."

"Don't listen to him," Jax snapped. "Kill him!"

Before the three bandits could rush in, Jerrell drew the blades from his sleeves, cocked, and threw both at the bandit to his left. The man dodged the first blade but caught the other in his shoulder. Jerrell charged toward the wounded man while the other two launched into action. He grabbed the staggering bandit's arm and pulled while spinning around, sending the man sprawling to the ground. A charging bandit swung a wild swipe as he tripped over his fallen comrade. To avoid the fatal strike, Jerrell leapt backward and landed on his backside.

Jax rushed in with an overhead chop. Jerrell rolled to dodge the attack and went over the riverbank lip as the blade struck the ground in a spray of dirt. Gravity caused Jerrell to slide and roll down the steep bank, his body breaking the branches of shrubs, which scraped his exposed skin. After spinning two full rotations, Jerrell lunged and grabbed hold of a tree root. His body swung around as the slope inverted, leaving him dangling from the root sticking out from a cavity of eroded shoreline. Just below, dark water rushed past a boulder jutting up from the river's surface. Hand over hand, he lowered himself the last couple feet, his boots finding safe footing on the boulder.

Since the earthen riverbank and shrubs along it blocked the view above, he could not see Jax or the other surviving bandits. However, their voices came from above, barely audible above the rush of the rapids.

A bandit asked, "Did he fall in the river?"

"I didn't hear a splash." Jax replied.

"Where is he?"

"You two, go down there and check."

"I just pulled a knife from my shoulder," one said.

The other added, "Why me?"

Jax growled, "I lead this band. Do it, or I will kill you myself."

Jerrell pulled his cloak around him and leaned into the shadows of the bank to hide himself. The sounds of broken branches and grunts came from above, slowly growing closer.

Jax called down, "Do you see him?"

"Not yet." The other voice was much closer.

Chunks of earth fell from the slope and plopped into the water to Jerrell's right. He pulled his hood back, reached behind his neck, and drew the blade he had hidden in his coat. It was his last knife, so he intended to make it count.

The sounds of the bandit coming down the riverbank grew louder. Then, a boot appeared, stepping on a root three feet from Jerrell. He gripped the knife and slammed it down, point first into the man's foot. His howl echoed into the night. When Jerrell yanked the blade free, the man jerked his foot away, slipped, and shrieked as he grappled for the man beside him, but it was too late. One pulled the other with him as they both plunged into the water. The current swept them away, flailing and crying for help. Their cries grew quieter until they were gone.

Silence loomed around him, and Jerrell considered what Jax would do next. Of the three options – come down the bank after him, wait at the top until he appeared, or hop on a horse and ride off – he suspected the man was all bluster and likely to behave like a coward when his cohorts were not there to witness it. Thus, he began hopping from rock to rock toward the bridge, hoping to find an easier way up. Shouts came from above, followed by the rumble of hooves. A moment later, a horse appeared on the arched bridge and raced across it at a gallop.

"Crap."

Unwilling to let the man get away, Jerrell slid his remaining blade into his boot and began scrambling up the steep slope, pulling himself up by grabbing hold of shrubs and digging his boots into the ground. He reached the top and raced across the quiet campsite. The horses were all gone, but Jax had ridden only one, which meant he had chased the others away to make things more difficult for Jerrell.

He spun around and found two of the bandits stirring, the men groaning as they fought to regain their faculties. Jerrell raced past them, pulled throwing blades from two men, picked up two more blades from the ground, and then ran to the road, where he headed in the direction opposite the bridge while holding tightly to the hope that one of the horses might have stopped after a short run.

A quarter mile later, he came upon a horse munching on a patch of tall grass along the side of the road. Slowing, he approached the steed at an easy walk to avoid startling it. When he drew close, he realized it was his own mount.

In a crooning tone, he said, "Hello, Inky." It was the name he had given the horse due to her black coat. "It's me, Jerrell." He scooped up the reins, hooked a boot in a stirrup, and threw his leg over the saddle. "I hope you are well rested, because we have a bandit to catch."

With a flick of the reins, a nudge of his knees, and a shouted "hi-yah," the horse burst into a gallop and raced down the moonlit road.

CHAPTER 15
ELEIGHTON

After galloping back to the bridge, Jerrell slowed his horse to a trot. He scanned the surrounding woods as he strained to pick up any sound. He saw no signs of Jax but worried the man might attempt a surprise attack. Tense and alert, he continued for another hour without spotting or hearing anything. Finally, he heard the low rush of water. Rounding a bend, another bridge came into view. Beyond it was a village, still dark and sleepy, although the hour was now closer to sunrise than sunset. At the foot of the bridge, he drew his horse to a stop and considered the situation. He closed his eyes and imagined himself as Jax.

Startled awake in the middle of the night, a single man had entered his camp, dispatched all seven of his companions, and forced him to flee. Jax would be tired and likely believed Jerrell was still on foot. The village was eight miles from the campsite, which would also give the man a sense that he had created enough distance to make this a safe place to rest. Like Jerrell, he would be tired and was unlikely to continue on through the night. *He is here. Somewhere.*

Choosing stealth, Jerrell slid off his horse and led her over to a fallen tree, where he secured the reins to a branch.

Patting the mare on the neck, he whispered, "Rest here, Inky. I'll be back once I recover my stolen items."

He crossed the bridge and slowed as he entered the village, which consisted of six buildings clustered near the road and a mill built on the riverbank. Beside the largest structure stood stables and a fenced courtyard with four wagons parked inside. A sign mounted above the door gave Jerrell the impression it was an inn, but the shadows made the sign illegible. *The inn is dark, and its owner and occupants asleep, so Jax would have gone elsewhere. Besides, he probably believed it would be the most likely place for me to visit.*

Attempting to enter an occupied house would have risked alerting the occupant, so Jax would have sought out an unoccupied place to sleep. That left only the mill and the building in the woods as likely hiding spots. Jerrell chose the mill first, creeping toward it beneath the moonlight. He ducked into shadow and snuck around the structure.

A rustle came from the shadowy trees behind the mill. Jerrell stood still while his heartbeat thumped in his ears. The snort of a horse followed, but nobody came rushing out to attack him. Ducking low, Jerrell crept toward the sound, crossing a small moonlit section before entering the woods. There, he found a horse tied to a tree.

He approached the steed and petted its nose. "Easy, boy." He didn't know if it was a boy or girl but doubted the horse would care.

Moving along the horse, he felt a saddle. Taking care to remain quiet, he opened the saddlebag and reached inside. His fingers fumbled with something hard before finding a grip. He withdrew a dagger with a gem on the pommel. *My blade!*

Switching hands, he reached in again and pulled out a fistful of cloth wrapped around a hard object. His heart leapt in anticipation. He unwound the cloth to reveal the golden bracelet. Now that it was safely in his grip, he considered his next move.

Inspired, he squatted and pressed the gem in his dagger. Blue light illuminated the forest floor. Nearby, he spied a rock the size of the bracelet, picked it up, and wrapped the cloth around it. He then stuffed the cloth back in the saddlebag and doused the light coming from his dagger.

With silent steps, he crept past the mill, crossed the bridge, and returned to his horse. He slid the dagger into the sheath on his hip and shoved the bracelet into his saddlebag before climbing back on the saddle. He flicked the reins and nudged Inky into a trot. The horse passed over the river and through the village. Even if Jax was awake and caught a glimpse of the horse riding by, the man would never suspect Jerrell had snuck in and stolen the objects hidden in the saddlebag.

A smile settled across Jerrell's face as he imagined Jax arriving in Eleighton, believing he was due a big payday only to discover his prized object had been replaced by a worthless rock. For that alone, Jerrell was willing to risk the bandit coming after him.

THE DIM GLOW of predawn shone in the east, warning of the impending sunrise. The view was soon blocked by trees as Jerrell rode his horse along a curved, uphill road. By the time he crested the rise, the sun peered over the edge of the distant horizon. In that light, he spied narrow trails of smoke rising from a city at the far end of a valley.

"Eleighton," he said aloud. "We made it, Inky. Soon, you'll have your fill of hay, and you can eat until you explode."

The road ran downhill for a while before leveling and running through a thick forest. As he crossed the valley, signs of humanity appeared – a small farm here, a cabin there, a plowed field, a fenced-in area where cattle grazed. The road led to a bridge that spanned a river with a farm nestled along the east bank. Once across, the road turned and ran parallel to the water. The trees thinned and buildings appeared to replace them. The view widened and he caught his first good view of the city.

Unlike the stone and brick structures found in the eight great cities and coastal cities, the homes and shops in Eleighton were crafted from wood. The buildings were spread out with trees and shrubs growing between them, unlike the compact, densely populated streets of Marquithe. The road Jerrell traveled divided the city in two and ran parallel to the river that meandered along the valley floor. The streets connected to the road ran uphill in both directions, each rooftop rising above the one before it. Southeast of the city, a cluster of manors hugged the hillside. *That must be where wealthy residents and wizards live.* In the opposite direction, a castle loomed over a rocky cliff. Beyond the city, the valley narrowed to a canyon with rocky cliffs overlooking a wooded floor. Columns of smoke rose from somewhere beyond his view, and the wind pushed the smoke away from the city.

The road led him to a square, where the Obelisk of Devotion stood dormant. Carts and wagons surrounded the obelisk. In the spire's shadow, farmers and merchants sold their products to the locals.

Beyond the square, the road split in two. A long, single storied building occupied the angled area between the two roads. A sign hanging above the door read The Rusty Fork. Another sign nailed to a post of the covered porch pointed right and read Stables in the Back. Jerrell guided his horse past the building into a dirt stable yard where a man knelt beside a wagon with one missing wheel. A thick log sat beneath the axle, holding it in the air.

The man looked up at Jerrell, squinting against the rising sun. "I don't recognize you."

"I just arrived in town."

"This early?" The man stood and dusted his hands off on his pants. His brown bangs covered his eyes, forcing him to push them aside. "Nobody arrives so early unless they ride all night."

Jerrell nodded. "Good guess."

"Ain't safe to be out at night in these parts. Bad things can happen."

"Yeah, I ran into some of those bad things." Jerrell climbed down. "Are you the stable hand?"

"That's right. The name is Jed."

"Well, Jed, Inky here is awfully hungry after our journey. Hay and a trough of water would do her wonders."

Jed nodded. "Very well. You are staying at the Rusty Fork?"

"I am. Sorry I can't give you any coin at the moment. I will have to pay you after I meet with Gurgan."

The man grunted. "The high wizard?"

"Do you know another?"

"Well, only his son and daughter, but she is away at the University, studying wizardly stuff, and Everett is just a boy."

"Good to know," Jerrell said in earnest before pointing toward the castle. "I assume that is where the high wizard lives?"

"Yessir."

"That is also good to know." He gestured toward the rear door. "Who runs the inn?"

"Ask for Basil. He will help you out."

"Wonderful. Take care of Inky for me. I will be back for her soon." Jerrell walked up to the back door, climbed the stairs, and ducked inside.

A narrow corridor led him to a dining room where four men sat eating breakfast. Jerrell claimed a table near a front window and sat with a sigh. He was exhausted and starved after a sleepless night. Worse, he had no coin for a room or a meal. *I hope Basil is a trusting man.*

A pudgy man emerged from the kitchen with a pitcher and headed toward the other occupied table. Although it was still early, sweat already darkened the man's pale green tunic. He wore a stained apron that might have been white at one time. Dark hair covered the sides and rear of the man's head while sparse strands shadowed his otherwise bald pate. Once finished at the other table, he crossed the room and approached Jerrell.

"Good morning, stranger. How may I help you?"

"You must be Basil."

"I am."

"I find myself in a bit of a bind. You see, I have a meeting with the high wizard today, but I am short on funds. Would it be possible to get a meal and room on credit? I will pay you double what I owe once Gurgan pays me."

The man grimaced. "You've no coin at all?"

"No. I ran into some bandits on the journey from Lionne."

Beads of sweat dotted the man's brow, one of which ran down his temple. "Bandits have been trouble of late, but they remain the least of our worries."

Jerrell frowned. "What worries you more than bandits?"

After a quiet moment of contemplation, the man said, "Let's just say, I recommend against going out at night."

Jerrell pressed the man, "Your stable hand mentioned something about that, but I can't say I understand."

Basil glanced across the room as two men entered. He turned back to Jerrell and spoke in a hushed tone. "People have been disappearing, there one day, gone the next."

"Perhaps they chose to leave Eleighton?"

"No. Something stalks the valley, something nefarious. You see, these people are found days later, dead. The worst of it – each had puncture wounds in their necks and their blood had been drained from their bodies."

Jerrell snorted. "You can't believe it is a vampire."

The big man grimaced. "The term has been whispered much of late. Whether I believe it or not, something is killing these people. It's your life to lose, but don't say I didn't warn you." The man gestured toward the door. "If you've no coin, I am going to have to ask you to leave."

"There must be some way we can come to an agreement."

"Do you have anything of value to offer?"

Jerrell was loathe to give up his dagger again, and the bracelet was out of the question. "I have a horse."

The man's eyes narrowed. "Where is this horse?"

"I left her with your stable hand."

"I will talk to Jed. If he has your horse, we can hold it until you repay me. If you haven't repaid me in three days, I will sell it to cover your expenses."

Jerrell nodded. "Done."

"Very well. Let me speak with him, and then I will return with a meal. What do you want to drink?"

"Do you have ale?"

"Isn't it a bit early to start drinking?"

Jerrell grinned. "From my perspective, I am starting about twelve hours late."

CHAPTER 16
CAPTIVE

Exhausted, Jerrell slept through most of the day, and evening was approaching by the time he exited the Rusty Fork. Although he had promised Basil he would return with the silver he owed, the innkeeper demanded he leave his horse as collateral. Without a horse or means to pay for a ride, Jerrell set out on foot.

The valley lay in shadow with the sun hidden somewhere beyond the peak above the castle. Jerrell headed toward the castle, following an uphill street lined by houses. Every home was made of wood; their front porches and peaked roofs were covered by cedar shakes.

When he came to the last house, the road turned and ran parallel to the hillside, rising until it reached a sharp turn, still bordered by pines and leaf trees. That switchback was the first of ten, and the thirty-minute climb left Jerrell gasping and sweaty. By the time he finally approached the castle gate, men were lighting torches on the castle wall.

A quartet of guards manned the gate, each dressed in leather armor with shining silver plates on their chest, shoulders, and bracers. Two stood holding halberds, the butt end on the ground while the blade end pointed toward the sky. The other two wore shields on one forearm while a sheathed sword rested on the same hip.

"Hold," said a guard with a sword and shield. "The high wizard is not holding court today. Do you have an appointment?"

"I have something I was asked to retrieve for the high wizard."

The man held a hand out. "Give it to me, and I will see that he gets it."

Jerrell snorted. "That is not going to happen."

"Why should I believe you? You could be an assassin for all I know."

"I could be Lord Malvorian for all you know."

The man grimaced. "You are not Malvorian."

"My, you are a sharp one, aren't you?" Jerrell sighed. "Tarin never mentioned any of this."

"Tarin?"

"Yes. He met me in Marquithe. He and I have a contract I am trying to fulfill."

The guards glanced at each other before the leader said, "We have never heard the name Tarin."

The reply confused Jerrell, and his brow furrowed as he rubbed his stubble-covered jaw.

"Listen," the guard said. "Come back tomorrow. Perhaps the situation will have changed, and he will be receiving guests again."

Jerrell frowned. *What situation?*

The guard continued, "If so, we will mark your name on the list, and you'll have a chance to speak your mind before His Grace. Until then, you are not getting inside the castle grounds. If we catch you attempting to sneak in, we will kill you on sight."

Sighing to himself, Jerrell turned and began his walk down the long, curved road, lined by trees thick with shadow. He rounded the bend of the first switchback and caught a glimpse of the city before trees again blocked the view.

The barkeep's warning replayed in his head, *I recommend against going out at night.* He glanced up toward the sky, darkening in the east as the sun set. It would soon be completely dark. The cover of darkness was normally welcomed by a thief, yet, he felt a chill at the thought of being stuck on the forest road at night with something nefarious lurking about. He did not believe in vampires, but he hadn't believed in the minotaur before facing it and the thing nearly killed him. *Real or not, I had better be careful.*

As he walked, Jerrell repeatedly found himself peering into the shadows of the surrounding trees for any signs of movement. Again and again, he rounded tight turns while the light of day slipped away.

In the last moments of dusk, Jerrell rounded the final bend and sighted the first home, a quarter mile ahead. Phantoms seemed to lurk in the shadows of the surrounding trees, setting him on edge. Driven by a sense of irrational urgency, he broke into a run, trying to keep to the moonlit portion of the road. Tall trees on the downhill side blocked the moon and covered a large section of the road in shadow. He ran into it while focusing on the moonlit road, a hundred feet ahead.

A flicker of motion in the shadows caused Jerrell to duck out of instinct. He was too slow. Pain flared from his head and shoulder, the impact of a blow that sent him stumbling to the road. He rolled along the gravel and lay face-down in the long grass beside it.

He blinked his eyes open as dots of white danced in his vision. The thumping in his head made it difficult to focus. Someone grabbed him and rolled him over. Through narrowed eyes, Jerrell focused on the silhouette of a man standing over him. The man tossed a thick branch to the ground as he stepped into the moonlight. Recognition came a moment too late.

"Got you, little bastard," Jax said. Then his boot struck the side of Jerrell's head, sending him into oblivion.

DARKNESS CLUNG to Jerrell like wet clay – slick, heavy, and difficult to shake loose. He struggled against it, his eyes opening to find his head a few feet above the ground and his body bouncing with each stride of a trotting horse. With every bump came a sharp, stabbing pain from his cracked ribs. Despite the pain, the weight of the darkness enveloped him and smothered all else.

Rough hands gripped Jerrell by the arms, causing him to stir. They lifted and pulled until his body slid from the saddle. Pain shot from his toes when his boots struck the ground. Two men lifted him, carrying him around a big building. His head bobbed as he struggled to fight off the threatening darkness. He attempted to wipe his eyes and discovered his wrists were bound behind his back. Looking down at his dragging feet, he found his ankles tied as well. He raised his head, blinking away the blur in his eyes. Jax walked five strides ahead and was entering a shadowy courtyard thick with trees.

The man stopped beside a pair of cellar doors, opening one before waving them forward. "Take him down. The master is waiting for us."

The two men continued to carry Jerrell. At the bottom, one fumbled in the impenetrable darkness. A squeak sounded as a door opened to reveal warm light. They dragged him into a storage room, surrounded by shelving, crates, and a line of barrels resting on a low platform beside the far wall.

A creak sounded again behind them as the cellar door closed. Jax walked past and approached the wall with the barrels. He lifted a barrel lid to reveal a brass lever. When he pulled the lever, a section of the wall and attached platform rotated, taking three barrels with it. A shadow-filled corridor lurked beyond the secret entrance. Jax continued forward, and the two men carried Jerrell through. At the end of the dark corridor, the bandit opened a door, and soft amber light seeped through. The men carried Jerrell through the third doorway and into a nightmare.

Torches mounted to the walls painted the long chamber with flickering light. To the left, a flight of stairs ended at a sunken area with a dirt floor. Chains hung from beams in the high ceiling. At the end of the chains were shackles secured to the ankles of two people – a man and a woman. Each hung upside down against the wall, their bodies limp and still. Around their necks were thick metal bands with silvery tubes running from them to a vat in the center of the space. A pool of dark liquid filled the vat while dark splotches marred the floor and walls. The smell was horrendous.

In the upper section of the room, where Jerrell, Jax, and the two men stood, was a stone altar, the top of its pale surface darkly stained. A silver tray and a nasty curved knife lay on the altar. On the stone tiled floor surrounding the altar was an eight-pointed star covered with bizarre, complex symbols, all marked in dark red. Dread clawed up Jerrell's spine. *Not this again.*

A heavy wooden table and shelves filled with books and exotic objects lined the wall beyond the altar. A thick tome lay open on the table, while a man in black robes leaned over it.

The man looked up at Jax with dark eyes – eyes Jerrell recognized.

"Tarin?" Jerrell muttered.

The robed man smiled. "Ah. Master Landish. So nice of you to join us." He walked around the table. "I must apologize for my deception. My name is Rostarin. The use of Tarin was a guise, allowing me to motivate you toward my own ends without the risk that you might identify me." He stopped before Jax. "I see you did not allow him to escape this time."

"As you predicted, I found him on Castle Road, returning to the city." Jax approached the table and dumped a handful of knives on it. "Here are the weapons we confiscated from him."

The wizard arched his brows. "Six blades?"

"And he knows how to use them," Jax shot Jerrell a scowl. "Proved that when he attacked my men."

Jerrell replied, "You are lucky. Had I not fallen down that riverbank, you would have felt the sharp end of my knife as well."

Clenching his fist, Jax made a move toward Jerrell but stopped when Rostarin's hand gripped his shoulder. When Jax turned back, Rostarin said, "Tell me you retrieved the artifact."

"Of course, Master Rostarin."

"Give it to me."

"As you wish." Jax held out his hand. In his palm lay the bracelet. "I pray it is sufficient for your needs."

Rostarin lifted the bracelet to the light of a torch, peering closely at the scrawl of enchantment along the bracelet's interior. "Enchanted, as I suspected." He turned toward Jerrell. "Did you have any trouble procuring it?"

Jerrell said, "Not at all. In fact, the last I saw, Montague was tied to his bed stark naked, while a party took place in his castle. I suspect his guests consider it a memorable night, while he might categorize it as a regrettable one."

Rostarin chuckled. "I wish I could have seen the look on Montague's face." He lifted the bracelet, torchlight reflecting off the metal surface as he twisted it. "If this boosts my abilities as they did for Montague, I will soon displace Gurgan. With the added power of sorcery, I may even try to challenge Malvorian himself."

Sorcery? Jerrell turned toward the altar and the bodies dangling from the wall. He suddenly realized what filled the vat. *Blood. His rites require blood.* He recalled Gerald Wrenthal's attempt to use sorcery toward his own ends. While Jerrell didn't claim to understand magic, he wanted no part of it.

"Since you have the bracelet, I will accept my payment and be on my way." Jerrell did his best to keep his tone steady despite his mounting anxiety.

Rostarin tilted his head, appearing to consider the request. "That would be the right thing to do...if you and I actually had a contract in place. Unfortunately, the one you signed at the Bureau was a forgery."

"What of the fifty gold?"

The wizard chuckled. "There was no gold. For all of your cleverness, you neglected to check with the Bureau after I presented the contract to you. Had you done so, my ruse would have been discovered at the onset."

Jerrell considered a few sharp responses but held back, instead asking a question with a reply he feared. "You got what you wanted, and I learned a painful lesson, but I fear your plans for me do not end there. What do you plan to do with me?"

"Ah. Direct as always. I must say, dealing with you has been refreshing. I will miss this."

"Miss what?"

"Your wit. I believe you know the answer to your question."

"You intend to drain me of my blood, as you have done to those poor people behind me."

Three slow beats echoed in the chamber as Rostarin clapped his hands together. "Bravo, Mister Landish. If only I had more like you in my employ. Well, ones I could trust."

"You can trust me."

"I think not. From you, I note a self-serving nature. In addition, you are brazen enough to take on a wizard – a quality I prefer to avoid in those who work for me. You see, I am meant to rise above other men, Gifted and Ungifted alike. I cannot risk you foiling my plans." The wizard circled Jerrell and approached the altar. "Besides, you should consider yourself blessed. Your blood will fuel the spell I intend to use against Gurgan."

Jerrell frowned. "You have the bracelet. Why not use that to boost your abilities? That should be enough to defeat a man like Gurgan."

Rostarin frowned and slid the bracelet on his wrist. He made a fist and Jerrell felt the tickle of magic. The wizard arched his brow and smiled. "The increase is impressive. If only my natural ability was sufficient, I might make do without the sorcery." He removed the bracelet and set it on the altar. "Unfortunately, more is required for me to rise to my destined position."

Jerrell sneered. "So, you turned to blood magic although it is forbidden and considered evil in the eyes of Farrow?"

The wizard slapped his hand on the altar. "You're damn right, I did. It was not my fault my father chose to dally with an Ungifted. Had both my parents held the spark, things would have been different."

This time, Jerrell snorted. "If you'd had a different mother, she would have had a different child, and you would have never existed."

Rostarin looked at Jax. "Do you understand what he means?"

The bandit shook his head. "No, master. It sounded like gibberish to me."

"That is because he is far too smart, and you are a witless dolt." When Jax opened his mouth to retort, the wizard flashed him a palm, stopping him. "Still, you performed your duty as prescribed. Continue to do so, and I will continue to reward you." He reached into his robes and withdrew five gold pieces, which he held out to Jax. "Take them. Three are for you. The others are for your companions. But before you leave, take the woman down to the city and drop her corpse into the square. She has been drained, and the discovery of her body will further fuel the rumors and fear, which works to our advantage. Once she is out of the way, chain Master Landish to the wall." He smiled. "I will drain his blood and prepare my ritual of elevation."

Jerrell swallowed hard, his thoughts racing, desperate for a means to escape his fate.

CHAPTER 17
BLOOD RITUAL

Forced to sit on the floor facing the wall while his wrists remained bound behind his back, Jerrell waited while shackles were clamped around his ankles. Chains secured to each shackle ran across the floor, up the wall, and over pulleys mounted to the thick beams overhead. Although Jerrell's head still ached, the fog clouding his thoughts had cleared. He had a firm sense of the gravity of the situation and remained vigilant, looking for some means to escape without resorting to panic.

Jax then lifted a larger shackle with two holes in the side. The man wrapped the metal ring around Jerrell's neck and then clamped it on. It was tight and made it difficult for Jerrell to turn his head.

Jerrell said, "While I appreciate the accessory, it clashes with my outfit. Do you have anything in a blue silk?"

Jax frowned at his companions, who both appeared confused. Far across the room, Rostarin chuckled. *At least the wizard understands my humor.*

Stepping back from Jerrell, Jax said, "Raise him up."

One of the men began to wind a winch on the wall – the same one used to lower the dead woman. The pulleys mounted to the beam above squeaked while the clanking chains pulled Jerrell toward the wall. When he reached it, the chains began to lift his feet, forcing his body to fall backward.

As he was raised farther off the floor, his back smacked against the wall until he dangled by his ankles. Once his head was five feet above the ground, the winch stopped. The man cranking the winch threw the lever beside it, locking it in place.

Jax approached Jerrell with a sneer. "Enjoy your last moments. Soon, you will be nothing but a lifeless corpse, like the others." The man turned toward Rostarin. "If you have no other need of us, master, I will head upstairs while Vern and Nate take the woman to the city square."

Rostarin tilted his head. "What's the matter, Jax? You don't wish to stay and witness the ritual?"

The bandit's jaw worked, but no words came out. The color drained from the faces of the other two men as well.

The wizard laughed. It was a chilling sound, bereft of humor. "Go on, you cowards. My magic is beyond your comprehension anyway."

The two men hastily scooped up the lifeless woman and carried her out the door, where Jax stood waiting, eager to leave. Once they were all beyond the doorway, Jax closed the door behind him, and the cellar fell quiet.

In the silence, Jerrell hung upside down. His face felt flush from the blood rushing to his head. With his hands still bound behind his back, his shoulders were sore as well. He worried that his extremities would soon grow numb from the lack of blood flow.

Across the room, Rostarin examined something in the thick book on his table. After a few minutes, he stepped back and peered at Jerrell from a distance.

"You asked what comes next." The wizard approached the altar and lifted the knife from it. He descended the short flight of stairs and eyed the blade, the metal edge reflecting a flash of torchlight when he twisted it in examination. "I will give you a choice." With a slow, methodical pace, he approached Jerrell. "I can insert the drain tubes into your jugular vein, as I have done with the others. Your heart will pump your blood out – the blood I need to complete my transformation. The tubes are narrow, and the process takes time. From what I have seen from the others – now approaching two dozen people – there is little pain, but the length of the process brings terror and despair before you eventually lose consciousness.

Even then, your body betrays you, pushing blood out until there is too little left to survive, and your organs cease functioning."

"That sounds wonderful," Jerrell said, "but I think I'll pass."

The wizard continued, ignoring Jerrell's sarcasm. "The other choice comes with this blade." He stopped a stride from Jerrell and held the knife in front of him. "With a well-placed cut, coming with a flash of pain, I can end your life in seconds and still collect the blood I require."

Jerrell had been watching Rostarin since his arrival in the wizard's twisted dungeon. The man was driven by an inferiority complex, and that was something Jerrell could use against him. "Even if you kill me, steal my blood, and perform your little ritual, you will never amount to anything more than a piss-poor wizard with feeble magic."

Rostarin snarled. "I will be a mighty wizard!"

"Gurgan will feast on you and leave you naked, bloody, and beaten for everyone in Eleighton to laugh at."

"Nobody will laugh at me! Never again!" The wizard stepped closer and raised his knife high, prepared to plunge it into Jerrell's heart.

Using everything he could muster, Jerrell tightened his stomach muscles and sat forward in a burst. His forehead smashed into the wizard's nose with a revolting crunch. The wizard fell backward and his head struck the rim of the vat with a resounding clang. The impact of the blow sent pain into Jerrell's forehead, down his face, and through his brain, causing his eyes to water. Spots filled his vision as his body fell limply back against the wall. His deep breaths slowly eased, and the spots receded, once again giving him an upside-down view of his surroundings.

Rostarin lay on the cellar floor with his arms splayed out. Blood covered the lower half of the man's face, a trail of which dripped to the stone tiles beneath him. The nasty knife rested near the man's feet, only a stride from the wall where Jerrell dangled.

Turning his head, which was not easy because of the metal collar, Jerrell spied the winch no more than four feet away. Beside it, the lock lever jutted out a foot from the wall.

After a few breaths, Jerrell bent sideways at the waist, and his body swayed on the chains. He bent the other way, adding to the momentum of his swing in the other direction. Again and again, he repeated the motion, each time swinging his body a little higher than his last attempt. Like a pendulum, Jerrell swung from side to side until he rose to mere inches from the winch. With the next swing, he bent at the waist and neck as much as he could, despite the metal collar. His head struck the lock lever with a clang. The lever lifted, releasing the winch as Jerrell swung back down. The floor suddenly raced toward him. He twisted to avoid landing on his head, and his shoulder struck the ground, eliciting a grunt and sending sharp pain through his cracked ribs. The chains followed, clanking loudly as they piled on the floor near his feet until the winch stopped. His body aching and his hands still bound behind his back, Jerrell lay still for a long moment before he opened his eyes.

Jerrell's feet were near Rostarin's, and the knife lay a couple feet from Jerrell's knees. Wiggling his body, Jerrell wormed his way across the floor until the knife lined up with his groin. He rolled over, rattling the chains shackled to his ankles. His hands, still tied behind his back, landed on the knife. The sharp edge bit into his finger and caused him to jerk in pain. A flick of his fingers spun the blade and allowed him to grip the hilt. He rolled on his side to face the wall and bent his wrist until the knife edge pressed against the ropes. Gripping the hilt with both hands, he sawed at the rope. The sharp blade soon cut through and the pressure on his wrists lessened. He shuffled his arms, and the ropes loosened further until he was able to yank his right arm free. He released a massive sigh.

He pushed himself up to a sitting position and began to loosen thumb-screws securing the clamp around his neck. The shackles on his ankles came next. He staggered to his feet and looked down at Rostarin.

The wizard's face was a mess and blood matted the hair on the back of his head. Jerrell knelt beside the man and felt for a pulse. The wizard shuddered and fell still.

"Dead," Jerrell said. "For your betrayal, your death was justified." He glanced up at the dead man still hanging on the wall. "For what you did to them, you deserved far worse. When you stand before Farrow, I hope he judges you harshly and you pay for the rest of eternity."

Jerrell had little regard for the gods. As far as he could tell, they felt the same for him. Justice, on the other hand, was an ideal he understood. He knew it was an odd perspective for a thief, but he was no ordinary thief.

He stepped over the wizard and climbed the stairs to the upper level, where he paused to touch the side of his head. His hand came away bloody. The other hand touched the other side, which revealed blood as well.

"I must look a mess. It's a good thing my admirers aren't here to see me."

He walked over to the table, scooped up the bracelet, and clamped it around his own wrist. Of course, it did nothing to him, but it seemed a safe place to keep it for now. He then collected his throwing knives and slid each into place before reclaiming his dagger.

Bloody, sore, and angry, he walked out of the dungeon, crossed the storage room, and climbed the stairs.

CHAPTER 18
JUSTICE

Once outside, Jerrell found himself on a wooded hillside above the city. Across the valley, he spied the torchlit walls of Eleighton Castle. A manor, larger than any commoner's house but modest for a wizard, loomed above the cellar entrance.

Jerrell followed a path cloaked in thick shadows and emerged in a gravel courtyard between an outbuilding (that he assumed was the stable) and the manor side entrance. When he tested the door, he found it unlocked. He carefully eased the door open to a narrow room with a wardrobe along one wall and shoes beside it. A corridor led him past a dark dining room, but the pale blue light of an enchanted lantern glowed somewhere ahead. He slowed and leaned against the wall just before the doorway. Moving quickly, he peered around the corner and jerked back to examine the image in his memory.

A stone fireplace dominated one wall of the sitting room. A sofa, two cushioned chairs, and a low table sat before the hearth. Beyond the sitting area was a small table with four chairs, one of which was occupied. In the pale light of the lantern, Jax gnawed on a chicken leg while his other hand hugged the bowl on the table before him. Nobody else was in the room.

Jerrell drew two throwing blades and stepped out into the doorway. "Hello, Jax."

The man jerked with a start, his eyes widening when he saw Jerrell. "What the...how did you escape?"

With slow, measured strides, Jerrell crossed the room. "I am impressed by Rostarin's scheme. I'll admit he tricked me into stealing the bracelet from Montague. He was smart to have you and your crew pretend you were simple bandits when you caught up to me. Your mistake was leaving me tied to that tree, alive. Once I caught up to you, your men paid dearly for it. Rostarin's mistake was sending you away tonight, thinking I was helpless just because I was chained to a wall with my hands bound."

Jax stood, his gaze flicking to his sword; it was still in its scabbard and leaned in a corner of the room. "What did you do to him?"

"To tell you the truth, Rostarin got much better than he deserved. By all rights, he should have seen his end on a gibbet with the entire city there to watch."

"He is dead?"

"As dead as it gets."

Jax lunged for his sword, but Jerrell was ready and loosed a throwing knife. The blade sliced through the man's forearm and struck the wall, pinning him in place.

"Argh!" the bandit cried out as his face twisted in agony as he reached for the knife hilt.

Jerrell took aim and loosed the other blade, driving it through the man's other hand.

Jax screamed.

While striding toward Jax, Jerrell drew his dagger and then burst forward, quickly closing the last few strides. He held the blade against the side of the bandit's neck, drawing blood.

"I warned you, Jax. You came after me anyway. However, since you only acted as a pawn in the wizard's twisted scheme, I'll give you a chance."

"What do you want?"

"I find myself low on funds. Where does Rostarin store his wealth?"

"His study. On the second floor. But it is protected by spells."

"What kind of spells?"

"I...I don't know. He warned me never to step foot in that room or I would experience a gruesome death."

Jerrell narrowed his eyes and considered the situation. Once deciding how to proceed, he nodded. "Very well. I need one more thing from you if you wish to live."

"Anything. I'll give you anything."

"I need a witness who can implicate Rostarin as the mastermind behind the recent disappearances."

"But...that will require me admitting my role."

"True. Which likely places your fate in the hands of the high wizard. Still, it'll give you a chance, and your cooperation might reduce your sentence." Jerrell shrugged. "Or, I can kill you right now and end your pain."

His breath coming in gasps, Jax appeared ready to faint until, finally, he said, "All right. Let me live, and I'll confess."

Jerrell smiled. "Wonderful." When he pulled his dagger away, the man visibly relaxed.

Jerrell yanked the throwing blade from the bandit's arm, and Jax fell to his knees, his arm and hand bloody as Jerrell stood over him. Raising his dagger high, Jerrell reversed his grip and drove the hilt down into the base of the man's neck. Jax collapsed in a heap, unconscious.

ONCE JAX'S wounds were bandaged and the unconscious man was tied to a chair, Jerrell climbed the stairs to the third floor. A moonbeam shone through the window at the far end of the corridor, the space between occupied by shadow.

Jerrell crept to the first door, slowly reached for the knob, and when he felt no tingling, swung the door open to reveal a bedroom. The four-poster bed lay empty, and the room was quiet. Jerrell was thankful that Rostarin wasn't married. Informing a woman she was now a widow was a complication he would rather avoid.

Moving along, he placed his palm against the next closed door. Again, he felt no magic, so he tested the door, this time finding it locked.

While dropping to one knee, Jerrell dug out his lockpicks. Moments later, the lock clicked, and the door swung open. He stood and took a tentative step into the room before spying an enchanted lantern dangling from a hook near the door. A twist of a knob activated it, painting the room in pale blue light.

Shelving filled with books covered the wall to the right. A curtained window loomed straight ahead, beyond an ornate desk. On the wall to his left, a tapestry depicted a faceless man in robes standing before a throng of thousands. A blue glow surrounded the man and he stood five times the height of other humans. In place of his face was a swirling lightning bolt. *Farrow,* Jerrell thought. Every god had a distinct likeness, making each unmistakable. Down the wall from the tapestry was a painting of Farrow hovering in the sky above Marquithe.

Lifting the lantern off the hook, Jerrell crossed the room with his other arm extended, concentrating on sensing some form of magic. A full circle of the room yielded nothing, causing him to stand in the middle with a frown.

"Jax claimed this room held the wizard's coin, but he was too scared to enter and check for himself. The question is, where is it hidden?"

He set the lantern on the desk, sat in the chair, and pulled out each of the three drawers. Nothing of note hid inside other than a parchment with a list of names. Twenty-some were crossed off, leaving a dozen unmarked. While interesting, the list held no monetary value, and Jerrell was desperately in need of coin – something which Rostarin no longer needed.

The shelving held nothing but books, so he crossed the room and lifted the painting off the hook. All that hid behind it was a bare, wood-paneled wall. Similarly, he found nothing behind the tapestry. He went to the window and pulled the curtain aside. The city of Eleighton slept beneath the starry sky, its peaked rooftops lit by moonlight on one side and covered in shadow on the opposite slope.

He backed from the window, and his heel caught the edge of the rug. Stumbling, he fell backward into the desk. The impact caused the lantern to rock and slide to the edge. Jerrell spun around and reached to catch it but was a moment late. The lantern struck the wooden floor with a hollow thud.

Jerrell frowned, circled the desk, and squatted to pick up the lantern. He stood and thumped his heel against the floor, hearing a distinct echo. A stroll across the room took him to the other end of the rug. He set the lantern on the floor and rolled the rug up until it was tight against the desk legs.

In the oak floor, he found a sawed-out panel with a knothole on one end. He slid a finger into the hole and lifted. The panel came away to reveal a recess two feet square and a foot deep. Three leather pouches rested in the shadowy recess. Jerrell lifted one out and shook it, hearing the distinct jingle of coins. The other two made the same sound, bringing him a smile.

"At least this headache was not for nothing."

He replaced the panel, unrolled the rug, and doused the lamp. With the three pouches cradled in one arm, he snuck out of the room and down the stairs. At the main level, he headed for the front door but stopped when a shadow passed by the curtained window beside it. He made out several voices – two men were approaching the door.

Jerrell hid behind the door. A key slid into the lock, followed by a click. The handle turned, the door opened, and the conversation suddenly became intelligible.

"...am thankful we are at the end of this."

"Hush," the other man whispered. "You don't want the master to hear you."

The men stepped inside. "You heard what Rostarin said. He plans to complete the ritual tonight, and we are unlikely to see him anytime soon."

The door closed and Jerrell swung, smashing the three sacks of coins into the back of one man's head. As the man toppled over, the other spun toward Jerrell. With a backhand swing, Jerrell drove the three sacks into the side of the second man's head, causing him to stumble. His forehead struck the door with a crack, and he collapsed beside his companion.

Jerrell stood over them, watching for any signs of movement. Other than the rise and fall of their chests, both men remained still. The pair working with Jax had worried Jerrell. He had wondered if he would have to hunt them down. Finding them at the manor before he left was a boon, even if it did require a little more work.

He sighed. "Now, to find something to tie them up with. After that, I am returning to the inn and curling up in bed." At that moment, nothing sounded better than sleep.

CHAPTER 19

HEROES

His plate cleaned, Jerrell pushed it away, and sat back as Basil approached his table.

The big man stopped and looked down at him with a grunt. "You sure can eat for a little man."

"I had an active night with no dinner. If it makes you feel any better, I am stuffed."

"I have no doubt. You finished two plates of eggs, ham, and biscuits."

"And both were excellent."

Basil collected Jerrell's plate. "I must say, I had my doubts when you said you would pay me."

Rising to his feet, Jerrell clapped the heavyset man on the shoulder. "Jerrell Landish repays his debts. If you don't believe me, you could ask Wizard Rostarin."

"You know Rostarin?"

"Let's just say he and I have met. Although, when you next hear his name, I suspect it won't be in a flattering context."

Brow furrowed, Basil asked, "What does that mean?"

Jerrell patted the man's cheek. "It means Rostarin was a very bad man."

Turning, Jerrell headed toward the inn's front door, which stood open.

From behind him, Basil called out, "Was? What do you mean *was* a bad man?"

Whistling as he stepped out into the mid-morning sun, Jerrell strolled down the street, pausing at the first intersection to watch a cluster of armored guards approach a building and knock on the door. A woman answered, spoke with the guards, and let them in. Across the street, another cluster of guards emerged from a building and then moved on to the next house.

They are searching for something. Jerrell wondered about the reason for the search, but not for long. Soon, he headed down the street, took the first left, and walked up to the front door of the city jail. He entered to find a heavyset city guard lounging behind a desk with his feet up and his hands cradling his head. The man's eyes were closed, and his bearded chin rested on his breastplate. Beyond him lurked a long room with three barred jail cells on each side and a barred window at the far end. The cells appeared empty, the building quiet.

Jerrell crept up to the desk and pounded his fist down on it. The man's eyes shot open, his arms flailing as his chair tipped backward. With his feet pointing toward the ceiling, the man toppled to the floor with a crash, breaking his chair in the process.

The guard rolled to his hands and knees and gasped. "What happened?"

Sitting on the edge of the desk with his arms crossed, Jerrell said, "You were sleeping."

Stumbling to his feet, the guard huffed. "I would never sleep on duty."

A door opened to the side of the room and three guards raced out with weapons brandished. Two wore only smallclothes, while the third was dressed in armor.

"What was that noise?" one exclaimed.

Jerrell shrugged. "I was only getting this man's attention."

"Who are you?"

"My name is Jerrell Landish. Perhaps you have heard of me?"

The guards looked at each other and shook their heads.

Sighing, Jerrell said, "I happen to be a famous...specialist."

"Famous?"

"A what?"

"Never mind." Jerrell stood and rested his hand on the shoulder of the guard he had woken. "What is your name?"

The man's eyes flicked toward his fellow guards. "Layton."

"Well, Layton, today is your lucky day. I am here to give you the chance to be heroes."

"Heroes?"

"I assume you are aware of the disappearances – people missing, their bodies found days later with puncture wounds on their necks, the blood drained from their lifeless corpses?"

One of the other guards narrowed his eyes and leveled his sword at Jerrell. "How do you know about the drained blood?"

"Because I was nearly a victim of the madman who caused this trouble."

"You know who is behind it?"

Grinning, Jerrell asked, "Have you heard the name Rostarin?"

EVERYTHING IN ROSTARIN'S manor was as Jerrell left it, only louder. When the city guards opened the front door, calls for help came from inside. The guards entered, and Jerrell followed them to the sitting room where Rostarin's three henchmen were tied to three separate chairs. To ensure the men remained that way, Jerrell had also tied each chair to another major piece of furniture.

As anticipated, Jax and his two companions began confessing the moment they spied Jerrell. All three blamed Rostarin and claimed they were forced by the wizard to do his bidding. Jax went so far as to declare he had been ensorcelled and had no control of his own free will. Jerrell knew better and suspected High Wizard Gurgan would as well.

Jerrell then guided the guards around the outside of the manor and led them down to the cellar. A voice inside his head screamed at the thought of revisiting the wizard's dungeon of terror, but he needed to see the situation all the way to its resolution. It was his ticket to an exclusive audience with the high wizard.

When he removed the barrel lid and pulled the lever to the secret door, exclamations of surprise echoed from the guards. After he led them through the door and into the room beyond, their reaction was far more pronounced. One swore to Farrow and began to pray aloud. Another covered his mouth, his eyes wide in horror. Layton gagged, fell to one knee, and proceeded to empty his stomach, the contents of which splashed to the floor in front of the altar.

"Now, do you believe me?" Jerrell asked.

The only guard who had refrained from reaction descended the stairs and knelt beside Rostarin's corpse. "You killed him."

"I was upside down and chained to the wall with my wrists bound while he came at me with a knife. It was him or me. What would you have done?"

The guard looked down at the dead wizard. "Frankly, I have no idea. Still, I can hardly fault you for it. I only wish he could have stood trial and received the public execution he deserved."

Despite the grim surroundings, Jerrell chuckled.

The guard stood with a grimace. "I fail to see any humor in this atrocity."

"Sorry. It's just that I told one of Rostarin's thugs the exact same thing. However, dead is dead, and the world is better off without this particular wizard."

"Can't say I disagree."

Suddenly eager to leave, Jerrell said, "As I said earlier, I wanted to offer you the chance to be heroes. Get together, craft your story, and make my part in this whatever you wish, so long as you get me a meeting with the high wizard."

Layton, now recovered, asked, "You wish to meet with Gurgan?"

"Yes, but in private rather than in his public court."

The guards looked at each other and shared a nod.

Relieved to be finished with the dungeon, Jerrell headed out the door. "I will wait outside."

~

WITH ROSTARIN'S henchmen locked up in the city jail, Jerrell rode in a wagon, seated between Layton and a man named Ivan, the latter guiding a two-horse team up the winding hillside road. Ivan wore a brown vest over his sweaty, cream-colored tunic. A brown hat with a broad brim shaded his face from the late morning sun. The man was about a decade older than Jerrell but was of a similar height with a lean, muscular build.

The ride allowed Jerrell's mind to wander, and he found himself thinking about the bracelet he had stolen from Montague. His recent interactions with wizards concerned him. Each had proven self-centered and consumed by ambition with little regard for others. He worried it was a rampant trait of the ruling class. *If so*—he gripped the bracelet hidden beneath his sleeve—*this object holds enough power to upset the balance of power. In the wrong hands, innocents could suffer, and it would be my fault for allowing it to happen.* The troubling realization made him reconsider his plan to sell the artifact.

By the time the wagon rounded the last switchback and the castle gate came into view, he had made his decision. The bracelet, regardless of its value, would remain a secret and stay in his possession until he was confident it would not make this already cruel world even worse.

The wagon stopped at the gate; the guards posted there approached, led by the same man who had turned Jerrell away the prior evening.

"Good morning, Ivan."

"Hello, Natal."

"You are a bit early today. And why the passengers?"

The wagon driver shrugged. "The city watch added a little something to today's delivery."

"Good day, Sergeant," Layton said. "The city guard has solved the crimes that have plagued our valley. The fiend behind the disappearances has been caught."

The sergeant arched his brow, his gaze leveled at Jerrell. "This man is a vampire?"

Jerrell snickered until Layton elbowed him.

Layton explained, "This man was nearly a victim himself. The city guard raided the killer's dungeon early this morning and saved him just in time."

"So, you caught the vampire?"

Jerrell rolled his eyes, but allowed Layton to reply.

"There was no vampire behind this killing spree. It was a wizard who had turned to dark magic."

"A wizard?"

"Yes. Rafael Rostarin."

"Rostarin?" Natal snorted. "That sniveling swine? It's difficult to believe he had it in him. Is he locked in the city jail?"

"The men working for the evil wizard are in cells, but Rostarin occupies the back of this wagon. We wish to deliver him to the high wizard, so he may witness for himself that the reign of terror has ended."

The sergeant frowned and approached the side of the wagon bed, half of which was filled with crates and sacks, the other half occupied by a still form lying beneath a blood-stained sheet.

He lifted the sheet, peered beneath it, and snorted. "His face is a mess."

"Yeah. A blow to the face broke his nose."

The man dropped the sheet. "Why not bring him in alive?"

Layton stammered, so Jerrell interjected. "The strike to the face caused the wizard to fall backward and crack his head against the rim of a metal vat, which killed him. Had they not acted instantly, I would be dead. The man had a knife against my throat."

A grunt was Natal's only reply. The sergeant motioned to the guards at the gate. "Let them in!" He turned back to the wagon. "Ask for Lieutenant Dandon. He is running today's exercises."

The guards parted, and the wagon rolled into the castle grounds.

A gravel bailey waited inside, bound by walls on three sides. Straight ahead, an arch led beneath the castle. The wagon rolled across the bailey, passed beneath the spiked portcullis standing above the arch, and headed into the shadows beneath the fortress.

The tunnel itself was thirty feet wide and four times as long. Brick columns connected by arches supported the structure, looming fifteen feet above. Closed doors waited on both sides of the tunnel, while daylight seeped in from both ends. The clang of clashing swords and the thuds of arrows echoed in the shadowy confines, as if a battle were taking place. The wagon rolled toward the far end and emerged into another gravel yard encompassed by the castle walls.

Stables loomed to one side while a sand sparring yard waited to the other. Dummies made of wood and straw, bales of hay, and paper targets filled with arrows stood along the far castle wall. Two armored guards traded blows in the sparring yard, their swords careening off each other's weapons and shields. Swordsmen attacked the practice dummies while archers loosed arrows at their distant targets.

The wagon pulled into the shadows of the stables before stopping. The guard and the wagon driver hopped down and strolled to the rear of the wagon while a tall man in a midnight blue uniform approached. Everything about him – from his deliberate stride to his puffed-up chest to the thrust of his chin – spoke of arrogance.

As usual, Jerrell responded to arrogance with irreverence. "Are you Lieutenant Hard On?"

The man frowned at Jerrell. His eyes were as dark as his hair. In his early thirties, he had a serious scowl and an intense gaze that took Jerrell in from his boots to his face all with an air of supremacy. "It is Lieutenant *Dandon*." The man turned toward the wagon driver. "Ivan. What are these two men doing here?"

Layton spoke before Ivan could reply. "Good morning, Lieutenant. We caught the man behind the recent murders. We are here to meet with the high wizard."

The man furrowed his brow while gazing at the sheet-covered corpse. "He is dead?"

The man's condescending attitude rubbed Jerrell the wrong way. "Perhaps you would like to snuggle beneath the sheet with him to find out?"

Dandon's frown deepened. "You've a mouth on you."

"Yes, but I only kiss girls with it, so don't get any ideas."

Ivan snickered, earning him a scowl from Dandon.

The lieutenant turned to Layton. "Who is this indolent arse?"

Jerrell said, "I prefer the term *clever*."

Layton hurriedly said, "He is a witness to the fiend's crimes."

Jerrell added, "And I was nearly a victim as well."

Dandon snorted. "It appears the killer chose a poor time to fail." He gestured toward Layton and Ivan. "Pick up the corpse and follow me."

The two men lifted Rostarin's corpse from the wagon bed and carried him to a door beneath the castle. Dandon opened the door, leading them up two flights of stairs. A corridor brought them to a small room with a cot in the center, where they placed the dead wizard.

"Ivan, you are free to go. The porters are downstairs, and they will help you unload your wagon." Dandon pointed toward Jerrell and Layton. "You two remain here. I am going to inform His Grace of what has transpired."

With Layton leaning against the wall, Jerrell waited, wondering what might happen next. He preferred to be in control of all situations, but yet again, such was not to be when meeting with the high wizard. He worried that Gurgan might be as bad or worse than the other wizards he had met. Thus far, Paloun was the only one who had not tried to kill him.

CHAPTER 20
A REQUEST

An hour passed before Lieutenant Dandon returned. This time, he was not alone. A pair of guards stopped outside the door, bracketing it while additional footsteps echoed in the corridor. A tall man in dark blue robes entered the room, his presence regal even without a crown. His brown hair was combed back from his high forehead to his neck. A streak of gray ran the length of his long brown beard, giving him an aged appearance despite the alertness in his gray-green eyes.

Another man trailed behind him, dressed in a dark blue uniform with silver stripes down the arms like Dandon's but with a silver star sewn to the left breast of his coat. The man also stood tall with a lean build and broad shoulders. While the lieutenant appeared in his early thirties, the lines on the other soldier's face and the graying hair above his ears marked him as north of forty.

Dandon said, "These men claim to have caught the murderer, Your Grace."

The robed man eyed Jerrell. "You were the one they freed?"

Jerrell nodded. "Yes, Wizard Gurgan."

The lack of title caused Dandon to scowl, but everyone remained silent. "Your name?"

"Jerrell Landish."

The wizard arched a brow and then turned to Layton. "Who lies under the sheet?"

Beneath the high wizard's steely gaze, Layton kneaded his hands and shuffled his feet. "It is a wizard, Your Grace. His name is Rostarin."

"Rafael Rostarin?"

The guard nodded. "Do you wish to see him?"

"I suppose I had better confirm his identification."

Layton lifted the sheet, revealing Rostarin's bloody face.

Gurgan nodded. "That is him." He took a deep breath. "Let us go down the hall and have a seat. I want to hear the entire story." He turned and left the room with the uniformed soldier in his wake.

"Well," Dandon said when nobody else moved. "Don't keep the high wizard waiting."

The guards rushed out of the room and Jerrell followed. They turned a corner, climbed a flight of stairs, and came to a large open room with windows overlooking the valley. In the middle of the room, four wooden chairs arranged in an arc faced a desk. Gurgan navigated around the desk and settled in the padded chair behind it.

"Please. Sit."

Jerrell claimed one of the end chairs while Layton sat beside him.

Gurgan gestured toward Layton. "What is your name?"

"Layton, Your Grace."

"Please, Master Layton, describe in detail what transpired. Leave nothing out."

Layton went on to tell the story he and the other guards had agreed upon. Two men were witnessed disposing of a woman's body late at night. They were followed and arrested at Rostarin's manor. When the guards reached the dungeon, Rostarin was in the middle of a dark magic ritual and about to sacrifice Jerrell. They rushed in and stopped him just in time, killing the wizard in the process. He then described the horrors found in the cellar. When Layton finished, the wizard sat back in his chair with his tented fingers against his lips.

After a long moment of silence, Gurgan turned toward Jerrell. "Is this true?"

"I can't see any fault in Layton's story."

Gurgan smiled. "I see." He sat forward. "Tell me, did you find anyone else in the manor?"

Jerrell frowned, unsure of why Gurgan was asking him. "Other than the dead man and woman, I saw only Rostarin and his three hired hands."

The high wizard turned to the uniformed man standing at his side. "Captain Fossie. See that this guard and his comrades are rewarded. Craft a formal announcement to reassure the populace that the murderer has been caught and executed. Be sure to note that he was merely a misguided wizard and not a vampire. However, that announcement and the information of the killer's capture are not to be shared outside of this room quite yet." His stern gaze met the eyes of every man in the room. "You are to keep this information confidential until I choose to release it."

Jerrell frowned. *Why would the wizard not wish everyone to know that the threat had ended?*

The captain nodded. "Yes, Your Grace."

"Good." Gurgan said with a nod. "Layton, you and your fellow guards will receive the reward of twenty gold pieces offered for the killer's capture. Give me a couple days, and I will have it delivered to the city jail."

Twenty gold? Jerrell had not considered the possibility of a reward, and this one was significant. Still, he had made a deal with the guards and was not about to betray them.

Layton grinned. "Thank you, Your Grace."

"We are finished here. You are all dismissed...except Master Landish. I must speak with him alone."

Dandon said, "Is that wise, Your Grace? We know nothing of this man. He is armed and could be..."

Gurgan clapped his hands and thunder shook the room. He spoke with a commanding tone. "Must I remind you? I am high wizard here. Seven Gifted challengers have discovered the lethality of my abilities. I can and will protect myself if so required." He then turned to Jerrell. "Which I find doubtful, for Master Landish has no reason to wish me harm."

Jerrell shook his head. "None in the slightest."

The wizard sat back and smiled. "See. All will be well. Now, off with the rest of you."

The room emptied, but the door remained open. Gurgan extended a hand toward it, and the hair on Jerrell's arms stood on end. The door slammed closed, leaving him trapped in a room with a wizard. Again.

From behind his desk, Gurgan stared at Jerrell in silence. Jerrell maintained a relaxed exterior despite the discomforting weight of the wizard's scrutiny. The wizard tapped on the desktop, his nail echoing against the wood in the otherwise quiet room.

Gurgan stilled his hand and narrowed his eyes. "I have heard tales involving the name Landish of late."

Jerrell restrained a grin. "You have?"

"The name was mentioned in connection with a certain young Orenthian wizard's rise last fall. More recently, someone with the name Landish was credited with unraveling a murder plot against a respected business-woman whose family has a long and respected history with the Bureau of Trading." He cocked his head. "I assume you are familiar with these events."

At last, my name is known elsewhere. "Manipulating Jakins to ease Paloun's ascension might appear a challenge to others, but it was easily executed for someone of my abilities. Rescuing Sorenna Souton, dispatching her assassins, and tracking down the man behind the plot required extreme combat skills and a keen analytical mind." Jerrell pressed his hand to his chest. "I happen to be blessed with both."

The wizard snorted. "You certainly don't lack for confidence."

"In my line of work, confidence is requisite, but so are caution, patience, and daring."

"What, exactly, is your line of work?"

"To tell you the truth, I find it difficult to give my current profession a title. I consider myself a specialist of sorts, able to take on assignments others might find daunting or confounding. I am not a large man, so others often underestimate me, which I use to my advantage. I can pick any lock and sneak into any stronghold. I notice things others miss and reach logical conclusions faster than most. Call it what you like, but you'll find nobody better at what I do."

Gurgan nodded. "As I had hoped."

The high wizard's gaze fell to his lap, and he released a sigh, his shoulders drooping in defeat. He stood and walked to the window to stare down at the city. A heavy silence clung to the room, leaving Jerrell anxious to interrupt it with a question, a quip, or any words at all.

With his back still facing Jerrell, Gurgan asked an unexpected question. "Do you have any children, Mister Landish?"

"No. I am unprepared to raise a child. Even if I was, I don't know that I would want one."

Gurgan turned toward him. "You have no woman in your life?"

"None for more than a night or two."

The wizard smiled. "Someday, you may meet a woman who captures your heart and refuses to relinquish it. Should that come to pass, I suspect your view on raising offspring will change."

Jerrell was doubtful either would happen but chose not to argue the point. "If you say so."

The wizard appeared to measure him with his gaze. "I sense an arrogance about you, Jerrell, which is understandable for someone of your age and accomplishments, but do not discount the wisdom of your seniors. A smart man absorbs such knowledge when possible. If I only knew when I was your age what I know now."

Jerrell frowned, recalling a similar conversation with a grizzled warrior less than two years prior. He had to admit that the man taught Jerrell a thing or two. "Perhaps there is wisdom in your words."

Gurgan smiled. "Well said."

"But why did you ask if I have children?"

The wizard's smile wilted as quickly as it had bloomed. "That is why you are sitting before me now."

Sensing a solemnness to Gurgan's mood, Jerrell remained silent.

"I have a daughter named Ydith who studies at the University on Tiadd.

In two years, she will complete her training and return to Eleighton as a master wizard."

"You must be proud of her."

"Of course. But she is not the subject of this discussion. Rather, it is my son, Everett. At thirteen, he has just begun his transformation from child to man. Part of that process is the awakening of the Gift inside him. Those abilities currently remain beyond his control, but that will change with time." The wizard's gaze dropped to the floor. "However, it is time I fear he lacks." He clenched his fists and when his eyes next met Jerrell's they were filled with fire. "Everett has gone missing. I want you to help me find him."

CHAPTER 21

INVESTIGATION

The wizard's statement regarding his son caused an instant shift in Jerrell's mood, his boasts quickly forgotten and his interest fully piqued.

"How long has Everett been missing?"

Gurgan plopped into his chair and rested his forehead in his hand. "We became aware of his absence three days ago. When he didn't show up to meet his tutor, she went to him and found his room empty. There was no sign of a struggle and no clue as to what might have happened."

Jerrell tried to place himself in the position of a thirteen-year-old living in a castle – a far cry from his own experience as a youth. Yet, he knew others who had fled abusive or overbearing situations. "What was your relationship with Everett like?"

Frowning, the wizard asked, "You suspect me?"

"You asked for my assistance, so I am gathering facts, not attempting to imply guilt."

"I love my son and have done everything I can to pave a path of success for him while attempting to fill the hole left when my wife died."

"Which was when?"

The man looked down at his desktop, but Jerrell noted a far more distant look. "Yvette died during Everett's birth. The midwife did what she could, but there was no wizardess nearby to save her."

"Wizardess?"

"A female wizard. They are far more skilled at healing then male wizards. My wife could mend a broken arm in seconds, yet it takes all my skills to heal a hangnail."

"Why was a wizardess not present?"

"Eleighton is a remote city in the mountains. Our population barely reaches three thousand. Few wizards choose to live here, and of those few, many live elsewhere during the cold winter months, which is when he was born."

Jerrell considered the information and asked another question. "Who knows of his disappearance?"

"Only Everett's tutor, Audette, my head steward, Frederick, Captain Fossie, Lieutenant Dandon, and myself."

"Why so few?"

"Because...I fear someone with access to the castle had a hand in it. Keeping it quiet helps me to keep the perpetrators off balance."

"Surely, you have searched for him."

"Yes, but under the guise of searching for the man behind the recent murders. That search began here at the castle, the day Everett disappeared. I have sixty men under my command, and every one of them was involved, forced to check in every room, closet, cabinet, and hiding space large enough to hold a person. They were told to report anything of interest but found nothing of Everett.

"The next day, the search expanded to the city, where the men moved from building to building conducting a detailed inspection. Under my direction, they began with the manors across the valley, homes of my most likely rivals."

"Including Rostarin?"

The wizard nodded. "His family estate is one of the three still owned by wizards."

"And the others?"

Gurgan frowned. "Both are wealthy families who use the manor as a summer home and stay in Lionne during the winter. They are likely to return in the coming weeks since the weather has turned, but the manors are currently empty." He ran his hand through his hair. "Anyway, after searching Rostarin's home, they found nothing, so my soldiers moved down to the valley floor and continued the search. They are to complete their search of the city today."

"So they missed the secret entrance in Rostarin's cellar?"

"It appears so."

"It was a brilliant design," Jerrell said. "If you didn't know what to look for, you would have missed it."

The wizard narrowed his eyes. "You make excuses for my men. Why are you trying to protect them?"

"I...don't know."

"Is it for the same reason you allowed the city watch to claim that they killed Rostarin and saved you when it is clear you killed him and saved yourself?"

Jerrell blinked. "You knew?"

"I suspected...until now." Gurgan smirked.

Chuckling, Jerrell said, "Well played."

"You still haven't answered the question."

Considering his response, Jerrell said, "I made a deal with the city watch and did not want to be saddled with the potential issues surrounding the death of a wizard. Depending on the man who governs the area, someone like me might find themselves on a gibbet for killing a wizard, regardless of the man's own guilt."

The wizard nodded. "That is true, but not in Eleighton. I make every attempt to treat individuals based on their own merit and not the amount of metal in their blood."

"That is a relief."

"Now, back to my son. Will you help me?"

"I will do what I can. However, I require your support."

"I will give you coin, men, whatever you need."

"I require unfettered access to the castle grounds. Inform whoever you need to that I am your special guest, and I have full privileges to come and go and do as I wish."

"Done." Gurgan stood and held out a hand, waiting until Jerrell stood and shook it. "Please find my son."

"I will do my best."

"I offered twenty gold pieces for Rostarin's capture. I will give you twice that if you return my son to me. Alive."

THE HEAD STEWARD, dressed in a black coat and clasping his hands behind his back, led Jerrell down a corridor on the fourth floor of Eleighton Castle. The man stopped, turned toward Jerrell, and gestured toward an open door.

"This is Everett's room."

"Thank you, Frederick."

The head steward stood stiff, his white hair slicked back, the tips of his white mustache twisted into a coil. He wore a black coat and seemed to have his hands permanently clasped behind his back. While elderly, he moved well enough. More importantly, Gurgan appeared to have full faith in the man and had asked him to give Jerrell any assistance he needed.

A moment of silence lingered while Frederick stared through the doorway with a sad look in his eyes. "There were numerous moments that boy tested my patience. He was often loud and sometimes destructive. Sixty soldiers live in the lower levels, yet the castle feels empty with neither Everett nor Ydith present." He turned toward Jerrell. "I pray he returns soon."

The pain in the man's voice struck a chord. Jerrell patted his shoulder. "I will do what I can, but you mustn't tell anyone why I am here. If asked, just say that my stay is High Wizard Gurgan's way of making reparations for the pain inflicted by Rostarin."

"Ah, the murderous wizard. I can comfortably speak for everyone in Eleighton when I say I thank you for capturing him."

"I..." Jerrell was about to correct the man but changed his mind. "You are welcome. Now, go and do whatever you normally do. Remember, I am only a guest."

"As you wish, Master Landish." The man walked off, leaving Jerrell alone.

The room was as Jerrell had expected. A bookshelf stood against one wall, a king size, four poster bed along the opposite side. The forest-covered mountainside was visible through sheer curtains covering the windows opposite from the door. A small stone fireplace sat between the two windows, dark and dormant. The bed was unmade, giving the room a lived-in appearance, although it had remained empty for three days.

He entered the room and began his search with the desk by the bookshelves.

AN INSPECTION of Everett's room yielded nothing, so Jerrell headed down the corridor and knocked on the door to the neighboring room.

A woman's voice came from inside. "I am coming."

The door opened to reveal a brown-haired woman roughly Jerrell's height and a dozen years his senior. Her green eyes scanned him from head to toe. She had full lips and pale skin, giving her an attractive appearance, which was spoiled only by her haughty expression. "Who are you?"

"My name is Jerrell. I am staying here for a few days and thought I would stop by and say hello."

She pressed her lips together and glanced down the corridor before replying. At the far end, two guards stood outside the door to Gurgan's office.

Gripping the door as if she was prepared to slam it shut, she turned back to Jerrell. "I am Audette."

"You are Everett's tutor?"

Her expression darkened further. "I am."

"May I come in?"

Audette grimaced. "Just know that a scream will bring a dozen armed guards."

She does not trust me. He smiled, hoping to disarm her with his charm. "Do not worry. You have nothing to fear from me, pretty lady."

Rather than melt at his words, her frown deepened. Still, she stepped aside, and he walked past her, finding a room much like Everett's but with a smaller bed and a round table and chairs where the boy's desk would have been.

Jerrell approached the window and peered outside. Tall pines covered the hillside beyond the castle walls, their shadows growing longer as the afternoon waned.

Without turning around, he said, "I heard you were the first to discover that Everett was missing."

"You know about that?"

He spun around to find her standing in the middle of the room, her hands clasped at the waist of her gray dress. "The high wizard informed me of his situation. Do not worry, I understand his wish to keep the information confidential."

She glanced toward the open door while kneading her hands.

"Is something wrong?"

"No. I...just feel uncomfortable talking about this with the door open. His Grace wishes to keep this private. Perhaps I should..."

"Leave it open." The woman's behavior had been odd from the start. He hoped leaving the door open might keep her off guard. "Do not worry, my visit will be brief."

Audette nodded. "All right."

"Your room is adjacent to his. Did you hear anything strange on the evening before his disappearance?"

Her brow furrowed, but she spoke her response in an even tone. "Not that I recall."

"And when did you realize he was gone?"

"He normally comes to my room to begin instruction right after breakfast. When he didn't show, I went to His Grace and informed him."

"Curious."

She blinked. "What is curious?"

"If he usually ate first, shouldn't someone from the kitchen or wait staff have noted him not showing up for breakfast?"

"I am not sure." She blinked. "He sometimes foregoes breakfast or swings by the kitchen to grab something if he is running late."

Her explanation made sense, but something still bothered him – something he could not identify.

"Other than tutoring, what is your role here?"

Audette shook her head. "Unless Everett returns, I fear the high wizard will relieve me of my position. I will be forced to leave and find new employment."

His questions finished, Jerrell walked to the door. "Thank you for your time. I will return if I need more information."

"Do you think you can find him?"

She has figured out the intent of my questions. "I know I can. I just hope I do before it is too late."

He walked away, heading toward his next appointment.

ALTHOUGH THE DOOR STOOD OPEN, Jerrell knocked. The two men inside, both leaning over a table, looked toward the door. They scowled when they saw him.

"Come in," Captain Fossie grumbled.

Jerrell entered the chamber and surveyed his surroundings. A map of Farrowen covered the wall to his right; books, scrolls, and charts filled the shelves on the left wall. A desk stood before the shelves, a vacant chair behind it. The dining chairs had been pushed aside, leaving the table in the middle of the room open on all sides other than where Fossie and Dandon stood.

Approaching the two uniformed men, Jerrell noted that a map of the valley lay on the table. The detail was impressive, with the location of every building in Eleighton noted by a red square. Upon each square was a copper coin.

"Are you placing bets?" Jerrell asked.

Dandon looked down at the map. "The coins represent buildings that have been inspected."

"And…"

"You know as well as we do that nothing has been found."

Fossie asked, "Why are you here?"

"I am curious and wish to help."

Dandon snarled. "You leaving to allow us to focus would be most helpful."

Fossie rested a hand on his lieutenant's shoulder. "At ease, Dandon. He is Gurgan's guest. It will do no harm for him to join the conversation."

With a scowl, Dandon grumbled. "Fine."

"Now," Fossie said, "since every building in town has been searched, where do we go next?"

Dandon tapped on buildings deeper into the valley. "We start with the smelting facilities and then move on to the mines."

"A fair amount of forest covers the valley between here and the mines," Fossie noted. "I suggest we search there first, so we don't have to worry about anyone moving him back into the city while our men are down in the mines."

"Good point, Captain."

The men continued their discussion while Jerrell listened and watched their every movement. He did not like Dandon, and it was obvious the man reciprocated the sentiment. *I hope he is behind it. Still, it is best to keep an open mind. Wishing for his guilt won't help me save the young man.*

Like his visit with Audette, Jerrell departed after a few minutes and went in search of his next interview.

A NARROW MOONBEAM shone through the gap in the curtains, providing just enough light to give shape to the furniture in the chamber. Unable to sleep, Jerrell lay in a soft bed, almost too soft, and stared up at the ceiling while thinking about what he had seen and heard during his investigation. After what felt like hours, he sat up, deciding he needed a drink to calm his mind.

He pulled on his breeches and slipped his tunic over his head before heading out the door.

Enchanted lanterns illuminated the corridor, which stood empty in one direction while a pair of guards waited outside the high wizard's chamber in the other. Audette and Everett's rooms were sandwiched between his and Gurgan's. Jerrell narrowed his eyes and wondered how Everett could have been taken from his room during the night if the guards were always present and posted so close.

He turned and walked to the stairwell. The stone steps felt cold beneath his bare feet. As he passed the third floor, he heard a door close. He froze. The swishing of approaching skirts followed, so he rushed down to the next landing and hid. The scuff of slippered footsteps entered the stairwell and then began an ascent.

Jerrell climbed up and peered around the corner, just in time to spy Audette in a bathrobe as she rounded the bend at the landing. Curious, he stuck his head into the third-floor corridor and found it empty. He closed his eyes and recalled the number of strides he had heard after the door. With his eyes still closed, he imagined himself as Audette while replaying her movement and counting down the time between the door shutting and her footsteps on the stairwell. He then stopped and opened his eyes to find a closed door with a star on it. *Fossie. Interesting.*

Turning, he returned to the stairwell and descended to the second floor, in search of the kitchen.

CHAPTER 22

BETWEEN THE LINES

By the time Jerrell arrived for breakfast, morning sunlight streamed through the open window of Gurgan's private, fourth-floor dining room. The high wizard sat in the lone occupied chair, the other nine empty and pushed neatly beneath the dark wooden table in the center of the room. Frederick stood beside a buffet table, his chest thrust out and heels pressed together. An attractive female servant stood at his side. Her red curls were tied back in a bun, her blue eyes alert, her pale skin smooth as porcelain. Jerrell's attention lingered on the woman, drinking in the curves outlined by the snug bodice of her gray dress. When Gurgan's gaze lifted to the doorway, Jerrell entered.

"You are late," Gurgan noted. "We were to break our fast an hour after sunrise."

As Jerrell approached the table, he found the wizard's plate nearly clean and the pale liquid filling only the bottom of the wizard's goblet.

"I had difficulty falling asleep last night," Jerrell explained, "and although I left the curtain open, so the sun would wake me, my body decided it was not ready to wake until moments ago."

Gurgan gestured toward the chair before Jerrell. "Sit."

After hesitating for a moment, Jerrell claimed the indicated seat. He disliked facing away from a door; it went against his nature. It was also one the reasons he was still breathing.

Frederick and the female servant both turned toward the buffet, followed by the sound of utensils clanking against dishes. Moments later, the chief steward approached the table and set a plate before Jerrell. When he stepped back, the woman leaned over Jerrell to set a goblet before him. She held a carafe in each hand.

"Would you care for apple juice or milk?"

Jerrell shared his best smile. "I'll take anything you have to offer."

She blinked and appeared flustered before returning his smile.

While she may not be the smartest girl, my interest doesn't lie in her quick wit. He decided to help her out. "While I'd prefer cold ale, apple juice will be fine."

"As you wish." She filled his goblet and stepped away.

Gurgan said, "Frederick, Mara, you are both excused. Please close the door when you leave. I wish to speak with Mister Landish in private."

"Yes, Your Grace," Frederick bowed and led the woman to the door while Jerrell continued to watch them over his shoulder.

When the door closed, Jerrell turned to Gurgan. "Where was *she* yesterday? I thought I had met your entire staff and I am unlikely to forget a pretty face."

"Mara was away from the castle, visiting her blind mother for the day. The poor girl spends her earnings on her mother's rent, care, and food. I give her one day off each week to spend with the woman."

"Don't those days create complications for your staff?"

"Oh, they manage well enough. Frederick is a stickler for details and makes it work."

Jerrell glanced up at the wizard. Gurgan's comments revealed much about the man beneath the robes.

The high wizard said, "I hear you were busy yesterday."

"Yes. I visited dozens of chambers and spoke with everyone on your staff...except for Mara."

"Did you observe anything that might help locate my son?"

"Yes and no."

"What does that mean?"

"Yes, I learned much, but I don't know where your son is…yet. However, I am getting a feel for who might be behind his disappearance. Like you, I suspect someone on the inside orchestrated it, but I am not ready to point fingers quite yet."

The high wizard frowned. "What can you tell me?"

Jerrell had expected the question. "Are you aware that Audette and Captain Fossie are having an affair?"

"Huh," Gurgan grunted. "I had suspected as much."

"It doesn't bother you?"

Gurgan stroked his beard, considering his response before speaking. "Including the barracks below, more than seventy people occupy this castle. Yet, it can be a lonely place, as I have found in the years since my wife's passing. If two people can find solace in each other's arms without it affecting their jobs, I will allow it. The fact that they have kept it discreet tells me they are not yet prepared to publicly commit to a long-term arrangement. Thus, I do not ask."

Jerrell was disappointed. He expected the discovery to be a nugget of unexpected information for the wizard to swallow.

"What else have you discovered?"

"Well, Fossie and Dandon are planning to resume the search today, starting with the smelting facilities and surrounding forest. It sounds like they will move on to the mines tomorrow."

"I expected that as well." Gurgan nodded. "The closest mines are three miles from the city. Some are more than twice that distance. The valley might be narrow, but that is still a lot of ground to cover. We can only send thirty men out at a time since a minimum of ten active guards must be on duty to protect the castle at all times. With three shifts, that removes half of my troops from the search."

"That makes sense." Jerrell pushed his eggs around with his fork while his mind raced. Something had bothered him from the start. Motive. That concern sparked his next question. "Do you have any enemies who might wish to get to you by harming Everett?"

"I would have put Rostarin at the top of such a list. His family and mine funded one of the iron mines, which means the income derived from it is split between our two estates. If he removed me and my line, that would have given him a path to claim my title while doubling his wealth. You see, that mine was his only income, while I have investments in a smelting facility and chromium imports that are used to turn the iron into steel."

Jerrell nodded. "I believe killing you and erasing your entire family may have been that mad wizard's scheme. With the sorcery he intended to use… along with other things"—Jerrell was reluctant to expose the capabilities of the bracelet—"he believed his magic would have been greatly augmented, at least enough to challenge and defeat you."

Gurgan snorted. "He couldn't even get into the University. For him to gain enough strength in the Gift to become a threat…well, that would have been something unexpected and most impressive."

Yet, Rostarin was dead and Everett was still nowhere to be found. "Assuming it wasn't him, are there any others who might wish to come after you?"

Stroking his beard while furrowing his brow, Gurgan considered the question. "I must admit, Malvorian and I do not get along."

"The wizard lord?"

Gurgan grimaced. "That man who does not deserve his station." A fire flared in his eyes. "If I had the means, I'd kill him and spare Farrowen from his selfish madness."

While interesting, the wizard's response did not answer the question. "But would he come after you?"

"Not as long as I continue to send a wagon full of iron ingots to Marquithe every week."

Jerrell arched his brows. "Why does he require so much iron?"

"He won't tell me directly, but I have observed that he is building a new garrison in Lionne and expanding the one outside of Shear. I can only speculate on his reason."

"War?"

"Good guess. The only question is against who?"

A knock from behind caused Jerrell to turn toward the door.

"Come in," Gurgan said.

The door opened to reveal Lieutenant Dandon. "Permission to enter, Your Grace?"

"Yes. Come in, Lieutenant."

The uniformed man approached the table, flashed Jerrell a scowl, and then extended his hand toward Gurgan. In it was a crumpled parchment with writing scrawled on it. "This was found on the road outside the gate. Twine tied to a rock the size of my fist."

Gurgan accepted the paper, read it silently, and fell back into his chair with a groan. His fingers raked down his face while his sorrowful eyes stared into the unknown.

After a moment of silence, Gurgan looked up at Dandon. "Continue today's search as planned. I must consider this and decide how to proceed."

The lieutenant thumped his fist to his chest. "Yes, Your Grace." He left the room and closed the door behind him.

After looking over the note one last time, Gurgan extended it toward Jerrell, who accepted it without comment. He straightened the paper and read the stilted, poorly written text.

HIGH WIZARD GURGAN,

We have your son. He is well and will be returned if you follow these instructions.

One hundred twenty gold pieces are to be placed in a sack. That sack will be delivered to the obelisk one hour after Devotion. It must be left at the foot of the obelisk, and the delivery man is to depart. If any soldiers or city guards are seen in the area, your son will die. If anyone follows the sack after it is claimed, your son will die. If any wizard is involved in this transaction or if we detect any magic of any kind, your son will die.

If we collect the gold, Everett will be freed tomorrow morning, allowing you to reunite with your youngest offspring.

Be warned, we will accept no deviation from the instructions above. Betrayal will be met with swift and deadly force.

. . .

After reading the note a second time, Jerrell looked up to find Gurgan still staring into space. *The man is understandably distraught.*

Breaking the silence, Jerrell asked, "Do you even have that many gold pieces?"

The man blinked and nodded. "It will put a strain on my coffers, but it is within my means."

"I assume you intend to pay them."

"Unless today's search turns up something useful, I don't see any other choice."

"It has to be me," Jerrell said. "I need to deliver the ransom."

"What? Why?"

"The note said no soldiers, no wizards, no magic. You need someone you trust."

"What makes you think I trust you?"

Jerrell rolled his eyes. "I am sure you have investigated everything I have done since arriving in Eleighton. When did I get here? Where did I eat? Where did I sleep?"

Gurgan narrowed his eyes before replying. "You arrived two days ago and checked in to Basil's place. He said he had to forward you coin for your meal, but you paid him back."

"Right. When was your son taken?"

"Two days before you arrived in the city."

"So, you know I had nothing to do with it. Who else can you eliminate from suspicion?"

Gurgan sighed. "Nobody."

"See. It must be me." Jerrell grinned. "Besides, I have a plan."

The wizard's face darkened. "Your plan had better not put Everett in greater risk."

Jerrell leaned closer to the wizard and gripped his forearm. "Think, Gurgan. Read between the lines."

"What does that mean?"

Hoping to avoid saying it out loud, Jerrell tried another approach. "Put yourself in the position of the kidnappers. Imagine you are holding someone captive...someone you wouldn't care about except for the coin they are worth. Once you receive the payment, what would you do? Would you let that person free, where they might be able to identify you and send people after you? Or would you kill that person and be free of such concerns?"

As the realization came over Gurgan, his eyes widened, and the color drained from his face. "Oh, no."

CHAPTER 23

MACHINATIONS

The heels of Jerrell's boots echoed softly in a quiet corridor.

He slowed as he approached two guards standing beside a closed door. "The high wizard summoned me."

One of the guards replied, "Hello, Landish." The man knocked, paused for a breath, and then turned the knob. The door opened a few inches. "Go on in. He is expecting you."

"Thanks." Jerrell pushed the door open and entered Gurgan's study.

The high wizard occupied the chair behind the desk, his gaze turning from the window to Jerrell. "You wanted to visit me once I had the gold ready." Gurgan gestured toward the twelve stacks of coins on the desktop. A hint of sorrow darkened his tone. "Here it is."

"If I may, I would like to borrow twenty coins."

"May I ask why?"

"I have an idea that might help us catch the conspirators, but I won't know if it will work until I speak with your blacksmith."

"Very well."

Jerrell slid a stack of coins off the table. The heaping pile filled his palm. He dumped the coins into an empty sack before adding the second pile. Cinching the sack tight, he lifted it, making the coins jingle. The weight of twenty gold and the way the light reflected off the edges of the coins sent his heart fluttering. There was a time where such a sum was beyond his wildest dreams. *Odd how your perspective changes.* In the past two years, he had handled five times as much – an astounding amount of wealth. He now also knew how easily such wealth was lost.

"I will be back this afternoon."

A quick trip down three flights of stairs took him to the door leading outside. He exited the building and crossed the quiet castle yard. Circling behind the stables, he approached an open building. The repeated peal of a hammer on metal steadily grew louder. In the shadows, a blacksmith wearing a heavy leather apron hammered a glowing sword blade. The man glanced up at Jerrell, completed two more pounds, and thrust the blade into a vat of water. A hiss and a cloud of steam puffed into the air.

In a friendly tone, Jerrell said, "Hello, Logan."

A grimace appeared in the man's thick black beard. Standing six feet tall with broad shoulders and a barrel chest, Logan appeared both imposing and power-ful, so the grimace likely scared off most people. Jerrell was not most people.

Logan growled. "I already answered your questions yesterday."

"No questions this time," Jerrell shook his coin purse. "I have a job for you."

The smith's expression softened. "What kind of job?"

"I am not sure if you are capable. It'll require more finesse than muscle."

"Just because I am stuck repairing weapons and armor all day doesn't mean I can't create finer pieces."

"Well, there is some creation here, but also modification."

"Go on."

"Can you quickly craft a mold?"

He frowned. "How large?"

Jerrell opened his coin purse and pulled out a gold piece. "This big."

Furrowing his heavy brow while staring at the coin, Logan said, "You want me to create a counterfeit coin?"

"I knew you were a smart man."

Grunting in reply, Logan added, "You are in luck. I happen to have a block of copper I had been saving for a special project. With it, I can have a mold ready in short order."

Jerrell smiled. "Wonderful. But first, I'd like you to use iron."

"What for?"

"You'll find out."

WITH THE BLACKSMITH busy at work on one aspect of his plan, Jerrell crossed the yard. He spied a wagon rolling through the gate, and his smile broadened at the sight of the driver. *Sometimes, my luck astounds even me.*

He stood beside the castle entrance and waited as the wagon rolled toward him. The driver pulled on the reins to stop his team and stared down at Jerrell.

"Hello again, Ivan," Jerrell said.

"I see you are still here."

"I see that you've a keen gift for observation."

Ignoring the jibe, Ivan said, "Can you get a porter to help me move these goods into the cellar?"

"Never mind the porters. I will help you unload."

Ivan shrugged. "Suit yourself."

They walked to the back of the wagon, where Jerrell waited while Ivan opened the tail gate.

"This is heavy," Ivan said as he pulled a crate toward him. "Grab the other side."

Gripping the wooden crate with both hands, Jerrell lifted with a grunt. "You were not exaggerating. What is in this thing?"

"Potatoes. Over a hundred pounds."

Ivan backed toward the door with Jerrell following. They waited as the wagon driver opened it, then stepped inside and descended a flight of stairs, which led them to a cellar with a dirt floor.

"Let's set it down over there." Ivan nodded toward the wall on their right.

They set the crate down and dusted off their hands. When Ivan headed toward the stairs, Jerrell gripped his shoulder, stopping him.

"Hold on."

"What is it?"

"I have a proposal for you. How would you like to have dinner with me tonight at Basil's place?"

Ivan's brow furrowed, and he gave Jerrell an odd look. "I am flattered, but I'm not interested in men."

Jerrell laughed. "No. It's nothing like that. I only wish to meet you there, buy you dinner, and have you perform a simple task. I'll even pay you two silver pieces." Tapping his own chest, Jerrell added, "Besides, you only wish you could have a lover with my physique and skills."

Ivan snickered. "What is this task you need done?"

"I'm glad you asked. First, you will meet me at the Rusty Nail immediately after Devotion. We will eat, drink an ale or two, and then..." Jerrell went on to explain Ivan's role in his plan.

WITH THE AFTERNOON waning and the sun partially eclipsed by the mountains to the west, Jerrell hurried across the castle yard and climbed the stairs to the fourth floor. He marched down the hall, heading straight toward Gurgan's study where two guards waited. The men didn't even bother asking him a question. Instead, they knocked, opened the door, and stepped aside.

Jerrell walked in to find Gurgan staring out the window.

The wizard turned around. "Where have you been? We will be out of daylight soon."

"I have your gold." Jerrell jingled the sack in his hands. It was heavy and much fuller than when he left the wizard's office earlier that day. The weight felt good.

Gurgan frowned. "That appears to be more than twenty gold pieces."

Jerrell grinned. "It's one hundred twenty coins."

"How..."

"Don't worry. Nobody will be the wiser, so hold on to the rest of your gold and let me do my job."

"I hope you know what you are doing. My son's life depends on it."

"I will do everything I can to save him. At the same time, I am also taking steps to catch whoever is behind this twisted plot." Jerrell glanced out the window. The wizard was right about one thing. Night was fast approaching and the ride to the city would take some time. "I need to get my cloak, but first, can you request a carriage to drive me down to the city?"

"Very well. Get your cloak. The carriage will be waiting."

With the sack of gold in one hand, Jerrell rushed out of the room while Gurgan called for his guards to fetch his driver.

Jerrell sat alone in the carriage with a pack at his side. The sack of gold had a blanket around it to dull the noise and had required force to stuff into the pack, causing the canvas to bulge.

By the time the carriage reached the bottom of the hill and rolled into the city, darkness had all but claimed the valley. The driver pulled up to the Rusty Nail and stopped. With his hood over his head, Jerrell climbed out and then sent the man back to the castle.

He stood in the street, staring at the Obelisk of Devotion four blocks away. He did not have long to wait.

A beam of blue light shot across the sky, struck the top of the obelisk, and caused the spire to burst into blue flames. People poured out of the surrounding buildings, dropped to their knees, and began to chant the prayers that fed their wizard lord, Malvorian.

As the minutes passed, Jerrell constantly surveyed the people around him, noting Ivan's presence but seeing nothing that appeared odd and no one watching him. The beam of light faded and the fire went out. Everyone rose to their feet and headed on their way. Jerrell followed Ivan and five others into the Rusty Nail.

An hour later, a cloaked man emerged from the Rusty Nail. With his hood raised and a full pack over his shoulder, the man stood in the moonlit street and glanced both directions. He appeared unaware of the person hidden in a dark doorway across the street.

The man set off toward the square in the heart of Eleighton, while his stalker followed at a distance. Upon reaching the empty square, the man with the pack approached the tower, steered to shadowed side, and squatted at the base. Seconds later, the man emerged from the shadows without the pack and returned down the street from whence he had come, unknowingly passing the watcher who was masked in the darkness beneath the awning of a shop.

The watcher waited, carefully monitoring the departing man while frequently glancing back toward the obelisk. When the cloaked man drew near the Rusty Nail, the watcher emerged from the shadows and headed across the square.

CHAPTER 24
STEALTH

On the moonlit rooftop of a two-story home, Jerrell leaned against a stone chimney, hidden in its shadow. His position provided a clear view of Eleighton City Square, the obelisk in its center, and the street on the opposite end where Ivan, dressed as Jerrell, headed back toward the Rusty Nail.

When Ivan's footsteps were too distant to hear, another cloaked form emerged from the night, crossed the square, and faded into the shade of the obelisk. A moment later, the person returned, clutching a pack tightly while heading toward the street below where Jerrell stood.

With the apex of the rooftop between him and the street, Jerrell hurried across the roof, reached the eave, and jumped to the neighboring roof. He repeated these movements, rushing across rooftops and leaping over gaps until he came to the end of the street. He then climbed over the apex and eased down the front side of the roof until he spied the cloaked figure walking along the otherwise empty street. The person entered the crossing below Jerrell. The added light from the moon and his closer proximity to the person made it clear that Jerrell followed a man with a tall, lean frame.

The man continued down the street and entered the second house on the right.

Jerrell squatted beside the eaves, swung his legs down, and dropped to the porch awning below. From there, it was a short jump to the ground. He rushed along the empty cross street and examined the front of the building. With the door closed and a curtain covering the window, he could not see inside. He snuck into the narrow gap between the building and the neighboring home, where he spied dim light coming from a second-story window.

A downspout ran down the side of the house, just beyond the window. Jerrell gripped it and pulled himself up, pressing his feet against the house while scaling hand over hand until he was even with the window. Then he reached out, grabbed the top of the shutter, and swung himself over. Hanging with his feet twelve feet above the alley, he peered inside.

Four men were visible through a gap in the curtain, all in a line along one wall and facing the same direction. They wore mismatched leather armor and dark cloaks. Two had swords on their hips, the others wore daggers. A muffled voice came from a fifth person beyond Jerrell's view. He strained to hear the words.

"...are to inspect the mines tomorrow. Now that we have our payment, we must kill the boy before he is found. If he is allowed to live and identifies us to Gurgan, the wizard will hunt us down and see us hanged."

An arm appeared in the gap, holding out a small sack, which was placed in the hand of one of the men. "This is your cut – ten gold for each of you and ten for the others. Once the boy has been dealt with, I suggest you leave the valley. The gold should be enough for a fresh start." The back of the cloaked man blocked the view for a breath. "Go now. Take care of the boy. I must return before I am suspected."

All five men turned and filed out the door.

By then, Jerrell's hands and arms were sore from hanging in such a precarious position, and his grip loosened. He pushed himself from the window, causing the shutter to swing back around. With one arm, he reached for the downspout. When he let go of the shutter, his other hand slid down the pipe, causing him to hurriedly scramble. He missed and fell, landing feet-first before falling to his backside and striking his elbow on something. His feet, elbow, and arse all stung as he sat up. A noise came from the street. The cloaked man had already passed.

Jerrell climbed to his feet, crept down the alley, and peered toward the square. The man's cloak swirled around him as he walked swiftly with the pack over his shoulder. With purposeful strides, the four men headed out of town in the other direction.

Crap. I can't follow both. After brief consideration, he emerged from the alley and headed down the street leading toward the mines, careful to stay in the shadows beside the buildings. A few hundred feet ahead of him, four men traveled along the moonlit road, on their way to kill the high wizard's son.

THE JOURNEY to the mines took longer than Jerrell anticipated. He took care to remain quiet and keep his distance. He could not alert the men that they were being followed, not until he knew where Everett was being held. More than once, he feared he had lost them; dozens of gravel paths wide enough for a wagon branched off the primary route. Alone on the moonlit road, surrounded by trees and darkness, he would stop and listen, straining to hear beyond the rustle of the wind. Distant voices or the crunch of footsteps revealed that the men had not turned from the main path, causing him to rush ahead with a fast walk, while carefully avoiding any heavy steps that would alert them to his presence.

An hour after leaving the city, Jerrell stopped at the junction of a side path. Long grass and weeds occupied the gap between two dirt ruts running off into shadow. The crack of a branch came from down the dark path. Jerrell followed it, hoping the noise had been from the men and not a moarbear. He had heard tales of the ferocious beasts that left him anxious.

Shadows consumed his surroundings; the trees leaned in. Nature had begun to reclaim the ground, and Jerrell was certain the path he followed was rarely traveled. The dark road ran uphill, turning repeatedly before the trees fell away and a rocky hillside came into view. A few hundred feet ahead, he spied movement in the shadow of the hill. He remained in the trees, waiting as light bloomed in a rock alcove. One of the men held an enchanted lantern while the others removed two panels from a boarded-up tunnel entrance. The man with the lantern ducked inside, and the other three followed. Once the last man ducked through the gap, Jerrell emerged from hiding and approached the tunnel entrance. Ten feet tall and just as wide, worn gray boards covered the opening except for the two-foot-wide gap. Utter darkness loomed beyond the opening.

Jerrell drew his dagger and pressed the gem on the hilt. A soft blue light shone from it. With the dagger held in front of him, he stepped into the tunnel, praying he was not entering a trap.

A DOZEN STRIDES into the tunnel, Jerrell reached a pair of metal rails connected by flat boards spaced a few feet apart. He followed the rails deeper into the mountain as the tunnel began to rise. The tunnel split in two, causing Jerrell to pause and douse his light. Pale light came from the path with the track. He followed it uphill and around a bend. The light grew brighter, eclipsed by numerous silhouettes.

He tailed them along a meandering route, always heading uphill and passing numerous branching paths, some of which also had tracks like the one on the ground beside him. After a quarter of a mile, a warm light appeared ahead, and the men faded from view. Voices arose, with numerous men talking. Jerrell crept forward, listening as he approached the light.

"...finally came back, Marcus. I never realized how much I would miss the sun."

Marcus replied, "The boss chose to wait until yesterday to send the ransom note, hoping to draw more gold from Gurgan."

"And?"

"We each get ten gold for this little caper. Gather around and take your cut."

Jerrell had reached the mouth of a large cavern. A cart with four metal wheels sat in the middle of the cavern, mounted to the metal track. At the far end, a bonfire illuminated the area. Smoke from the fire rose to an opening in the cavern ceiling, a hundred feet above. Numerous ledges overlooked the cavern, one near where Jerrell stood appeared twenty feet high. Another one twice as high protruded from the opposite side of the cavern. A wooden lift dangled beside the nearest ledge, suspended by a thick rope attached to a pulley mounted near the rocky roof.

The four men Jerrell had followed had been joined by five others. They huddled in a circle at the far end of the cavern. The coins clinked as one man divided the contents of the sack. Bedrolls lay on the floor beside their bonfire, along with a pile of packs and ten jugs. On the cavern floor below the ledge, a dozen strides from Jerrell, a boy in torn robes sat against the rock wall. The boy's arms were tied behind his back while ropes secured his ankles together. Bound and gagged, the boy stared at the kidnappers with terror-filled eyes.

Shadows clung to a narrow side tunnel beside Jerrell. The floor inside the tunnel rose steeply with tall steps carved into the floor. Curious, he ducked into the tunnel and spied light above. He quietly scrambled upward and found himself in another part of the cavern. Beside him, another tunnel led to darkness. On his hands and knees, he eased along the lowest ledge and peered down at the kidnappers.

"Ten gold each?" one of the men asked with a smile.

Marcus explained, "The boss promised this scheme would be worth it."

"I wonder how much he kept," another man said.

"It was his plan, and he risked far more than any of us. He deserves his, same as we do."

"Now what?"

"Now it is time to end this and leave the valley."

"You mean?"

Marcus drew his sword and turned toward Everett. "Yes."

Jerrell leaned forward and saw Everett below him. The boy's eyes gaped in fear, and he struggled against his bonds. Backing up, Jerrell lifted his gaze to the lift, which hung nearby. His gaze followed the rope from the lift to the pulley high above, then back down to where it was secured to a metal loop in the wall several strides away. Jerrell quickly stood, pressed his dagger to the rope, and began to saw at it. At the same time, Marcus stalked toward Everett.

Two strides from Everett, Marcus stopped and stared down at him.

"Sorry, boy. It is nothing personal. While I am sure you would promise not to identify us if we allowed you to live, it is a risk we cannot take." He pointed his blade at Everett. "I will make it quick."

The man raised the sword high, preparing for a fatal strike. Jerrell's blade severed all but the last strand of rope, which snapped. A high-pitched squeal echoed in the chamber as the pulley spun and the lift plummeted. Marcus looked up, but he was too late – the lift crashed down, crushing him. The man's sword arm stuck out from the wreckage, momentarily twitching. The sword fell to the cavern floor beside the unharmed teen.

The remaining eight kidnappers stared with wide-eyed shock.

"What the blazes?" one man exclaimed.

Another pointed up at Jerrell. "Look!"

"Intruder!"

"Get him!"

With his free hand, Jerrell reached into his sleeve, drew a throwing blade, and loosed. The knife plunged into an enemy's chest, causing him to stagger and fall.

The two men with crossbows lifted them and took aim. Jerrell dropped to the ground just before the bolts struck the cavern wall. The men then scrambled toward the tunnel he had used, so Jerrell sprung to his feet and ran into the tunnel off the side of the ledge. Five strides in, he squatted, drew a throwing blade, and stood ready. As the first man climbed onto the ledge, Jerrell loosed, and the knife sailed into the man's stomach. The man clutched at it, stepped backward, and fell into the man behind him. Both tumbled out of sight.

"He has more knives," someone called out.

"Reload those crossbows."

Expecting the enemies would now advance with more care, Jerrell turned and hurried along the dark tunnel.

CHAPTER 25

FRACAS

The glow of the gem in Jerrell's dagger extended only a few strides before him as he hurried along the twisting tunnel. At the first branch, he took a side path that angled backward. The ground turned to an upslope as the tunnel curved back around. When it finally leveled, he spied light ahead.

The tunnel opened to a ledge four stories above the chamber he had just fled. Leaning over the edge, he spied Everett still propped up in a sitting position, bound and gagged. The destroyed lift lay beside him. Beyond it, three kidnappers stood while a fourth lay on the floor, clutching his bloody stomach, his eyes clenched tightly in pain.

Jerrell had killed two and wounded a third, all of whom were in the chamber with the four upright men. *That leaves two. They must have entered the tunnel and are pursing me.*

"What do we do?" one man asked.

"Shane and Barnum will take care of the intruder."

"What if he doubles back here?"

"Then we will deal with him. Ricard, watch the tunnel up there," the man pointed toward the lower ledge across the cavern from where Jerrell hid. "Pike, watch the entrance."

"What about you?"

Gripping his sword, the man gestured toward Everett. "I am going to end the boy. Like Marcus said, we can't leave him alive to identify us."

Jerrell backed away from the ledge and stood in the tunnel mouth. He had to think fast. Halfway between the upper tier where Jerrell stood and the one across the cavern hung the free end of the severed rope. The other end remained secured to the roof of the destroyed lift. Out of time and lacking other ideas, Jerrell bit down on his dagger blade, charged toward the ledge, and leapt.

Forty feet above the cavern floor, Jerrell kicked as he sailed through the air and began to fall. Reaching out, both hands grabbed the dangling rope. The rope jerked with his weight and swung forward from his momentum. The roof of the lift broke away from the rest and shot upward, the pulley squealed as Jerrell dropped toward the second story ledge. His feet found purchase, and he twisted around to find a man aiming a crossbow in his direction. Across from him, the lift's roof swung wildly. Jerrell released the rope and dove. The bolt flew over him and shattered on the rock wall. The pulley again squealed as the lift roof dropped down, struck the head of a swordsman, and knocked him to the ground as it crashed down with a mighty crack.

Jerrell drew a knife and threw it toward the man with the crossbow. His blade struck the man in the shoulder, causing him to twist and cry out.

One of the men went for Everett with his sword raised. Jerrell hurriedly drew the throwing blade from behind his neck and released it. The blade spun in a full revolution before it plunged into the right side of the man's neck. The sword arm came forward, but the hilt slipped from his grip. The weapon spun and landed point-down, piecing the man's foot. He screamed and fell to the ground beside the bound and gagged teen.

Jerrell pulled his dagger from his teeth, held it ready, and leapt toward the man urgently attempting to reload his crossbow. The man looked up, his eyes widening as Jerrell landed on him. They both crashed to the ground, the impact causing Jerrell to roll off while his dagger remained buried in the man's chest.

"You bastard!" the last standing swordsman shouted as he rushed forward with his sword over his head.

Jerrell rolled aside as the blade crashed down and struck the rock beside him. He scissor-kicked, one leg striking the attacker in the ankle, the other behind his knee. The man fell forward to his hands and knees. Weaponless, Jerrell grabbed a rock the size of his fist and swung hard while lunging at the man. The rock smashed into the man's head with a sickening crack. He collapsed face-first and did not move.

Scrambling to his feet, Jerrell scooped up the man's sword and hurried forward as the kidnapper with a throwing blade in his neck crawled toward Everett. With a lunge, Jerrell drove the sword through the man's back. He cried out and fell to his stomach. Suddenly, the chamber was silent other than Jerrell's gasps for air.

He knelt beside Everett, who stared back with wide, bloodshot eyes. "Are you all right?"

The boy nodded, wiggled, and strained against his bonds.

"Good. I am going to get us out of here."

The sound of footsteps came from above. *Crap. The other two are returning.*

Jerrell gripped Everett by the front of his robes and sat the teen forward while ducking low. With a grunt, he pulled the boy over his shoulders and stood. Although Everett was a decade younger than Jerrell, he was taller and likely outweighed him. *I can't carry him far and they are almost here.* He turned and spied the empty cart resting in the middle of the chamber. Jerrell staggered toward it and dumped the boy inside, so Everett was sitting in the bottom with his head just below the upper lip.

Jerrell spun around to retrieve his dagger from the dead kidnapper's chest, intent on using it to cut the boy's ropes. As he rushed back toward the dead man, a motion appeared on the ledge above.

"There he is!"

"He killed the others and has the boy!"

"Use your crossbow!"

Jerrell yanked the dead man off the ground and sat him upright, using the body as a shield. The bolt struck the corpse in the back with a thud. He gripped the hilt of his dagger and shoved the man away, freeing his blade.

"Get him!"

The remaining swordsman leapt off the ledge, straight toward Jerrell, who twisted away. The man landed on his feet but stumbled forward. Jerrell charged after the man and leapt, kicking with both legs. His heels struck the man in the lower back and sent him sprawling, his sword skittering free. Jerrell landed on his side, rolled with his feet beneath him, and rushed toward the man who crawled after his lost sword. With a forceful kick, Jerrell's boot struck the man in the face, flipping him over. Squatting, Jerrell sliced with his dagger, leaving a deep gash in the side of the man's neck. Blood spurted from the wound.

Spinning away from the dying man, Jerrell looked up to find the last kidnapper cranking his crossbow launch arm back. His eyes widening in alarm, Jerrell rushed over to the cart and began pushing it. The wheels squeaked at first and then gained momentum. As he crossed the room, he looked up again to find the man sliding the bolt into place. Jerrell had reached the downhill slope, and the cart began to roll faster. Jerrell let go and ran beside it, keeping the cart between him and the man with the cross-bow. The man raised his weapon, took aim, and Jerrell dove as he reached the tunnel mouth. A thwap sounded as the bolt released, followed by a thud as it struck the side of the cart. The cart raced past Jerrell and disappeared down the dark tunnel. He rose to his feet and gazed into the darkness for a breath. *I can't have anyone following us.* He turned around and stared into the warmly lit room, listening.

The sound of a crank came from the narrow opening in the side of the tunnel. The cranking grew louder. It was joined by footsteps, and both sounds grew closer. Jerrell pinned his back to the rock wall a stride from the opening. The crossbowman emerged from the tunnel and Jerrell lunged with a thrust of his heel, striking the side of the man's knee, and causing it to fold inward. A cry echoed as the man went down, his finger squeezing the trigger in his hand. The bolt shattered off the tunnel ceiling. Jerrell snatched the crossbow from the man's grip, raised it, and smashed it over his head, breaking the lathe off one side in the process. The man groaned, so Jerrell struck him again, this time with the stock. It collided with the man's forehead, causing the back of his head to bounce off the rocky ground. He did not move.

Jerrell tossed the busted crossbow aside and headed back into the fire-lit chamber.

Bodies were strewn about but none moved. He rushed around the room, retrieving his dagger and throwing blades, wiping each on a tunic or coat before returning it to its place. With every blade reclaimed and cleaned, he triggered the light on his dagger and headed down the dark tunnel, toward the entrance. As Jerrell made his quarter mile journey, he imagined Gurgan's reaction to his heroics.

For one man to take on and kill nine armed enemies and rescue the high wizard's abducted son from certain death...well, Jerrell's fame was certain to rise, along with his wealth. Satisfied, he followed the track to the end, where the silhouette of the cart stood out against the moonlight seeping through the gap in the boarded-over tunnel entrance.

"Sorry for the delay, Everett. I had to take care of business before I could return you to the castle." Jerrell approached the cart and shined his light inside. His spirits stepped off a cliff and plummeted into darkness. "Oh, no."

Everett's head lay against the side of the cart, his mouth still gagged. A crossbow bolt jutted from the boy's eye and blood stained the side of his face. The other eye stared with a glassy lifelessness.

Frustration, regret, and shock held Jerrell in stasis before his head dropped to his chest. After a few deep breaths, he rubbed his eyes dry. *Gurgan will be heartbroken.* The mere thought of telling the man his son had died made Jerrell's stomach churn. Despite everything he had done to save Everett, he was forced to say the three words he thought he would never say.

I have failed.

Pushing his sorrow aside, he took a deep breath and climbed through the gap in the boards.

CHAPTER 26

INJUSTICE

Slouched on a wagon seat with Ivan at his side, Jerrell fought off weariness while the horses pulled them up the hillside toward Eleighton Castle. Clouds dotted the awakening sky, but the land remained untouched by morning sunlight. When the castle gate came into view, the dread inside Jerrell's gut roiled. He was rarely fazed by tense situations where his own life hung in the balance, but this...

As the wagon neared the gate, Ivan pulled the reins, and the horses stopped shy of the guards posted there.

"You are early today," Sergeant Natal noted.

Ivan replied. "It was not my idea, and it is not a typical delivery."

The man looked at the wagon bed, its contents covered by a dark green canvas tarp. "What is it this time?"

Jerrell thumbed toward the wagon bed behind him. "Have a look for yourself."

The sergeant reached into the wagon bed, his other hand resting on the pommel of his sword. He lifted the tarp, and his eyes widened. "What happened?"

"I happened," Jerrell replied. "These men were holding Everett captive."

Natal dropped the tarp. "You found him?"

"Yes. He is the one wrapped in the sheet."

The color drained from Natal's face. "By the gods…"

"Do not worry. I will inform Gurgan. I only ask that you send someone to get him. We will wait in the bailey."

"Very well." Natal stared at Jerrell for a breath. "You are a brave man, Mister Landish."

"Bravery has nothing to do with it."

The response stirred up a question Jerrell had asked himself a dozen times over the previous three hours: *Why are you willing to risk the wizard's wrath?* He struggled to answer the question yet felt compelled to proceed anyway. A part of him screamed to flee Eleighton rather than face Gurgan, but he needed to see this through, regardless of the cost.

The sergeant pulled a guard aside and spoke with him briefly. The man ran off toward the castle. When the gate opened, the guards moved to the side of the road, and Ivan drove the wagon into the castle grounds. The wagon passed beyond the bailey and slowed when it reached the shadows beneath the castle. There, Jerrell and Ivan climbed down and stood near the rear of the wagon, waiting. A stillness seemed to grip the area; the morning was quiet with nobody, not even the guards, in sight.

The door to the castle opened. Two guards emerged, followed by Lieutenant Dandon, Captain Fossie, and High Wizard Gurgan.

The wizard glanced at the wagon before turning to Jerrell. "I was told you have urgent news."

"Yes."

"Did you make the exchange last night?"

"The sack of coins was left at the obelisk as instructed. Moments later, it was retrieved by a man in a dark cloak. I followed that man to a home near the western edge of town, where he paid four men and sent them off toward the mines while he headed back into the city."

The wizard frowned. "Paid other men? Why would he do that?"

"The men were to return to Everett's location and kill him. The boy had seen too much, and they feared he could identify them."

Gurgan gasped. "What happened?"

"I was alone and had to act fast, so I followed them. Roughly three miles out of town, they turned down a rarely used side road and approached a mining tunnel with a boarded-over entrance."

Dandon said, "It sounds like one of the abandoned mines."

Fossie asked, "Where are these men? Where is Everett?"

"I am getting to that," Jerrell snapped, irritated by the interruption. "Inside the mine were five more men and Everett, who was tied up and gagged. The kidnappers split up the coin and were about to kill the boy when I interrupted them. A frantic battle ensued. In the end, I escaped the mine." Jerrell took a breath. "Nobody else survived."

Gurgan gasped.

Jerrell stepped up to the wagon, gripped the tarp, and tore it back, revealing nine dead men in a twisted pile. Beside them lay another form, unmoving beneath a white sheet with dark red stains.

The wizard approached the wagon and reached toward the sheet, hesitating before lifting a corner. He flipped it over, revealing the corpse beneath it. Jerrell had closed one of Everett's eyes. A bloody, raw mess filled the other eye socket.

Gurgan began to sob, his shoulders shaking with each gasp. Nobody said a word. The wizard slid down to a knee and held his face in one hand while the other gripped the wagon. After a few minutes, the man wiped his eyes and turned toward Jerrell.

"You promised you would save him."

"I promised I would catch the culprits." Jerrell gestured toward the pile of bodies. "Well, they are dead. I did what I could to spare your son, but there were too many, and a stray crossbow bolt found him before it all ended."

Something invisible struck Jerrell, lifted him off the ground, and slammed him into the castle wall. Pain flared through the back of his head and his back.

Gurgan strode up to him. "Give me one reason I should not kill you."

"Once they had the coin, they intended to kill Everett and would have done so numerous times over had I not been there. It was a fluke that he died as we attempted to escape the last abductor. I did everything I could to save him. Unfortunately, it was not meant to be. Nothing you or I do will bring him back."

The wizard glared at Jerrell for a long tense moment, and then stepped back. The invisible bonds holding Jerrell vanished, and he fell to the ground, landing on his hands and knees. He climbed to his feet and touched the back of his head. His hand came away with a crimson streak.

Gurgan turned toward the wagon. "Does anyone recognize these men?"

Dandon said, "These are the guards you expelled from the castle last autumn, Your Grace."

The wizard spun on his lieutenant. "The ones who raped that woman in town?"

"Yes."

Turning back toward the wagon, Gurgan said, "I should have sent them to the gibbet."

"They are dead now, Your Grace."

"Yes. But at what cost?"

Captain Fossie cleared his throat. "Like the rape committed by these men, this atrocity occurred under my command, Your Grace. I have failed you."

Gurgan shrugged, his eyes downcast.

Fossie continued. "Pride and duty compel me to resign my position. Dandon can take my place. I will pack and be on a carriage before sunset."

The captain turned, entered the castle, and was gone.

Gurgan spoke without looking up. "I want you gone as well, Landish."

"About my payment..."

The wizard spun toward Jerrell with a sneer, his eyes flaring. "You dare to ask for gold?"

Jerrell was going to do so but changed his mind. "Given the circumstances, I was going to say you can keep it. After all, there is at least one conspirator I have not captured."

"As I said, it is time for you to return to Marquithe, Landish. I'd rather not see your face again."

Gurgan opened the castle door and went inside with his two guards behind him.

After a silent beat, Dandon said, "I can't say I didn't want to see you fail, thief. I just wish the cost had not been so steep." He turned and entered the castle, leaving Jerrell alone with Ivan.

"What now, Jerrell?" Ivan asked.

"I'll walk back to town. It will give me time to think. I need some food and a bit of rest before I leave Eleighton. Thanks again for your help, even if it did not work out."

Jerrell walked out of the castle yard and down the hill beneath a dark cloud of regret.

Eddard Fossie stood beside the door to his room, waiting while two porters lifted a chest from the foot of his bed. "Careful. My entire life is within that chest."

The two men labored beneath its weight as they shuffled past him and to the stairwell. Eddard was about to follow when he spied Dandon coming down the corridor.

"I was hoping you had not yet departed. I came to say goodbye, Captain."

Eddard shook his head and gestured at the black doublet he wore. "I am captain no more. That title belongs to you."

"You are a military man. What will you do?"

"It may be time for me to retire from conflict and live a simpler life."

"Well, whatever you do, I wish you well. I'll do my best to carry on here."

He clapped Dandon on the shoulder. "I am confident you will do well by Gurgan."

Eddard ducked into the stairwell and descended quickly, hoping to avoid another encounter with the high wizard. Once outside, he found a carriage waiting beside a wagon. The two porters stood in the wagon bed and hoisted the chest onto the carriage roof, causing the vehicle to shudder. Beside it sat two smaller chests, neither of which belonged to Eddard.

"Is everything ready?" he called to the driver.

"Almost, Captain. As soon as this chest is secured, we are free to depart."

"Excellent." Eddard opened the carriage door. "Let us be away. I'd like to make it to Marquithe the day after tomorrow."

Climbing in, Eddard pulled the door closed behind him and sat with a sigh.

The woman beside him slid a hand down his thigh. "It took you long enough."

He lifted her hand from his leg and patted it. "Give it a moment, my love. We will be out of this godforsaken city soon, and then, we no longer need worry about what others see or think."

Audette withdrew her hand and sighed. "Of course, you are correct. I am merely anxious to move beyond this charade."

He kissed her cheek and then whispered in her ear. "Just remember, we have thirty reasons why the charade took place."

She nodded. "I know."

The driver called out and the wagon burst into motion. Eddard watched through the window as the gate slipped past and was replaced by a wooded hillside. A smile bloomed on his face. After twenty-five years as a soldier, grinding and struggling, he was finally a rich man.

THE CARRIAGE ROLLED through the streets of Eleighton, passed through the square, and then turned east. The buildings gave way to trees as the sights and sounds of the small city faded away.

"We are free," Eddard said in relief.

Audette gripped his arm and leaned her head against his shoulder. "And together."

He allowed himself to enjoy her company. It would last until he was safely away from Eleighton and settled in his new city. When he chose to rid himself of her, the remaining gold would be his and his alone.

The carriage slowed to a stop.

With a furrowed brow, Eddard glanced at Audette, who asked, "Why are we stopping?"

"I don't know." He leaned over to the window and shouted, "What is wrong?"

The driver shouted back, "There is a woman and a child on the bridge."

"Go around them."

"I can't. The bridge is too narrow."

A breath huffed out of Eddard's flared nostrils before he opened the door and stepped out.

As the driver had said, a woman stood in the middle of the bridge. Dressed in a yellow dress and matching bonnet, she faced away from him while rocking her swaddled baby.

Eddard walked toward her, passing the horses before approaching the narrow wooden bridge. "Good afternoon, Ma'am."

She continued to hum and rock the child while facing away from him.

He stepped closer and gripped the woman by the shoulder. "I am sorry, but you need to move."

The woman spun around, dropped the bundle in her arms, and flashed a blade. Before Eddard knew what was happening, the tip was pressed against his jugular and biting into his flesh.

"Move and you die, Captain."

With a flourish, the person tore the bonnet away, revealing a mess of dark hair, amber eyes, and an unshaven face.

Eddard blinked in surprise. "Landish?"

CHAPTER 27
SHOCK

The shock on Fossie's face brought a grin to Jerrell's face. He held his blade steady. A wrong move would end the former captain and his preference was for Fossie to remain alive.

Raising his voice, Jerrell shouted, "Unless you want me to kill your lover, it is time to climb out of the carriage...Audette."

The carriage rocked and Audette emerged, moving slowly, her eyes pained, and her face etched in concentration while one hand gripped the door and the other held the rail beside the opening. She stumbled and groaned as she stepped down to the road. *What is wrong with her?*

Fossie overcame his surprise, and his eyes flashed in anger. "You have crossed the line, Landish. I will have you arrested and executed."

Jerrell chuckled. "I think not." Raising his voice, he shouted, "Layton!"

The city guard and three of his cohorts emerged from beneath the bridge and climbed up the riverbank. Two held crossbows, one leveled at Fossie, the other at the carriage driver. A third drew his sword and stood behind the former Captain of the Eleighton Castle Guard while Layton held his sword toward Audette.

Jerrell lowered his blade and patted Fossie on the cheek. "Don't move, or you will bleed, and she will die."

Using the dagger, Jerrell sliced at his yellow dress, which tore open to reveal his typical outfit. He shoved the bundle into Fossie's stomach, moved past the man, and approached the carriage with everyone watching.

"What is this about?" Fossie asked.

Jerrell turned toward him. "I intend to find the gold."

"What gold?" Fossie grimaced. "The porters packed my chest. You'll find only my own belongings inside."

Jerrell gripped the rail beside the door while lifting a foot to the step. "Oh, I have no doubt of that. However, who searched Audette's things?"

The man's gaze flicked to Audette but said nothing.

Once inside, Jerrell examined the interior. Although the chests were strapped to the roof, he doubted Fossie would risk storing the gold up there. It was simply too precarious of a location, at risk of bandits or of simply falling out during the trip. The same went for the small storage hatch on the rear of the carriage. No, he would find it somewhere inside.

He knelt and gripped the edge of one padded bench, lifting it with a creak. A blanket occupied a storage space that was otherwise empty. With the bench lowered, he moved to the bench on the opposite side and lifted it. The space below it was completely barren. He let it go, allowing the bench to drop with a thud as he stared into space, thinking. There was no other place to store the gold in the carriage interior, so where could it be?

Then, it came to him – the image of Audette struggling to climb out of the carriage. Still in her late thirties, she was neither old nor infirm.

Jerrell climbed out and approached Audette. Still holding his dagger, he knelt and gripped her skirts.

"What are you doing?" she yipped, aghast.

He flashed her a malicious grin. "I wish to see what treasure lurks beneath your skirts."

Fossie growled, "How dare you? She is a lady and above such depravity."

Turning his grin on Fossie, Jerrell said, "I will prove that she is far more depraved than she would have others believe."

He sliced with his blade and cut across the front of her skirts. He then yanked down, broadening the tear until it revealed her upper thighs down to her ankles. The bumps of flat disks lurked beneath bandages wrapped around her thighs. Jerrell eased his dagger beneath one of the wrappings and sliced it open. A dozen golden coins fell and struck the cobblestone street in a flurry of clinks before settling.

"Well, well," Jerrell said as he lifted a coin. "What do we have here?"

Fossie scowled. "I suspect it is her life savings."

"I think not."

Jerrell walked to the side of the road, picked up a small granite stone, and began using the sharp edge to scrape at the coin's surface. After a dozen strokes, he stopped and dropped the rock.

Grinning, Jerrell strode over to Fossie and showed him the coin. "See the silver beneath the gold? That is steel. You see, this coin is counterfeit."

One of the city guards said, "Possession of counterfeit coins is a crime."

"I suspect these coins are also uniquely marked with Logan's brand beneath the gold surface. Should that prove true, Fossie and Audette will soon find themselves on the gibbet for the abduction and murder of High Wizard Gurgan's son."

The color drained from Fossie's face. Audette's eyes rolled up and she collapsed in a heap.

"Shackle them," Jerrell said. "It is time to return to the castle."

Captain Dandon led Jerrell down a castle corridor he had not visited. At the end, the uniformed man paused before a closed door and looked back over his shoulder. "To be clear, he remains quite distraught and might lash out. Don't expect me to defend you."

While Jerrell still did not like Dandon, he respected the man's honesty. "I can take care of myself."

Dandon opened the door, and Jerrell followed him into the castle temple.

Made of dark gray bricks, the building was modest in size. Thick beams three stories above supported the high ceiling. Rows of wooden benches able to seat no more than a hundred people bordered the aisle down the center. At the far end of the room was a dais, an altar, and a ten-foot-tall statue of Farrow, his muscular body capped by a lightning bolt rather than a human head. Above the statue, a circular stained-glass window provided light. A multicolored sunbeam shone through it and landed directly upon a still form lying on the altar.

Kneeling on the dais was a man in black robes. Upon hearing their entry, the man growled over his shoulder. "I told you I was not to be disturbed!"

Dandon stepped aside, creating distance between himself and Jerrell. "I apologize, Your Grace, but the thief demanded to see you."

Gurgan stood and spun around, his eyes flashing while sparks of raw magic arced from his fingers. "I said I never wanted to see you again, Landish."

The edge in Gurgan's tone would have caused Jerrell's hair to stand on end if the wizard's magic had not already done so.

Remain steadfast, Jerrell told himself. "I do not wish to trouble you in your time of grief."

"Yet here you stand."

"I have come with a gift. While it will not bring your son back or ease your pain, it might provide a modicum of justice."

The sparks faded away. "What is it?"

"Layton!" Jerrell shouted. "Bring them in!"

The four city guards escorted Fossie and Audette into the temple. Both were shackled with their hands behind their backs. She still wore her ruined dress, her shift and one bare leg visible below the tear in her skirts. Bandages remained wrapped around the other thigh.

Gurgan strode toward them with a furrowed brow. "I thought these two had left the city."

Jerrell said, "They tried, but the city watch and I arrested them at the bridge."

"Arrested?"

With a flourish, Jerrell dumped the sack of coins in his hand. They bounced off the dark blue rug and settled. "We caught them with these."

"Gold?"

Jerrell squatted, picked one up, and showed it to Gurgan. The surface was scratched, revealing silver beneath. "They are the coins Logan crafted for me. Each is counterfeit with a steel core. Each is also marked with Logan's brand." He gestured toward the tutor. "The rest remained strapped to Audette's leg, proving these two were responsible for your son's abduction and murder."

Fossie interjected. "I don't know anything about those coins. Audette must have been the one behind the plot."

Jerrell snorted. "I suspected you would pass off the blame, as I also suspect you planned to rid yourself of Audette once you were safely settled elsewhere."

Audette gasped.

Turning to Gurgan, Jerrell explained, "It was a man who met with the former guards last night. While the voice was muffled through the glass and difficult to identify at first, I am sure it was him. I would be shocked if the entire thing had not been his idea. He used Audette's loneliness to manipulate her into aiding him, and they likely intended to blame it all on the supposed vampire. That plan was foiled when Rostarin was exposed."

The woman blurted out, "It was Eddard's plan." Tears ran down her face. "I was tricked into it, and before I knew it, there was no way out. Everett was not supposed to die. We were to be far away when he was discovered, but Eddard changed the plan."

Fossie snapped, "Shut up, you sniveling wench!"

"Enough!" Gurgan roared.

Everyone stood still, the room silent.

Gurgan turned to Dandon. "Captain, take these two down to the dungeon and lock them up. We will assemble a gibbet in the city square tomorrow and execute them at sunset."

Audette collapsed to her knees and sobbed hysterically, her hands over her eyes. Fossie gazed down at the floor, his shoulders slumped in defeat. The guards collected them and followed Dandon out the door, leaving Jerrell alone with Gurgan.

The wizard sighed, his gaze fixed on the door as it closed. "I never suspected betrayal would sting so sharply. At least I will have justice." He turned to Jerrell. "I thank you for that."

"I wanted justice as well – for you, your son, and for the stain this mess has left on my reputation."

Gurgan's brow furrowed and he gave Jerrell a nod. "I had not intended to pay you, but your diligence deserves something. Follow me, and I will reward you before you depart for Marquithe."

The wizard walked out the door. Jerrell cast one last glance toward the altar where Everett lay and then followed.

After a three flight climb and a myriad of corridor turns, they came to the wizard's office. Gurgan approached his bookshelf, closed his eyes, and held his hand before a thick tome. The book shook violently and then settled. Only then did the man remove it. Turning toward Jerrell, he opened the book and dropped it on the desk.

The book's pages had been glued together with the interior bored out to create a cavity. A dark blue pouch rested in the recess.

"Take it," Gurgan said. "Inside, you'll find twenty gold pieces. You've earned it."

Jerrell tentatively reached for the pouch. Not sensing any magic, he scooped it up. The weight felt pleasing. He untied the laces and peered inside. Golden edges shined back at him. *This wizard is different. He has displayed integrity and compassion.* He made a decision, sat in the chair before the desk, and removed his boot.

"What are you doing?" Gurgan asked.

"I have a gift for you." Jerrell pressed the tiny release and the bracelet around his ankle came free. He slid it on the desktop, the gold glittering in the afternoon sunlight. "It is enchanted to augment the magic of the bearer. Montague used it to kill High Wizard Garue and gain his position in Lionne. However, he is an arrogant, self-serving man and does not deserve such a prize. I pray you will use it more wisely."

Gurgan picked up the bracelet, eyed the silver inscription inside the band, and nodded. "I thank you." He clamped it on, and Jerrell felt the tickle of magic crawl across his skin. The wizard's eyes widened. "With such power, I might challenge Malvorian himself."

After putting his boot back on, Jerrell stood. "If that is the case, please leave me out of such plans. I have already upset one wizard lord and intend to avoid repeating that mistake." He walked out the door without another word.

~

AFTER TWO LONG days of cross-country travel, Jerrell rode Inky through the gates of the city he now called home. Unlike the peaceful seaside port of Lionne and the quiet wooded hillsides of Eleighton, the thriving pulse of Marquithe made the city feel alive. Two weeks had passed since his departure, and he realized how much he missed it. *Opportunity lies within these walls. I just need to find it and take advantage of the situation.* His new office at the Bureau had elevated his position, and while he had hoped to use his success with Montague and his exploits in Eleighton to enhance his standing, he worried that Everett's death would negate any positive impact they might add.

He rode at an easy walk along the twisting streets bordering the estates of wizards and wealthy merchants. The path took him to the square outside of Marquithe Palace, where the Tower of Devotion stood as the tallest point in the city. He passed the palace walls, crossed another square, and entered a shadow-covered street thick with people.

The now-familiar sights and sounds called to him. He passed his favorite bakery, the smell of fresh baked rolls taunting him and sending his stomach into a frenzy. Yet, he resisted, knowing that Frella would have a meal waiting for him at the Blue Hen. Three intersections later, the tavern came into view. He pulled in front of it, dismounted, and tied his horse to the post outside the door.

With anticipation stirring in his stomach, he entered the building. It was busy. The scent of roasted chicken greeted him although the patrons ignored him standing in the entrance. The door to the kitchen opened and Frella emerged.

She smiled as she crossed the room with a platter in her hand. "I see you finally decided to show up."

He grinned. "I can tell you missed me."

The woman snorted. "You have too high an opinion of yourself."

"You might be the first to say it, but I doubt you are the first to think it."

"That much is true." She walked past him and unloaded the tray, placing the plates on a table before four men. She spoke to them briefly and then turned back toward Jerrell. "I must say, I am disappointed in you."

His smile slid away. "How come?"

"You went and got married, and I was not invited to the wedding."

A guffaw spurted out. "Married? Me? Never."

She furrowed her brow. "If not your wife, why is a woman living in your apartment?"

"Woman? What woman?"

"Blonde. Pretty...perhaps too pretty."

"While I like the sound of that, I don't know about any woman in my apartment."

"In that case, you have a surprise waiting upstairs."

Tossing his hunger aside, Jerrell spun on his heel, headed out the door, and went straight toward the alley. At the entrance, a man on the ground reached out and grabbed his leg, stopping him.

"Jerrell. I've been waiting for you."

"Hello, Urlan."

"There is a woman, Jerrell. She is upstairs right now."

"As I have heard."

As Jerrell walked away, the beggar shouted, "I have been watching for you as we agreed!"

But you allowed a woman into my apartment?

"You owe me, Jerrell!"

Ignoring the man, Jerrell passed the window he usually used to enter and headed for the wooden staircase at the far end of the alley. He climbed the stairs, careful to pass over the loose step, something Jerrell had done on purpose. At the top, he was again careful not to lean on the railing as he went to the door. Beside it, he squatted and used his picks to unlock it. When the knob turned, he readied himself and shoved it open while stepping aside. The bell attached to the door chimed, joined by the thwack of two crossbows loosing. A pair of bolts sailed through the doorway and struck the wall across the alley.

Whoever she is, she left this trap armed. Curious, Jerrell entered the apartment.

Nobody occupied the sitting room – the sofa and chairs were vacant, and the bear trap beneath the window was open as he had left it. The kitchen appeared clean and unused as well, so he headed down the hallway, checked the bathing room, and found it empty. The door to his bedroom was closed. It had been left open before his departure. He leaned with his ear against the door and listened, hearing nothing. With care, he turned the knob, stepped aside, and threw the door open.

The soft blue light of an enchanted lantern illuminated the bedroom. On the bed was a woman with blonde hair, blue eyes, and flawless skin. Her full lips were pursed, and she held a book on her lap. One of Jerrell's tunics covered her torso, leaving her legs exposed from the thigh down. The laces of the collar were loose, which allowed him a glimpse of the valley between her breasts.

She was gorgeous, and he recognized her immediately.

"You!" Jerrell growled.

"Hello, Jerrell. I am so glad you are back."

"I never got your name in Yor's Point."

"Oh, you got a name, just not the real one. You may call me Haelynn."

He entered the room, drew his dagger, and held it in front of her. "It is time for you to talk, Haelynn."

She smirked. "You only just arrived, and you already whip your weapon out and wave it in front of my face?"

He ignored the risqué comment. "I want to know what you did with the fifty gold pieces you stole from me in Yor's Point."

CHAPTER 28

A MARRIAGE PROPOSAL

J errell stared into Haelynn's eyes. Like calm cerulean waters, they reflected confidence despite the tip of his dagger hovering just shy of her exposed cleavage.

Her full lips turned up in a smirk as she gently pushed his weapon aside. "I no longer possess your gold, Jerrell."

"Where is it?"

She cupped his cheek. "Can't we discuss this later? You've only just arrived, and I thought we might have some fun. After all, you passed out on me last time."

"That is because you drugged me."

Her smiled widened. "You figured that out."

She gripped his tunic and pulled him closer while leaning in. Their lips met. Hers were soft, warm, and quickened his pulse.

After a moment, he forced himself to pull away, suspicious. "While I find you attractive, I must know why you are in my apartment."

Haelynn stuck out her lower lip. "Why ruin the fun?" She pulled her legs in and shifted so she was kneeling on the bed, giving him a clear view down the deep V of the unlaced tunic she wore. His tunic. "Can't we discuss that later?"

Her hands found the laces of his breeches. His gripped them, stopping her.

"Why are you here, Haelynn?"

She sighed and fell back on the bed, the bottom of the tunic rising to expose her sculpted thighs. Her blonde hair was sprayed out across the bed, framing her beautiful face. In a sultry tone, she asked, "Are you sure you don't wish to play first?"

"I am tired, hungry, and smell of horse after two days in the saddle. Had you caught me at another time, I doubt I could've turned you down, but right now, I just want to eat, bathe, and enjoy a good night's rest in a real bed."

Sitting up on her elbows, she nodded. "I could eat as well."

"In that case, let's go downstairs, and we can discuss this over a meal."

Haelynn rolled over, slid her hand beneath the pillow, and pulled out a long, thin sheath, which revealed the hilt of a dagger.

Jerrell narrowed his eyes. "What were you intending to do with that?"

"A girl must take steps to protect herself." She slid off the bed and lifted the black dress hanging over the headboard. "Give me a moment to dress myself."

Jerrell shook his head. "I think not. Until I know what is going on, I am not letting you out of my sight."

She shrugged. "Suit yourself."

With an arched brow, she stared at him while pulling the tunic up over her head and tossing it to the bed. The shadows clung to the contours of lean muscle on her legs and arms. Her narrow waist and flat stomach accentuated the curves of her breasts and hips. As he drank in the view, Jerrell's body reacted, his pulse hammering in his ear, his breeches feeling all too tight. She stared back with a smirk.

Slowly, she picked up the dress and stepped into it, slipping it up her legs and then swaying her hips from side to side as the dress snaked up to her waist. One arm slipped through, followed by the other before she began lacing up the bodice. Her dark red corset followed – she laced it tightly before spinning it around, so the laces were in the back. The entire process invigorated Jerrell. He regretted turning her offer down.

Lastly, she strapped the stiletto dagger and sheath to her thigh. When she dropped her skirts, the dagger was hidden from view.

"I am ready," she said. "Let's go get some food."

His belly full and his plate empty, Jerrell sat back and sipped on a tankard of ale while watching Haelynn eat. She cut the last of her pork chop from the bone, lifted it to her mouth, and slid it off the fork with smooth grace. When he glanced around the room, he found more than one man watching her, and he could not blame them. Her beauty shone in the dimly lit tavern like a guiding star on a dark night. Even the way she chewed oozed sensuality.

He turned back toward her as she dabbed her mouth with a cloth napkin. "Now that dinner is over, perhaps we can attend to business?"

"If that is what you wish."

Jerrell shook his head. "I see what you are doing."

She blinked. "Whatever do you mean?"

"You are the one who sought me out, yet you make it seem as if you are my guest and doing me a favor."

A subtle smile was her only response.

"My question is, do you attempt to manipulate me on purpose? Or are you so used to twisting men around your finger that such machinations come without thought?"

"Nicely observed. This is the Jerrell I expected in Yor's Point."

"You caught me on a bad day, deep in my cups and fresh off a fight with some unruly sailors." He pressed her. "And you never answered my question. Another of your bad habits."

"I prefer to call my habits tools of self-preservation."

Tired and lacking patience to continue the dance, Jerrell cut straight to the point. "Explain why you are here."

She glanced around. While half of the tables were occupied, nobody sat near enough to hear them. It was why Jerrell had selected the table in the corner, far from the door and the bar.

"I caught word of your success with Sorenna Souton. Interestingly, I hear you now operate out of an office in the Bureau."

"I do."

"As far as I can tell, you are the first in our profession to channel your skills into such legitimacy."

"*Our* profession?"

She smirked. "You are a thief, Jerrell. Don't deny it."

"So you admit you are one as well."

"I am what I am."

"And I suspect you are quite good at it. After all, you fooled me and stole my gold."

"I am sorry about that." Her gaze lowered for a breath before rising to meet his. "It was only business, so I hope you won't take it personally."

He was about to retort and then considered what he would say to her had the tables been flipped. While she must have sought him out back then as well, it was likely only for the gold. He would have done the same thing.

"Fine. I will accept that, but it doesn't explain why you are here now."

"Speaking of which, where have you been? I waited a week for you to return."

"I had business in Lionne and then in Eleighton. I had planned to return sooner, but things did not go as expected." The image of the crossbow bolt in Everett's eye flashed through Jerrell's mind. He wished he could go back and do things differently, but that was impossible. As far as he knew, not even magic could alter events of the past.

"Lionne?" She tilted her head. "Were you by chance responsible for the incident at Lionne Castle?'

"Incident?" He was curious what she had heard.

Leaning in, she said, "Rumor has it that High Wizard Montague was found stark naked and tied to his bed. They say this occurred during a masquerade ball in a castle filled with guests, and when freed, he claimed he was drugged and robbed by a man dressed as a woman. Surely, you must have heard of this."

"As I said, I was in Eleighton for much of the past week, and word of this incident has yet to reach the remote mining town." He smiled. "However, I may have had a hand in that scandal."

"I knew it." Her eyes sparkled with excitement as she smiled at him. "I've never met a thief who would dare to cross a wizard as you have done with Montague, Jakins, and Kylar Mor."

Jerrell narrowed his eyes. "How do you know about Jakins and Mor?"

She sat back and shrugged, another distracting sensual motion. "We all have secrets, Jerrell."

He frowned at her response, irritated by her lack of transparency. However, he had done nothing to conceal his recent exploits. If anything, he had used them to bolster his fame, so her knowledge of his actions could have been attained with minimal effort.

Choosing to move along, Jerrell said, "You still have yet to tell me why you sought me out."

Leaning over the table, she said in a hushed tone, "The situation in Marquithe has changed since you left."

"What situation?"

"A guild has risen, led by a dark and mysterious man."

He frowned. "What sort of guild?"

"A guild of whores, beggars, assassins, smugglers, and thieves."

Jerrell had worked for such a guild during his later years in Fastella. He had resisted joining them, and by doing so, earned himself their enmity. Eventually, he had been forced into joining lest he wake up dead one morning.

"I don't like the sound of that."

"Many of us feel as you do, but this man possesses enough gold to place himself in a position of strength. He appears to own the city watch and various members of the Midnight Guard as well."

"Lord Malvorian's private army?" Everyone in the city knew the Midnight Guard. Its men had a reputation as skilled warriors, handpicked by the wizard lord to protect Marquithe Palace and its ruler. Beyond that, the special force was known for their unrelenting loyalty. "Is this only a rumor or can it be verified?"

She shook her head. "It does not matter. Enough believe it and, for that reason alone, have willingly joined the guild and now apply pressure on those of us who have yet to relent."

"And where do you stand?"

Haelynn stared at the table for a long moment before replying. When her eyes rose to meet his, they mirrored the sorrow in her tone. "I have been beholden to another in my past, forced to do as I would not choose. I wish to avoid such a situation, and that is why I came to you."

"What do you expect me to do about it?"

She reached across the table and grabbed his hand, holding it in hers as she pulled it against her chest. "I suggest we work together, Jerrell."

Despite the distraction of her physical contact, he shook his head. "I work alone."

"Yes, in the past, but can you stand against the thieves guild alone?"

"My office in the Bureau gives me legitimacy other thieves don't possess."

"Yours is no longer the only office there."

"What?"

She released his hand. "The man who runs the guild now has an office on the top floor, in one of the dark rooms along the back."

"The fifth floor?" Jerrell frowned. His was only on the second level and among the open, less-private offices.

Haelynn stood. "As you have personally experienced, I possess unique skills, ones I believe would complement your own abilities. Together, perhaps we can stave off the pressure applied by this new guild. Think on my proposal, Jerrell. I will soon return for a response."

"You are leaving?"

"Yes. There is...something I must deal with, and I have put it off for far too long already."

He realized he was sad to see her leave but was unwilling to say so. "You mentioned this new guild leader numerous times, but you never mentioned his name."

"Nobody knows who he is, but those in the guild call him the Whispering Man."

CHARLATAN
FOR HIRE

CHAPTER 1
THE WHISPERING MAN

Midmorning on an autumn day, Jerrell strolled down the sunlit streets of Marquithe, navigating around puddles and hopping over rivulets left by the prior evening's storm until he reached a broad square with a fountain in the center. The square was packed with people purchasing goods from carts and wagons. After slipping past the crowd and the fountain, he approached the massive five-story building bordering the south side of the square. A pair of guards searched him for weapons, claimed his dagger and four of his throwing blades, and bid him a good day. He stepped into the Marquithe Bureau of Trading and took the stairs to the second level.

Little of this routine differed from any other morning since his return from Eleighton. That is, until he reached his office.

Two burly men dressed in leather armor stood beside the sofa. One had a bald head and black goatee. The other sported shoulder-length brown hair and a heavy brow. The bald man was six feet tall with a barrel chest and bulging arms, bare from the shoulders down. The other was even taller, with a long, lean frame and a nasty scar across his left cheek.

Jerrell frowned. "The Bureau clerks did not mention guests."

The bald one grunted. "The clerks are paid to ignore us."

"Huh." Jerrell held out his hand. "In that case, I am waiting."

The bald man furrowed his brow. "Waiting for what?"

"For you to pay me, so I can ignore you as well."

The lean man grimaced. "How about we pay you with our fists and see if we can silence your wise arse mouth?"

"You might try. Others have, some of whom could knock your arse right out the door. Still, none have succeeded."

The man took a step toward Jerrell but stopped when his bald partner put a hand against his chest.

"Keep yourself together. The boss wants to talk to Landish, which would be difficult if you knock him unconscious."

The lean man then nodded toward Jerrell. "You are to follow us to a meeting upstairs."

"If I decline?"

The bald one sneered and cracked his knuckles. "Please do."

Jerrell considered his options, and although he wanted to show the blowhard that he was no pushover, his curiosity demanded he comply. "Fine. I am interested to see what this is all about."

The bald man sighed. "Follow me."

He pushed past Jerrell, and the taller tough gestured for him to follow.

With the bald tough leading and the tall one trailing, Jerrell made his way to the stairwell and began his ascent. They passed the third and fourth floors, each filled with people brokering deals. When they reached the top level, the bald man led Jerrell down a narrow corridor. Doors lined one side of the hallway. A trio of toughs stood outside the closed door near the end.

The bald man knocked. A male voice answered through the door. "What is it?"

"It's Van. Sorry to bother you, sir, but Gosling and I found Landish and brought him as you requested.

Moments later, the door opened, and a woman exited. She was tall and graceful, her blonde hair falling across bare shoulders, drawing all eyes to her dipping neckline and partially exposed assets. *Haelynn. Where has she been all this time?* An entire season had passed since he had eaten with her in early summer. *And what is she doing here?* Her blue eyes locked on Jerrell's, and her eyelids tensed in a silent message, *Pretend to not know me.*

"What are you looking at?" she asked.

He decided to play along. "I see a beautiful woman who could use the company of someone handsome, clever, and talented."

Her gaze looked him up and down. "Do you know such a man?"

"You are looking at him."

"I think not."

She turned and headed toward the stairs, her hips swaying overtly in her tight black dress while Jerrell and the five bodyguards watched.

What are you up to, Haelynn? Despite the time that had passed since he last saw her, Jerrell had not forgotten her offer. He had even tried to seek her out, but nobody seemed to know where to find her.

Chuckling, the bald tough said, "You only wish you could bed a woman like her."

I bedded her once and turned her away the second time. Jerrell wished he could say the words aloud and throw them in the irritating blowhard's face. *She wants to keep our relationship a secret*, he realized. Why? He was not sure, but he suspected he would find out soon enough.

The man prodded him toward the open door. "Go on in."

Jerrell entered a dark room illuminated by a single candle flickering in the far corner. In the center of the room, a hooded man sat alone on a sofa, facing the door.

Among his other assets, Jerrell had been blessed with keen eyesight and could see in the dark better than most. However, the man's back to the candle left his features masked by shadow.

"Sit," the man said in a hushed voice.

Jerrell sat on the chair across from him. A low table occupied by two cups and a carafe sat between them. Although the door was closed behind Jerrell, he ached to reposition himself so he could watch it. Just knowing it lurked behind him made him itch between the shoulder blades.

"What's wrong, Mister Landish?" the man whispered. "You seem uncomfortable."

Rather than give the man satisfaction, Jerrell decided to turn the conversation around. "You continue to speak in a sultry tone. Are you trying to bed me?"

The man grunted. "I heard you were brash."

"And I heard you believe you control Marquithe."

The man sat forward and snapped. "Damn right I do."

"I am happy for you, but you do not control me."

Leaning back, the Whispering Man chuckled.

Jerrell narrowed his eyes. "Why do you laugh?"

"I was warned you would be difficult."

"And I was warned that you would try to convince me to join you. I have experience working beneath the thumb of a guild leader. I left that life behind years ago, and I have no intention of returning to it."

The man tented his fingers to his chin. "Ah, yes. I hear you hail from Fastella and were once Cordelia's lapdog."

"I was no lapdog. She and I had an agreement. It ended when I no longer needed her, so I left the city and found a new home."

"Yes. You wasted a year in Yor's Point, drinking, gambling, and bedding women."

He knows about that as well? Jerrell shrugged. "I don't consider those activities a waste of time, especially since I happen to be rather skilled at all three."

A quiet fell over the room, the mysterious man appraising Jerrell, who waited to see where the conversation would lead.

Finally, the man leaned back and said, "Over the past year, you've made a name for yourself. I must admit, I never considered an office at the Bureau until you opened yours. It requires a bold thief to announce his services to the public, but I can do bold as well as anyone."

"Then, why hide your identity?"

The man stared at Jerrell for a long, silent beat before nodding. "That is the first good question you've asked. You see, masking the identity of the man behind the guild allows me certain freedoms I would otherwise lack, no different than your old employer, Cordelia."

Jerrell had tracked down Cordelia's true identity only to discover she was a middling wizardess and a widow. The other wizards thought little of her, but she ruled the underbelly of Fastella and likely had more power – the power of influence, not the power of magic – than any of them other than Lord Taladain.

The man's explanation made sense. "Since we both occupy offices in the Bureau, I don't see why I would choose to work for you."

"When was your last contract?"

"What?"

"When was the last time a guest even visited your office?"

Jerrell grimaced. Two full seasons had passed since Tarin's fake contract sent Jerrell off to Lionne. Not one appointment had occurred since.

The man chuckled again. "If you won't respond, I will answer for you. Half a year has passed since your last appointment. Yet, I take on and issue contracts regularly. Why do you think that is?"

"I would guess that you paid someone off."

"I heard you were intelligent. Pay attention, and you will soon see the truth of it. If you wish to remain in business within Marquithe, you will do so under my direction."

"And if I decline your offer?"

"You will change your mind. It is only a matter of time."

Jerrell stood. "Sorry, but I enjoy my independence."

"Have it your way, Mister Landish. For now."

Jerrell turned to the door, opened it, and pushed past the five brawny men guarding it.

CHAPTER 2
A WARM WELCOME

Oblivious to the noisy surroundings of The Tawdry Tankard, Jerrell replayed his conversation with the Whispering Man. Again. It had bothered him all day and well into the night.

A hand on his shoulder drew him from his reverie.

"Are you even listening to me?" asked a man in his late twenties. He pushed his straw-colored bangs aside. "If you are going to ignore me, I might as well be drinking alone."

Jerrell shook his head. "Sorry, Kolbert. I am just a bit distracted."

"I'll say. You've hardly touched your ale, while my mug is empty. If I didn't know better, I'd think you were ill."

Jerrell lifted his tankard to his lips and took a swig. The ale had warmed. After swallowing, he set the mug down. "I'm afraid I am unlikely to be a fun drinking companion tonight."

"What is bothering you? Is it your lack of clients?" Kolbert waved to the waitress as she walked past with four tankards in her hands.

"Yes...and no." Jerrell considered telling Kolbert about his situation but worried that the new crime lord might target his business as well. "I am just trying to decide how to improve the situation." He tipped the tankard up again, intent on finishing it. When he reached the bottom, he lowered the cup and wiped his lips dry.

The waitress returned, her hands now emptied. She wiped sweat from her brow with the back of one hand. "You boys want another round?"

Kolbert smiled. "You know us too well, Iesha."

With black hair and coppery skin, Iesha was among the few Hassakani in the city. She had a lean build, but her corset was tight enough to cause her modest bust to bulge into her low neckline.

She smiled and arched a brow while her dark eyes stared at Kolbert. "You come here three nights a week, Kole. Every time, you eat and wash the food down with ale. It would be strange if I did not know when you want another round."

He smiled. "You notice how often we visit?"

Iesha put a hand on her hip. "Look. This place is busy, and I've many tables to serve. Do you need anything other than two ales?"

His smile faltered. "No. Just the ales."

She held a palm out and Jerrell dropped three coppers into it. Spinning around, she weaved through the crowd, toward the bar. Kolbert's gaze followed her the entire time.

Jerrell nudged Kolbert. "Why don't you just ask her to dinner?"

The man's green eyes turned toward Jerrell. "What do you mean?"

"You are attracted to her."

"What makes you say that?"

Rolling his eyes, Jerrell said, "It is obvious. You eat dinner here three nights a week, and you all but drool every time she walks by."

Kolbert glanced across the room. "Do you think she would say yes?"

"You will only know if you try. What is the worst that could happen?"

"She could say no."

"And where would that leave you?"

"Alone, I guess."

"You are alone now."

"Yes, but...I still harbor hope. If she says no, I won't have that either."

Jerrell sighed, reached across the table, and gripped his friend's shoulder. "If she shows no interest, then you can move on and find another woman to pine after. There are likely a thousand young, single women in this city. If not Iesha, another would be happy to share your bed."

Kolbert shared a shy smile. "You think so?"

"I know so. You just need to place more confidence in yourself, and everything will be just fine."

Iesha reappeared through the crowd carrying two foam-capped mugs. She approached the table with a smile. "Here are your ales, boys."

Jerrell reached for a mug with one hand while the other poked Kolbert beneath the table.

"Ouch," Kolbert shot Jerrell a look.

Iesha made to turn away but stopped when Kolbert tugged her skirts. She turned back with an arched brow. "Did you need something else?"

"Yes."

"What?"

"Um. You, I guess."

She frowned. "I am not for sale. Head two blocks over if you wish…"

"No." Kolbert shook his head. "That's not what I meant."

"Then what?"

"I would…I was wondering…"

Unable to continue to watch his friend struggle, Jerrell interjected, "Kolbert here is interested in buying you dinner."

"I had dinner hours ago."

Kolbert found his words. "Not today. Another time. We could go wherever you like."

Iesha cocked her head and narrowed her eyes. "You are interested in…me?"

Grinning broadly, he simply nodded.

She looked him over, from his black boots to his gray breeches to his purple coat. When her gaze returned to his still-grinning face, she nodded. "All right. I am game. I happen to be off work tomorrow evening. Meet me here after Devotion."

Jerrell's brow furrowed. "You want to eat here?'

Iesha snorted. "I'd rather eat just about anywhere else, but we need to meet somewhere." She spun away and headed back toward the bar.

Hoisting his mug, Jerrell held it out toward Kolbert. "See. She said yes. You'll get your chance to impress her. Don't mess it up."

He took a swig and wiped away the foam. With Kolbert's problem solved, Jerrell's own worries resurfaced, eating away at his thoughts until they were completely consumed.

AFTER EMPTYING MORE ales than he could count, Jerrell's troubled thoughts quelled, or perhaps, were drowned. He and Kolbert stumbled to the exit and emerged to a dark street. They patted each other on the back, said goodnight, and headed in opposite directions. Even drunk, Jerrell was not worried about finding his way back to his apartment. The walk had become routine and often occurred without his conscious notice.

He reached a dark intersection – the enchanted lantern on the pole shattered and dormant. It happened frequently enough that he was not alarmed, however, it was at the corner where he was to turn. Rounding the bend, he walked down the dark alley running one hand along the wall to steady himself.

Movement appeared in a shadowed doorway beside him. On instinct, Jerrell ducked, and the blow glanced off the top of his head. He landed on his hands and knees. Before he could react, a boot smashed into his midriff, knocking him to his side. A second kick followed, striking him in the back. Another shadow appeared above him, joined by a fist striking his face. He covered his head with his arms and curled into a ball while blows landed again and again, hitting his back, arms, and head.

By the time the attack had stopped, Jerrell was gasping for air and wincing at the pain. Moments of silence passed before he lowered his arms and looked up. Four shadowed silhouettes stood over him. One held a dagger – Jerrell's dagger.

"The streets are no place to be on your own." The man gripping the dagger leaned down toward Jerrell, his voice a harsh whisper. "This city is not a place to be on your own. I suggest you reconsider your situation.

Imagine how safe you would feel if you always had a friend watching your back. Think on it, or we may meet again."

The man slammed his fist down, driving the dagger into Jerrell's thigh. Pain shot through his leg. He clenched his teeth and groaned. The four attackers walked off, leaving Jerrell alone in his pain. He stayed on the ground for a few minutes, each breath accompanied by a stabbing ache in his cracked ribs. Finally, he forced himself into motion. Beaten and bloody with his dagger still sticking from his thigh, he rose to his feet and staggered down the dark alley.

ALTHOUGH CLOSE TO HIS APARTMENT, the distance had never felt so great. Each step was agony, every breath ragged. His surroundings wavered with every movement, but he focused on remaining upright, fearing a fall would render him unable to get up again.

Somehow, Jerrell dragged himself up the alley stairs outside his apartment. At the top, he fell to his knees, dug into his coat, and found his lock picks. With forced concentration, he picked the lock and pocketed the picks. A turn of the knob and the door swung open, taking Jerrell with it. He fell to his stomach, and the bell on the door rang, but no arrows sailed above him. Confused and delirious from the alcohol and the subsequent assault, he looked up to find the crossbows disconnected from the rope running to the door. *I know I armed that trap when I left.*

Stumbling to his feet, he yanked the dagger from his thigh and staggered inside. The living room was dark and appeared empty. A door down the corridor squeaked open, and soft light seeped into the room.

"Jerrell?" a woman's voice asked.

Haelynn. "Yeah," he croaked. "It's me." He closed the door behind him, leaned against it, and locked it. He hurt everywhere, and his leg felt warm below the gaping wound.

The light grew brighter until Haelynn turned the corner. When she held the lantern up, her eyes grew wide. "What happened?"

He smiled, and his torn lip stung. "After a year in Marquithe, I finally met the welcoming committee."

Haelynn drew closer and lowered the lantern, allowing him a good look at her. She wore a cream-colored shift that clung to her curves. Normally, that image alone would have sent his blood pumping. In this case, he felt dizzy.

Jerrell held a hand to his forehead. "I think…"

The room spun and the floor rushed toward his face. His chin struck the wooden floorboards and blackness caved in.

CHAPTER 3

DENIED

J errell swam in a sea of agony. The waters were as thick as syrup and tinted the color of blood. He stroked hard, struggling to reach the surface.

One eye flickered open to a warmly lit room. The other eye was swollen shut. A blonde angel sat at his side and used a cool sponge to dab his forehead.

"There you are," she said.

He raised his head and found himself naked in a copper tub. Crimson water filled the tub, covering his lower body. "How'd I get here?"

"It wasn't easy, but I figured I needed to clean your wounds. How do you feel?"

"Like the refuse in the alley outside." He shifted and pain shot through his torso, causing him to wince. "My ribs are broken."

"I am not surprised. The bruises look horrible."

He lifted a hand that felt like lead and touched his chin. It hurt. His fingertips came away bloody.

"You cracked your chin open when you fell," she explained.

His leg burned and body ached...everywhere.

"I need help," he croaked.

"That's why I am here."

Thoughts warred with the fog in his head. "A healer. Send for a healer."

She frowned. "What wizard is going to come here for any price?"

Jerrell smacked his lips. His mouth felt dry, and he felt like he might throw up. "Forca. Send for Portia Forca. She…" Black spots danced before his eyes. "Owes…" The room spun. "Me…"

Darkness swallowed all thought.

A BELL RANG. Jerrell opened his eyes. He was shivering, and his teeth were chattering. He lay on the hard floor beside the tub. An enchanted lantern hung from the hook on the wall, bathing the room in soft blue light. Despite the heavy blankets covering him, he was freezing.

Shuffling came from down the hall. The bell rang again as the door closed.

A voice was speaking in the distance. "He is this way."

Footsteps drew closer until Haelynn appeared in the doorway. She moved aside to reveal another blonde, shorter and in her mid-thirties. While Haelynn had a long, slim build with enough curves to draw Jerrell's attention, the other woman's form was nothing but curves…significant curves. He noticed this despite his chill wracking his body and the pain clouding his thoughts.

Portia Forca pushed past Haelynn and knelt beside Jerrell. She rested her palm to his forehead. "He is burning up and his face is a mess."

"He was beaten and stabbed," Haelynn said. "I bathed him, trying to clean his wounds. It took everything I had to get him in the tub and then back out. I dried him off, covered him, and left to find you."

Portia pulled Jerrell's blankets aside, exposing him. He hugged himself tightly – his teeth chattering. His ribs ached and thigh throbbed.

"You bandaged his leg?"

"I had to. It would not stop bleeding."

Leaning close to Jerrell, Portia cupped his cheek. "It was wise of you to send for me, Jerrell. Brace yourself. The healing will require much from your own body."

Her hand slid up to his forehead. She closed her eyes, and a tingle ran across Jerrell's skin. He began to shake and his back arched, lifting all but his head, shoulders, and heels off the floor. The healing took hold, knitting his skin closed and melding his bones back together. Jerrell gasped for air, feeling overwhelmingly hungry, but then his strength fled, and he collapsed as sleep overcame him.

A NOISE CAUSED Jerrell to stir. He was in his own bed. A strip of sunlight shone through a gap in the curtains, informing him it was midmorning. He sat up, exposing his bare torso. A brief inspection confirmed he was completely naked beneath the covers.

He heard it again – someone moving about the apartment. His sheathed dagger hung from a hook near the door just beyond his grasp. Taking care to remain silent, he slipped out of bed, drew the blade, and tossed the sheath on the pillow. His bare feet made no sound as he crept toward the living room. When he neared the end of the corridor, he realized someone was in his kitchen, just beyond his view. The scent of smoked ham wafted toward him, causing his stomach to cry for sustenance.

He snuck past the two crossbows pointed toward the door, keeping close to the wall. At the corner, he paused before leaping out with his blade ready.

"Eek!" Haelynn jerked backward and dropped the tray in her hand.

The tray hit the floor, causing the plates on it to bounce. Eggs, ham, and biscuits splattered on Jerrell's bare feet.

Hand on her chest, she said, "Jerrell! You startled me."

He lowered his blade. "You are still here?"

"Yes, I..." She glanced at the floor. "I went downstairs to get you food. Portia said you would be starving when you woke." A smirk appeared. "I never expected you would sneak up on me with your weapon waving about."

He followed her gaze and realized he was stark naked – and that she was not referring to the dagger in his hand. "Perhaps I should put some clothes on."

"Good idea. I'll see what I can salvage of the food."

After donning a fresh change of clothes, Jerrell returned to the kitchen. Haelynn sat at the table with a tray of food in front of the opposite seat.

He claimed the chair and began eating frantically.

"What happened last night?" she asked.

After washing down the food with a drink of water, he said, "The Whispering Man met with me yesterday. He tried to convince me to work for him rather than continue running my own enterprise. When I declined, he said I would change my mind. I suspect he sent his henchmen after me to teach me a lesson. Unfortunately, I was drunk and not paying attention, so they got the better of me."

She snorted. "I'll say."

He took a bite of a biscuit, chewed, and swallowed. "The man has taken steps to intercept potential clients before they even reach me. I've not seen a single client since last spring. Now I understand why."

Haelynn frowned. "What are you going to do?"

Jerrell grimaced. "I have spent time beneath the thumb of a crime lord and found it was not to my liking." He stared into space. "Just when I had created a legitimate business, this man seeks to destroy it."

She reached across the table, placing her hand on his. "What if we worked together?"

"You suggested that once before. Then, an entire summer passed without a word from you. I thought you had left the city and gone on your own way."

"I told you...I had to take care of something. It just took much longer than I had expected."

"Why were you meeting with the Whispering Man yesterday?"

She shrugged. "Same reason as you. He forced a meeting and sought to retain my services."

"What did you tell him?"

"That I would think on it."

"And if he discovers you are in league with me?"

She smiled. "I am not afraid if you aren't."

Jerrell stared at her for a long moment, considering how she had cared for him on a night he might otherwise have died. He might be able to trust her, at least a little bit. *I just hope I don't regret this.*

He nodded. "Very well. Let's do this together."

Her smile widened and her eyes sparkled, making the room appear three shades brighter. *My, she is stunning.* Despite his reservations of a partnership, he realized how easy it would be for this woman to manipulate a man. That skill could be leveraged, but it didn't solve his immediate problem.

"Now, how do we find a client?"

She stood. "I don't know, but I suspect you will figure it out."

His gaze followed her as she walked to the door. "Where are you going?"

Pausing to look over her shoulder, she said, "Unlike you, I did not bathe last night. I also got very little sleep. You think on our little problem while I rest, bathe, and deal with some other issues. I will find you in a few days."

She exited the apartment, leaving Jerrell alone with his thoughts.

THE SUN WAS WELL into its decent by the time Jerrell made it to the Bureau. When he reached the second floor, he went straight to Kolbert's office, sat down, and told the man what had happened. Of course, Kolbert was shocked and concerned about the attack but thankful Jerrell had recovered. Jerrell did not reveal the name of the wizardess who had healed him, only that she had likely saved his life. He also excluded Haelynn and her role from the story. Even if he had agreed to work with her, Jerrell wished to keep her role a secret.

Then came the more complex subject. How was he going to gain clients? As the streets outside the Bureau darkened, Kolbert and Jerrell exchanged ideas.

"If you were in a similar position, how would you go about securing clients?" Jerrell posed.

The young man scratched his head. "Well, as someone who trades in fabrics, I guess I would begin with the tailor shops in the city. That way, I could strike individual deals and consolidate demand. Then, I'd make some trips to Balmoria and Hassakan to meet with cloth makers and place the orders with them directly."

Jerrell grinned. "You would seek out the clients yourself?"

"Yeah, I guess I would."

"Then that is what I will do."

"How is that going to work?"

"Well, I'll start with the wealthy." Jerrell stood. "Thanks, Kolbert. I feel better now."

"While I am meeting Iesha tonight, we could meet for drinks tomorrow."

With a shake of his head, Jerrell said, "Until I have this situation under control, I intend to keep my mind sharp."

"No ale at all?"

"Frightening, isn't it?"

"Yes."

"I'll stop by sometime tomorrow. Until then, take care."

"Where are you going now?"

"I wish to make a quick visit upstairs."

Jerrell soon found himself on the fifth floor, heading down a dark corridor in the back. Three brawny men stood outside a closed door, chatting and laughing. As Jerrell approached, one noticed him. The bodyguard's smile melted, and he blinked in confusion. The other two men spun around to face Jerrell. Their knuckles were bruised from a recent scuffle.

Jerrell flashed them a smile. "Good afternoon, gentlemen. Is it not a wonderful day?"

One of the men stammered, "How...what are you doing here?"

"I came to see your master. Is he in?"

"Yes. He is just..."

The door opened and a tall man with shoulder-length black hair emerged. He wore a long black coat over a brown tunic and a wide-brimmed black hat to match. With a bulbous nose, a heavy brow, and a fat chin, he was one of the ugliest people Jerrell had ever met.

The man looked Jerrell up and down. "You must be Jerrell Landisss," he hissed. "I've heard talesss about you."

Jerrell eyed the man warily. "And who are you?"

"They call me Whissstler." He flexed his hands, as if eager for a fight. "I am the best bounty hunter in the Eight Wizardomsss."

"Huh. I've little time for bounty hunters."

"Jussst pray I am never paid to hunt you down." Whistler smiled. It was not a friendly sight, made worse by his three missing teeth. "Or you will dissscover just how ussseful a bounty hunter can be."

Turning, Whistler walked off, leaving the doorway open. Jerrell sauntered into the room. As before, the Whispering Man sat in the far corner with a flickering candle behind him.

"Master Landish. I did not expect to see you so soon. You look...well."

"I slept soundly and woke refreshed."

The Whispering Man did not take the bait, instead pretending he knew nothing of the assault on Jerrell. "Have you reconsidered my offer?"

"Not at all," Jerrell said in a glib tone. "I simply wished to thank you. The warm reception I experienced last night convinced me to remain independent. You see, I could not stoop to working for a snake who would send henchmen after someone and nearly kill them just to get his way."

The man's clenched fists shook, and anger seeped into his tone, giving his whispers a harsh edge. "You will go broke waiting for clients, Landish."

"Which is why I do not intend to wait, you horse's arse." Jerrell spun toward the three bodyguards. "Next time, you had better kill me if you have the chance. Otherwise, you may not live to see the sunrise."

He walked down the dark corridor, whistling a happy tune.

CHAPTER 4

THE ONE-EYED JOKER

"And, in summary, if you find yourself in need of..." Jerrell paused as he gazed over the crowded hall. Hundreds of eyes stared back at him. "If you need the help of someone cunning, someone who possesses rare skills, seek out Jerrell Landish."

Palkan Forca stood at Jerrell's side and addressed the room full of wizards. "Thank you, Mister Landish. The members of the Marquithe Wizards Guild will consider your offer and seek you out should the need arise." Beneath his breath, he added, "We are even now, Landish."

"Yes, we are," Jerrell replied in a quiet voice. "Congratulations on your recent rise to guild leader." He patted the tall wizard on the shoulder and jumped down from the dais.

All eyes were on him as he strolled down the center aisle, opened the hall doors, and stepped outside. He paused in the entrance hall and considered their response, or lack of one. No questions. No feedback. Nothing.

The door opened. Portia Forca emerged as her husband's voice echoed in the guild hall. When the door closed, his voice faded, and the room fell quiet.

"That did not go well," Jerrell muttered.

"It was not so bad," she assured him.

"I felt like an idiot up there. I can't even properly articulate what it is I do."

"You explained how you foiled Souton's assassination attempt, something most, if not all of them had heard of. Your efforts to capture the abductors of High Wizard Gurgan's son also caught their notice. Even if he rules a remote city like Eleighton, Gurgan is a known and respected wizard."

"Still, some of my more challenging exploits were the ones your husband forbade me to share."

Portia rubbed his arm. "At least I was able to convince him to allow you to speak."

"Thank you for that. I appreciate it."

"I told you before, if you need something I can provide, I will do my best to make it happen."

He took her hand off his arm and squeezed it. "I must be going. I am to meet Haelynn for dinner."

She gave him a kind smile. "She seems like a nice woman. Are you and she...?"

"What?" He shook his head. "No. We are just colleagues."

The wizardess arched a brow. "She is far too fetching to mean so little to you."

"Well, I'd be lying if I said I didn't find her attractive. I am just...being careful."

"Don't be too careful, or you'll miss all of the fun."

He laughed. "I am bewildered how a wonderful woman such as yourself ended up with a stuffy old bore like Palkan."

Her smile faltered, her gaze going distant. "He was not always this way. There was once a time when the two of you might've been friends. Of course, you were still a boy back then, so I guess it wouldn't have worked anyway."

He strode to the exit. "I suspect we will meet again. Until then, I wish you the best, Portia."

"You as well, Jerrell."

He stepped out into the evening air. The sky was light, but darkness crept in from the east while the sun was nowhere in sight. *Devotion will soon begin. I had better hurry.* Haelynn had proven difficult to track down, so he didn't dare miss their meeting time.

～

FAR ACROSS THE CITY, Jerrell ducked into the One-Eyed Joker and was met by raucous laughter, chatter, and cajoling. He had visited the tavern on two other occasions – both had included numerous rounds of dice – and each time he had left with more coin than when he had entered. It was a dingy place and came with the patrons one might expect. Thus, both evenings had also concluded with a fight. Jerrell gave as well as he got but had left with a bloody nose on one occasion and a black eye and cracked ribs on the other. This time, he had no intention of gambling or starting a fight – he had other concerns to address.

In the dim torchlit interior, he pushed through the crowd while scanning his surroundings. The taproom smelled of stale ale, unwashed bodies, and other, much more unsavory, odors. Through a gap between two groups, he spied a cloaked and hooded figure alone at a table in the corner.

He pushed his way past a pair of burly men harassing a barmaid and approached the table. "I must admit, I had doubts about you actually showing."

The figure lowered her hood, revealing blonde hair, blue eyes, and a face far too pretty for such an ugly crowd. "It was I who requested this meeting."

"That's what bothers me." He sat down across from her. "You disappear for weeks at a time, and nobody knows where to find you. It is difficult for someone as attractive as you to remain invisible, but you do a commendable job. I had begun to wonder if you were a figment of my imagination."

Haelynn smiled. "You think I am attractive?"

"You know I do. I suspect even the chair you sit on is excited about your arse touching it."

She chuckled. "You are a true rogue, Jerrell."

"I'll not deny it."

A barmaid approached the table. A long brown braid was draped over one bare shoulder, a dark green dress covered much of her thick body, and her cream-colored corset was cinched tight enough to make her breasts appear as if they were about to explode.

Jerrell smiled at her. "Hello, pretty lady." He was not attracted to her round, freckled face or turned-up nose, but he knew the effect kind words and a friendly smile were apt to elicit.

The woman smiled, revealing a gap between her front teeth. "Welcome to the Joker. Would you care for ale?"

"Ale sounds good." He glanced across the table. "Make it two."

Haelynn shook her head. "No. None for me."

Jerrell smirked. "If I had thought you wanted one, I'd have ordered three."

The waitress laughed. "That'll be two coppers."

He handed her three. "See if you can find clean mugs, please."

"I will be right back." She turned and slipped through the crowd.

Haelynn asked, "Have you found any clients yet?"

Frowning, he shook his head. "I've visited nearly every office in the Bureau. Many appear confused about what I do. Others scoff and send me away without posing a question."

"What about the local wizards?"

"After weeks of trying, I finally was able to gain an audience with the Marquithe Wizards Guild this evening."

"And?"

He shrugged. "And I was met with vacant-eyed stares. While they are now aware of me, I doubt anything will come of it anytime soon."

"I am disappointed in you, Jerrell. I thought you would be more convincing at this," she said in a level tone.

He snapped, "Do you have any better ideas?"

A smirk turned her lip up. "Actually, I have one idea."

"I am listening."

Haelynn leaned over the table, giving him a view down the front of her dress. He forced his eyes to her face.

She whispered, "I hear the enchanters are meeting with Lord Malvorian tomorrow afternoon."

"So?"

"I don't know what the meeting is about, but it sounds as if the enchanters are angry with him. Where there is a disagreement, there is also an opportunity. It might be worth investigating."

He frowned. "Why all the secrecy?"

"Because...I discovered this information last night during pillow talk. If the man I was with knew I told anyone, he would have me killed."

While Jerrell still didn't trust Haelynn, he didn't want to see her dead. *It must have been someone with power.* It was an intriguing nugget of information, especially since he knew so little of her.

"Where do you go?"

She frowned. "What do you mean?"

The barmaid returned with two ales, set them down, and then walked away.

Jerrell leaned over his mugs and looked Haelynn in the eye. "You disappear for weeks at a time, and nobody seems to know where you are or when you will reappear. If I didn't know better, I'd think I was partner to a ghost."

Her gaze dropped to the table as she sat back. "I live dual lives, Jerrell. This one is dangerous. The other is far more likely to see me killed. It is best if you do not know."

When she stood, he grabbed her hand. "I am sorry. Don't leave."

"What do you want from me, Jerrell?"

"Stay. Have a drink or two."

"And then?"

"Perhaps you would be interested in coming back to my apartment?"

"I thought you were not interested."

He snorted. "I'd be lying if I said I wasn't interested. I merely thought it best to take things slow after what happened in Yor's Point."

"Are you saying you trust me now?"

"I am saying, I am willing to try."

She sat back down and smiled. A simple smile on a beauty like her would stir the blood of any virile young man. Jerrell was no different. He drank his ale while enjoying the view, and when the barmaid returned, Haelynn ordered him another along with a glass of wine for herself. They shared small talk, and she laughed at Jerrell's stories.

Soon, they were walking down the street. Jerrell had his arm around her, and Haelynn had her head on his shoulder. When they reached his apartment, he led her inside and closed the door. She kissed him and he responded in kind. He tore his coat off, and her hands found their way into his tunic while he unlaced her dress. His pulse raced as she kissed his neck.

She eased back into the moonlight, dropping her dress to the floor. The moonbeam gave her skin a milky appearance, while shadows clung to the undersides of her breasts and the contours of her lithe body. He tore his boots and breaches off before tossing his smallclothes aside. The two of them stood a stride apart, both naked and panting in a moment of unspoken tension. In his ear, Jerrell's heart thumped out a strict demand – *take her, Jerrell.*

So, he did.

~

JERRELL WOKE to the morning sun streaming through his bedroom window. He rolled over and found himself alone in bed. The room was a mess. All was quiet. He stood and walked down the corridor, not caring that he was naked. His clothes remained strewn about the living room, but nobody else was in the apartment.

"She left me again."

It was an odd feeling to be the one left behind when it was usually he who left before the woman woke. It was he who often avoided telling others where he lived or when, if ever, he would be seen again.

"Damn that woman," he swore while returning to his bedroom.

The conversation from the prior evening came to him, and he recalled her mention of the meeting between the enchanters and Malvorian.

"I need to find a way into the palace." He opened the chest at the foot of the bed and pulled out a flat sack. He reached inside and removed a long gray beard. "I have been waiting to wear this."

Excited at the idea of donning a new personality, he began to dress.

CHAPTER 5

A FLY ON THE WALL

Bent over and walking with a limp, Jerrell approached the palace gate. His view was blurred by the round wire-rimmed spectacles resting on the tip of his nose and the bushy eyebrows glued above his eyes. Ahead of him, a line of farmers, merchants, and citizens waited to enter the palace grounds.

The gnarled staff in Jerrell's hand thumped with each step. The wind whipped around his tattered robes and tugged at the bent, cone-shaped hat on his head, forcing him to grip the brim with his other hand lest it fly away – something he could not afford since the long gray hair draped to his shoulders was attached to the hat. A rope draped over his shoulder lay hidden beneath his robes chafed at his neck.

He stopped at the end of the line and grimaced while awaiting his turn. The line advanced slowly while a clerk recorded each name in his ledger. A farmer in a broadly brimmed brown hat joined the line behind Jerrell. In his arms, he held a brown hen.

Curious, Jerrell asked in a cackling voice, "Why the chicken?"

The man grunted. "She is all I have left after a pack of rock wolves raided my henhouse."

"So, you brought the chicken to the wizard lord?"

"Well, I don't expect Lord Malvorian to see me himself. I plan to ask a magistrate to declare a royal hunt. After all, it makes no sense to purchase a new rooster if the wolves might return."

While the farmer's argument had merit, it gave Jerrell an idea of the type of complaints a magistrate or wizard lord might have to address. *Governing sounds like a big pain in the arse. Why would anyone wish to subject themselves to such a tedious life?*

When his turn arrived, Jerrell stepped forward with a labored motion accompanied by a groan.

The clerk spoke in a nasal tone. "State your name."

In a wheezing voice, Jerrell replied, "I am Jernigan the Learned."

The clerk frowned. "The what?"

"The *learned*, you dolt. I am a scholar of some repute."

With a roll of his eyes, the clerk wrote in his ledger. "What is your reason for attending court?"

Pressing a hand to his chest, Jerrell said, "I wish to start a new school in Marquithe. It will be a home for young merchants and wizards who wish to become tomorrow's leaders."

"Fine. You are to attend Magistrate Aldon's court. It is in court room two. Wait until your name is called."

"Aldon?" Jerrell snorted dismissively. "I must meet with Lord Malvorian."

The clerk sighed. "Don't be foolish. The wizard lord is a busy man."

"Too busy to care about the future of his fair city? Nonsense. I insist on seeing him."

The guard standing beside the clerk interjected. "Just move on, old timer. We've no patience for your nonsense." He gripped Jerrell's sleeve and dragged him through the gate.

Jerrell stumbled to a stop, huffed, and straightened his hat. "How dare you treat me like some common street rat?" Thrusting his chin out, Jerrell limped ahead.

He crossed an open square and headed toward the largest structure in the city.

Marquithe Palace was a network of interconnecting buildings. At one end stood the Temple of Farrow, a building in the shape of a peaked arch, the front adorned by a massive circular window facing the moon in the eastern sky. Like the domed Temple of Gheald in Fastella, which Jerrell had attended on numerous occasions, the building was extensive enough to hold thousands.

Connected to the temple was an arrangement of buildings with rounded turrets, bridging the temple to the palace itself. The palace was four times the size of the temple, consisting of arches, blocky buildings, and spires stretching to the sky. The tallest tower stood at the center, and its top glowed with a deep blue flame. Jerrell had to admit, the palace was impressive.

He climbed the stairs, then stopped and glared at the guard by the entrance. The man grunted, opened the door, and waved him inside.

The receiving hall was massive with a tall arched ceiling and stained-glass windows along the front. Black marble tiles covered the floor, its polished surface reflecting light from the enchanted lanterns mounted to the walls.

In the corners closest to Jerrell, stairwells descended into darkness. Beyond the stairwells, doors lined both sides of the hall, each standing open except at the far end, where a pair of armed guards blocked two doors with sour expressions on their faces. People shuffled into the open doors while clerks in dark blue coats marked names in their ledgers.

The throne room must be behind the doors at the far end of the hall. However, the guards would make entry difficult. Rather than heading to the court room as he had been directed, Jerrell shuffled to the wall beside the entrance and began digging through his clothing as though looking for something. When the door opened and the farmer in the brown hat entered, Jerrell extended his staff and hooked the man's ankle. He fell face-first with a grunt and slid across the tiles. The chicken in his arms tumbled across the floor, righted itself, and burst into a run.

The eyes of everyone in the hall followed the startled hen as she clucked, hopped, and scurried around the vast chamber. Taking advantage of the distraction, Jerrell ducked into the dark corner stairwell and faded from view.

~

With his costume removed and safely hidden, Jerrell slipped out of a storage room with the coil of rope over his shoulder. He followed a dark corridor, guided by the flickering light of a torch. It brought him to an intersection where another torch beckoned in the distance. That torch led him to a stairwell, which he ascended, slowing as he neared the top. He peered around the corner and found an empty corridor leading to another stairwell. Again, he climbed, this time passing three landings before the stairs ended, where he paused and reflected on his conversation the prior evening with Haelynn.

~

"What can you tell me of the palace throne room?" he had asked as they lay in bed together.

Her breath tickled his bare chest. "It is a hall big enough to seat a thousand people. A dais occupies the front, upon which rests a wooden throne. The main entrance is in the back with a side entrance on one side of the throne. To the other side is an antechamber with no exit."

He imagined the layout in his mind. "So, these two doors are the only ways into the throne room?"

"Yes, other than the lift."

"The lift?"

"It is located behind the throne. The lift shaft rises beyond the throne room's domed ceiling before climbing up into the Tower of Devotion."

He rubbed his jaw. "That offers some possibilities."

"I should note that the lift is powered by magic only the wizard lord of Farrowen possesses."

Jerrell frowned in thought. "This lift passes through the palace roof?"

"It does." She ran her finger down his chest. "If we are finished with business, perhaps I could interest you in more pleasure?"

"I might be convinced."

Her lips met his as her hand tracked down his torso.

Footsteps drew Jerrell from his reverie. He slipped into an alcove behind a statue and remained still. A guard dressed in silver plate armor marched past, his head hidden beneath a silver helmet. The man's midnight blue cape swirled behind him as he faded down the otherwise empty corridor.

When the man turned the corner, Jerrell snuck out, to search for another stairwell.

With the rope still over his shoulder, Jerrell emerged from the curved stairwell into a small room. Daylight seeping through a narrow window revealed a wooden ladder rising to the ceiling. A trapdoor above the ladder was the only other way out. He scaled the ladder, opened the trap door, and peered outside. The trap door led to the roof of a circular tower, the top of which was surrounded by a waist-high wall. Nobody was on the tower, so Jerrell climbed out and crawled to the wall to peer over it.

He found himself eight stories above the palace grounds. The palace itself appeared even larger than he had anticipated, stretching out to the north and south. To the northeast was the throne room's domed roof. Beside it, the Tower of Devotion extended another hundred feet up. The azure flame of Farrow burned in the open chamber at the top, capped by a pearl-colored dome supported by a ring of pillars. During Devotion, that flame would intensify to an inferno that consumed the tower's upper reaches. After many centuries of this nightly occurrence, the tower and the dome above remained pristine and unblemished. Jerrell wondered how hot the flames were and what might happen should he attempt to touch them. *Focus, Jerrell,* he admonished himself.

He rounded the tower at a crouch while peering over the wall. An iron-rung ladder secured to the tower's outer wall led down to the palace roof, two stories below. He swung one leg over the wall, found the first rung, and began his descent.

Once on the palace roof, Jerrell ran toward the Tower of Devotion. Ten-foot-tall open arches in the circular tower wall revealed the empty interior. Each arch was supported by a pair of stone block pillars, three feet thick and just as wide. He slowed as he drew close and leaned forward to peer through the nearest arch.

An open shaft led down into the palace. At the bottom, six stories below, was the empty lift. It was nothing more than a rectangular platform with a pedestal on one end. Thick chains ran from the lift and up the side of the shaft, rising into an opening two stories above Jerrell. The opening was the size of the lift, and the hollow tower innards were visible through it. At that same level, an enclosed bridge supported by arches led to a blocky building – likely where Malvorian and the other palace officials lived.

The sun appeared to be beyond its apex and beginning its descent toward the western horizon. *The meeting with the enchanters will begin any moment.*

A bell chimed from the depths of the shaft, spurring Jerrell into action.

He slid the rope from his shoulder, looped one end around the nearest stone block pillar, and began feeding it down into the shaft. When about ten feet of rope dangled into the throne room, he tied it to the pillar, securing it in place. He slipped on his leather gloves, and gripping the rope firmly, he began to lower himself down the shaft with his boots pressing against the stone walls. The sound of male voices came from below, their words muffled.

Five, ten, fifteen feet of stone slipped past as Jerrell eased himself down. As he neared the room's opening, the conversation became louder. When the wall ended and open air began, he flipped his legs up, wrapped the rope around one of them, and lowered himself another couple feet. Upside down and hanging four stories above the floor, he peered into the massive throne room.

A man with black hair, a thick black beard, and dressed in shimmering silver and midnight blue robes sat on the throne below him. A pair of guards bracketed the door at the side of the chamber. Rows of benches bordered an aisle running down the center. A quintet of men in black robes stood in the aisle. A man with a long gray beard was speaking.

"...is the meaning of this?"

The man on the throne, who could only be Lord Malvorian, replied. "Whatever do you mean, Olberon?"

"You know very well that silver is the core ingredient to any enchantment. How are we supposed to continue supplying enchanted items to the southern wizardoms if we cannot acquire silver?"

"Ah. I see. You believe that your lack of supply is my problem. That is where you are mistaken."

"For centuries, our tower has been guaranteed a steady supply from the Souton Mines."

"Guaranteed? Do you have this in writing? Did I sign such an agreement?"

The old enchanter grimaced. "You know the way of things, Malvorian."

"The way has changed. I have a wizardom to govern and you enchanters have long made it clear that you are not my subjects, although your tower stands within my city. You will need to solve your supply problem without me. My subjects have other needs that require my attention. You are on your own."

Olberon's face turned red, and he shook with constrained fury. "If our supply runs out...what then?"

Malvorian sat back with a nonchalant shrug. "I suspect you will have some spare time on your hands."

The enchanter stomped forward. "How dare—"

The instant Malvorian thrust his hand forward, Olberon lurched and shot up into the air, not stopping until he was suspended in the cavity of the dome high above the throne room floor. The wizard lord stepped away from his throne while arcs of blue lightning crackled from his clawed fingers.

"No!" Malvorian roared. "How dare *you*! I am wizard lord here, anointed by Farrow himself. The magic you enchanters wield is meaningless to my might. Generations of your kind will come and go while I persist. Challenge my patience again, and I will destroy you all."

The four enchanters on the floor cowered and fell to their knees. High above them, Olberon's face turned as pale as his beard. The old man stammered, "P...please, Your Majesty. I did not mean to offend you."

Malvorian smiled. "That is more like it."

He waved his hand and Olberon fell. The old man screamed as he plummeted toward the throne room floor. Again, the wizard lord reached out, this time using his magic to stop Olberon a mere foot from the carpet. A breath later, Malvorian dropped his hand and Olberon landed on the floor.

The old man lay still other than the rapid rise and fall of his chest. He stumbled to his feet while sweat ran down his pale face.

Malvorian said, "Time for you to leave, Olberon. At some point in the future, your shipments of silver will resume. Until then, I do not wish to see your face."

The enchanters scurried out of the room. When the door closed, Malvorian turned toward the corner of the room.

"Wexall. What do you know of this?"

A man emerged from the shadows and approached Malvorian. He was as tall as the wizard lord, with a powerful, athletic build of a warrior but wore the telltale robes of someone who wielded magic. His brown hair was slicked back and a trimmed beard covered his sculpted jaw.

The newcomer replied, "I've heard rumors that silver deliveries from Souton have come to a stop. When queried, Roka claimed that the issue was temporary and that the miners were seeking new veins to tap."

Malvorian growled. "I don't like it. This is the first I have heard of Souton Mines running low on silver."

"I believe further investigation is warranted, Your Majesty."

"As do I. See that it is done, but covertly. If you find something underhanded, I do not wish to alert anyone involved."

"What of Roka?"

"If I discover he is lying, I will make an example of him. I cannot have the other high wizards believing they can betray me."

Wexall bowed. "As you wish, Your Majesty."

"Thank you, Chancellor." Malvorian circled the throne. "While you are at it, tell Thurvin to tighten the web. It is time the fly fell under our control."

"We've made numerous attempts, but this fly is crafty, persistent, and difficult to catch."

"In that case, try something different, something even this fly would find impossible to overcome." The wizard lord stepped on the lift and put his hand to the pedestal.

A hum arose as the lift headed straight toward Jerrell.

Oh, crap.

CHAPTER 6
WIZARD LORD

The lift holding Lord Malvorian, the most powerful wizard in Farrowen, rose toward Jerrell as he dangled upside down. Being caught spying on the wizard lord was something he desperately wanted to avoid.

Jerrell unwound his leg from the rope, and his lower body fell, stopped only by his gloved hands gripping the rope. The movement sent the rope straight toward the chains connected to the lift. Hurriedly, Jerrell yanked his dagger from its sheath. When he neared the chains, he drove the dagger through a gap in a link. The dagger wedged and moved with the chain, rising while Jerrell held tightly to the hilt. The stone walls slid past as he was carried upward.

He glanced down to find the top of Malvorian's head twenty feet below. The wizard lord stared vacantly into space, his mind preoccupied. Jerrell prayed the man would not look up.

Jerrell readied himself as the arches drew closer. The opening appeared, and he lunged for the rope, gripping it with his free hand. He wiggled and pulled, yanking his dagger free, which sent him swinging toward the pillar while hanging by one hand. By that point, Malvorian had glimpsed the end of the rope. His gaze turned upward in time to see Jerrell swing his leg onto the ledge surrounding the lift. The wizard's eyes widened in alarm.

"What is this?" Malvorian roared.

Jerrell spun from the tower and burst into a run across the palace rooftop, his thoughts scrambling for a means of escape.

Climbing the tower to reach the trap door was out of the question, yet the palace roof was too high for him to jump without dying or suffering great injury.

He glanced over his shoulder as Malvorian thrust a hand out and released a bolt of lightning. Expecting this, Jerrell altered his path at the first hint of movement. The lightning missed him and struck the tower, sending a blast of chipped stone through the air.

As Jerrell neared the edge of the rooftop, six stories up, the trees of the gardens came into view, and he leapt. Another bolt of lightning shot over him as he plummeted toward a Cypress tree. He widened his arms to wrap them around the tree while turning his face to the side. The boughs of the uppermost branches slid through his arms until Jerrell finally stopped eight feet below the tip. The narrow tree bent under his weight, tipping him forward. A crack resounded as the trunk snapped in half. Again, Jerrell fell, this time clinging to the severed tree trunk as he sped headfirst toward the ground. The tree tip struck the turf, and a jolt shot through it, shaking Jerrell loose. He flipped and landed on his back in a shrub while the broken tree bounced beside him.

Jerrell lay still, attempting to catch his breath. Somehow, he still gripped his dagger. He sat up and realized he was also still in one piece. Distant shouts of alarm sounded. He scurried behind a hedge and began crawling toward the palace. The thuds of approaching footsteps and clanking armor came from the other side of the hedge.

From the rooftop, Malvorian yelled, "There was an intruder on the roof."

A guard called back from the garden. "Where did he go?"

"He is down there somewhere, you idiot! Find him!"

At the far end of the hedge, Jerrell reached the palace wall. A side entrance was nearby, and the guard manning the entrance stood ten strides from the building, his attention on his comrades rushing into the garden and his back to the door.

Creeping along the wall, Jerrell made for the door, pulled it open, and slipped inside.

~

ONCE AGAIN DRESSED as an old man and leaning heavily against his staff, Jerrell emerged from the dark stairwell and strode into the palace receiving hall.

A guard at the front door furrowed his brow. "Why were you downstairs, old man?"

In a crotchety tone, Jerrell snapped. "I was told there was a privy down there."

"A privy?"

"Don't judge me. Just wait until you are my age. You'll find your bowels are far less predictable."

The man blinked. "Did you find one?"

"I am sorry to say it was too late." Jerrell grimaced. "I've gone and soiled my robes."

The guard's eyes widened. He covered his mouth and nose with his free hand, the other still gripping his halberd.

Jerrell stroked his beard. "I don't suppose the magistrate will wish me to wait in his courtroom now?"

The guard shook his head while still covering his nose. "I think it best if you return another day."

With a disgruntled snort, Jerrell nodded. "You are likely correct. I will return to my shop and clean up."

The guard stood aside, pushed the door open, and waited as Jerrell limped past him. Just for show, Jerrell held one hand to his rear, as if attempting to hold things together. When the door closed, he descended the stairs and crossed the square, the thud of his staff striking the ground in time with each limping stride.

As Jerrell neared the front gate, he glanced to the side to find a pair of guards running across the square, straight toward him. A flutter of panic tickled his stomach, but he kept his steady, plodding pace and passed the guards manning the gate as the onrushing squad drew close.

"Someone broke into the palace grounds and was seen on the roof," a guard blurted out between gasping breaths. "Lord Malvorian has ordered a search of the…"

The man's voice faded beneath the din of surrounding traffic as Jerrell crossed the square outside the palace walls and headed toward the safety of a busy street.

SEATED at a table at the Blue Hen, Jerrell used a chunk of bread to wipe the last of his beef stew from the bowl before him. He popped the bread in his mouth and chewed while he continued to mull over the meeting between Malvorian and the enchanters. The lack of silver supply had caused problems for the enchanters, but every problem created an opportunity for someone smart enough to solve it.

He looked up as a tall, shapely woman in a black dress and red corset approached his table. "I wondered if weeks or seasons would pass before I saw you again."

Haelynn sat across from him with a smirk. "Did I hurt your feelings by leaving while you slept?"

Jerrell snorted. "Hardly. It just irritates me that you proposed a partnership and then you come and go without informing me when I might see you again."

"Now you know how it feels."

"What is that supposed to mean?"

"Have you ever told others where you will be and when they might next see you? What of the women you've bedded and abandoned in the middle of the night?"

"That is different. First, I've never worked with a partner. Second, the women I left in the middle of the night knew I was there for sex and nothing more."

She arched a brow. "You think there is more between us than sex?"

"Being business partners makes it more than just sex. If that is part of the business arrangement, you'll find no argument from me, but if we are to work together, I need you to commit to it rather than just appearing when you see fit."

Her blue eyes stared at him for a long beat before she nodded. "Fine. I will prove you can trust me."

"Good."

"Were you able to gain entrance to the palace today?"

"Yes. I found out why the enchanters are upset with Malvorian."

"And?"

He smiled. "I believe there is ample opportunity to take advantage of the situation."

"As I had hoped."

Jerrell downed the last of his ale and stood. "Let's go up to my apartment, where we can discuss this in private."

She rose to her feet and slid her arms around his neck. "Perhaps we could engage in other, more interesting business first?"

He grinned. "I like the way you think."

He wrapped his arm around her, and they headed toward the exit.

CHAPTER 7
A DEAL BROKERED

A carriage carried Jerrell and Haelynn down the streets of Marquithe. The Bureau of Trading came into view as they crossed the sprawling square before it. The view narrowed dramatically when the carriage entered another busy street.

Jerrell turned from the window to the woman at his side, her hand resting on his knee. He enjoyed the contact but would never say so. More so, he enjoyed the view. No matter how Haelynn dressed, styled her hair, or even without makeup, she never appeared anything less than gorgeous. But, on this occasion, wearing her hair in a bun with stray blonde locks dropping down to her neck, she was stunning. The dark makeup outlining eyes the color of the sea, smears of rouge highlighting perfect cheekbones, and dark red gloss painted on her full lips made her appear as if she had stepped out of a painting. Her dark red gown had ruffles on the upper arms and a cut leaving her shoulders bare while giving others an enticing view of her cleavage – Jerrell couldn't decide where to look. If she had such an effect on him, how would the enchanters respond when they saw her?

The carriage brought them down a street that gently turned from west to south as it sloped uphill. Moments later, the carriage slowed to a stop. The interior rocked when the driver climbed down.

The driver opened the door and stood aside. "We've arrived, Master Lancomb."

"Thank you, Raymond." Jerrell stepped down and placed his black top hat on his head before turning back toward the door. Extending a hand, he said, "Come along, my dear."

Haelynn's gloved hand reached for his, and she lifted her ruffled skirt while stepping down. Once on the street, she stood beside him. The difference in their heights felt a bit odd. Even without shoes, she stood a couple of inches taller than Jerrell. When wearing heels, he found his eyes even with her chin, making it more natural for him to glance down at the gap in her neckline than up to her eyes. *Be honest, Jerrell. You were more likely to stare at her chest than her eyes anyway.*

Haelynn looped her arm around Jerrell's, pressing her body against his, which added to the distraction he was forced to ignore as he shifted back into character.

Tipping his hat to the driver, Jerrell spoke in a formal tone. "Remain here with the carriage, Raymond. Lynnette and I will be finished shortly."

"Yes, Master Lancomb." Raymond bowed as Jerrell and Haelynn turned away.

The Enchanter's Tower loomed above them, eclipsing the midday sun. The rough gray stone structure stood ten stories tall. Over a hundred feet in diameter at the base and gently narrowing as it rose toward the sky, the tower housed dozens of enchanters and thousands of magical objects. A sister tower stood in Anker, the capital city of Kyranni. Those were the only two outposts outside of the enchanters' home island of Cordium.

A pair of guards stood outside the open door, watching Jerrell and Haelynn as they approached.

Stopping before the door, Jerrell said, "Good day, gentlemen."

One guard glanced at the other before replying, "The store is open. Go on in. We've a fine array of enchanted items to purchase."

Jerrell waved his hand. "We are not here to shop. My partner and I wish to meet with Master Olberon."

One guard turned to the other. "Do you know of any meetings scheduled for today?"

The man shook his head.

"Master Olberon is not expecting us," Jerrell said. "But I assure you, he will want to meet with us."

"I am sorry…"

"Tell him we have access to silver."

The guard blinked. "Silver?"

"Lots of silver."

The guard nodded. "Very well. Come inside. You can wait in the store while I speak with the master enchanter."

Still arm in arm, Jerrell and Haelynn followed the man inside. The guard took an immediate right, passing a desk before climbing a stairwell that curved along the building's outer wall. A black-robed old man seated at the desk counted coins while a male customer waited. When the transaction was finished, the customer hoisted an enchanted lantern and walked out the door. Jerrell turned to examine the rest of the room.

Oddities displayed on shelves, in glass cases, and on stone pedestals, occupied an open space supported by a ring of thick columns made of the same gray stone as the tower walls. A handful of patrons milled about the room, each escorted by a young man in black robes. One such young man, no older than twenty, approached Jerrell and Haelynn. He wore a silly grin while ogling Haelynn.

"May I help you, miss?" the young man said, completely ignoring Jerrell.

Haelynn smiled and released Jerrell's arm. With the same hand, she cupped the young man's arm and pulled herself close. "I haven't visited this shop before, but I've heard you have some real treasures."

"Oh, yes. We have magical items ranging from enchanted lanterns to augmented staffs."

"I would love to see such a staff."

Still grinning, the young man nodded. "I would be delighted to show you my staff…I mean, *a* staff."

The two walked off, leaving Jerrell alone. Everyone in the store paused to watch her. Jerrell waited until footsteps came from the stairs. The guard reappeared in quick descent and approached Jerrell.

"I will escort you and your partner upstairs. Master Olberon has agreed to see you."

~

AROUND AND AROUND THE TOWER, they ascended, passing three closed doors and a half-dozen windows before arriving on the fifth-floor landing. The guard opened the door and stood aside, allowing Jerrell and Haelynn to walk past him.

Much of the level consisted of a single open space dominated by a long oaken table in the middle. Ten chairs surrounded the table, each occupied by a man in black. All were much older than Jerrell. Among them was a man he recognized from the throne room. The man stood from his end of the table, his eyes fixed on Haelynn while a grin appeared inside his long gray beard.

"My, my," Olberon said as he crossed the room and took Haelynn's hand. "Decades have passed since this tower has been graced by such beauty."

Haelynn batted her eyelashes and blushed. "You flatter me, Master Enchanter."

While Jerrell was happy for Haelynn's presence to distract the old men, he didn't want to stray too far from the purpose of their visit. He extended his hand. "Thank you for agreeing to see us, Master Olberon. My name is Tyrell Lancomb." Olberon shook his hand. "And you have met my lovely partner, Lynnette Parks."

The enchanter nodded, turned, and circled the table to the one open seat. "My guard tells me you have something of value to offer."

"As I understand, you require silver to properly enchant objects."

"We do."

"Rumor has it that Lord Malvorian has cut off your supply."

Olberon grimaced. "Where did you hear that?"

Jerrell twisted one of the ends of his waxed mustache. "Men of means have eyes and ears where others do not. I am certain you are aware that knowledge can be as powerful as any army."

The master enchanter glared back at Jerrell for a long, silent moment, and then chuckled. "Too true, Mister Lancomb. Too true."

Jerrell pressed forward. "Just how much silver do you require?"

The old man turned to the man beside him, who was at least two decades younger than Olberon. His head was bald and a single gray streak ran down his long black beard. "Horsham. How short are we on our silver reserves?"

Horsham's dark eyes narrowed, a moment passing before he replied. "At the current rate, our supply might be consumed in two weeks, three at most."

Olberon shook his head. "And we typically carry a full year's worth to be safe."

"Which is?"

"A ton."

Jerrell blinked. "A ton of silver?"

"Yes."

Glancing at Haelynn, Jerrell asked, "And how much would you be willing to pay for a ton of silver?

Without hesitation, Olberon said, "Two hundred gold pieces."

Jerrell's heart fluttered and his palms began to sweat, but he showed none of his excitement. He was no mathematician, but he was sure two hundred gold pieces exceeded the value of raw silver. "If we were able to deliver a ton of silver, can you actually pay such a sum?"

"We have the gold and will pay it if you can deliver the silver."

This is it, Jerrell thought. *If we can pull this off, I will have more wealth than I ever thought possible.* Splitting it with Haelynn would still yield him one hundred gold pieces, with which he could easily avoid falling beneath the Whispering Man's thumb.

"Expect to hear from my associate soon. His name is Jerrell Landish, the greatest thief in the Eight Wizardoms. If anyone can procure that much silver in such a short time, it is him."

CHAPTER 8

CROSSED AT THE CROSSING

A mile outside of Marquithe, Jerrell neared a split in the road, pulled the reins, and slowed his stallion to a stop beneath gray autumn skies. The horse was a piebald with black patches amid a field of white, which was why Jace named the steed, Patches. Rather than stand still, Patches shifted and stamped his hooves. The man who sold him the horse had warned Jerrell that the stallion was rambunctious. It felt as if the animal longed to gallop across the open fields bordering the road rather than settle for a walk or even a trot.

He turned his steed as Haelynn's horse neared him. Her gray wool cloak billowed behind her while the skirts of her black dress rode up to expose smooth, shapely calves.

"Whoa, Inky," Jerrell crooned.

The black mare slowed to a stop and Haelynn sighed in relief. The woman leaned over the saddle, gripping the reins with one hand and the saddle horn with the other, her knuckles white.

With slumped shoulders and her golden hair hanging over her face, she turned to Jerrell. "Let's go back to the city and pay for a carriage."

He grimaced. "I can't believe you've never ridden a horse before."

"I grew up in the city and until recent years, never had a reason to leave. When I have traveled, it has always been in a carriage or on a wagon."

Jerrell glanced back toward the city, considering her request once again. He had gone out of his way to find the man who had purchased Inky from him, knowing the horse was mild-tempered and would be easy for Haelynn to ride. He had never anticipated it would be her first experience in a saddle. Midmorning was fast approaching, and he was loathe to lose any more time.

Finally, he shook his head. "To go back, sell the horses, and then find a carriage driver willing to drive us to Souton would take too much time. In addition, we are short on funds and the cost of a three-day carriage ride is beyond what I am willing to spend. We need to save the remainder of our coin for our caper once we arrive."

"You need to stop fighting the horse and remember what I told you. Sit up straight but keep your back relaxed. Hold the reins gently and keep your feet firmly in the stirrups. Remain calm and move your body to the rhythm of your horse. Feel the way she is walking and let her rock you from side to side without resisting. If you are too tense, you are more likely to bounce and be thrown off balance."

She pressed her lips together and stared at him. "You are going to make me do this, aren't you?"

He just wanted to keep moving. "Just get through the day. We should reach Castor's Crossing by nightfall. There, we will find a hot meal and a soft bed."

"I can already tell that I am going to be sore."

Jerrell nodded. "I suspect so."

"In that case, you owe me a back rub tonight."

Any reason to place his hands on her body was agreeable to Jerrell. He suspected it might lead to other, more interesting activities, which made the idea of massaging her all the more enticing. "If we make it to the inn as planned, I promise you the best back massage you've ever had."

He turned his stallion around and urged it into a trot, choosing the southwest branch while glancing toward the route that led south to Palla-nar. He had yet to take that route and visit the southern-most wizardom. He wondered if he would ever have a reason to do so.

TREES WITH LEAVES OF GOLD, amber, and crimson lined the sides of the road, the fields surrounding Marquithe all but forgotten. The road ran down the middle of a flat basin that was twenty miles wide and bordered by two ranges of hills. Jerrell and Haelynn both rode at an easy walk. It had been a long day, made longer by Haelynn's frequent need for breaks. Darkness tainted the gray skies. The day was nearing its end when they rounded a curve to see Castor's Crossing.

Two dozen buildings lay clustered along a riverbank. The road ran alongside the buildings before coming to an intersection – one route continued parallel to the river, the other led to a bridge over it. At the junction was a two-story wooden structure with a porch along the front and stables in the back. The sign mounted to the porch awning read Castor Cottage.

Jerrell pointed toward the building. "That must be the local inn. Let's hope they serve ale."

Haelynn groaned. "Let's hope they have hot baths."

He smirked. "Is that an invitation?"

She snorted. "Find your own bath. I just want a hot soak before you rub my back. I am already sick of smelling like a horse."

"What of dinner?"

"I'll eat in the tub."

They circled the building and rode up to an open stable door. A man in dark green trousers emerged. The sleeves of his stained tunic were rolled up to his elbows, his hands covered in muck.

Jerrell pulled on the reins, stopping Patches before climbing down.

"You stayin' at the inn?" the man asked.

"We are." He handed the man the reins. "They've had a long day and will need hay, water, and rest. Take care of them and it'll be worth a silver piece."

The man's smile revealed two missing teeth. "They will be treated like royalty."

"Wonderful." Jerrell turned to see Haelynn slowly lift her leg over the horse and ease herself down to the ground.

She pressed her hand against her backside and groaned. "My arse might be broken."

"From what I've seen, it was already cracked." He smirked at his own humor.

Rather than laugh, Haelynn gave him a flat-lipped glare. "Watch it, or you won't be seeing it again."

He slid an arm around her. "My, you are grouchy."

The two of them headed toward the inn's rear entrance.

She replied, "That is because you are trying to kill me."

"Now you are just being dramatic." He opened a door that emitted a vile squeak. "Let's have a drink. It will improve your mood. Then, you can bathe."

SHOUTS STIRRED JERRELL AWAKE. He rolled over to find Haelynn climbing out of bed. Dressed only in her shift, she ran to the window and peered outside.

He rubbed his eyes. "What's all the ruckus?"

"There are men in the stable yard, chasing off the horses."

"What!" Alarmed, Jerrell rolled out of bed.

Haelynn shrieked and rushed toward him. On instinct, Jerrell swept the quilt off the bed and held it wide as she flew into his arms. A rock crashed through the window, shattering it and sending shards spraying across the room. He used the quilt-covered woman to shield himself as glass flew past. Pain flared as numerous chunks cut his exposed forearms.

Jerrell opened the blanket and looked at Haelynn, whose head was buried in his shoulder. "Are you hurt?"

She lifted her head. "I am fine."

A flaming arrow shot through the broken window and struck the door. Another followed, striking the curtains before embedding itself in the wall. Jerrell raced over to it and used the heavy quilt to smother the fire. Screams arose elsewhere in the building while shouting continued outside.

He then turned to Haelynn. "We need to get out of here!"

Jerrell scooped up his breeches from the floor and pulled them on, not even bothering to lace them. He quickly slipped on his boots, pulled his tunic over his head, and threw on his jacket. By then, Haelynn had donned her dress, but it remained unlaced in the front.

He grabbed both their packs before heading to the door, where he paused to glance toward Haelynn. By then, she had donned her cloak and tucked her corset under her arm.

She nodded. "Let's go."

He eased the door open as black smoke swirled past. At the end of the corridor, the flicker of flames illuminated the stairwell.

Closing the door, he said, "We will have to leave another way."

"What of the men outside? They shot arrows at us."

After brief consideration, he said, "Wait in here a minute. Perhaps they will leave." He shoved the packs into her arms. "Until then, stay away from the window."

"Where are you going?"

"I saw at least one other couple staying here. I am going to see if anyone needs help."

He tore the door open, darted through, and slammed it behind him. Swirling smoke filled the corridor, so he dropped to a crawl. When he reached the room next door, he tested the handle. It turned and the door opened. The room was empty. The door across from him opened to reveal a tall man with graying brown hair. He held his trousers to his waist, his naked upper body exposing thick arms and a bulging stomach. A small woman stood behind him, the straps of her shift visible above the blanket wrapped around her waist. Both were easily twice Jerrell's age.

Smoke poured into the room, and the man began to cough.

"Get down!" Jerrell cried.

The couple dropped to the floor.

"The inn is on fire. You need to flee. The stairwell is impassible, so you will need to go out a window." Jerrell pointed across their room. "Yours is over the front porch. Open it and climb out. I'll be right back."

As the man closed the bedroom door, Jerrell turned toward to his own room and discovered the spreading flames were now licking the walls near the door. He scurried over, gripped the hot knob, and opened the door to find Haelynn seated on the bed with her dress laced up and the corset beside her.

Jerrell rolled into the room and swung the door shut. Rising to his feet, he snatched the quilt from the floor and wrapped it around himself.

"Grab the packs," he called to Haelynn. When she had them, he hugged her close, so the quilt covered them both. "Come on. We are going out a front window. The smoke is bad, so hold your breath."

He paused for her to inhale, forced her to duck with him, and tore the door open. Hot flames licked the doorframe. Jerrell lifted the quilt over both their heads and rushed her through the doorway. They stumbled against the corridor wall and raked along it until they reached the next door. Jerrell opened it and they fell into the room. Whipping the quilt off him, Jerrell kicked the door closed. The quilt smoldered, so he used its own weight to smother the flames.

Jerrell looked up to find the window still closed and the couple hurriedly dressing themselves. "What are you doing? I told you to go out the window."

The man buttoned his dark green coat. "It is an autumn night and cold outside, so we thought we should get dressed."

After unlatching the window, Jerrell swung it open. "You do realize this is a matter of life and death, right?"

"Well,"—the man glanced at the woman— "we noticed you took the time to dress."

Jerrell rolled his eyes and pointed toward the door as smoke seeped in through the narrow opening beneath it. "We have little time. I am going to climb out onto the porch roof. Follow me and I'll help you. Dally and you will die."

He threw a leg over the sill, twisted, and dropped down to the porch roof. With the sill just below his armpits, he said to Haelynn. "Give me the packs."

When she handed him the packs, he slung both over one shoulder and took her hand. She hiked her skirts high and slid one shapely leg through. He gripped her thigh with his free hand, lifted, twisted, and set her down.

Despite the angle of the roof, she gracefully stood and nodded to him. "Thanks."

"Go down to the eave and drop to the ground while I help these two."

The woman came through the window first. Her petite frame was even lighter than Haelynn's, which made sense since she was only five feet tall. Hacking and coughing from the smoke that now filled the room, the man followed and proved to be both the most difficult and clumsiest among them. By the time Jerrell had him out of the room, flames were burning through the door.

Jerrell shuffled down to the eave and dropped the two packs – Haelynn caught them both. He then gripped the edge, twisted, and lowered himself until he was hanging by his outstretched arms. From there, the short drop was easy. Helping the older couple down was not.

Once they were all safely on the ground, the woman hugged Jerrell. "Thank you so much, young man. If not for you, my husband and I would have died."

The man added his thanks. "I own a trading business in Souton. If there is anything you need, show up at Marlowe & Sons and ask for Desmond."

"Who is Desmond?'

The man thumbed himself. "I am Desmond Marlowe. This is my wife, Marnie."

"Nice to meet you, Desmond, Marnie. My name is Jerrell Landish." Stepping back, Jerrell said. "Sorry, but we must be going."

He gripped Haelynn by the elbow and led her around the building.

"What are you doing?" she asked.

"We need to climb on our horses and ride out of here...assuming the men who started this fire are gone."

When Jerrell neared the rear of the building, the firelit stable yard came into view. The yard was empty, and someone leaned against the open stable door.

Intent on helping, Jerrell crossed the yard with Haelynn in his wake. When he drew close, he saw it was the stable hand. The man's tunic was covered in blood, his head drooped to the side, and his slumped body lay still. Jerrell squatted beside the man.

"He is dead." He glanced back toward the inn. Flames had consumed the rear of the building and would soon devour the rest. "I am afraid the inn's owner also did not make it out." Rising to his feet, he inspected the stable's interior. It was empty. "And our horses are gone." He recalled the shouts that woke him. "Whoever did this either stole the horses or chased them off."

"Do you think they targeted us?"

Jerrell snorted. "For this inn to be assaulted on the only night we stayed here is too great a coincidence. This was planned, and we were the targets. I am sure of it."

"Why?"

"To stop us from reaching Souton is my guess."

"Who would do something like this?"

"Malvorian? The Whispering Man? Another rival or enemy you have yet to reveal? It could be any of them."

She scowled at him. "You still don't trust me."

"I didn't say that."

"I was nearly killed tonight!" She thrust her finger into his chest. "If you think I had something to do with it..."

He cupped his palm over her mouth. "Will you hush?" Leaning close, he said, "You are right. I am sorry."

When he removed his hand she said, "Do not cover my mouth again. Ever. If you do, I will bite you."

Jerrell grinned. "You promise?"

A drop of water landed on Jerrell's face. Before he could mention it, two more struck his head. The sky opened, and it began to pour. Jerrell gripped Haelynn's hand, and they raced through the open barn door.

CHAPTER 9

THE ROAD TO SOUTON

Flames chased Jerrell down a long corridor. No matter how fast he ran, heat raged against his backside. He glanced over his shoulder as an explosion shook the building. A massive ball of fire burst down the corridor, certain to consume him.

Jerrell sat up with a gasp. He blinked in the darkness and turned toward the closed stable door, where a strip of daylight shone through the narrow gap.

In a groggy tone, Haelynn asked, "What's wrong?"

He rubbed his eyes. "Just a dream. Don't worry about it. I see daylight. We had better start moving." He reached out and felt through the hay until he found their packs.

She sat up, her face ghostly in the dim light. "I don't hear rain."

"Thank the gods. I hate traveling in the rain." Jerrell hoisted both packs over his shoulder, crawled to the edge of the hay loft, gripped the ladder rails, and climbed down. When he reached the dirt floor, he called up, "Come down. I'll help you."

Haelynn appeared above him, her skirts swishing as she descended. He reached up and held her by the hips, guiding her until she reached the bottom. She turned toward him and slid her hand around his back. "You were quite heroic last night."

"I only did what had to be done."

Her hand slid down the small of his back as her lips met his, giving him a soft, warm kiss that lasted just long enough for his body to react. When she pulled back, she said, "I'll properly thank you when we next have access to a bed."

Jerrell shrugged. "I'll not argue with that."

"Truly? For once, no argument from the great Jerrell Landish?"

He turned to the door. "I do not argue that often."

"Only when you feel you are right and others are wrong."

He swung the door open to the dim light of dawn. "I must admit, that happens quite often."

The dead stable hand still lay just outside the door, his empty eyes staring up into the sky. His clothes were wet, and puddles dotted the otherwise empty stable yard – evidence of the evening storm. Across the yard, was the wreckage of the inn. The sight of the scorched, collapsed remains instantly dampened Jerrell's mood. *People died last night because of me.* He corrected himself. *No, I did not set the fire, and I never asked for anyone else to do it.*

Jerrell turned toward Haelynn, who had pieces of straw sticking in her blonde locks and clinging to her gray cloak. He picked a few strands from her hair and tossed them aside. In return, she smirked and did the same for him.

After dusting themselves off, they walked to the cobblestone road and glanced in both directions. The village was quiet, and the road empty.

"You got your wish," he said.

"What wish?"

"You won't have to sit in a saddle today."

"But I never said I wanted to walk."

He smiled. "That is why you should take care what you wish for." He waved her to follow. "Let's go. We are about sixty miles from Souton."

She caught up to him. "You want me to walk sixty miles?"

"Well, I am certainly not going to carry you."

"You are hilarious. Please tell me you have a better idea."

"We will walk until something better comes up and should be able to cover twenty miles today if we keep a good pace. Even if we must travel on foot the entire way, it will only take three days."

"Three days? What about food?"

"I have enough trail rations to make it through today. When we reach the next village, we will eat and restock. If we are lucky, we will find a better means of travel by then."

"You intend to steal horses?"

He considered it and shook his head. "You clearly hate riding, and I prefer to not listen to your incessant complaints about it, so I'll find another way."

Her voice rose in pitch and volume, her tone aghast. "Incessant?"

Jerrell chuckled. "It seems I struck a nerve."

"You had best take care, or I'll strike you."

"Promises, promises."

BENEATH THE AFTERNOON SUNLIGHT, Jerrell followed the road as it wound up a steep hillside. The sun had grown hot, and the steady evaporation of the prior evening's storm meant humidity. Jerrell's tunic was damp with sweat and clung to his body, and his coat, which he had long since removed, hung over his arm.

Haelynn walked at his side, her jaw set despite her gasping breaths. To her credit, she had not complained once all day – not about the food, the walk, or even the weather.

As they crested the hill, the view expanded. Tree-covered hills and valleys extended for miles in all directions. To the distant south and east, mountains loomed ahead of them. Somewhere in those mountains was the mining town of Souton.

An approaching wagon rumbled behind them. Three wagons had passed them during their journey from Castor's Crossing, but all of them had headed northwest toward Marquithe.

She gripped his arm, stopping him. He turned to find her hair clinging to her sweat-covered brow.

"What is it?" he asked.

Between gasping breaths, she said, "Finally, a wagon heading south."

"What do you intend?"

"I intend to get us a ride."

He frowned. "You look a bit of a mess."

She used her cloak to dry her face before tousling her hair. She then unlaced the front of her dress to her sternum. By the time the wagon appeared, she was standing in the middle of the road with a hand on one hip, her chest thrust out, and her cloak over one shoulder.

The wagon drew closer. The driver had broad shoulders and a thick brown beard. Beside him sat an older man in a dark green coat and a petite woman in a flowery dress. Jerrell recognized them immediately.

The driver pulled on the reins, stopping a few strides short of Haelynn. She sashayed around them and spoke in a pleading tone while dragging her finger down her chest to draw the man's eyes. "I am a poor, lonely woman seeking a strapping, heroic man who might give me a ride to Souton."

Jerrell laughed as he approached her from behind. "Didn't you see who sits beside the driver?"

Haelynn grunted. "Isn't that the couple from last night?"

He walked past her and stopped beside the wagon seat. "Good afternoon, Mister and Missus Marlowe."

The woman nudged the man. "Look, dear. It is our hero from last night."

Mister Marlowe nodded. "That it is." To Jerrell he asked, "What was your name again?"

"Landish. Jerrell Landish."

"That's it. Please, call us Desmond and Marnie. I see you two have made it quite far on foot."

"Yes. Fourteen miles by my guess." Jerrell patted the side of the wagon bed. "You found a ride."

"It is one of ours." Desmond patted the driver on the shoulder. "This is Miles. He drives for us and was coming through Castor's Crossing. We joined him for the journey to Souton, since our own wagon and horses were nowhere to be found."

"How fortunate."

"Would you care for a ride?" Marnie asked.

Jerrell nodded. "We would love a ride."

"I apologize, but the wagon seat is full."

"We would be happy to ride in the back."

Haelynn grimaced but said nothing as she headed to the back of the wagon.

Joining her, Jerrell extended a hand. "Let me help you in."

"I will pass."

"Why?"

She jumped up and tipped herself over the gate of the wagon bed, landing amid a cluster of crates filled with produce. "I have had enough of your help today."

He climbed in and sat across from her. "I don't know why you are cross with me."

The wagon lurched into motion as Haelynn crossed her arms over her chest. With her dress still partially undone in the front, the effect was both pleasing and distracting, bringing a smile to Jerrell's face.

She grimaced. "Why are you grinning?"

He leered, making it obvious.

She glanced down at her chest, her frown deepening. "Sometimes, I find you utterly annoying."

"What did I do?"

Pressing her lips together, she glared at him. "First, I was forced to ride a smelly, unruly beast all the way to Castor's Crossing—"

"Unruly? Inky is about as mild-mannered a horse as you'll ever meet."

"—then, rather than enjoy a good night of rest, our inn is attacked and burned to the ground – we escape the fire only to be caught in the rain—"

"I found us shelter."

"—wet and smelling like I attempted to bed a campfire, I was then forced to sleep in a hayloft—"

"Better than in the rain."

"—we wake the next morning, and rather than a hot meal, I am reduced to eating dried meat and old, crusty hard rolls while walking twenty miles—"

"I found us a ride after only fourteen miles."

"—and when I finally get us a ride, I am stuck sitting on a hard wagon bed that is sure to numb my arse and leave it bruised for the next few days—"

"If you like, I'll rub your arse tonight."

"—I am sore, sweaty, dirty, and I stink. I am sadly in need of a bath and a change of clothing—"

"I'll happily join you for a bath. I might even be convinced to take you shopping once we reach Souton."

"—The worst of it? None of these trials seem to affect you."

His smile melted. "Wait a minute. You are mad at me because I am not all salty and upset like you are?"

"Yes, and it makes me sick."

Jerrell shot a look of appeal toward the driver's seat, where Desmond and Marnie Marlowe sat, both looking back at him. They had obviously been listening the entire time.

Marnie smiled and shook her head. "Ah, to be young and in love."

Desmond nodded. "I recall when we had such passion."

She touched his cheek. "We still have plenty enough passion, Dez. Remember last night?"

The old man smiled. "I suspect our heat is what set the inn on fire."

The lady laughed. Jerrell grinned. Haelynn snorted and, somehow, scowled even harder.

THAT NIGHT, they were forced to camp in a meadow just off the road, further adding to Haelynn's displeasure. After a breakfast consisting of hot porridge and day-old biscuits, the wagon continued south into the foothills. The mountains were painted in the warm shades of autumn. The road meandered between hilltops often going up and occasionally dropping into shallow valleys. Soon, the hills gave way to mountains where dozens of switchbacks brought the wagon up to a saddle nestled between two snow-capped peaks. Beneath blue, late-afternoon skies, the wagon finally crested the rise. The trees bordering the road parted, and Jerrell caught his first glimpse of Souton.

Surrounded by towering mountains, the mining town hugged the shore of a lake of the same name. Even at a distance, the placid waters reflected a puffy white cloud found in the sky overhead. A castle stood at the far end of the lake, its gray battlements appearing like an enormous outcropping of rock amid the surrounding pines. The city itself appeared no larger than Eleighton.

The wagon rolled down a gentle slope, the trees obscuring the view.

Jerrell called out, "How long before we reach the city?"

Over his shoulder, Miles said, "We will be there within two hours."

Turning to Haelynn, Jerrell said, "At least we will be blessed with hot food and a warm bed tonight."

She nodded, her irritation apparently eased. "And a bath. Don't forget the bath."

He grinned. "I am looking forward to that the most."

A smirk appeared on her lips. "I suppose I will let you join me. I realize you've done your best, and none of this was planned."

"I am relieved to hear you admit it."

Haelynn waggled a finger at him. "Be careful, Jerrell. I could change my mind."

Relieved to see her in a better mood, he held his palms up. "I will be good...at least, until you want me to be bad." He cocked his head and arched his brow at the last statement.

She laughed. "You are incorrigible."

"I'd say the same for you."

Shrugging, she said, "We all have our issues."

Jerrell sat back, feeling pleased. The journey had not gone as he had planned, but after an unexpected fire the first night, the next two days had proven to be uneventful. He planned to spend a quiet, pleasant evening with her, and when he woke the next morning, he would plan their next caper.

CHAPTER 10
MARLOWE & SONS

Towering purple peaks blocked the late afternoon sun, casting Souton Valley in shadow. Streaks of clouds stretching across the deep blue sky reflected in the still waters of the lake in the heart of the valley.

The wagon rolled past houses built along the shoreline and brought them to an intersection. In one direction, the crossroad ran down the spine of a peninsula. Walled estates stood to either side of the road. Within those walls were lakefront mansions, each with a private dock. In the other direction, a gravel road wove past buildings and up toward the mountain to the west.

Once past the intersection, the wagon continued into the business district. They passed a general store, a tailor, a cobbler shop, a butcher, a wig shop, a tool shop, a baker, and finally, an inn.

Jerrell crawled past the crates and tapped the wagon driver on the shoulder. "You can drop us off here. We will stay at the inn."

Desmond scoffed. "Nonsense."

His wife said, "We cannot have our hero paying for a room when we have the space. You will be staying in our home."

Jerrell imagined the four of them packed together in a modest home, unable to spend time alone or to work on his scheme. *They will have us drinking tea and knitting hats while sitting on rocking chairs.* "We appreciate the offer, but..."

Desmond held his palm toward Jerrell, stopping him. "We insist, and that is the end of it."

Sighing inwardly, Jerrell crawled back to sit across from Haelynn, who wore a smirk. "What?"

"I find it funny that the great Jerrell Landish was just put in his place by a sweet old couple."

"What do you suggest I do? Stab them?"

"You wouldn't. Murder is not your style."

His brow furrowed. "I've killed plenty of people."

"Under different circumstances, but that doesn't mean you are a killer."

"What about you?"

"I can take care of myself."

"I've no doubt. How many have you killed?"

"Enough. Take care. I may soon add another name to the list."

"Me?"

She smirked. "Don't worry, Jerrell. If I had wanted you dead, it would have happened long ago."

The wagon rolled to a fenced-in yard on the lake side of the street. Inside the yard was a U-shaped red and white building with a dozen stable doors. The driver guided the horses through the open gate and into the dirt yard, where he stopped his team. Jerrell spied a long sign above the building – the words Marlowe & Sons were painted in red.

"Here we are." Desmond jumped down from the wagon seat and extended a hand to his wife.

Jerrell hopped over the wagon gate and then helped Haelynn down. He then asked, "Do you need help unloading the wagon?"

Desmond shook his head. "Miles will take care of it in the morning. Let's go in the house. We are overdue for a hot meal."

"A hot meal does sound wonderful," Jerrell had to admit.

"Follow us." Desmond took his wife's hand and circled the stables.

They came to a stone path bordered by pines, where Jerrell glanced over his shoulder. Miles stood by the wagon, watching them with narrowed eyes, but quickly turned away from Jerrell's gaze.

The path led toward the lake, which was visible through gaps between towering trees. After a short walk, the trees parted to reveal a log home over a hundred feet long, its roof covered in cedar shakes. Six stone chimneys rose from the building, brown smoke coming from the largest.

Desmond and Marnie headed straight for the building. Upon reaching it, the man stepped onto the porch and reached for the door. He opened it, passed through the doorway, and called out, "Atzori! We are home!"

Jerrell shot Haelynn a questioning look, stepped inside, and surveyed his spacious surroundings.

A vaulted ceiling supported by a matrix of log beams stretched the width of the house, easily spanning sixty feet. A massive stone fireplace dominated the center of the room with ten-foot-wide passages on either side of it. To the near side of the fireplace, a spacious sitting room had two sofas and a quartet of chairs arranged in an arch around the fireplace. Failing daylight seeped through the high windows overlooking the sitting area.

Desmond and Marnie removed their coats, draped them over hooks on the wall, and headed across the room with Jerrell and Haelynn close behind them. To Jerrell's surprise, the fireplace had an opening and mantle on each side. In front of it was a long wooden table with benches along the sides and chairs at each end. A chandelier with a dozen lanterns hung above the table and provided warm light. The wall beyond the table was made of broad windows that provided a gorgeous view of the lake.

The door to the side of the room swung open and a middle-aged man with graying, curly black hair, brown skin, and a broad white grin emerged. "Master Marlowe. Mistress Marlowe. You are back." The man wiped his hands on his stained apron.

"There you are," Desmond said with a smile. "We have guests, Atzori. Please meet our new friends, Jerrell and Haelynn."

Atzori nodded. "Pleased to meet you."

Jerrell nodded. "You as well. I am surprised to find a Kyranni in a remote Farrowen mining town."

"It's a fine place to live – much better than the humid jungle or life in the

Murguard. Let's just say that even after a decade in this peaceful town, I still endure nightmares."

Desmond sniffed. "Based on the delicious scent in the air, we must have arrived in time for dinner. Will we have enough to feed everyone?"

"The boys are all back, and you know how they eat. Thus, I prepared sufficient potatoes, carrots, and hard rolls to feed an army. Lamond had a good day on the lake and came back with two dozen walleye. He is out back baking the fish as we speak." He pointed toward the window and Jerrell spied an outbuilding with gray smoke rising from it. "Now, if you will excuse me, I must take the next batch of rolls out from the oven before they burn."

Atzori ducked back into the kitchen as the front door opened. Jerrell turned to find a bearded man a few years his senior step inside. He was joined by a woman with a young girl in her arms and a boy trailing behind her.

Marnie squealed, "Garmond!" she rushed over and hugged the young man before turning to the woman. "It is good to see you, Alicia." After hugging the woman, Marnie kissed the child in her arms.

Desmond scooped up the boy and hugged him. "How is my favorite grandson?"

The door opened again and another man in his twenties entered with a woman on his arm. Her belly was distended and appeared ready to burst. It was immediately apparent that the two men were brothers. Another round of hugs and kisses followed. The sound of a door opening came from down the corridor, and a dark-haired man Jerrell's age appeared, a grin splitting his neatly trimmed beard. He wore thick leather gloves and gripped a pan filled with baked fish, their heads removed but still covered with scales.

"Lamond!" said Marnie. "The fish smell delightful."

"I am glad you think so, Mother," he said as he strolled through the room, "because dinner is ready."

"Wonderful!" Desmond chimed. "Now that everyone is here, let's fill our plates, so we can finish eating before Devotion begins. Once we are all settled, I will introduce our new friends."

The man with the fish entered the kitchen and everyone else followed, leaving Jerrell alone with Haelynn. They both stared silently at the swinging door while the ruckus of eight happy people came from the neighboring room.

In a detached tone, Jerrell said, "I grew up an only child. When my mother died, I was alone."

"You knew your mother? I didn't even have that." There was an uncharacteristic sorrow in her voice.

"I guess we will find out what being around a family is like."

"I suppose."

He took her hand, led her through the door, and entered the busy kitchen.

THE DINNER PROVED to be as delicious as it smelled. The meal included a full round of introductions, followed by steady chatter. Jerrell learned that Desmond and Marnie's two eldest sons drove wagons, making deliveries to surrounding farms, villages, and sometimes even Marquithe. Their youngest son spent his days maintaining wagons – replacing rotted boards, broken axles, and worn wheels. He also cared for the horses and, whenever possible, spent time on the lake, fishing.

When he had cleaned his plate, Jerrell sat back and sipped his white wine while daylight slowly faded outside. "The stables appear too substantial for a mere three or four wagons and eight horses," he commented to Desmond.

Desmond nodded. "Not so long ago, we had six drivers, with wagons and teams to go with them."

"What happened to reduce your company size?"

Desmond frowned, his eyes dropping to his lap. "Politics happened."

"What do you mean?"

"Decades ago, I struck a deal with High Wizard Roka to take over the business of delivering silver to Shear, Lionne, and Marquithe. Often, the buyers were the enchanters. They use a lot of silver in their work."

"So I've heard."

The old man continued. "While the precious cargo required me to hire guards to protect it, the deliveries paid handsomely and easily covered the additional expense. That business allowed me to grow this company and buy this house. Before long, I had more business than I could manage myself, so I bought a second wagon, two more horses, and hired Miles. Rather than continue to drive to Marquithe and the coast, I handled the local deliveries so I could spend time at home with my family while Miles handled the more distant deliveries. Years passed, and competing traders died or moved away. Soon, my business was the only one in the valley, and I had five drivers working for me. When Garmond turned fifteen, I began sending him on local deliveries. Two years later, Belmond began doing the same, and I changed the company name to Marlowe & Sons. And so, our company thrived until this past spring."

"What occurred then?"

"A Hassakani trader named Yamal Razak came to town."

Jerrell frowned. "A Hassakani?"

"Yes. At first, I found it odd that Razak chose to move his business to Souton. Then, the man brokered an arrangement with High Wizard Roka and everything changed. Since this agreement, Razak has had exclusive rights to all silver deliveries. My only trips to the mine now involve the removal of oxen manure."

"Oxen manure?" Haelynn scrunched her face in disgust.

"Yes. Oxen are used at the mines to power the machine that crushes stone. With four oxen working at a time and four shifts, there are sixteen oxen defecating day after day, so the manure piles up."

Jerrell rubbed his jaw, turning the information over in his head and wishing to move past the nasty subject of manure. "Have you tried to negotiate a new deal to put Marlowe & Sons back in charge of the silver deliveries?"

"I have made numerous attempts, but what am I to do?" Desmond shrugged. "Roka will not even meet with me to discuss the situation. I have even sent missives offering to lower my price for deliveries, but they go unanswered."

An azure glow came from the window as a beam of blue light shot across the lake and ignited the obelisk beside the castle.

"Devotion begins." Desmond stood. "Let's head out to the deck and say our prayers to Lord Malvorian. I only hope the mosquitoes are not bad tonight."

Jerrell followed the family outside while he reflected on Desmond's tale. He now had an idea as to why silver was suddenly difficult to obtain, but he was no closer to figuring out how to get his hands on a wagonload himself. *Tomorrow, I will conduct my own investigation.*

MEANDERINGS

The mosquitoes turned out to be worse than Jerrell had anticipated, leaving welts on his exposed hands, neck, and even his cheek. When Devotion ended, Desmond and Marnie's two eldest sons and their families departed for their own homes. Lamond and Desmond headed to the stables to speak with Miles while Marnie escorted Jerrell and Haelynn to their quarters. With an enchanted lantern to provide light, she took them down a short corridor on the same end of the house as the kitchen. It led to a spacious bedroom with a vanity, mirror, wardrobe, dormant fireplace, and copper tub. A hand pump stood beside the tub, the pipe secured to it descending through a hole in the floor. Their packs sat on a bed large enough for them to share.

Marnie said, "This used to be Garmond's room. Since he and Alicia bought their own house, it is now seldom used." She set the lantern down on the vanity and turned toward Haelynn. "I suspect you would like a bath."

Haelynn nodded. "Very much so."

"Use the pump to fill the tub. I already instructed Atzori to boil a pail of water. Jerrell, if you visit the kitchen, I suspect you will find it ready. Add that to the water in the tub until the temperature is to your liking. A bar of soap and two towels are on the shelf below the vanity."

"Wonderful," Haelynn said. "Thank you, Marnie."

Marnie walked to the door. "If you need anything else, ask Atzori, but do so soon, before he retires for the evening. Breakfast is served shortly after sunrise."

The door closed, leaving Jerrell and Haelynn alone. He walked over to the water pump and lifted the handle. After a few pumps, water began to pour into the tub.

Haelynn sat on the bed and sighed as she removed her shoes. She dug through her pack while Jerrell continued to fill the tub, pulling out a fresh shift and laying it on the bed before rising to her feet.

"You heard her. We will need that bucket of hot water."

"We?"

She arched a brow. "You expressed an interest in sharing the bath."

He grinned. "I am certainly interested." After a few more pumps, he walked to the door. "I'll be right back."

Once in the kitchen, he found Atzori wiping down the counter. "You are here for the hot water, no?"

"Yes, I am."

The big man handed Jerrell thick leather mitts. "Use these when you lift the pail off the stove."

Jerrell slipped the gloves on, reached over the hot fire, and gripped the handle of a five-gallon metal bucket filled with boiling water.

"Take care not to spill on yourself. It'll burn you something fierce."

Grunting as he eased toward the door, Jerrell said, "I'll do my best to avoid it."

When he returned to the bedroom, he found Haelynn in her shift, pumping water. The tub was now one third full. She stopped and stepped away while he poured the steaming water into the tub. He set the hot pail and mitts on the fireplace hearth and turned to see Haelynn, now completely naked, slide into the water.

"Can you hand me the soap?" she asked.

Jerrell retrieved the bar of soap and handed it to her with a grin.

She arched a brow. "Are you enjoying the show?"

"Very much."

"I thought you were going to join me."

He sat on the bed and tore his boots off. His clothing quickly followed.

Haelynn scooted to the middle of the tub. "Sit behind me, so you can wash my back."

Jerrell gestured toward himself. "All right, so long as you don't mind getting poked in the backside."

She smirked. "Tell little Jerrell to relax. It isn't time for him to play yet."

"Little?" Jerrell slid into the tub. "That is hurtful."

Haelynn laughed, and he realized it was the first time in days he had heard her laugh. "You know what I meant." She handed him the soap.

He sat behind her, dipped the bar of soap in the water, and began to wash her back.

Haelynn said, "I have never been around a family like this, or really any family at all. They seem so...happy."

Jerrell nodded, having noticed the same thing. "I know what you mean."

"It makes me long for a family of my own."

"You could find a man and get married."

"Is that a proposal?"

He snorted. "Not from me."

She looked over her shoulder with a hurt look in her eyes. "Would I be such a poor choice?"

"It's not that. I just never intend to marry, neither you nor any other woman."

Haelynn sighed. "I am not surprised."

He stopped washing her and put his hand on her upper arm. "What is wrong?"

"I just feel...so alone."

"I am literally sitting with you in a tub intended for one person."

"No, I mean...these people, they look out for each other. They support each other. They know, regardless of what happens, they will return to a home filled with love. I've never had anyone love me, or anyone to love back."

"I can love you for a night," he offered.

"You speak of sex."

"I do."

"There is no love in sex."

Despite her thoughts about sex mirroring his own, Jerrell was sad to hear her say it. He recognized an emptiness existed in relation to sex, as if it *could* mean something more if only he could figure out the origin of the emptiness.

She then added, "Often, sex is just a tool I use toward my own ends."

"Is that how it is with me?"

"That first time back in Yor's Point, yes. More recently, it has been for my own pleasure." She shrugged. "After all, a girl has needs too."

"Well, tonight we have each other and a soft bed, so how about I attend to those needs." He pulled her hair aside and kissed her neck, his lips working their way up to her ear, where he whispered, "Your back is clean. I thought I might wash your front now, and we will see how things go from there."

She turned toward him and smiled. "As you wish."

Their lips met, and Jerrell's heart hammered in his chest.

After breakfast the next morning, Jerrell and Haelynn bid the Marlowes a good day with the promise to return for dinner. They followed the shaded path past the stables and stopped at the edge of the road.

Jerrell said, "I am going to poke around a bit at the mine and see if I can come up with any ideas."

"Try not to get into trouble."

"Unfortunately, I can make no promises. What are you planning?"

"I am going to visit a tailor."

"A tailor? What for?"

"To choose some material and to take some measurements."

"You are getting a new dress?"

Haelynn produced a gold coin. "You are buying it for me."

"Is that mine?"

She smiled. "I snatched it from your coin purse while you were sleeping."

"You mean you stole it."

She stuck her lower lip out. "Don't you want me to look my best?"

"I find it difficult to picture you looking anything less than spectacular."

Haelynn patted his cheek. "You are charming when you want to be. However, if I am to be of use to you, I need to look the part."

"What part?"

"One of us needs to talk to Roka and ferret out the motivation behind his deal with Razak."

Jerrell found himself nodding. "It would be helpful to know."

"Do you expect me to visit a high wizard dressed like this?"

He looked her up and down. While her appearance satisfied his tastes, it might not be suitable for an engagement with the ruling wizard class. He sighed and dug out another gold coin. "Fine. You might consider a wig as well, just to complete your ensemble. Try not to spend it all."

"You can't put a price on perfection, Jerrell."

"We don't need perfection. We only need good enough." He eyed the way her dress clung to her narrow waist. "Besides, you could wear a burlap sack and still look beautiful."

Her smile widened. "Sometimes, you say the sweetest things."

"If you would like to thank me tonight, I won't argue."

"We shall see how the day goes. Good luck." She turned and headed toward the shops they had passed coming into town, her backside swaying with each step.

Get moving, Jerrell. He tore his gaze away from her, turned, and headed down the road away from the town center.

Large and small homes stood among the trees from one side of the road to the lake. The forest dominated the other side of the road until Jerrell came to a tall wooden picket fence. A gate made of long boards connecting spiked wooden posts stood open, revealing a dirt drive bordered by trees. Above the gate was a wooden sign spanning two posts: Razak Trading Company.

Jerrell peered through the gap in the trees beyond the gate, where the dirt drive ran uphill to an open gravel yard. In the yard, a wagon was surrounded by half a dozen armed men dressed in red tunics and loose-fitting black trousers tucked into tall boots. A pair of large barns bordered the yard – one was connected to a two-story farmhouse. Beyond the buildings, horses grazed in a fenced meadow.

Two men emerged from one of the barns, each leading a horse toward the waiting wagon. They hitched up the team. One man climbed onto the wagon seat and snapped the reins. The wagon rolled down the drive with three guards jogging on each side. The guards all appeared to be Hassakani, many with facial hair and scimitars. Those not armed with swords had a bow slung over one shoulder and a quiver over the other.

Jerrell waited to the side of the road as the wagon rolled through the open gate, turned south, and headed down the road with the guards keeping pace beside it. Curious, Jerrell followed the wagon at a walk until it was a quarter mile ahead of him. He then removed his coat and broke into a jog.

THE ROAD SPLIT – a cobblestone path led east toward the castle and a gravel road headed toward the mountains. The wagon took the latter, and Jerrell followed it, keeping pace at a distance in the hopes of avoiding attention. When he came to a hill rising hundreds of feet and spied the wagon rounding a turn above him, he slowed to a walk, gasping for air with each plodding step. After what felt like miles, he crested the hilltop and caught his first view of the mine.

The road wove down a hillside into a narrow canyon surrounded by gray rock walls. Shadow covered the canyon floor where carts, wagons, and men moved about. Miners entered one of three tunnels before fading into the dark opening. Two walls, each about three stories tall, obscured any passerby's view of the compound. In between the two walls were wooden buildings with angled roofs, half of which were encased by wrought iron fencing with spikes at the top. Armed guards strolled along the top of the outer wall.

Razak's wagon and the escort of guards stopped outside the iron barred gate of the outer wall. The gate swung open, and the wagon rolled inside. When the gate closed, the guards who had been escorting the wagon split off while the wagon continued toward the inner wall.

Jerrell headed down the hill toward the mine for a better look.

The area before the outer wall had been cleared of trees, although a number of stumps remained. The wall ran from cliff to cliff, creating a man-made barrier while nature provided suitable protection for the mine on the other three sides. A dozen guards with bows paced the top of the wall while others were visible through the open gate.

Jerrell approached the outer gate.

"State your business," said a brawny guard several inches taller than Jerrell. The leather vest stretched tight across his barrel chest left his thick arms bare, and his hand comfortably rested on the pommel of the sword at his hip.

"I am looking for a job," said Jerrell.

"You want to work in the mine?"

"That is the general idea."

"It's a hard life."

"I've already lived a hard life. I'd like one that pays better and includes regular meals."

"Oh, you'll find food here. Most of it is edible, but not much more than that."

Jerrell was unfazed. "Who do I speak to about working here?"

"Go on in, continue past the inner gate, and enter the first building on the left. Someone there will help you out. Tell the guard at the inner gate you are seeking work."

The guard waved his arm and the gate swung open. Jerrell strolled through and into the gap between the two walls. The fenced-off buildings stood on one side, while six buildings without barriers stood to the other. The inner wall had two gates ten feet apart, one large enough for a wagon, the other human sized. Jerrell headed toward the smaller one and explained his purpose to the guard who let him inside. Heading directly for the first building on the left, he stepped inside and paused inside the doorway.

The building had an open interior with six posts running in a straight line down the center. To one side of the posts were ten tables with long benches. The six Hassakani guards sat at one of those tables, eating. The scent of hot porridge hung in the air, causing Jerrell to frown. *I hate porridge.*

He turned to the other side of the building, where three men stood behind a counter. All wore stained aprons. Two were cleaning pots while a third watched Jerrell approach. "Hello! I am seeking work."

The man wiped his thick fingers on the apron. "We don't need another cook."

"No. I want to work at the mine."

"If you want that, you had better talk to the captain."

"Where would I find him?"

The man thumbed toward a walled room in the corner of the building. "In his office."

"Thanks."

He walked past the counter and approached the closed door to the room. When he knocked, a voice came from inside. "What is it?"

"I am seeking work."

The door opened to reveal a middle-aged man with a shorn head and a brown goatee. He looked down at Jerrell with a frown. "Mining is hard labor. You look a bit small."

"I'm stronger than I look."

"Well, I happen to have a job suitable to your size." The man grunted and then extended a hand. Jerrell shook it. "My name is Hulik, Ray Hulik. Around here, folks just call me Captain."

"I am Jered Standish."

"Well, Jered, let's get you to work."

CHAPTER 12
MEET GARCON

Jerrell exited the mess hall, following Hulik, who led him to one the four warehouses built on the far side of the inner wall. An elderly man with a gray beard and wisps of gray hair covering his otherwise bald head emerged from the shadows and approached them.

"Mornin', Cap'ain." The old man's smile revealed several missing teeth. "What can I do for ya?"

"Good morning, Eagle. This is a new hire who needs supplies."

The old man looked at Jerrell. "He is a bit small but looks fit enough. Might make a fine mouser."

"My thought as well."

"I'll be right back."

The old man limped off, and Hulik turned to Jerrell. "We will outfit you, so you can start working straightaway. The pay isn't great, but it comes with a roof, a bed, and all the food you can eat, assuming you can stomach what our cooks call food."

Even if the guard at the gate and Hulik hadn't disparaged the food, Jerrell had never expected fine dining, but he had a more important question. "What is a mouser?"

Hulik smiled. "You'll soon find out."

The old man emerged from the closet with a cart, its wheels squeaking as it crossed the room. The cart carried a coil of rope, leather gloves, a leather harness, a wrapped bundle, a small hammer, and a strange metal helmet. When the old man reached Jerrell, he handed him the helmet. Jerrell turned it over and found a padded interior. On the front was a small rectangular metal cage with glass panels.

"This looks like...an enchanted lantern."

Eagle nodded. "That's right. Put it on. Pull the lever on the side of the lantern, and it'll give you light."

Jerrell placed the helmet on his head. The weight felt odd. When he tipped his head forward, the helmet slid down over his eyes.

"Buckle the straps, and it'll stay in place."

He tilted the helmet back and secured the straps beneath his chin.

Eagle then handed him the harness. "Step into this and strap it around your waist."

Jerrell did as asked, slipping each foot through the harness before pulling it up. Once buckled, the man handed him the coil of rope, a small hammer, the bundle, and the leather gloves.

"Good luck to ya." Eagle turned and pushed the cart back toward the storage room.

Hulik patted Jerrell on the shoulder. "Come on. I'll introduce you to the shift leader."

Jerrell walked across the compound beside the big man. "What's in the bundle?"

"Metal spikes."

While Jerrell was still unsure of his role as a mouser, a picture had begun to form.

They circled an enormous structure in the middle of the compound. The structure consisted of a thick pole in the middle, rising up from a ring of twelve-foot-tall stone arches. A ramp ran up to the top of the arches, where four oxen walked along the flat top of a circular wall. One end of a heavy beam was strapped to each of the beasts – the other end was secured to the thick pole, causing it to spin. Jerrell spied men dropping chunks of sparkling gray stone in a gap between a massive metal gear and a plate with thick metal teeth. As the pole and gear turned, the rocks were ground between the gear teeth and those of the plate, causing them to shatter. Other men sorted the crushed rock, shoveling it into two piles, one that glittered and another that was a dull gray. As they rounded the structure, Jerrell spied a trio of wagons lined up outside it, two piled high with rock and a third with oxen manure.

"What was that operation?" Jerrell asked when the noise of the contraption subsided in the distance.

"The crusher. We use it to separate silver from worthless rock."

They reached the tunnel mouth and entered thick shadows. A track ran down the middle of the tunnel, reminding Jerrell of the ore mine outside of Eleighton. Spaced out every ten strides, beams supported by posts bracketed the tunnel. An enchanted lantern hung from every third beam. Sixty strides in, the tunnel opened to a massive cavern. A broad ledge encircled the chamber, overlooking a pit six stories deep. The pit was empty, but the walls showed pick marks that left Jerrell wondering how much work it had taken to dig such a massive hole.

Jerrell and Hulik followed the track along the ledge, circling to the far side of the chamber before fading into a tunnel on the opposite side. A squeaking sound grew louder, until a cart appeared from the tunnel and rounded the cavern, forcing Jerrell and Hulik to step aside. Dull and shiny gray rock filled the cart. It rolled past, reached the other tunnel, and faded from view.

The tunnel system and track reminded Jerrell of his desperate fight to save High Wizard Gurgan's son, Everett. When they came to a cart sitting alone at the mouth of a branching tunnel, he imagined Everett sitting in the cart, his head leaning against the inside, a crossbow bolt jutting from his destroyed eye. The incident had affected Jerrell more than he was willing to admit. He was not used to failure. Worse, he had failed the boy, an innocent bystander caught up in a scheme for gold. Jerrell understood the desire for wealth, but he did not understand how anyone could kill an innocent teen to attain it. Gold came and went, something he had experienced, but life was simply too precious to toss aside with such calculated callousness.

They came to another chamber, even more extensive than the last.

Jerrell whistled in awe. "This place is big enough to house Marquithe Palace."

"Yes. It is a sight to behold." Hulik added, "I suspect that the entire city of Marquithe might fit in this network of caverns."

Beneath a dome of rock, dozens of terraced levels overlooked an underground canyon. On each terrace, groups of men chipped away at the rock walls while others used shovels and their hands to load rubble onto one of two dozen lifts. Those at the top hoisted the lifts to the top where workers emptied them into carts on the track.

"Come along." Hulik headed down a rock stairwell built into the side of the cavern.

Jerrell followed the man past two terraces. When he reached the third level. Hulik led him across a long, narrow terrace, toward a burly dark-skinned man shouting orders to three men loading a lift. Once the lift was full, a man called up and the lift began to rise.

The dark-skinned man turned and nodded toward Hulik as he drew near. "Welcome, Captain. It's been days since I've seen you down here."

"How is the operation going, Leshonn?"

"Well enough, but I fear we will exhaust the silver deposits in this cavern by the end of the year." The man's gaze shifted to Jerrell. "Who is your companion?"

Hulik clamped a heavy hand on Jerrell's shoulder. "Meet Mister Standish. He was just hired to be your new mouser."

"Wonderful. I hope he lasts longer than the last one."

"The man still hasn't shown?"

"No. He set off to explore a new section five days back."

"Five days? You think he is dead?"

"Either that or he escaped."

Alarm shrieked in Jerrell's ears, telling him to run. "Why would he want to run?"

Hulik said, "Many of the men who work down here are convicts, sentenced to work here rather than waste away in prison. All convicts remain chained and under the watchful eyes of a guard. However, we needed a mouser and none of the free men volunteered, so we found a pris-oner about your size and set him to the task."

Leshonn added, "Mousers work alone. While the entrance he used was under watch, he may have found another way out and decided to pursue freedom."

Jerrell said, "I can understand that."

Hulik gestured to Leshonn. "I will leave Standish in your hands. When the day is done, we will sort out his sleeping arrangements."

"I already have a place to sleep," Jerrell said.

"Sorry, but rules are rules. Everyone who works in the mine stays in the barracks. No exceptions. Don't worry. We will house you with the guards, not the prisoners."

Jerrell frowned. "You didn't say that before I took the job."

"You didn't ask. Best of luck down there." Hulik clapped Jerrell on the shoulder and then headed back toward the stairs.

"Come along, mouser. Let's get you a companion, and I'll show you the new tunnel."

JERRELL DESCENDED a wooden ladder into the depths of the massive cavern. It was the third ladder he had taken after descending a dozen sets of stairs. When he reached the bottom, he gazed up at the rock dome a thousand feet above.

"Yes," Leshonn spoke in a wistful tone, "the cavern can appear over-whelming at first. Given time, it seems to shrink until it feels more like a dungeon cell."

"If that is how you feel, why do you continue to work here?"

The big man stroked his white beard. "Truth to tell, I don't know where else I could go. Old soldiers like myself are of limited use. I am through killing, be it humans or darkspawn. Here, I have a purpose."

"Which is?"

"To keep these men alive." He motioned Jerrell forward. "Let's go speak with Adrion."

The lowest level was darker than the others – thick shadows clung to the rock like moss. It was also empty...until Jerrell spied an old man sitting on a wooden rocking chair, humming to himself. A table holding a pitcher and a cup rested to one side of the man, a cot to his other side.

"Who is it?" the old man asked when Leshonn and Jerrell drew near.

"It is me, Adrion."

"Welcome, boss."

"I brought you a new mouser. His name is Standish."

The old man tipped his rocking chair forward and stood, groaning in the process. White hair covered his head and a long white beard hung down to his chest. His skin was pale and his eyes milky.

"Welcome, mouser."

"Thanks," Jerrell said, still unsure what this was all about.

"Come. Let's see who will be joining you."

The old man moved with shuffling steps, his hand extended before him.

"What's wrong with him?" Jerrell asked.

"Mostly, he is old, but also, he is blind."

"Why is he down here then?"

"I'll let him tell you."

The old man stopped and turned toward Jerrell. "Many years ago, I was a thief. Some say I was the best thief in the world. Young, arrogant, and skilled, I believed I could steal anything from anyone...until I decided to take a precious bauble from Lord Malvorian. That small mistake cost me everything. I was captured, imprisoned, and given a choice: Volunteer as a sacrifice in the Darkening ceremony or spend the rest of my life toiling in the mine. I chose the latter." The old man chuckled. "Despite everything, I won."

"You won? How is this winning?"

"Oh, I've seen men come and go. Many die here while others leave because they miss the sun. The prisoners rarely last a decade. I've been down here for seventy years. My time runs short, but that is still sixty years longer than Malvorian believed I would live. Who knows? Perhaps someone will soon do the world a favor and end his magic-fed existence. Outliving him would fulfill my final wish."

The old man turned and shuffled off. Leshonn gestured for Jerrell to follow. A cage made of wooden poles and a grid of wires sat at the far end of the floor. Inside the cage were dozens of mice ranging from gray to white.

Adrion felt at the cage, found the latch, and opened the door. He reached in, bending low while holding his palm just above the floor. "Come along, my pretties. Who is ready to go on an adventure?"

The mice gathered around his hand and swarmed over one another until one snuck onto his palm. Adrion stood upright, closed the cage door, and turned to Jerrell.

With the mouse sitting in his extended palm, Adrion said, "Meet Garcon, your new partner."

CHAPTER 13

THE MOUSER

Jerrell stared apprehensively at the mouse in the old man's hand. "Does he bite?"

Adrion shook his head, his wispy white beard wavering like a feather in the wind. "These are not ordinary mice. I raised them myself, so they are used to humans. If anything, he will treat you like you are his mother."

"Mother? I lack the equipment for that job."

The old man laughed and handed the mouse to Jerrell. "No need for breast feeding or anything like that. Just share whatever you eat with him, and you'll be fine."

The mouse snuck onto his palm and stood on its hind legs. Its beady little eyes stared back in curiosity.

"This mouse is my partner?" Jerrell asked. "How does that work?"

"Mice are far more sensitive than humans. They have incredible hearing and fragile lungs. If Garcon suddenly becomes frantic, take heed. It likely signals danger such as a tunnel collapse or some other threat. If he grows lethargic, it could indicate a lack of breathable air. You see, these underground caverns often contain toxins that will slowly poison your body. You might not notice it until it is too late."

The mouse crawled up Jerrell's arm in rapid movements spanned by brief pauses.

Jerrell asked, "Does everyone have a mouse?"

Leshonn snorted. "The miners hardly need them. Mousers on the other hand..."

Garcon reached Jerrell's shoulder and seemed to settle in. "Again, you use the term mouser. What, exactly, is my job?"

"Come along. I'll show you." Leshonn clapped the old man on the shoulder. "Thanks, Adrion. Have a good day."

"Take care, boss."

The mouse now sitting on his shoulder, Jerrell followed Leshonn to the ladder, where they ascended to the terrace twenty feet above. Rather than heading toward the next ladder, the two crossed the uneven floor toward a crew of five men, two pounding at a rock wall with their picks, two shoveling up the finer rubble, and the last loading chunks of stone into a large wooden bucket. Ropes connected to the bucket rose through the shadows. Three lanterns on the ground surrounding the work crew provided light to the immediate area. The rhythm of repeated thuds grew louder as Jerrell drew near the group.

"Rollie!" Leshonn shouted.

The men stopped working, turned toward Leshonn, and set their tools down. Sweat covered the exposed skin of arms bulging with thick toned muscle. The tallest wiped his brow. He appeared to be in his mid-thirties with pale skin, blond hair, and blue eyes.

The man nodded. "Hi, boss."

"Hi, Rollie." Leshonn turned to the others. "Take a break. Drink some water. I need to borrow your team leader for a few minutes." The men dropped their tools and tossed their gloves aside, strolling over to a pile of packs beside the wall. Turning toward Rollie, Leshonn asked, "Can you show me to the tunnel where we lost our last mouser?"

"Sure thing." He hoisted one of the lanterns. "This way."

They followed an upslope and entered the mouth of a shallow tunnel. When they came to the end, Rollie squatted and pointed toward a dark recess in the gray rock. It was five feet wide and no more than a foot tall. The light in his hand did not reach the far end. "We broke through here a week ago. The last mouser went in and never returned."

"Thanks, Rollie." Leshonn turned to Jerrell. "Your job is to explore the extent of the caverns." The man held out a chunk of white stone. "Use this to mark your direction, so you can find your way back. If you happen across any veins of silver, mark those as well. When you are finished, report to me. If you need to scale something steep, use the spikes and the hammer. If you need to go down, use the rope. Just pay attention to your mouse. Your life depends on it."

"You want me to go in there?" Jerrell had spent plenty of time in tight spaces but worried about what might be lurking in the darkness.

"You asked for a job. This is it. Think of it as an adventure."

"An adventure," Jerrell repeated the word, hoping to ease his worries. He sighed. "Fine."

"Remember to pull the lever on your helmet lamp. Without light, you won't get far."

When Jerrell reached up, the mouse scurried behind his neck and settled on his other shoulder. He found the lever and pulled it down. Soft blue light shone in front of him, illuminating the two men.

"Good luck," Leshonn said.

The other man's brow furrowed as he stared at Jerrell. *He seems happy it is not him. How did I get myself into this?* Jerrell's eagerness to inspect the mine had led him much deeper than anticipated.

He squatted, crawled into the opening, and then fell flat against his stomach. With his head down and turned to the side, he pulled himself into the narrow gap and toward the darkness.

THE GAP RAN DEEPER than Jerrell had expected. His metal helmet scraped along the rock, his head turned sideways, the lantern light extended in front of him. He repeatedly slid forward, wondering when it would open to a wider chamber.

The mouse crawled onto his neck and slipped inside his coat. Although the creepy sensation made his skin crawl, he forced himself to keep advancing.

The thought of the mountain of rock above him, and what would happen should it collapse, ate away at his courage. His heart began to thump, and his breaths came in gasps – he was eager to be out in the open. Just when he considered turning back, the tunnel ceiling began to climb. He lifted his head to find himself at the entrance to another cavern. Crawling forward, he dragged his legs out of the tunnel and climbed to his feet.

The cavern ceiling was three times Jerrell's height. In one direction, boulders led to a high tunnel. In the other, a hole lurked in the cavern floor. The mouse popped up from Jerrell's collar and crawled onto his shoulder. It sniffed the air but did not appear alarmed.

Jerrell stood over the hole, squatted, and shone his light down. The bottom was too distant for it to reach. A faint rush came from below, causing him to frown. *It sounds like…water.* He considered going down but recalled the opening at the other end of the cavern. Given a choice, he preferred going up first.

He crossed the cavern. Its walls were a dark gray with a tint of blue, and Jerrell scrambled up the first boulder. One led to another, and soon, he was forced to duck lest he hit his head against the cavern ceiling. He squatted and approached the opening – a winding tunnel sloped upward.

JERRELL CAME to yet another intersection, the fifth in thirty minutes, and used the chalk to mark his way back. One path led down into what appeared to be a cavern. The other was a vertical shaft rising into darkness.

Tired and unsure of his next direction, he sat on a rock, dug into his pack, and removed a hard roll. He tore a chunk off and popped it into his mouth. High-pitched chatter came from his shoulder, drawing his attention to the mouse, which paced back and forth.

"Are you upset about something?" Jerrell recalled the guidance Adrion had given. "Oh. You want a bite?" He tore off a small piece and held it out to the mouse. Garcon stood on his hind legs, took the bread, and began to eat.

Jerrell finished the roll and took a swig of his water. He then poured a little into his palm and held it up to the mouse. Garcon scurried onto his hand, slurped up the water and returned to his shoulder.

"Huh," Jerrell shook his head. "That is actually pretty neat. I would have never thought it, but I kind of like you, Garcon."

Deciding he needed some air, Jerrell unstrapped his helmet and lifted it off his head. He wiped one hand through his sweaty hair while the other set the helmet on his lap. The lever bumped against his leg, dousing the light. Darkness crashed in, enveloping him.

"Crap."

He lifted the helmet, turning it over in his hands while searching for the lever. The mouse chattered in his ear, causing him to look up. A dim light was visible at the distant end of the shaft above him. Then, he felt an eddy cool his forehead.

"It's a way out." Excited, he donned his helmet, flipped the lever, and buckled it tight.

Rising to his feet, he found a handhold and began to climb. Ten feet up, he found a metal spike driven into the rock. He stared at it in a moment of confusion before realization struck. "The last mouser climbed up this way."

He gripped the metal spike and pulled himself up before finding another. Soon, he came to a ledge and crawled onto it – and the light became brighter. Another thirty feet of careful climbing brought him to a small cave. Through its opening, bright sunlight beckoned. He emerged into a narrow crevice with rock walls on three sides. Heading in the open direction, he scrambled up a boulder and the view opened to a tree-covered valley. A lake occupied the heart of the valley. Homes lined its shore and a castle was visible at one end.

His gaze shifted to the land below the hilltop where he stood. Within seconds, he knew his position.

"I am standing above Razak's property." He smiled at the irony.

A plan began to form, and while pieces of the puzzle remained undiscovered, a sense of confidence washed over him.

Jerrell removed his helmet, the rope, and the rest of the gear he had been given, storing it in the mouth of the tunnel before turning away. "Come along, Garcon. I want to introduce you to the Marlowes. But first, let's see if anyone is home at Razak's."

CHAPTER 14
WIZARDESS GARUE

Haelynn Broga turned and examined herself in the mirror. The bright red curls tumbling over her shoulders distracted her briefly. While the wig was suitable to her skin and eye color, it made her already-striking appearance unforgettable, which was the point. She turned her attention to her new dress, a pale green material that went perfectly with her pale complexion while nicely complementing the wig. The tight bodice pushed her breasts up and created notable mounds exposed by the low neckline. The form-fitting cut clung to her flat stomach, followed the curve of her hips, and then flared to skirts of green with white ruffles.

"The alterations look good," she said.

The tailor, a short man twice her age, surveyed the dress while slowly circling her. He stopped behind her, running his hands down her torso before rounding to stand in front of her. His hands started at her hips, crawled up to her breasts, and gently squeezed them. She arched a brow and glared at him. It was the type of behavior she had endured countless times since blossoming at far too early of an age.

"The bodice appears a bit tight in the bosom," the man noted.

In a flat tone, she said, "It is fine as is, so I suggest you remove your hands before I break your fingers."

He jerked backward, his brow furrowing. "I was merely…"

"I know what you were doing. You do as well. Perhaps I should discuss it with your wife."

He blanched. "That will be unnecessary."

"In that case, I should be going. How much do I owe you?"

"You had a gold piece…"

"If you will not be reasonable, I will circle around to your back door and see if your wife is home."

"I meant to say that I have change if you intend to pay with the gold piece."

"And the price for the dress?"

"Six silver pieces."

The clopping of hooves and the rumble of wheels came from outside. She turned toward the window as a team of horses settled in front of the shop. "Make it five."

He frowned. "You are a hard woman."

"You have no idea." Haelynn slid her fingers into her bodice, removed the gold coin, and handed it to the man. "I will wait for my change."

The tailor headed toward the back room with her gold piece. After a moment, he returned with a handful of silver. She accepted the change, grabbed her old dress off the hook on the wall, and headed outside.

A carriage waited outside, and the driver watched her with interest. She looked up and found the sun high overhead, her entire morning spent in the tailor's shop. Still, the afternoon was hers. Recently bathed and in a new dress, she was ready for her midday appointment.

Haelynn approached the carriage. "It is about time. You kept me waiting for nearly an hour."

The driver frowned. "I was paid to arrive at midday."

"Which occurred an hour past."

He looked up into the sky. "I don't…"

She snapped. "You dare to argue with a wizardess?" Her persona would not allow argument from an Ungifted. Embodying the character she portrayed was critical, something she had learned from Jerrell.

The man clamped his jaw shut, fear replacing the anger in his eyes.

"Take me to Souton Castle." She climbed into the carriage, sat back, and stared out the window as the carriage rolled down the road.

Shops, homes, and trees passed by. The stables of Marlowe & Sons appeared, and she caught a brief glimpse of Desmond and Marnie's home, stirring memories from earlier that morning.

AFTER RECEIVING the coins from Jerrell, Haelynn had walked down the road and entered the stables of a carriage shop. Inside, she found the driver tending to his horses.

"Pardon me," she said in a demure voice. "I need to hire a carriage for my mistress, Wizardess Garue."

The man nodded. "You've come to the right place."

"She has a morning appointment with the tailor in town and wishes to be picked up at noon."

"Where is she going?"

"The castle."

He arched a brow. "Wizardess Garue has a meeting with High Wizard Roka?"

"Yes, after which she will need a ride back to town."

"Easy enough."

Haelynn handed the man five silver pieces. "This should cover the costs. If you do your job well, she will undoubtedly reward you."

He pocketed the coins. "I look forward to it."

Haelynn left the stables and returned to Desmond and Marnie's house. The sitting room and dining room were empty, so she walked to the kitchen and found Marnie and Atzori seated at the counter, holding steaming cups of tea.

Marnie sat back and smiled at her. "Hello, Haelynn. I did not expect you back so soon. I hope your stay in Souton is going well."

Haelynn's smile came naturally. She genuinely liked Desmond and Marnie. Somehow, the couple made her feel like a normal person. "I enjoy it here."

Atzori said, "I made tea. Would you like some?"

Marnie added, "There is leftover breakfast as well. You ate so little this morning."

"No, thank you." Haelynn did not eat much. She found no joy in food. There was little in life she enjoyed. "Marnie, I was hoping you might be able to help with some womanly items."

The woman stood, took Haelynn's hand, and said, "Of course, dear. What do you need?"

"Do you have rouge?"

"Ah. You wish to impress your man."

Men are easy, but wizards require additional finesse. "Yes."

"Come along. I will get you fixed up."

With her cheeks reddened, lips painted, and eyes outlined with kohl, she once again departed, this time heading for the wig shop she had noticed when she had ridden into town.

THE CARRIAGE TURNED SHARPLY, stirring Haelynn from her musings. She pulled back the curtain to discover the carriage following a cobblestone road that ran along wetlands at the south end of the lake. Beyond the reeds stretched the open water, a handful of fishing boats between her and the north shore, eight miles away. The carriage crested a small rise, and the castle came into view. Surrounded by walls of gray stone, the castle grounds occupied a small peninsula with three sides bordered by water. She released the curtain and sat back, focusing on her role as an entitled wizardess.

The carriage slowed to a stop, and male voices carried inside. Moments later, a man in armor appeared at the carriage door.

When the man knocked, Haelynn drew back the curtain and arched a haughty brow. "Yes?"

The guard adjusted his helmet, revealing a heavy brow and a hooked nose. "Pardon me, miss, but who are you and what business do you have at Souton Castle?"

"I am Wizardess Shyla Garue. My father was the high wizard of Lionne until Montague so vilely murdered him. I wish to offer High Wizard Roka an alliance and...more."

"Welcome, Wizardess. My name is Horton. I am a lieutenant in Roka's guard. I will escort you inside and introduce you to His Grace. However, since your appearance is unscheduled, I cannot guarantee you an audience."

She pressed her lips together in obvious irritation. "Very well."

The man jogged ahead, and the carriage lurched into motion, quickly rolling through the gates. The carriage turned toward the lake and came to a stop. The door opened to reveal Horton waiting outside.

Haelynn lifted her skirts and stepped out. She stared up at the castle. Modest in size, the structure appeared quite old and made of the same gray rock as the wall.

"If you will follow me, Wizardess." Horton led her toward the shadowy alcove at the front of the castle. Inside the alcove was an arched door made of heavy oak, reinforced with iron plates.

She swept through the doorway into a circular entrance hall. Spiral stairs on her right climbed the wall while a doorway beneath them led to a dimly lit room. The guard headed up the stairs, his armor clanking and the sword on his hip swaying with each step. Haelynn lifted her skirts and ascended after him. They passed an arched opening at the second story and continued to the third, where the man led her down a long corridor, illuminated only by the light from the stairwell behind her and a window at the corridor's far end. Just before the window, he passed through an open doorway. She followed, pausing at the entrance.

With a high ceiling, the chamber was forty feet long and half the width. A long dining table with ten chairs stood empty in the heart of the room. The stone fireplace at one end of the room was dormant – a pair of doors on the opposite wall opened to an incredible view of the lake.

Haelynn and Horton crossed the room and stopped in the doorway leading outside. A man in his mid-thirties sat at a table on a balcony over-looking the lake. With brown hair and hazel eyes, the man's chiseled face gave him a handsome appearance. His robes were sky blue with silver light-ning bolts sown on. They were trimmed in black and had a sash to match. He was not alone.

Seated across the table was a swarthy man with black hair and a goatee trimmed to a point beneath his chin. Even seated, it was obvious that the man was tall and broad shouldered. He wore a fine black coat over a white tunic. His puffy black trousers were tucked into his boots. When the man looked at Haelynn, she froze for a breath. *Hassakani.*

The wizard looked at his guard. "Who is this beauty, Lieutenant?"

Haelynn replied. "My name is Shyla Garue. My father was high wizard of Lionne."

Horton added, "Sorry for the interruption, Your Grace, but she insisted on meeting with you."

Roka stood and absently waved Horton off, his gaze fixed on Haelynn. "I can always make time for a fellow Gifted, particularly one who is so pleasant on the eyes." He gripped her hand, bent, and kissed it before smiling up at her. "It is a true pleasure to meet you, my dear."

Despite the chill that ran down her spine, Haelynn forced a smile. "You as well, Your Grace." She turned toward the other man. "And who is your companion?"

"Do not worry about Mister Razak. He was just leaving."

The swarthy man grimaced, clearly unhappy about being dismissed. He stood, cinched his coat, and dipped his head. "Thank you for your time, Roka. Just remember our agreement. We both have much to lose should we fail to deliver."

The wizard's smile slipped away. "You'll have everything that was promised."

Razak pushed his way past Horton and disappeared inside.

"Escort him to the gate, Lieutenant," said Roka.

"Yes, Your Grace." The guard departed, leaving Haelynn alone with Roka.

The wizard reclaimed his seat and gestured toward the one across from him. "Please. Sit. Have a drink with me. It has been too long since I've shared an afternoon with a beautiful woman. Who knows? If things go well, perhaps we can spend more time together."

Haelynn sat and smiled. "You flatter me, Your Grace."

You conniving snake.

CHAPTER 15
THE COST OF CURIOSITY

Jerrell peered through a gap between pine boughs. A two-story farmhouse and adjoined stable occupied the hilltop clearing beyond them. Below the house was an outbuilding with a door standing open. A man with a sword on his hip strolled out from the building and approached the two men guarding the gate. The distance was too great for Jerrell to hear their words, but it was obvious that they were deep in conversation.

With the guards distracted, Jerrell turned to his companion and spoke in a hushed voice. "I see a cellar door behind the house. It seems like a good way to sneak in. What do you think?"

The mouse's beady eyes stared at Jerrell while it sniffed, wiggling its nose and whiskers.

"Right, then. Let's go."

He snuck through the trees, remaining parallel to the clearing until the house blocked him from the men at the gate. Easing between two blueberry bushes, he emerged from the woods and approached the house. In the back, a pair of doors angled up from the ground. He gripped one and pulled it. It shook but did not open. Frowning, he gripped it with both hands and strained. The result was the same, and there was no lock visible.

"It must be barred from inside," he muttered to himself and the mouse. Lifting his gaze to the window he sighed. "I guess we will do it that way."

Approaching the window, Jerrell cupped his hand to shield himself from the sunlight and peered into an empty dining room. He drew his dagger, stuck its tip in the gap between the two panes, and jiggled it until the latch lifted. Sheathing the dagger, he swung the window open and jumped up, so his waist bent over the sill. Seconds later, he was standing beside a round dining table with a mouse on his shoulder. An open doorway waited in each direction.

With soft steps, he crept to the doorway that peered into the kitchen. The room stood empty, the oven cold. A narrow door on the other side of the kitchen likely led to a pantry.

Turning, he crossed the dining room and poked his head through the other doorway. It opened into a foyer leading to the front entrance. Across from the dining room was an empty sitting room, the fireplace dark. A stairwell stood along the wall on the opposite end of the sitting room.

Jerrell crossed the room and quietly ascended to the second story. A long corridor ran the length of the building with open doors to either side. The first was a small bedroom, the bed unmade, as was the room across from it. He passed three more bedrooms before coming to a door at the end of the hall. It led to the largest bedroom – the bed was made, and the room clean yet clearly lived in. He spied a stack of papers on the desk by the window, taunting his curiosity.

He crossed the room and picked up the first paper. It was a letter written in Hassakani – a language he could not read. A seal of red wax embossed by a signet ring graced the bottom of the letter. The signet was immediately familiar – it was the symbol of the Hassakani flag.

The next sheet of paper was also written in Hassakani, but the third he was able to read – an agreement between Razak and High Wizard Roka, giving Razak exclusive rights to the silver mine.

The fourth sheet and a few beyond it proved to be the most useful – they provided a list of scheduled deliveries. Jerrell discovered that empty wagons were brought to the mine and picked up days later, loaded and ready for delivery. And then, he found records of the wagons' destination.

"Shear?" He rubbed his jaw. "Why was Razak delivering silver to Shear?"

It was an odd list of names – *Hassaka's Spirit*, *The Red Spear*, *A Lark's Song*, *Stolen Breeze*, and *Urgent Horizons*. At first, he thought them the names of inns, but then realized another explanation made more sense.

"Ships. Those are the names of ships." He glanced at the letters with the red seal. "Razak is shipping silver from Shear to Lord Sarazan in Hassaka. It appears Roka has struck a deal behind Malvorian's back."

Voices outside caused Jerrell to jerk with a start. He set the papers down and pulled the curtain aside to find a tall, swarthy man dressed in a fine black coat approaching the house with three guards at his side. The man's dark eyes rose to the window and widened at seeing Jerrell.

Oh, crap.

HAELYNN LAUGHED at something Roka said. It was a forced laugh, one she often used with men to make them believe they were charming. Having been chased off the balcony by the midday sun, the two now shared a sofa in the sitting room. The doors stood open and the breeze from the lake cooled her. She was thankful – the wig was stifling, and she longed to tear it off.

She playfully swatted at his leg. "You are a scoundrel, Your Grace."

He downed the remainder of his wine. It was his third goblet. She lifted the carafe from the table in front of her and refilled it.

"Please, my dear. We have spent half of the afternoon together. There is no need for titles. Call me Westin."

"Westin?"

"It is my name. Westin Roka."

"Ah. A fine name. Distinguished too."

"You think so?"

Her hand slid up his arm. "It is not surprising that you rose to high wizard."

"Yes, but Souton is a small city, nothing more than a village, really. If not for the silver mine, we'd have nothing but trees and a location for the wealthy to visit during the summer."

She pretended to sip her wine. It was a wonder that he had not realized how little she actually drank, since the carafe was nearly empty. Setting her goblet on the table, she turned toward Roka, giving him a full view of her cleavage, enhanced by the tightness of her bodice.

"I have a proposal for you."

"I thought your visit might have a purpose other than laughing at my jokes."

"You've proven to be a surprise, I must admit, but I did come here with business in mind."

"Which is?"

"Souton is beautiful, and the silver mines surely offer some attraction to someone such as yourself, but would you not be more interested in controlling the vineyards of Lionne? You currently live in a castle beside a lake, but what of one overlooking the sea? Rather than harsh, cold winters in the mountains, would you not prefer mild ones on the coast?"

"You offer me rule of Lionne?"

She ran a hand up his chest, her lids half closed, her voice sultry. "With my help you could defeat Montague and control the most desired district in Farrowen."

He tilted his head in apprehension. "What is in it for you?"

Her expression darkened. "That snake murdered my father."

"So it is about revenge."

"Yes. Although...perhaps...you might consider a longer lasting union."

His brow arched. "Marriage?"

"I see the way you look at me."

His smile said as much. "I'll admit it is a tempting offer, but I have reason to believe I can be more than high wizard."

Haelynn frowned. "More? The only higher position is..." She gasped, her eyes growing wide. "You wish to become wizard lord?"

Roka said, "Who would not desire the might of a god? Who would not seek to extend life to many times that of a mortal man?"

"Surely, you do not believe you can challenge Malvorian. He wields the Gift of Farrow. His magic is too great for an ordinary wizard to overcome."

"Then I shall become something more than ordinary."

She sat back and crossed her legs, intentionally exposing her smooth calf. "I would very much like to hear more."

"I've already said too much." He sipped his wine.

She stared at him for a long moment considering her next move, now that their conversation had reached an apparent conclusion. "Then, may I ask another question?"

He reached over and slid his hand up her shin. "Enough talk," he said in a throaty voice. "I have longed to touch you since the moment we met."

When he leaned in, she planted a hand on his chest. His hand slid up her leg, but she gripped it, stopping him just above her knee. She whispered, "One last question, then you and I will shed ourselves of these clothes."

Roka sat back, his brow furrowed. Haelynn slid a dress strap down her shoulder, pulling down a corner of the bodice in the process. His eyes went to her chest and his expression turned from doubt to longing.

"There was a serving girl who worked in Lionne Palace when I was young," Haelynn said. "We were close once but had a falling out. She left Lionne, and last I heard, she was headed for Souton. I thought you might know of her whereabouts."

"While only a few thousand people live in the valley, I do not know them all. However, many work at the mine and none are women."

"She would be in her twenties, blonde with blue eyes. As a girl, she drew as many compliments as I did, some even said she resembled me, although I am Gifted and she a mere servant."

"I do know a woman who fits that description. What was her name?"

"Rylynn."

He chuckled. "I thought as much."

Haelynn's breath caught in her throat, her heart racing. "Where can I find her?"

"I am sorry, but she is no longer here."

"Where is she?"

"Sarmak, I expect."

"Sarmak? Why would she go to Hassaka?"

"She was part of the agreement I struck with Lord Sarazan."

Rage burned in Haelynn's gut. "You sold her like a slave?"

He snarled. "How dare you question my actions?"

Haelynn slid her hand up her skirts, found the hilt of her stiletto, and readied herself. She forced the anger from her face. "I am sorry," she crooned while her hand stroked his cheek. "Let's forget the entire thing."

When she leaned in to kiss him, he pursed his lips, ready. She lunged with her blade, straight toward his chest. He yanked his arm in and the blade careened off the goblet, piercing his hand rather than his chest.

Roka shrieked in rage and pain. An invisible force blasted into Haelynn, launching her over the sofa arm and sending her sprawling to the floor. She pushed herself up to find him standing over her with blood dripping from his hand.

"You bitch! You cut me!"

She crawled to her hands and knees, still gripping the knife. "Allow me to end your pain."

He thrust a hand toward her. Invisible ropes wrapped around her and lifted her off the floor.

"Guards!" Roka exclaimed. "I captured an assassin!"

CHAPTER 16

AN EXPLOSIVE MOMENT

By the time Jerrell closed the second-story window curtain, it was too late. Razak had seen him.

Outside, someone shouted, "Intruder!"

Hesitating for a breath, Jerrell pulled the curtain back again to gauge the reaction of Razak and his men. Razak stood in the same spot, pointing and calling out orders. To Jerrell's surprise, dozens of armed men burst from the outbuilding door. *They are using that building as a barracks.* The connection hit him in an instant, along with the realization that he had better flee.

Turning from the window, he raced out of the bedroom, sprinted the length of the hall, and rushed down the stairs. All the while, Garcon gripped firmly to Jerrell's shoulder, the mouse's sharp claws digging through the leather and piercing Jerrell's skin.

When he reached the main floor, Jerrell heard voices outside and a key sliding into the front lock. The entryway stood between him and the open window he had used to break into the house, making his initial route impossible to retrace. Instead, he rushed over to the door beneath the stairs, praying it led where he expected. He tore it open and darted into the shadows. As he pulled the door closed behind him, the front door opened, and men rushed in.

Standing in darkness, Jerrell pulled out his dagger and clicked the gem in its pommel. Pale blue light bloomed to reveal a steep stairwell. He held the blade before him and descended as quickly as he could without making any noise. The mouse crawled over his collar and found its way beneath his coat, as if hiding from danger.

At the bottom, he came to a closed door. A test of the knob proved it to be locked, so Jerrell knelt and dug out his lock picks. Above him, a thunderous herd of footsteps pounded up the stairwell to the second floor. A bead of sweat ran down his forehead as he found the first tumbler. Shouts came from above as men rushed from room to room, searching for him. His armpits were damp and sweat ran down his ribs. The second tumbler tripped. Deciding he was out of time, he twisted the picks, hoping a third tumbler was not present. The knob turned. He pushed the door open, slid into the cellar, and closed it behind him a beat before the door at the top of the cellar stairs opened.

Jerrell locked the door while shouts echoed in the stairwell outside. He spun around and found a barrel, which he tipped on its edge and rolled toward the door. He lifted the barrel up. It rocked as it settled in place. The rumble of footsteps came from outside the door, quickly growing louder. Jerrell leaned against the barrel and shoved until it collided with the door. At that moment, the knob shook as someone attempted to turn it. The person shouted for a key. With a moment to consider his next step, Jerrell turned and held his dagger up to inspect his surroundings.

The barrel he had moved was one of about two dozen. He pushed on a few of them and found each to be full and heavy. Beyond the barrels were stacks of long wooden crates, all of them sealed. He spied a crowbar resting on a crate and used it to pry open one of the crate lids. It took a few moments and a bit of effort before the nails gave and the lid lifted off. He set the crowbar down. The box was filled with scimitars, light reflecting off their oiled blades. Frowning in thought, Jerrell stood and approached shelves with burlap sacks, some longer than three feet, others not more than two feet. He cut open one of the longer sacks and pulled a wooden bow from it. Inside were five more bows. It immediately became clear that the smaller bundles were arrows. There were dozens of bundles and dozens of arrows in each bundle.

"This place is an armory."

The hammer of footsteps came from the stairwell, again urging Jerrell into action. He pushed past more shelves and found another collection of barrels near an ascending stairwell. At the top of the stairwell, a narrow strip of light outlined the gap between the two closed cellar doors.

Jerrell pushed past the barrels blocking the stairwell entrance and ended up tipping one over. The lid popped free. Dark, viscous liquid poured out. The liquid gave off a strong odor, one Jerrell had smelled before.

"Naphtha?" He swept his gaze over the barrels, counting fifteen nearby. When added to the barrels on the other side of the cellar, the total approached forty. "That is enough to do a lot of damage."

The door on the other end of the cellar opened and dim light seeped into the room. Jerrell immediately doused his light and crouched low.

A voice came from the stairwell he had descended just minutes earlier. "Is he down there?"

"I don't know. I can't see a thing," a closer voice replied.

"Grab a torch," someone said.

"I've got one," a third voice said.

Footsteps descended, bringing warm light with them. Realizing he was about to be caught, Jerrell ascended the back stairs, felt for the horizontal doors, and found a heavy wooden beam holding them closed. He pulled at the beam, and it came free, falling into his arms. He staggered and grunted at the weight. The beam fell to the stairs and tumbled to the bottom, making a terrible ruckus.

"He's in the back stairwell!" a man cried out.

Out of time, Jerrell threw the cellar door open to bright daylight. When he popped his head out, a guard swung his sword, attempting to cleave Jerrell's head from his body. He ducked beneath the strike and reached into his sleeve. In a burst, he charged out and dove aside as the scimitar crashed down, barely missing him. Loosing with a side-arm throw, Jerrell's throwing knife spun and buried in his attacker's stomach. The man clutched at the hilt and staggered backward. Jerrell followed with a kick to the side of the man's knee, felling him.

Shouts came from inside the house, both upstairs and below ground. Jerrell rose to his feet as footsteps echoed up the back stairwell. He waited a breath, unsure of what to do. A brawny, swarthy man gripping a scimitar emerged from the stairwell. He was trailed by a leaner man holding a torch in one hand and a sword in the other. A window on the main floor opened, and a man appeared with his bow ready.

Desperate and afraid he might be unable to escape, Jerrell charged toward the brawny man at the top of the cellar stairs. He leapt high and kicked out with both feet, driving his heels into the man's muscular chest. Jerrell bounced off and fell to the ground. The brawny man stumbled backward into the man holding the torch, knocking him down. The torch went tumbling.

Jerrell burst into a mad dash, racing away as quickly as possible. He had made it only a dozen strides before the torch reached the bottom and ignited the spilled naphtha. A whoosh of hot air struck Jerrell as the accelerant turned to an instant inferno. Then, the first sealed barrel ignited.

A staccato of explosions shook the ground. The force of the blast launched Jerrell off his feet and sent him tumbling through the air. The last thing he saw was the sky before he landed in a thicket, and everything went black.

A BELL RANG, and rang, and rang, and rang...as if stuck in the trailing sound of the final chime. The incessant noise was pervasive, jumbling Jerrell's thoughts. He floated in a warm sea, somehow breathing despite being underwater. How it was possible, he could not say. A light shone somewhere above, his surroundings amber, red, and brown. Something tracked across his cheek and was gone. He tried to swim toward the light, but he was caught in an ocean of molasses, his arms like lead, his feet bricks. Ever so slowly, he drew closer to the surface until, finally, his eyes blinked open.

A pair of beady eyes stared back, giving him a start until he remembered

Garcon. The mouse climbed down to his chest, allowing Jerrell a clear view of his surroundings.

He lay on his back, all but enveloped by the leaf-covered branches of shrubbery rising four feet above him. Beyond the shrub, white puffy clouds dotted the blue afternoon sky.

A crackling fire burned somewhere nearby, just close enough for Jerrell to feel the heat on the top of his head. He bent his neck to look toward it. Through the shoots of the shrub, he spied fire, the extent of which was frightening. A shadow eclipsed the flames as a man walked past, just a stride from Jerrell's hiding place. Another man joined the first. Despite the ringing in Jerrell's ears and the roar of the flames, he could just make out their voices.

"Did you find anything?"

"No. He either died in the explosion or is long gone."

"Either way, Razak is not going to like it."

"Who do you think the man was?"

"An agent, I would guess."

"Sent by who?"

"I'll let Razak speculate."

"Come on. Let's go tell him."

The men walked off, leaving Jerrell alone.

He sat up with a groan. His body ached and the ringing in his ears annoyed him, but he was whole and alive. Moving in the opposite direction of the burning house, he crawled through the shrubs and into the forest. Once on his feet, he scurried off, intent on giving Razak's land a wide berth while making his way back to the road. *I need to find Haelynn and discuss what I discovered today.* As he wove through the woods, he wondered what she had learned in her meeting with Roka.

CHAPTER 17

A CRATE OF POTATOES

It was midafternoon by the time Jerrell returned to the Marlowe ranch. Miles and Lamond stood in a stable stall entrance, deep in discussion.

With his ears still ringing, Jerrell approached the two men. "Good afternoon."

When they turned toward him, Miles said, "You look a mess. Did you start a fight with a tree?"

Jerrell dusted dead leaves from his hair and noted the tears in his coat. "Damn. I love this coat."

Lamond asked, "Where'd you go today, anyway?"

With a shrug, Jerrell said, "I was out exploring."

Garcon crawled out from his coat and peered at the two men.

Lamond pointed. "You've got a mouse in your coat!"

"Oh, yeah." Jerrell opened his hand for the mouse, who crawled onto his palm. "This is Garcon."

Miles narrowed his eyes. "It looks like one of the mice they give to mousers in the mine."

"You know about that?"

"You can't live in a small town like Souton and not know about the mine."

Jerrell chuckled. "Yeah. It appears I have a job there. Garcon and I explored a new tunnel and had a little side adventure on the way. Have either of you seen Haelynn?"

"No." Lamond shook his head. "She hasn't returned from the tailor shop."

A hint of worry niggled at Jerrell, causing him to frown.

Lamond said, "If you've been in the mine, I assume you haven't heard what happened."

"Something happened today?"

"First, there was a massive fire at Razak's ranch. The house and attached stables burned to the ground. He also lost a few wagons in the blaze."

Jerrell nodded. "I saw the fire." *My ears still ring from the explosion.*

Miles asked, "You wouldn't know anything about that, would you?"

"Can't say I do."

The man grimaced while eyeing Jerrell.

Lamond said, "Irving then came by with his carriage and told us that some woman attempted to assassinate High Wizard Roka."

"What?"

"As wild as it sounds, he claims that he drove this woman to the castle himself. After Roka captured her, Irving was questioned to see if he was somehow involved. The man feared he might be thrown in the dungeon with the wizardess."

"Wizardess?"

"I know, it sounds crazy, but Irving insisted it was true. He also claimed she was going to be held until tomorrow. Roka intends a public execution, likely to discourage future assassination attempts."

A lump of dread settled in Jerrell's gut. "This woman...did Irving describe her?"

Lamond laughed. "You needn't worry. Your wife could not have been involved. This woman had a head of curly red hair. Apparently, she was a wizardess from Lionne."

While neither described Haelynn, both were quite possibly part of her guise to gain entrance.

"Is there a wigmaker in town?"

"Yes. Two buildings down from the tailor shop your wife visited this morning. Why do you ask?"

"Oh, I am just curious." Jerrell backed away. "Speaking of the tailor, I think I'll make a visit and see if Haelynn is finished."

~

Sore, tired, and frustrated, Jerrell opened the front door to the Marlowes' house to find Marnie and Atzori in the sitting room, chatting.

"Welcome back, Jerrell," Marnie said. "How was your day?"

He ignored her question. "Where can I find Desmond?"

She frowned. "He should be in his office in the back of the house."

"Thanks."

He crossed the room and entered the corridor leading away from his bedroom. After passing three open doors, each leading to a vacant bedroom, he approached the last door. It was cracked open, so he knocked.

"Yes?" Desmond's voice came from inside.

When Jerrell pushed the door open, he found Desmond seated at a desk placed before a window offering a pleasant view of the lake and valley beyond it. Inside the room, shelves overflowing with stacks of papers covered one wall, while a painting of Desmond and his family graced the opposite one. Their appearances indicated the painting was at least ten years old. Below it were two wooden chairs with green velvet cushions.

The old man turned toward him. "Ah, Jerrell. To what do I owe the pleasure?"

"No pleasure, I am afraid." After closing the door, Jerrell crossed the small room and plopped down in a chair with a sigh. During his walk back from the wig shop, he had considered the situation and had reached a reluctant conclusion. "I hate to get you involved, but I need your help."

Desmond set his quill down, his expression serious. "I am listening."

"I assume you are aware of today's assassination attempt."

"Yes. Lamond told me no more than an hour past."

"It was Haelynn."

The man's brow furrowed. "I don't think so. Lamond said the woman was a red-head and a wizardess."

"She was wearing a disguise."

"As a wizardess?"

"I am aware of the penalty for impersonating a wizard, however, it is no worse than the price she will pay for trying to kill Roka."

"Are you sure it was her?"

"I have just returned from a visit to the wig shop. An attractive blonde purchased an expensive wig of red curls early this morning."

"That does sound like her, but why would she try to kill Roka?"

"I don't know. She was only supposed to visit and dig for information."

"Information about what?"

"The mine, the silver deliveries, the deal with Razak..."

Desmond arched his brows. "You thought to help me regain my contract for silver deliveries?"

While the old man's situation had nothing to do with the true reason for her visit, Jerrell allowed him to believe otherwise.

"There is more, but the less you know, the safer you will be should things turn even worse."

"Worse?" Desmond exclaimed. "They plan to execute your wife tomorrow morning. What could be worse than that?"

"Trust me. That is just the beginning of what could go wrong. However, Haelynn's situation is why I am here and why I need your help."

Desmond nodded. "Anything."

"I need a way into the castle grounds. Today."

"Today?" The old man glanced out the window. "It'll be dark in a few hours."

"Which is why we must come up with a plan and execute it quickly. I assume you deliver goods to the castle?"

"I did, until Razak appeared."

"And how did you gain entrance?"

"I produced a signed order."

"Do you have any old ones?"

Desmond stood and approached the shelves. After digging through a stack of papers, he held one out to Jerrell. "Here, but I don't know how it will help you."

Jerrell took the paper, looked it over, and nodded as a plan began to form. "This is perfect."

"But it is old, and the date is wrong."

Jerrell went to the desk, dipped the quill in the inkwell, and leaned over the order. In moments, he stood back, satisfied with his work. "There. All set."

Desmond stood beside him. "You changed the date."

"I know."

"That is illegal."

The comment earned the old man an eye roll from Jerrell. "Of course it is illegal, but it is necessary to make our plan work."

"What *is* our plan?"

"It starts with one of your wagons, driven by Lamond. He will make the delivery at sunset today, when the sky is darkening."

"Why Lamond?"

"Unlike your other sons, he has no family of his own."

"What about Miles?"

Jerrell shook his head. "I am sorry, but I cannot place my trust in someone who is not part of your family." Something about the man also bothered Jerrell, but he chose to avoid the issue.

"But I've known Miles for many years..."

"It doesn't matter."

"All right. If Lamond drives you, what are you delivering?"

Jerrell shook the altered order. "This."

"Potatoes?"

"I don't have enough potatoes."

"Please tell me you know where to acquire some quickly."

"Of course."

"Wonderful. But first"—Jerrell grinned— "do you own any large crates?"

~

Desmond Marlowe sat on the bouncing wagon seat with Lamond at his side. Nervous sweat dampened his armpits, and he worried he might say or do the wrong thing. As an open and honest person, he had little experience with plots and schemes, yet Jerrell appeared to be a master plotter. Desmond wondered just what the man's background was. If the circumstances were different, he would have denied Jerrell's request to get him into the castle. However, something was amiss in Souton. Until he understood the details behind Razak and High Wizard Roka's arrangement, he was willing to bend the laws. His curiosity demanded it.

The wagon rounded a bend, and the castle walls came into view. The setting sun shone upon the castle's upper reaches while the rest remained blanketed in shadow. As the team approached the gate, Desmond stared up at the archers busily lighting torches along the top of the wall. A drop of sweat ran down his ribs, and his hands shook, but despite his anxiety, he had insisted on joining Lamond on the delivery. If anything went wrong, he would assume responsibility and spare his son, who still had his entire lifetime in front of him.

Thus, with a large crate of potatoes in the wagon bed, they had set out to make the false delivery.

The wagon slowed outside the gate, and Horton approached with another guard at his side. Desmond thought, *Please, Farrow, do not let me mess this up.*

"Good evening, Desmond," Horton nodded and turned to Lamond. "I see your youngest is with you as well."

"How are you faring, Horton? It has been a while."

"Things are well enough, despite a bit of excitement here today."

"I heard there was trouble. Was His Grace injured?"

"The wench stabbed his hand before he was able to stop her."

"Did it cause you any trouble?"

Horton gave Desmond a worried look. "Thus far, it doesn't look like Roka is seeking to apply blame. I do hope he is satisfied with her capture, so my men and I can remain unscathed."

Desmond frowned as he realized Horton might be blamed if Jerrell's plan were to succeed. He liked Horton and did not wish him harm. Roka was another story.

Horton asked, "Why are you here?"

Desmond waved his order in the air. "We're to deliver a load of potatoes."

"You? All deliveries have been awarded to Razak."

"Did you not hear about the fire?"

"I saw the plume of smoke and heard Razak's house burned down."

"Yes. Three of his wagons were scorched as well, and he is still chasing down horses that escaped during the fire." Again, he waved the order toward the guards. "I am making today's delivery in his stead."

Horton frowned, tore the order from Desmond's grasp, and examined the note. He handed it back. "Go on in. You know where the cellar door is located. I'll send a man over to open the door and escort you."

Desmond nodded. "Thanks, Horton."

Lamond looked at Desmond, their eyes meeting briefly before he snapped the reins and the wagon rolled through the gate. Beneath his breath, Desmond said, "I feel bad lying to Horton."

Lamond nodded. "He is likely to feel Roka's wrath should this go as planned."

"I know, but it cannot be helped. Roka has made his bed and must suffer for it."

The wagon rounded the castle and stopped in a narrow courtyard between the main structure and the outer wall. The two men climbed down, rounded to the rear, and opened the tailgate. A guard jogged up the drive and stopped beside the castle side door.

"Ready?" Desmond asked as he gripped the crate. It was three feet square, and a heap of potatoes stuck up from the open crate top. A half-dozen loose potatoes rested in the wagon bed, having fallen out during the drive.

"Ready."

"Lift."

The weight of the crate caused Desmond to grunt. He gripped the bottom with one hand and the side with the other, staggering as he backed toward the entrance. The guard opened the door and stood aside as Desmond and Lamond passed through it.

Once inside, the guard opened another door, exposing a stairwell descending into shadow. Lamond backed down it while Desmond followed, gripping the crate – his arms were beginning to flag. By the time they reached the bottom, Desmond ached to be relieved of the heavy crate.

The guard pointed. "Set it there."

Eager to do so, Desmond squatted and set one corner on the dirt floor before tearing his hand out from beneath it. The crate tipped down with a thud.

He stood and dusted off his hands. "I will go up and find Bertram, so he knows about the delivery."

The guard shook his head. "No. It is late, and we'd like to close the front gate, so you had best head back home. Once you are in the wagon and on your way, I'll notify the head steward myself."

Unable to do anything but comply, Desmond took one last look at the crate before nodding and heading up the stairs.

Once outside, he and Lamond reclaimed their seat on the wagon and rode out toward the gate. *May Farrow be with you, Jerrell.* Desmond wondered if he would ever see the man again.

CHAPTER 18

DUNGEON CRAWL

Crouched in a tight ball, his knees on the bottom of the crate, his rear against one side, his tucked head against another, Jerrell remained still despite his desire to break free. The potatoes covering him smelled of dirt. The cellar likely did as well.

The thumps of footsteps arose as men scaled the stairs. The door clicked shut and the cellar fell silent. Unable to put up with his restraints any longer, Jerrell rose up on his knees, spilling potatoes out onto the cellar floor. The room was dark with dim light coming through a high, narrow window above a row of shelving.

He stood, climbed out of the crate, and stretched. He was still sore from the explosion earlier in the day. Hiding in a cramped position for twenty minutes had not helped the situation. Once sufficiently stretched, he dumped the rest of the potatoes from the crate and set it back in place. He then lifted a sack of flour from a shelf and dropped it into the crate, tucking the top end down so it filled the entire bottom half. Moving quickly, he began collecting potatoes from the floor and tossing them into the crate. When he had finished, the crate appeared much as it had when Jerrell was hiding inside.

A noise came from the stairwell. Jerrell launched into motion. He scurried across the room and hid in a dark corner past the shelving.

The door opened and pale light streamed into the room.

"See." Jerrell recognized the voice of the guard who had escorted Desmond and Lamond. "A crate of potatoes, just as I told you."

Another voice huffed. "I must be getting old. I don't recall placing an order."

"Well, Horton confirmed the order was legitimate."

A sigh followed, and the old man said, "I don't dispute it. I merely find it disheartening to know how my memory has begun to fade."

"No offense, Bertram, but if I am doing as well as you when I am your age, I will be happy."

Bertram laughed. "No offense taken. Come on. Devotion will begin soon, and I've a dinner to serve when it is finished."

The door closed and soft footsteps faded into the distance.

Jerrell emerged from his hiding spot and looked up at the window. *Devotion. That is the time I need to find Haelynn.* He stared through the window toward the darkening sky, waiting for the telltale blue light to appear.

THE WAGON ROLLED beneath the portcullis and out of the castle grounds. Desmond glanced at his son, whose gaze reflected the same anxiety that roiled in his own stomach.

Daylight clung to the western horizon, but stars already twinkled in the twilight and night would soon be upon them. The wagon continued to rumble down the road. As it eased around a gradual curve, Desmond glanced over his shoulder, spying the castle gate just before the trees obscured the view. When he saw nobody following, he breathed a sigh of relief. The view narrowed as trees standing along the road cast the wagon in thick shadow.

A ghostly form appeared in the gloom, bouncing rhythmically as it drew closer. Desmond blinked, wondering if his eyes were playing tricks on him — they were not a keen as when he was younger. A white stallion materialized.

Its rider wore dark clothing. Five other horses emerged from the shadows, trailing their leader, whom Desmond suddenly recognized. He gripped Lamond's wrist and motioned for him to stop.

The rider on the white horse halted beside the wagon. "What are you doing out here, Marlowe?"

Desmond replied, "We were merely making a delivery, Razak."

The swarthy man grimaced. "You know about my exclusive contract with Roka."

Shrugging, Desmond said, "I had an order to fill, so I made the delivery. Perhaps Roka worried you were otherwise occupied considering the accident at your ranch today."

"It was no accident." Razak growled. "A man broke into my home and set it ablaze. Seven of my men died in that fire."

"I am sorry to hear that. Did you catch the man behind it?"

"Not yet. You wouldn't happen to know anything about it?"

"Me?" Desmond shook his head. "Nothing at all."

Razak waggled a finger. "If I discover you have any ties to what happened, I swear I will see you skinned alive and your head on a pike atop the castle ramparts."

Desmond forced a swallow. Razak was a hard man who lacked humor, and his threat elicited disturbing images.

"I will be watching you, Marlowe. But now, I must be going. Devotion is about to begin, and I've a dinner meeting with the high wizard immediately afterward." Razak kicked his horse into a gallop while his guards followed.

Lamond spoke first. "I think it was Jerrell."

"What do you mean?"

"I think Jerrell may have caused the fire."

Desmond frowned, recalling Jerrell's silence when questioned about the fire. "Whether it was him or not, we can do nothing about it now. I'll worry about it if he and Haelynn return to our house."

~

THE AZURE GLOW on the battlements informed Jerrell that the flame of Farrow had been lit. With Devotion underway, he opened the cellar door and headed up the stairs. Easing the door at the top open, he peered into an empty corridor illuminated by a torch on the wall. He crept to the corner and came to a much longer hallway, where three torches mounted to the wall held back the surrounding shadow. He put an ear to each door he passed before opening it and peering inside. After nine doors, he reached the end of the corridor and peered around the corner.

Another short hallway led to an open door leading outside. Through the opening, he spied numerous guards kneeling and chanting the words of Devotion. Two doorways stood between Jerrell and the one leading outside. He snuck along the wall and peered through the first doorway to find a room with rows of bunk beds on one side and a pair of long tables and benches on the other. *This must be where the guards live.* He continued toward the door leading outside, hoping none of the guards would turn around before he passed. He turned the knob and eased the door open to reveal a dark stairwell illuminated by a torch at the bottom.

He slipped inside, closed the door behind him, and descended with silent footsteps. At the bottom, he poked his head around the corner. A torchlit room waited at the end of a corridor. He crept toward it, the dirt crunching softly beneath his careful footsteps. Just shy of the torchlight, he paused.

The room appeared to be octagonal in shape with another corridor directly across from Jerrell. A table and two chairs sat in the middle of the room. Each of the visible walls had doors of iron bars, one of which stood open. A burly man with long blond hair stood in the cell doorway, his back to Jerrell. While dressed in the same armor as the other guards, the man wore no helmet.

A male voice came from the depths of the cell. "Why fight it, sweetie? You know you want it."

A woman's voice replied, "You disgust me."

Haelynn. Jerrell crept forward as a ruckus came from the cell, followed by a slap.

The man in the doorway said, "Hurry up, Wallace. I'd like a turn before Devotion is over."

Haelynn squealed as a scuffle erupted in the cell.

Picking up a chair, Jerrell lifted it and charged. The burly man in the door turned as Jerrell swung at him. The chair struck the man's forehead with a loud crack and shattered. He collapsed in a heap while splinters of the broken chair struck the walls and fell to the floor.

Haelynn lay on a pallet in the cell, the front of her dress torn open. On one knee beside the pallet, the lean guard had his breeches unlaced. When the man looked up at Jerrell, she kicked him in the groin. The jailor doubled over, his breath expelling with a whoosh while his eyes bulged. Jerrell lunged for the man, gripped the back of his leather armor, and shoved him forward, driving him headfirst into the wall. The sickening crack of his skull striking stone preceded the thud of his body collapsing to the floor.

Jerrell looked down at Haelynn. It was odd to see her with red hair, but he tossed that detail aside. Her cheek was red, her eyes as well. "Are you hurt?"

She pushed herself to a sitting position. "You arrived just in time." Rubbing her face, she worked her jaw. "The bastard slapped me. Twice. If I still had Silverthorn, I'd have skewered him."

"Silverthorn?" He held out a hand and helped her to her feet.

"My stiletto. Roka confiscated it when I stabbed him."

"You got him?"

She grimaced. "Only his hand."

While Jerrell wanted to know why she had tried to kill the wizard in the first place, urgency forced the thought aside. "We had better hurry and get out of here. Devotion will end soon."

"You don't need to tell me twice."

As soon as she was out of the cell, Jerrell rolled the bigger unconscious guard inside, took the key ring off his belt, and locked the cell. He then approached another locked cell and tossed the keys through the door. "It should take a while to free the jailors. Let's go."

Jerrell hurried down the dark corridor with her trailing. At the top of the stairs, he pressed his ear to the door. Laughter echoed down the corridor.

"Oh, crap."

"What's wrong?" she asked.

"Devotion has already ended, and the guards are returning to the barracks." He gestured. "Let's head back down and try the other direction."

Once beyond the dungeon cells, the corridor grew dark, so Jerrell used his dagger to provide light. The path opened to a room with chains on the wall. Posts stood in the middle of the room while whips hung from hooks on the wall near them. Dark splotches of dried blood marred the walls, the posts, and the ground beneath them.

Haelynn said, "This place gives me the creeps."

"Same here. Be thankful they didn't hold you captive here." He approached the closed door at the far end of the room. It was locked. "Perhaps I threw those keys away too quickly."

"Can you open it?"

Jerrell snorted and dropped to one knee. "Give me a moment." Seconds later, the door swung open. He pulled his picks from the lock and stood. Beyond the door was another stairwell. "Let's hope it leads someplace quiet."

He led the way with the gem in his dagger pommel providing light. They climbed not one, but two flights of stairs before arriving at a closed door. Again, he listened but heard nothing. Carefully, he eased the door open and peered through the crack. The light of the enchanted lanterns revealed a corridor beyond the door. It appeared empty other than a laundry cart, so Jerrell began to tip-toe down the hallway.

When they reached the cart, they heard a noise from the room beside it, causing Jerrell to stop in alarm. Standing still and holding his breath, he identified a female moan from beyond the door. Another moan followed, this one slightly higher pitched. A man's voice joined in.

Haelynn whispered, "Someone is having fun in there."

"And a better day than I've had." Jerrell put his hand on the knob. "But their day is about to grow much worse."

He threw the door open to a small bedroom. On the edge of the bed was a blonde female servant with her skirts hiked up to her waist. Her legs wrapped around a man who was standing with his trousers around his knees, his bare backside to the door.

When she saw Jerrell, the woman yipped, and her eyes widened.

The man looked over his shoulder. "What are...oof"

As the man spoke, Jerrell raised his dagger, pommel down. A hard chop to the back of the man's neck caused him to fall forward, right on top of the woman. He did not move.

Flipping his dagger in his hand, Jerrell leaned close to the woman. "Sorry to interrupt your fun, but we are desperate and need something from you. If you resist or call for help, I will cut you. Understand?"

The woman nodded.

"Good. What is your name?"

"I...Iris."

"Pretty name for a pretty woman." Jerrell meant it. While a bit lean for his tastes, she was attractive, her features resembling Haelynn. "And what is his name?"

"Harris."

"Iris. Harris. Got it." He said the names aloud. "This can't be comfortable for you, so I am going to start by moving Harris aside." He grabbed the back of the man's dark blue coat and flipped him off her. The unconscious servant bounced off the bed and landed on the floor in a sitting position, his nakedness visible to all.

Haelynn closed the door. "I can see what she likes about him."

Jerrell snorted. "It's not *that* impressive."

She smirked. "Jealous?"

"No, I..."

Haelynn laughed and patted his cheek. "You have nothing to worry about, Jerrell. Now, tell me we are bothering them for a reason other than to ogle."

"Now that you mention it..." He turned to the woman. "Please remove your clothing."

"What?" she said, aghast. "Please don't..."

He flashed a palm, stopping her. "We need your clothing and nothing more."

CHAPTER 19
UNCOMMON SERVANTS

Dressed in a dark blue coat and matching trousers, Jerrell pushed the laundry cart down the castle corridor. Haelynn wore a white apron over a rather plain blue dress, but it was near impossible for her to appear anything but plain. With her jaw set in determination and her hands clasped at her waist, she marched down the corridor at his side. Their own clothing was hidden in the cart's bin.

"I hope nobody finds that couple before we are away from the castle." she said.

"Let's hope that does not happen. I tied them well, and with the gags, they can do little more than moan and mumble."

A smirk teased her lips. "Isn't that how we found them in the first place?"

He chuckled. "Yes, but others are unlikely to intentionally walk in on such activity."

A heavy-set, dark-haired man in a stained white apron emerged from a door at the far end of the corridor. When he spied Jerrell and Haelynn, he threw his hands up. "There you are. Have you forgotten about tonight's dinner?"

Jerrell looked at Haelynn. Her blonde hair was in a bun, her red wig long discarded. While her chest tested the seams of her bodice, she otherwise looked enough like Iris to pass at a cursory glance, especially in dim light.

Likewise, Jerrell had taken a blade to his cheeks to remove the stubble. Clean-shaven and dressed as the steward, he had wet his hair to tame it, combing it with a part down the middle to appear more like Harris. He stood a couple inches shorter than the steward, but that could not be helped.

Jerrell turned to the cook. "We have laundry—"

"The laundry can wait. The food is ready. Get in here, so we don't keep His Grace and his guest waiting."

The cook disappeared through the doorway, the door swinging closed behind him.

"What do we do?" Haelynn asked in a hushed voice.

"We play along as Iris and Harris. If the lighting is poor, perhaps he won't notice."

"Let's hope not."

Jerrell pushed his way through the door and passed into a narrow prep room. Sacks, crates, pots, and pans filled the shelves along one wall, while a counter covered with a dirty cutting board, flour, and three empty bowls stood along another. They crossed the room and entered a kitchen illuminated by the cool light of an enchanted lantern on one end and the hot fires of an open oven on the other, the flames from the oven providing dim, flickering light. One man pulled a pan with baked fish from the oven, turned, and slid them onto plates held by the cook who had found Jerrell and Haelynn. The cook spun around, set the plates on a long platter, and dropped a couple hot rolls onto it, joining the mashed potatoes, asparagus, and fish already there. A carafe of red wine and two goblets waited on the counter near the plates. When finished, the cook placed two metal domes over the plates and stepped back with a nod.

"All set." The cook dusted off his hands. "The rest is up to you."

Jerrell picked up the platter of food and headed back to the door he had entered through.

"Where are you going?" the cook asked. He pointed toward the stairwell across the kitchen. "The dining room is that way. Bertram is waiting for you."

"Of course. I don't know what I was thinking." Jerrell crossed the room to the stairs, where he waited while Haelynn collected the carafe and goblets.

At the top of the stairs, they emerged in a corridor. Two guards bracketed a door at the end.

Under his breath, Jerrell said, "It looks like we have no choice but to continue the charade."

"What if someone recognizes me from before...or realizes that I am not Iris?"

"Just try to remain out of the light and shield your face when you are near someone. People seldom pay attention to servants."

Jerrell led the way past the guards and into the dining room. A long dining table stood in the heart of the room while a sofa and two chairs surrounded a fireplace built into the far wall. The flickering light of flames bathed the two seated men as they engaged in quiet discussion. Jerrell assumed the wizard must be Roka, and immediately recognized the other as Razak.

An old man in a black coat approached Jerrell and spoke with hushed urgency. "You were expected minutes ago."

Whispering, Jerrell said, "Sorry. We got distracted...Bertram."

The man squinted at Haelynn. "Are you well, Iris? You appear a bit peaked."

Even in the dim light of the candles, Haelynn's cheek appeared red. Jerrell realized he had forgotten about the scuffle in the dungeon. "Should we set the table?" he whispered, hoping to distract the man.

"Are you daft? You know you must wait until His Grace is seated." Bertram quietly crossed the room and stopped near the sitting area, where he waited.

Jerrell strained to hear the conversation, but it was all mumbles and grumbles until Roka stood abruptly.

"What? You can't be serious," the wizard exclaimed.

"I am. It's gone. All of it."

"And the man who caused the fire?"

Razak raked his fingers down the side of his face. "I don't know. He either died in the blaze or escaped. It is difficult to know, since naphtha-fed flames burn hot enough to melt steel. Anyone caught in it would have been incinerated."

The wizard stared into the fire. "This cannot be coincidence. Someone knew of our plans and sought to sabotage them."

"That is my thought as well."

The crackle of the fire filled the ensuing silence. Turning from it, Roka looked toward the old man. "Dinner is ready, Bertram?"

The old man bowed. "Ready to be served, Your Grace."

"Come, Razak. Let us eat and discuss this further." Roka crossed the room.

Razak stood and followed the wizard to the table. Both appeared visibly upset.

As the wizard neared the table, he clutched his bandaged hand with his unharmed one. The steward stood behind Roka's seat and pushed it in as he sat. Razak pulled his own chair out and took a seat beside the wizard.

The old man gestured toward Jerrell and Haelynn.

"Don't look either of them in the eye," Jerrell reminded her, "and for the sake of the gods, don't stab anyone this time."

She grimaced but held back any retort.

Jerrell placed the tray down on the table, lifted the two plates from it, and set one down before Roka, the other before Razak.

"You have a familiar look about you," Razak said while staring at Jerrell.

The head steward replied, "Harris and Iris have been part of the staff since late summer. You have likely seen them during a prior visit."

Haelynn placed the goblets on the table, filled each with wine, and set the carafe down before backing away.

The wizard said, "This will be a private dinner. You are all excused."

Bertram gestured toward Jerrell, turned, and left the room. He and Haelynn followed and met the old man in the corridor.

"It looks like you two can retire early tonight. Do try to be on time tomorrow morning. If I must come looking for you, it will be trouble." He pushed his thick spectacles up his nose, spun on his heel, and walked away.

AT THE BOTTOM of a dark stairwell was a door leading outside. With Haelynn's hand in his, Jerrell stepped out into the cool night air. Moonlight shone down on a flagstone path curving through pines. Beyond the trees was the castle wall.

A gravelly voice disturbed the tranquil scene. "Who goes there?"

Jerrell turned as an armored figure emerged from the shadows. "It is Harris and Iris."

"Why are you dressed like that?"

Jerrell was again dressed in his regular clothing, while Haelynn had wrapped a cloak found in the maid's bedroom around her torn dress. "We don't wish to catch a chill, and our uniforms are hardly made for outdoor activities."

"Activities?" The man grunted. "What are you about?"

"It is a beautiful evening for a stroll about the castle grounds."

"A stroll?" The man sounded doubtful.

Jerrell leaned closer and lowered his voice. "Bertram disapproves of us being...together. We merely seek some time alone. We hoped to find some privacy so we could...you know."

The guard chuckled. "That, I can understand."

"I hoped you would."

Jerrell patted the man on the back, wrapped an arm about Haelynn, and escorted her down the path. They came to a split, one route leading around the castle, the other toward the rear wall — they took the latter route. The path curved again and was enveloped by shadows of the surrounding trees. Inviting light beckoned ahead. Reaching the shadow's edge, the wall again in Jerrell's view, he pulled her to a stop.

The lake was visible through the iron bars of a man-sized gate in the wall, however, in the shadows, he identified the dark silhouette of a guard.

Jerrell pulled Haelynn close and whispered in her ear. "Can you distract him?"

"What are you asking?"

"You know what I mean."

"Then, what?"

"I'll sneak up behind him and knock him out."

Her scowl revealed her opinion of his plan. Yet, she removed her cloak and shoved it at him. Her torn dress revealed enough of her chest to draw anyone's attention and would likely have the man drooling. "I've had a rather trying day and would prefer not to have some smelly guard's paws on me, so please do not dally."

She strolled down the path, and when she stepped into the moonlight, the guard started. Her skirts swirled as she glided toward him, her lips pursed.

"Who goes there?" the guard choked out.

In a throaty voice, she replied, "A lonely woman seeking a strong man to satisfy her needs."

The man emerged from the shadows and removed his helmet to reveal shorn hair. With broad shoulders and thick arms, he stood a head taller than her and could not have been older than his mid-twenties. The guard rubbed his eyes and blinked, as if he could not believe what he saw.

Haelynn walked right up to him and placed a hand on his breastplate while staring up into his eyes. "Do you find me attractive?"

The man stammered. "I...I don't...I mean...yes."

She arched her brow. "Have you been with a woman?"

"Of...of course." The hand gripping his helmet dropped to his side.

Her hand slid higher, cupping his cheek before slowly rotating herself toward the wall and forcing his gaze to follow. "So, you know your way around a woman's body?"

Now that the man's back was toward him, Jerrell snuck forward, lifting Haelynn's cloak with both hands spread out. Haelynn took a step back from the guard and slid her dress down to bare one shoulder then the other, further exposing her chest. A demure smile followed.

When he was a stride from the guard, Jerrell flipped the cloak high and dropped it over the man's head. He hurriedly snatched the helmet from the man's hands. The guard tore the cloak off and spun around as Jerrell swung. The helmet struck the guard in the nose, causing him to stagger. Following with as hard a backhand swing as Jerrell could muster, the helmet careened off the side of the guard's head, resulting in a noisy clang that rang throughout the garden. The guard toppled over, forcing Haelynn to dodge lest she be crushed beneath him. He struck the flagstones with a clatter.

A shout arose in the distance, followed by others – Jerrell recognized the last two sentences.

"The prisoner has escaped!"

"Noise at the rear gate!"

Haelynn pulled her dress back over her shoulders. "Not very subtle, Jerrell."

Jerrell squatted beside the guard and unhooked the keyring from his belt. "That was louder than I had expected. Hurry and grab your cloak. They will be coming this way."

He fumbled with the keys while stepping over the guard. The first key did not fit. Footsteps hammered in the distance, quickly drawing closer. The second key slid in the lock, but the rust made it difficult to turn. Jerrell jiggled the key and applied more pressure. It finally turned. The gate swung open as two guards appeared down the path.

Darting through the gap, Jerrell waited for Haelynn and then slammed the gate shut. "Get to the boat!"

The guards raced closer with swords ready as Jerrell reached through the gap in the bars. He gripped the key, turned it, and pulled it from the lock. The lead guard leapt over the fallen man and thrust, his sword sliding between the bars, straight toward Jerrell's chest. A twist of his shoulders caused the blade to slide past him, but it was a narrow miss. Jerrell backed away from the gate still holding the keyring.

The guards shook the gate, but it held. One turned to the other, "Get Horton. He has the other key."

Jerrell spun away and saw Haelynn already on the dock. He raced down stone stairs to the shoreline and onto the dock as she climbed into one of the two rowboats moored there. Drawing his dagger, Jerrell cut the second boat free and gave it a hard shove. He spun around and moved toward the first boat as an arrow buried itself in the dock. Shadows moving atop the wall warned him that more arrows would soon be coming.

Jerrell cut the rowboat free and pushed hard against the rail, propelling the vessel away from the dock as he leapt in. The small boat rocked when he landed in it. Two more thwaps came from the wall. A pair of splashes sounded beside the hull as the arrows hit the water. As he lifted the first oar, Jerrell slid the pivot pin into a hole and then reached for the other oar. With both in place, he settled on the middle seat, gripped the handles, and began to row toward the western shore, intentionally moving away from the reflection of the moon.

"Quiet out here," he said in between strokes. "Noise carries over open water."

A loud creak echoed in the night. Guards poured out of the gate and down to the dock.

A male voice exclaimed, "They took a rowboat."

"And cut the other one loose," said another voice.

"Where are they?" a third asked.

"Does anyone see them?"

"Spread out along the shore."

Now a few hundred feet out, Jerrell continued to row in long, steady strokes, while Haelynn wrapped her cloak around herself and curled up in the bottom of the craft. By land, the Marlowes lived three miles from the castle. Crossing the lake would reduce the distance, but not by much. Resolved to row the entire way, he tore off his coat and loosened his tunic. It would be drenched with sweat by the time he reached the Marlowes' dock.

CHAPTER 20

CONFESSIONS

Chatter echoed in the dining room and carried through the closed bedroom door, waking Jerrell. He opened his eyes to morning light filtering through the closed curtains. A groan slipped out as he sat up and swung his legs off the bed. His shoulders were sore, his back tight, and a faint ringing replayed in his ears, reminding him of the prior day's explosion.

A hand touched his bare back. "Are you well?"

Over his shoulder, he said, "I feel like a dragon chewed me up and spit me out."

Haelynn said, "There is no such thing as dragons, silly."

He considered her statement for a breath before responding. "I sometimes wonder what is real and what is myth. Perhaps the creatures of legend were once more than legend. I mean, the tales originated from somewhere, right?"

"Where is this coming from?"

"I don't know. It's just...the accounts I have heard from soldiers who fought in the Fractured Lands, well, those monsters *must* be real. Why not other creatures as well?"

"So, you believe in goblins, trolls, and whatever else is reported to occupy the Murlands?"

"Although I've not seen them, I've met others who have. The stories and descriptions are too consistent to be invented."

"Well, true or not, I for one am glad I have yet to see them. Enough monsters surround me as it is. Roka, for one."

He turned toward her, the covers pulled up to her midriff, leaving her upper body covered only by her thin shift. Although she was stunning and exuded sensuality without effort, he had seen her manipulate others with ease, so he reminded himself to remain wary although part of him wished to take her. Again. However, mention of the high wizard awoke a question that had been sleeping for too long.

"Why did you try to kill the wizard?"

"Which wizard?"

He arched a brow. "You've tried to kill more than one?"

She ran her hand down his torso, the sensation launching his pulse toward the sky. "We were both exhausted last night. Now it's morning, and it would be a shame to waste the opportunity."

Jerrell grappled with his urges, pushed them aside, and gripped her wrist, stopping her just shy of his lap. "You are avoiding the question."

Her lower lip stuck out in a pout. "You don't want me?"

"Don't be foolish, Haelynn. So long as blood flows through my veins, I will want you. However, I've discovered that what you want can sometimes be bad for you."

She bit her lip coyly. "Do you want me to be bad, Jerrell?"

He rolled his eyes. "Tell me, Haelynn. Why did you stab Roka?"

She glared at him in defiance. A long moment passed, but then she sighed. "Fine."

Finally. "I am listening."

She sat up on one elbow. "I lied to you."

"I am not surprised, but what about?"

"I do have family. A sister, younger than me. Prettier as well."

"Prettier? I find that difficult to believe."

"Thank you, Jerrell, but it is true." Her gaze grew distant. "I was twelve when my mother disappeared. Although I was young, I was able to take care of myself. At only eight years old, Rylynn relied on me for food, shelter, and guidance. We survived on the streets for three years, and then, she disappeared. I spent much of the next decade searching for her, but without luck until a week ago when a contact in Marquithe informed me of a young blonde being held in Souton Castle."

"Your sister?"

She nodded. "The name the man gave me confirmed it."

"Where is she?"

"When I confronted Roka on the subject, he informed me that she was no longer in Souton. Like a cow given in exchange for a plot of land, he had sent Rylynn to Lord Sarazan in some deranged agreement."

"Sarazan? Hassaka's new wizard lord?"

She nodded, her expression dour.

Jerrell whistled. "That further proves Roka is in league with the Hassakani."

"It certainly appears so."

"And you tried to stab him because he shipped your sister halfway across the world?"

Haelynn grated, "That duplicitous bastard deserves to die."

Jerrell held her hand. "I am sorry about your sister, but trying to kill him like that...you nearly got yourself killed instead. Your death would do nothing to help her."

She relaxed with a sigh. "I know. I was just so angry. I lost my head and nearly ruined everything."

"Well, there is nothing we can do about it now." His stomach growled, reminding him that he had missed dinner the prior evening. "By the sounds of it, breakfast is waiting out there. You are likely as hungry as I am. Let's get dressed, eat, and figure out our next step."

A small gray form crawled over the edge of the bed and stood on its hind legs to chitter at Haelynn. She shrieked, rolled toward Jerrell, and squirmed past him, onto the floor.

Rising to her feet, she backed away. "Kill it!"

He laughed. "I am not going to kill Garcon."

She hugged herself while staring wide-eyed at the small creature. A shiver wracked her body – creating an even more distracting scene to cloud Jerrell's mind.

"Garcon?"

"It's his name."

"You named a mouse?"

Jerrell reached out and scooped the mouse off the bed. "He is friendly. See?"

"Mice are filthy creatures that spread disease."

While petting the mouse, he warned, "Watch what you say. You are going to hurt his feelings."

"Get rid of it, Jerrell."

"I will not. He is my friend, and I still have need of him."

Her brow furrowed. "You are serious."

"I am, but do not worry. You won't have to deal with him for much longer."

~

ONCE THEY HAD DRESSED, Jerrell and Haelynn walked into the dining room where Desmond, Marnie, Lamond, and Atzori sat in quiet discussion. The number of empty plates made it clear that five others had already eaten and departed.

Marnie smiled at them. "Good morning. You two certainly slept in today. Was it a late night?"

Before Jerrell could reply, Desmond spoke. "Marnie. Atzori. Can you fix a plate of food for our guests?"

Husband and wife shared a silent exchange before she stood. "Come, Atzori. Let's heat up breakfast so they can eat."

She picked up a pair of plates while the servant gathered the rest before following her into the neighboring room.

When the kitchen door swung closed, Desmond gestured toward the table. "Please. Sit. We have something to discuss."

Jerrell and Haelynn sat beside the old man. Jerrell asked, "What is this about?"

Desmond's gaze shifted to Haelynn. "I am glad to see you are freed from your incarceration. Did they harm you?"

She smiled. "Thank you, but I have been treated worse."

"I did not hear you enter last night. It must have been late."

Jerrell said, "It takes a while to row across the lake. I'd guess it was midnight by the time we crawled into bed."

Lamond cleared his throat, drawing his father's attention.

Desmond met his eyes and said, "Yes. Right, then." He turned toward Jerrell. "Listen. We want to know if you caused the fire at Razak's ranch yesterday."

"I did cause it."

The man jerked back in surprise, blinking twice before he said, "If you thought burning down the man's house would help me—"

"No." Jerrell shook his head. "It had nothing to do with your situation."

"Why did you do it, then?"

Jerrell had debated how much he was willing to tell the men. Their assistance had been vital in getting him into the castle, but he had already put them at risk. *Still, they deserve the truth.*

"I must confess something." He glanced at Haelynn, who narrowed her eyes. "Haelynn and I came to Souton intent on stealing silver."

"Stealing? Are you telling us that you're thieves?"

"Yes...and no."

Lamond snorted. "What does that mean?"

"The silver is part of a contract we had taken out with the Marquithe Enchanters Guild. You see, their supply is about to run out, and without a delivery, they would be unable to craft enchanted objects. When they went to Malvorian, he disregarded them and told them to solve their own problem. He does not understand the depths of the trouble brewing here in Souton."

"Trouble?" Lamond frowned. "What sort of trouble?"

"The deal between Roka and Razak goes beyond mere transport of silver. Yesterday, I snuck into Razak's house and poked around a bit. On his desk was a list of scheduled deliveries, along with ship names. Hassakani ships."

Desmond's brow furrowed. "You believe Razak is shipping the silver to Hassaka?"

"Yes. It is part of the bargain between Roka and Lord Sarazan."

"Why would Roka make a deal with the wizard lord of another nation?"

"He seeks to overthrow Malvorian."

"What?" Lamond exclaimed. "That is insane. Everyone knows wizard lords are impossible to kill."

"Not impossible, or thrones would never change hands."

Desmond sat back and ran a hand through his thinning gray hair. "Hold on. How did you come to this conclusion? Surely not just because of the silver."

Haelynn said, "Yes, Jerrell. Please tell us how you know this."

The prior evening had offered little opportunity to talk, so Jerrell had yet to share the details with her. "When I was in Razak's house, he spotted me peering out the second story window. It was too late for me to escape the house unnoticed, so I hid in the cellar. It was filled with weapons – hundreds of swords, hundreds of bows, and thousands of arrows. In addition to the weapons, there were dozens of barrels filled with naphtha."

"Naphtha?" Haelynn asked. "What is that?"

Desmond said, "It burns hot and when pressurized, can explode. The miners use it to open up new tunnels. I still have a few barrels I procured before I lost my contract to Razak."

Jerrell nodded. "A guard came after me as I exited the outer stairwell. When he fell down those stairs, his torch ignited the naphtha. The house exploded, destroying the weapons and anyone unfortunate enough to be caught inside at the time."

Haelynn slapped her hands together. "That was what Razak and Roka were talking about last night."

Jerrell nodded. "Yes. I don't know who was going to wield them, but the loss of the weapons is a setback to Roka's plans. For now."

She grimaced. "My sister was part of Roka's bargain as well."

"It appears so."

Desmond said, "You are forgetting one important thing. Weapons, silver, warriors – none of those matter when facing a wizard lord. Someone must contend with Malvorian's magic and find a way to kill him despite his ability to heal himself."

"True." Jerrell recalled the bracelet he had taken from Montague and later gifted to Gurgan. "I believe that is part of Roka's bargain as well."

Haelynn said, "You aren't making sense, Jerrell."

He continued. "I happen to know of a magical object that can boost a normal wizard's ability so it approaches the powers of a wizard lord. While that particular object is far from here and unknown to Roka, another relic of a similar nature might exist elsewhere. I suspect Sarazan has promised Roka such an object. Perhaps that is why the high wizard sent your sister to Sarmak."

Desmond's eyes widened. "The high wizard traded a Farrowen woman to the wizard lord of Hassaka? That is revolting."

"Such a disregard for individual freedom is why Roka must be stopped."

The old man glanced at his son, who nodded. "We want to help you."

"This is dangerous, Desmond. People have already died. More might join them before we are through."

"Still, it is the right thing to do. And if it helps to get Razak out of our valley, all the better."

Jerrell grinned. "Actually, I was hoping you might offer to help."

Haelynn gripped his arm. "Are you insane?"

He took a deep breath and patted her hand. "You'd be the guest of honor at a public execution today if not for them. They got me into the castle without anyone realizing. They own wagons and know how to drive them. If we are to complete our mission, we need their help."

She crossed her arms over her chest, scowling. "I just hope you don't get either of them killed."

"I'll do my best to keep us all alive."

Desmond leaned closed. "Do you have a plan?"

Jerrell nodded. "I do."

The kitchen door opened, and Marnie appeared carrying a carafe of milk and two goblets. With the next swing of the door, Atzori emerged with two steaming plates. The scent of bacon reached Jerrell and his tongue began to water.

"I hope you are hungry," Atzori said as he slid the plates across the table.

"Starved," Jerrell said with a grin. He picked up his fork and began to eat.

Haelynn huffed. "Aren't you going to tell us, Jerrell?"

"What?"

"Your plan."

"All in good time. Now, eat. You'll need your energy."

CHAPTER 21

THE SETUP

The pale light from Jerrell's helmet lamp stretched before him, illuminating the narrow gap he slid through. The sounds of his grunts and the scraping of clothing across rock distracted him from the more distant sounds of metal tools striking stone. Above it all, a voice inside Jerrell screamed for him to turn back, to climb to the surface, and to return to the mining compound another way. Any other way. He ignored the voice and forged ahead, gripping the rock with gloved hands, and pulling himself forward inch by inch. Then, finally, he saw the cavern. After a few feet more of squirming like a slug, he emerged from the tunnel opening and breathed a deep sigh of relief. Garcon crawled out from beneath his collar and sniffed the air.

"Yes. We are back in your home," Jerrell said. He wondered if the mouse wanted to return to his cage with the others or if he would have preferred to remain as Jerrell's companion.

Twenty strides away, the work crew he had met the prior morning hammered at veins of silver. One of the men paused, wiped his brow, and turned toward Jerrell, his eyes widening. He reached out and stopped the man beside him. Soon, all five turned in his direction.

"Mouser, you are back," one man said.

"I figured you had died," another added.

A third man asked, "Did you find the last mouser?"

Jerrell stood and approached them. "I don't know anything about the last mouser, but I am very much alive."

"What did you find?"

"More than I had expected." Jerrell lifted his gaze toward the upper tiers. "Where can I find Leshonn?"

"Climb, mouser. He is somewhere above."

"Good. But, first, I need to go down and return this mouse to Adrion."

JERRELL CLIMBED nine ladders and thousands of stairs as he ascended from tier to tier. All along, the noise of picks and shovels striking rock serenaded him as men chiseled away at the stone surroundings.

Two levels below the top of the cavern, he followed a stone bridge the width of his arm span to a pillar thirty feet in diameter. On the pillar, he found a dark-skinned man bent over a table covered in papers.

Leshonn looked up at Jerrell's approach. "Mouser. I feared you had befallen the same fate as your predecessor." He examined Jerrell from head to toe. "You look like hell. Did you run into trouble?"

Jerrell wore the same clothes as he had on the prior day, but the day's events had taken a toll. The crawl through the tunnels and the tears from the explosion gave him a worn and ragged appearance. "I'd be lying if I told you yesterday didn't include its share of challenges. I nearly died more than once."

"The tunnels can be dangerous." The man nodded knowingly. "What did you find?"

Jerrell said, "Luckily, I found water."

"Water?"

"An underground river. It flows through one of the caverns."

"So you didn't run out of water. I bet you are hungry, though."

Jerrell grinned. "Starved."

"Well, we are nearing dinner time, so food will be waiting for you. But first, tell me more of what you found."

"The tunnels are extensive. Once through the gap, I found them going both up and down. I tried up first, which turned out to be a waste of my time, so I doubled back. The descent was steep and long. Had I fallen, there would be no one to tell the story since the shaft descended hundreds of feet. At the bottom, I followed the underground river and came to an open cavern. From there, I, again, continued until I reached a chamber nearly as impressive as this one. Veins of silver thicker than my waist reflected the light of my lantern. But there is more."

"More?"

Jerrell held out his hand. A jagged stone rested in his palm, the edges reflecting light.

Leshonn's eyes widened. "Gold?"

"Gold!" Jerrell feigned excitement.

The man took the rock from Jerrell's hand and turned it over. Undisguised lust sparkled in his eyes as he gazed at the nugget. *I've got him.*

"Was there more than this?" Leshonn asked.

"I chiseled that chunk off the cavern wall. A thousand times as much awaits us down there."

The man gripped the nugget, masking it in his dark hand. "You must not tell anyone of this. If word gets out uncontrolled..."

"I understand."

"Good."

"About that food, I've had nothing to eat since sometime last night. I even considered eating the mouse, but I didn't want to be alone. Anyway, I am starved."

"I'll walk you to the mess hall myself. I'll even tell the crew to feed you double since you missed dinner last night. Wait here a moment. I need to issue the order to shut down."

The man crossed the bridge, approached a rope dangling from a scaffold, and pulled it – a bell rang, echoing through the cavern. He then returned to Jerrell, waved for him to follow, and crossed the bridge, heading toward the stairs leading to the tunnel level.

By the time Jerrell stepped outside, pink-tinted clouds stretched toward the darkening sky in the east. The entire mining compound was draped in shadow that extended all the way to the lake.

He strolled across the gravel yard, past the crusher where oxen lazily circled on the scaffold's upper tier. In the pit below the scaffold, workers shoveled crushed rock into two different lifts. Three heaping piles – one of silver, one of worthless dull rock, and one of manure – now filled the trio of wagons beside the crusher.

A second bell rang – this time, the chime echoed through the narrow canyon. The workers dropped whatever they happened to be holding – a chunk of rock, shovel, or a broom. Some tossed whips aside and began removing the harnesses from the oxen.

When they entered the mess hall, they were greeted by the scent of beef stew.

Leshonn gestured toward the serving counter. "You go on and eat. I need to speak with the captain."

The dark-skinned man headed to the office door, knocked, and opened it.

"We need to talk."

Hulik's voice came from inside. "It's late. Can't it wait until tomorrow?"

"Not this. Our mouser returned and..."

The door closed, cutting off the sentence, but Jerrell knew what the discussion entailed – the subject was the first shoot of a carefully planted seed.

He approached the counter. "Fill me up. I'm starved."

While waiting for the cook to fill his bowl, Jerrell glanced toward the office. *I hope they don't decide to break the nugget open.* If they did, they would discover a granite core coated in melted gold. The allure of gold had the intended effect on Leshonn. He hoped the same from Hulik.

Holding a full bowl, Jerrell sat down at an empty table and began to eat, simultaneously considering the men's discussion.

Across the Eight Wizardoms, Souton was known as a source of silver. The men in charge of the mine had to mine the mineral and supply it as expected. Gold was another story. It offered men like Leshonn and Hulik a path to wealth without the wizard class knowing. Not even Malvorian would expect gold to come from the mines of Souton.

As Jerrell finished his stew and hard roll, the office door opened. Leshonn exited with a parchment in hand. Eager to discover what was happening, Jerrell rushed his bowl over to the counter and caught up to the man.

"Where are you heading now?" Jerrell walked in stride with the man.

Leshonn turned toward him. "I thought you were going to eat."

"I was hungry, so it went fast."

"Huh," Leshonn grunted and opened the door. "You never came back last night, so you haven't been assigned a bed yet."

"Not yet."

"Come on. I'll set you up with the guards. I need to bring this to them anyway."

"What is it?"

"An urgent requisition."

Jerrell's smirk was lost to the man since his gaze was fixed straight ahead. Across the compound, miners poured out of the tunnel. Some joked and laughed. Others appeared exhausted. The steady stream headed toward the mess hall, under the watchful eyes of guards.

At a man-sized opening in the inner wall, Jerrell and Leshonn were met by a pair of guards. The guards searched Jerrell's pockets and patted him down but found no silver so he and Leshonn strode straight to the guard barracks and walked in.

A middle-aged guard spied them and walked over. "To what do I owe the pleasure, Leshonn?"

"Hi, Bostic. I've an urgent order we need to fill. Are any of Razak's men around?"

"Yeah. Two are over there eating right now."

"Good, because we need Naphtha here tomorrow."

Bostic grimaced. "Naphtha? That is going to be a problem."

"Why?"

"Didn't you hear about the fire?"

"What fire?"

"At Razak's ranch. The naphtha stored there was destroyed. Every last barrel."

"What?" Leshonn ran his hand across his shorn hair. "Where can we acquire more?"

"Marlowe."

"Desmond?"

"Yeah. He used to supply it to us and might have a few barrels remaining."

Leshonn shoved the order at Bostic. "Take this and see if Desmond can fill it. The sooner, the better."

A BARREL OF FUN

The day waned slowly, since Jerrell had nothing to do. When he had approached Leshonn that morning, the man told him to relax and take it easy. He had earned it and would be paid regardless. Yet, it was not in Jerrell's nature to do nothing, so relaxing required more effort than work.

Ever so slowly, the sun moved across the sky while Jerrell poked around, chatted with workers in the mining compound, and reflected on his scheme. Thus far, things had gone according to plan, but Jerrell knew as well as anyone, plans were made to go awry. It was not a matter of if but when. Others might perceive such twists as a source of anxiety. For Jerrell, the anxiety came in the waiting for some unknown occurrence to send the plan into disarray. When it actually came to pass, well, that was when he was at his best.

Thus, when sunset was finally upon them, Jerrell headed across the compound toward the inner gate. As he passed the crusher, he glanced toward the wagon bed piled full of silver. It shimmered in the failing light and reminded Jerrell of what might be. Until he had spent time in the mine, he had not realized just how little silver came from a stone placed in the crusher. It took weeks to fill a wagon like this one. In the meantime,

Desmond's driver, Miles had hauled away two wagons filled with the worthless gray rock known as tailings in the span of just two short days. If the silver mine ran low, as it appeared it might soon, then what?

Jerrell approached the inner gate where he was met by two guards. "If you intend to search me again, do take care when you search my jewels. I expect gentle cupping and would prefer no fingers up my arse this time." He held his hands up. "I promise, I've shoved nothing up there. My preference is that it remains an exit only."

Felix, a guard he had met the prior evening, said, "Just stand still and we will do our jobs. Trust me – we don't enjoy it any more than you do."

The inspection went quickly and was far less invasive than Jerrell let on. When they were finished, he headed toward the guards' barracks, feeling punchy. As he reached the barracks, he spied a wagon pulling up to the outer gate. Desmond held the reins and an attractive blonde woman sat beside him. Jerrell smiled, opened the door, and went inside.

DESMOND DROVE a wagon up to the mine gate. A hard pull on the reins drew the team to a stop. Guards approached the wagon – both men he knew. One was Bostic, a burly, grizzled man approaching his middle years. The other was Walker, tall, lean, and no older than twenty-five.

"Good evening, gents." He smiled and handed over the order signed by Hulik. "I've a load of naphtha to deliver."

Bostic nodded. "Good evening, Desmond. It's been a while since I've seen you driving. Where's Miles?"

"He and Lamond had to make a run to Castor's Crossing and haven't made it back yet."

"Who is this pretty thing?"

Desmond turned toward Haelynn, seated at his side. "This is my niece, Lissa, visiting from Eleighton."

Walker stared at her with a silly grin while Bostic's gaze swept over her. Twice.

"It is nice to meet you," Haelynn said. "I've heard much about the famous silver mines of Souton, so when Uncle Desmond said he had to make a delivery, I jumped at the chance to join him and see the mine for myself."

Bostic shook his head. "I am sorry, miss, but no women are allowed inside the main compound."

"What do you have against women?"

"Me? Nothing. In fact, I find them to be quite wonderful company."

"Is it me, then?"

"No. You see, most of the men working in the mine are criminals, and those who aren't criminals have spawned from the dregs of society. It has been seasons or even years since many of these lowlifes have seen a woman, and if their eyes land on your beauty, I fear I won't have enough guards to keep you safe."

She pressed her hand to her chest, and said, "Oh, my. You mean they would attempt to take me like some taproom whore?"

"I am afraid so. Thus, I insist you remain with us in the safety of the barracks. When Desmond is finished inside, you may rejoin him. Until then, we will keep you safe." He flashed her a reassuring smile. "You have my word."

When she gave Desmond an apprehensive look, he laid his hand on hers. "It'll be alright. I won't be long inside. When I come back out, I will find you, and we will head home."

"You will escort me, Mister Bostic?"

He grinned. "I would be pleased to."

She descended from the wagon, took Bostic's arm, and waited as the man waved to another guard. "Open the gate!"

The chains clanked as the portcullis lifted up. The wagon rolled past the barracks and through the inner gate. Once inside the compound, Desmond pulled his wagon up beside the mess hall, stopped, and went in search of Hulik, but not until he cast a nervous glance at the barrels inside the wagon. All appeared identical, but that was a ruse. One contained something other than naphtha. He just hoped nobody noticed the difference.

～

Jerrell stood on a chair before a room filled with guards. The men laughed as he finished one joke and prepared the next.

"Have you heard the story of the two Pallanese woodcutters?"

One guard yelled, "They must be idiots!"

Jerrell grinned. "Pretty much, but sometimes, even idiots can be clever."

"Clever idiots?" The man laughed. "Let's hear it."

"All right. Here we go." Jerrell pretended to heft an axe. "One fine spring day, two Pallanese woodcutters were out chopping down trees. Spring being spring, the sky darkened, and it soon became clear a storm was rolling in. So, the woodcutters* packed up their things, hopped on their wagon, and headed down the dirt road toward their village.

"During the drive, they came upon a field of buttercups in full bloom. The driver stopped the wagon and the other woodcutter asked, 'What are you doing?'

"The driver pointed toward the field. 'Beautiful, isn't it?'

"The other nodded. 'That it is – so beautiful I wish we could show them to our women. It would surely inspire them, and we would be in for a wonderful night.'

"The first laughed. 'My thought as well, so how about we pick the flowers and bring them back with us?'

"'Pick them all?'

"'Every one of them.'

"So the woodcutters proceeded to uproot every single buttercup, stripping the field bare before piling them up in the wagon bed. When they finished, they climbed back into the wagon, the driver snapped the reins, and they continued toward the village.

"A lightning bolt rendered the heavens asunder and struck the road just before the wagon. The driver yanked on the reins, attempting to calm his team, but they charged forward, driven by fright. A figure appeared on the road, right where the bolt had struck – he was tall, muscular, and unclothed. The figure held up a palm and the charging horses stopped as if they had struck a brick wall. When the wagon settled, the driver asked, 'Who are you?'

"The towering figure boomed," Jerrell lowered his voice, "'I am your god, Pallan.'

"The woodcutters were dumbfounded, one stating, 'Oh, Pallan. We are mere woodcutters, yet you honor us with your presence.'

"The god bellowed, 'This is no honor. I am here to punish you. As my children, you are required to honor nature. Yet, you picked every single buttercup in that field.'

"One woodcutter looked at the other. 'We thought to gift them to our women.'

"The god would not have it. Again, he boomed, 'You have defiled nature with your excessive waste. As punishment for picking all of those buttercups, I sentence you to a full year without butter.'

"The woodcutters' jaws dropped in shock at such a harsh penance. Then, one leaned close to the other and whispered, 'Good thing we didn't pick pussy willows.'"

A beat of silence followed as the guards processed the story.

Then the room erupted in raucous laughter. Men slapped their knees and the backs of their neighbors. Jerrell snickered, knowing he had the room wrapped around his finger...until Haelynn walked in.

One by one, the guards took notice, often nudging those next to them. In the span of three breaths, all eyes were fixed on her.

Jerrell spoke in a loud voice. "My, my. Who is this beauty that has graced us with her presence? Come up here, so everyone can get a look at you."

Escorted by Bostic, Haelynn approached the table. The crowd parted for her, broad grins painted on the guards' faces. When she was beside the table, Jerrell squatted and extended a hand, which Haelynn accepted. Bostic planted his hands on her waist and lifted her up.

"You ready?" Jerrell asked under his breath.

"Always," she replied before spinning toward the crowd and flashing a smile.

Raising his voice, Jerrell said, "How about a little dance?"

She gave a demure smile. "I could dance if you wish."

"I wish!" The crowd laughed. Jerrell turned to them. "Everyone clap with me."

As he began to clap out a beat, others joined in. Haelynn gripped her skirts and swayed to the beat.

"That's it!" Jerrell cheered. "Let yourself go!"

The beat picked up and Haelynn spun, her skirts flaring. All eyes were on her, hair and skirts trailing as she turned, laughed, and swayed.

Jerrell jumped down and worked his way through the crowd, quickly forgotten as the men watched her with wolfish grins on their faces. As Jerrell reached the door, he glanced back to find Haelynn loosening the laces on her bodice. He opened the door and slipped out unnoticed, now that all eyes were affixed to her.

Moving with a purposeful gait, Jerrell marched toward the two guards posted at the inner wall. "You men are missing it."

"Missing what?"

"Did you see the blonde with Bostic?"

"How could we miss her?"

"She is dancing in the barracks. Last I saw, she was in the process of removing her dress."

The two guards looked at each other.

"If you would like to check it out, I can watch the gate."

The men grinned. "You would do that?"

"Sure."

They hurried off, moving at a near run.

Jerrell sauntered through the gate and headed straight toward the wagon standing outside one of the warehouses. Desmond stood beside the wagon, talking to Leshonn.

"...lucky I still had these five barrels," Desmond was saying.

Leshonn signed a sheet of paper and handed it back to Desmond. "I'll help you unload it, and you can be on your way."

"Hi, Leshonn," Jerrell said, drawing the man's attention. "I thought you might want to know that you are missing quite the show in the guards' barracks."

The man furrowed his dark brow. "Show?"

Jerrell leaned close and whispered, putting an emphasis on the words gorgeous, woman, and undressing. Leshonn's eyes grew wide. "Right now?"

"And I fear it will end soon. If you'd like to see, I can help unload the wagon."

The man looked at the barrels and then turned toward the gate, his gaze filled with longing. "Alright. I'll be back shortly."

He hurriedly marched off toward the gate, and Jerrell turned toward Desmond with a grin. "At least men are predictable."

Desmond shook his head. "I shouldn't be surprised, but I am. The prisoners could just walk out right now."

"While that would be a fun distraction, I do not think it necessary." Jerrell gestured toward the barrels. "Which one is he in?"

"The one without red on the metal band."

Jerrell hopped up into the wagon, gripped that barrel, and tipped it up before rocking it toward the open tailgate. "Sorry about this, Lamond. We'll try not to drop you."

WITH THE WAGON UNLOADED, Desmond returned to the driver's seat, snapped the reins, and drove out of the inner compound. Once near the barracks, he slowed to a stop. Jerrell and Bostic emerged from the building with Haelynn between them, a cloak over her shoulders.

Bostic stopped beside the wagon and turned toward Haelynn. "I am sorry that turned a bit ugly. The men...well, they can be eager. You gave them something they miss, and something to dream about. None of them will forget this anytime soon."

"Thank you, Lieutenant."

He held his hand out. She took it and allowed him to help her onto the wagon seat.

Desmond said, "The barrels are all in the warehouse. I'll be back in the morning to pick up the manure."

Bostic nodded. "And what of the tailings?"

"I am hoping Lamond will be back tonight. If so, we will take those as well."

As Desmond drove the now-empty wagon through the gate, taking

Haelynn and himself back to the ranch, concerns for Lamond and Jerrell roiled in his gut.

～

JERRELL CREPT through the dark barracks, passing dozens of sleeping guards. He reached the door and slipped out into the night. Moonlight illuminated the confines between the outer and inner walls outside the mine. With the outer portcullis closed for the night, the inner gate stood unguarded. There was no need for guards with the compound sealed and the prisoners locked away for the night. If any escaped, they would still need to go over the outer wall, since the inner one led to a dead-end canyon and the warrens beneath the rock. As a result, the outer wall was perpetually manned by guards, ensuring nobody entered the compound and no prisoner escaped it.

After creeping across the dark yard, Jerrell approached the man-sized utility door beneath the inner wall. It was locked, as expected, but locks rarely stopped Jerrell, and this one proved to be of little consequence. He set to picking it, and moments later, the door swung inward, allowing him to slip past it.

The inner compound was quiet without a soul in sight. Jerrell made his way to a warehouse in the shadow of the wall, opened the side door, and slipped into the dark confines.

"Lamond?" he whispered.

"Over here."

Activating the gem on his dagger, Jerrell held it up to find the man standing amid a cluster of barrels, one of which was opened.

"Did you have any trouble getting out?"

"Yes. It took more effort to break out than I had expected. I began to panic until the lid finally popped open."

"How long have you been waiting?"

"An hour or so." Lamond handed Jerrell a shovel and gripped a second one. "I found tools. Even then, it is bound to be a long evening."

"Let's move the empty barrel first." Jerrell said, setting his shovel aside to grab ahold of the barrel top.

They carried the barrel across the compound. Four wagons rested beside the crusher, one of which stood empty. They placed the barrel on the empty wagon and rushed back for their shovels. When they returned, both climbed into a wagon, its bed filled with tailings. Determined, Jerrell thrust his shovel into the rock and tossed a scoop onto the neighboring wagon. Lamond did the same, his scoop of rock spilling over the empty barrel. Again and again, they dug into the rock.

While the work was hard and Jerrell drenched with sweat, he dreaded the next step of the plan more than this. After all, what could be worse than shoveling manure?

"So, this tunnel we're supposed to use to escape the mine," Lamond asked, "how far is it?"

After tossing a shovel full of rock into the other wagon, Jerrell paused and wiped sweat from his brow. "It'll take us about half an hour to navigate through it and another thirty minutes to reach your father's ranch. Now, keep shoveling. Morning will be here soon enough, and we will have no time to sleep if we dawdle."

CHAPTER 23

SLEIGHT OF HAND

With the morning sun at his back, Desmond drove an empty wagon through the mine's outer gate, across the housing compound, and into the inner yard. The wall still blocked the sun from view, but the oxen were already harnessed, rounding the scaffold, and driving the mechanism that powered the crusher.

He pulled the wagon to a stop and climbed down while Lamond drove in on another wagon, which was empty as well. Desmond noted the bags under his son's eyes, the slump of his shoulders, and the lolling of his head. It had been a long, sleepless night for him and Jerrell – they had returned to the ranch just before sunrise.

Desmond's gaze turned toward the wall and the warehouse standing in its shadow – the same warehouse where he had delivered naphtha the prior evening. A trio of empty carts waited outside the warehouse. Hulik stood nearby, calling out orders as four men picked up the barrels and loaded them into the carts. *What will happen when they count one less barrel?* He then spied another wagon approaching the outer gate. In the seat was a coppery-skinned driver with a thick black beard. At the man's side was Razak. Seeing his rival reminded Desmond of Jerrell's instructions. *Keep to the plan, Desmond. Razak is a suspicious man, so use that against him.*

523

Desmond unhitched his team and walked the horses over to a wagon, its bed piled high with sparkling rock. He was hooking his team to the wagon as Razak's wagon rolled in through the gate. The rival trader glared at Desmond with undisguised hatred. The wagon stopped before Desmond's team, and Razak hopped down.

"What do you think you are doing?" Razak growled while stomping over to Desmond.

"Fulfilling my order, as any trader would."

"You are to take the worthless tailings and the manure. The silver is mine to haul."

Desmond frowned. "I am aware of that."

"Then, why are you hitching your team to the silver wagon?"

Desmond blinked in feigned surprise. He turned toward the wagon, peered at the load, and grunted. "Huh. I guess I am just used to the left-most wagon being filled with tailings."

"Clearly, that is not the case today, so move your team out of my way." Razak crossed his arms over his thick chest. "Move it, Marlowe. I don't have all day."

Desmond unhitched his team from the wagon and shifted them to the one beside it. Meanwhile, Lamond hitched his team to the wagon on the far end, piled high with oxen manure. When he was finished, Desmond returned to his seat, snapped the reins, and pulled the full wagon toward the gate, leaving the empty one behind. A moment later, Lamond's wagon of manure followed him through the inner gate. He slowed as he neared the outer gate.

Bostic approached the wagon. "It looks like you are all set. Just give me a moment." He walked along the wagon and dug into the pile of crushed rock. He let the rubble filter through his fingers and fall back to the gravel. "Looks good."

Lamond pulled up beside Desmond, the odor of manure wafting over. "You sure you don't want to switch wagons, Pop?"

Desmond chuckled. "I've spent enough of my days hauling manure. It is now your turn."

"I was afraid you would say something to that effect." He turned to the guard. "What say you, Bostic? You want a handful of oxen dung as well?"

Bostic snorted. "Not in the least."

"In that case, I'll be going."

"Oh, no," Desmond said. "You are riding *behind* me. I'll not be eating manure odor all the way back to the ranch." He glanced over his shoulder as Razak rode up in his wagon, a mound of sparkling silver jutting up from the wagon bed. "Let Razak smell it instead."

Bostic chuckled. "That arse might actually enjoy it."

They all laughed, Desmond's forced chuckles joined by nervous sweat. He snapped the reins and rode off, eager to be away yet careful not to show it.

"Thank you for everything," Jerrell said as he hugged Marnie. The petite woman felt like paper in his arms. "Don't worry. Your son will be back in a few days. Your husband and elder son, even sooner."

Haelynn hugged the woman and thanked her as well. With their good-byes complete, they carried their packs outside and down the path to the stables. There, they found Lamond alone on one wagon while Desmond and Garmond occupied another with Miles looking on.

"Are you certain you don't want me to make this delivery?" Miles asked.

Desmond shook his head. "I promised this load to Lord Horus and intend to see it through myself."

"Why would Horus want useless tailings?"

"He did not say." Desmond scowled. "So long as he pays, what does it matter?"

Jerrell led Haelynn to the Lamond's wagon, its bed still filled with oxen manure. He helped her up, her face pinching as she sat beside the driver.

"The smell is horrible. Can't I ride in the other wagon?"

Jerrell shook his head. "Not unless you wish to end up in Orenth."

She frowned. "I'd rather not."

He took a seat beside her. "In three days, we will be back in Marquithe, and this whole thing will be over."

"What of Roka?"

"Like I told you, he will get his. Give it time."

"Ready?" Lamond asked.

"Yes." Jerrell turned to Desmond. "I'll keep your son safe. Once he is rid of this manure, we will continue to Marquithe, so he can pick up the goods for a return run. You just deliver that load to Orenth before anyone catches up to you."

Desmond said, "Do you think Razak will figure it out?"

Miles frowned at the comment but said nothing.

"I don't know," Jerrell shrugged. "If he does, you had best be far away."

Lamond snapped the reins, the wagon lurched into motion, and Jerrell, Haelynn, and Lamond headed north, toward Marquithe.

Yamal Razak was in a sour mood.

As a military man, like any seasoned soldier, he had endured excessive hardship, both physically and mentally. When his new wizard lord had asked him to lead the efforts in Farrowen, over a thousand miles from his home city of Sarmak, he had accepted with pride and humility. It was a special mission, filled with secrets and duplicity. He possessed the right combination of skills, having led others in battle, performed covert operations…and having been raised by a father who was a trader. He was able to drive a wagon, he simply despised doing so. Thus, the sour mood.

With the reins in his grip and an armed soldier on the seat beside him, Razak drove the wagon north, toward Shear. A man armed with a crossbow sat beside him while six soldiers on horseback shadowed the wagon, their eyes constantly scanning the surrounding woods, wary of bandits. The load of silver was hidden beneath a dark green tarp, making it unlikely for bandits to guess at the wealth in the wagon bed. Still, that didn't mean someone from Souton might not follow and be ready to attack. The silver weighed more than a ton and would readily convert to gold coins should it be delivered to the right party. From time to time, in moments of greed, Razak wondered what his life might be like if he sold the silver and disappeared. However, an inner voice always reminded him of Sarazan's wrath should Razak betray him. *He is a cruel and vindictive man who would not rest until my head adorned a pike on the battlements of Sarmak Palace.* So, he ignored his own greed and focused on duty. In this case, his duty was to see the silver securely on a ship bound for Hassaka. It was why he had demanded to drive the wagon himself. After the destruction of the weapons, wagons, and the loss of the naphtha, he could not afford another misstep.

The day waned as the hills and forests of southern Farrowen slipped past, quiet and uneventful until midafternoon when a rider on horseback came up from behind, drawing the attention of the guards and Razak alike. The guards slowed their horses, drew their weapons, and waited in the road between the wagon and approaching rider. Over his shoulder, Razak watched as the rider drew near, hunched over the galloping steed. The rider sat upright and slowed his mount. *Miles?* Razak slowed his team.

"I must speak with Captain Razak," Miles said to the guards.

"What is this about?" a guard demanded.

"It's alright," Razak replied. "Bring him to me."

The guards followed as Miles rode up beside Razak's wagon. The man appeared winded. The horse thrice so.

"Something is wrong," Miles said.

Razak frowned. "What can it be, now?"

Miles shook his head. "I don't know for certain, but something is amiss." He panted. "Desmond seldom drives anymore and never for deliveries outside of the Souton region. Yet, he and Garmond are headed to Tiamalyn with a load of tailings."

"Tailings? That's just worthless crushed rock! Why would they haul it so far?"

"They wouldn't. Not unless someone was willing to pay for it."

Razak rubbed his goatee and considered the situation. His eyes widened in alarm as he came to a logical conclusion. Rising to his feet, he scrambled from the seat to the wagon bed and tore the tarp away. Sunlight sparkled off the silver. Unsatisfied, he lifted a shovel nestled beside the pile and thrust it into the crushed silver, scooping out a shovelful and then examining it. Dull gray rock was mixed in with the silver. He quickly dug through the pile, dumping load after load into the corner of the wagon bed, each scoop containing less silver than the one before. His shovel then struck wood with a hollow thud.

He tossed it aside and dug at the pile with frantic, urgent swipes. His actions soon exposed the round rim of a barrel. It was surrounded by worthless gray rock, the only silver on the top of the pile.

"We've been deceived." Razak spun toward the man still seated in the driver's seat. "Turn around and drive back to the ranch."

"Where are you going?"

Razak hopped out of the wagon. "The rest of us are heading down the east route." He approached a horse with a guard in the saddle. "Get down. I need your horse. You can ride back in the wagon with Hestian."

"Yes, Captain." The guard dutifully dismounted.

Once in the saddle, Razak turned the horse south. "The rest of you ride with me. We need to catch Marlowe before he reaches the Orenthian border."

WITH THE SETTING sun on his back, Desmond and his wagon rolled down the road leading toward Tiamalyn. It had been a long and uneventful day. Once again, he looked over his shoulder and found the road empty.

"Maybe Jerrell was wrong about Miles," he said, hoping his long-time driver was as loyal as he believed.

Garmond said, "I hope so. I always liked Miles. If he truly is a traitor... well, that would not sit well with me at all."

"Betrayal has that effect on a man."

"And if he is not a traitor?"

"Then this entire journey is a useless lark."

Garmond frowned. "I'd rather be home with Alicia and the kids."

"I know how you feel. It kind of makes this outing a losing proposition either way."

"And if Lamond and Jerrell make it to Marquithe without incident?"

Desmond grinned. "Razak will have lost, and we will be richer."

A rumble arose on the road behind them. Desmond turned toward it to find a half-dozen riders approaching at a gallop. The men were hunched over their mounts, the rider in the lead instantly recognizable as Razak.

"We have company." Desmond turned forward. "Just remember to act surprised."

Garmond looked over his shoulder and frowned. "Miles is with him."

Sighing, Desmond said, "I had hoped otherwise, but it appears Jerrell was correct about him."

Rather than stopping the wagon, Desmond pretended nothing was amiss, the wagon continuing forward. The riders drew even with it and then passed it. Razak leaned from his saddle and gripped the bridle of one of Desmond's horses, slowing the team. Once they had stopped, Razak turned his mount toward the wagon.

"What is the meaning of this, Razak?" Desmond demanded.

"You've gone too far, Marlowe."

"I had a contract to remove this rubble. I am free to do with it as I wish."

"True. With the rubble. With a load of useless crushed rock."

"I've found a customer who has use for such rock."

Razak dismounted and approached the wagon. "That would not be surprising. Silver is a highly desired commodity."

"Silver?"

Razak gestured toward the pile of rock. "Garmond. Climb in and dig."

Garmond scowled. "I will not."

Razak drew his scimitar and held it to Desmond's chest. "Then I will kill your father."

Desmond snarled. "You would murder your competition in cold blood?"

"It is your punishment for capital theft," Razak snapped back.

Desmond said, "Go on, Gar. Dig as Razak demands."

Garmond climbed into the wagon bed, lifted a shovel from the side of the rock pile, and thrust it into the pile. Bits of gray rock trickled down the sloped sides. When the shovel came free, a scoop of identical crushed rock filled it. He dumped the shovel load into the corner of the wagon and scooped another load. Again, and again, he repeated the process, yielding nothing but plain gray rock.

Razak lowered his sword and reached into the wagon, scooping a handful of rock and staring at it with a frown. "I don't understand."

Desmond restrained his smile. "What did you expect? We were contracted to haul a load of tailings, and that is what we are doing."

"But...where is the silver?" He spun toward Miles, his volume and tenor rising, "Where is the silver?"

Miles shook his head. "I don't know. I swear. There was just this wagon and the other, filled with"—his face turned white— "manure."

"Where is the other wagon?"

"With Lamond. He and two others are riding toward Marquithe."

Razak's voice rose in volume and tenor. "Marquithe? That is in the opposite direction! It is nearly sunset, and they have been riding all day, which places them two days ahead of us. Worse, our horses are spent." He ran a hand through his black hair. "How can we catch them in time?"

Miles said, "I don't know, sir."

Razak sheathed his blade and climbed back on his horse. He pointed toward Desmond. "If I find silver in Lamond's wagon, I am coming after you."

"He hauls a wagon of oxen manure and likely has already unloaded it at some farm along the way. Why would he have silver?"

Lips pressed together, Razak glared at Desmond. He then nudged his horse into motion and rode back the way he had come with his guards following.

When the horses were out of sight and the rumble of their hooves faded, Garmond sat down beside Desmond. "That was surprisingly satisfying."

"Yes." Desmond allowed a grin. "It seems Razak is having a very bad day. I suspect tomorrow and those that follow will offer him little solace."

CHAPTER 24
WEALTH

"We've a delivery to make!" Jerrell insisted.

The guard at the gate threw his arms wide. "This is a city, not a farmer's field. Who within these walls would want a load of crap?"

Jerrell had expected resistance from the guards but was not about to relent. "It was requested by the enchanters. Why, I have no idea."

"The enchanters?"

"Come, now. Those crazy old men remain locked in their tower, where they conduct their strange, unknowable magic. They are odd, mysterious, and the most secretive lot in the Eight Wizardoms. I cannot guess why they want a load of oxen dung, but my job is to see it delivered."

One guard looked at the other, doubt etched in their expressions.

Jerrell tried again, taking another approach. He sighed deeply, allowing his frustration to show, his volume lowering as if he were nearing defeat. "Listen. Do you think we would be riding around with this rather fragrant, disgusting load on a lark?" He put his arm around Haelynn. "Do you think this beautiful woman would endure this stomach-turning stench if she had a choice?"

Her large blue eyes pleading, Haelynn said, "I beg of you. Let us in, so we can be rid of this foul load. I don't know how my business partner convinced me to accept such a nasty contract. Worse, he somehow tricked me into riding with him. The sooner it is over, the better. At this point, I feel as if the odor has permeated my skin. I may have to bathe three times and burn this dress just to be free of it."

Jerrell added, "You have my word, we will proceed directly to the Enchanter's Tower, relieve ourselves of this odiferous burden, and will return to our homes to scrub the stench off the wagon and our own bodies."

The sergeant took a deep breath, his nostrils flaring before he nodded. "Fine. Just go straight to the tower and be done with it. If anyone asks, you tell them you entered the city through the north gate. I'll deny you having passed this way."

Haelynn smiled, leaned forward, and took the sergeant's hand. "Thank you, sir. I am in your debt."

The man smiled. "I am happy to help. If you are ever seeking company, you can find me at the Storm Cell on evenings I am not on duty."

"I will remember that."

Lamond snapped the reins, and the wagon rolled through the gate.

Rather than take a circuitous route along the inside of the city walls, the poorest quarters found in Marquithe, Jerrell had Lamond head for the luxurious estates of wizards and wealthy merchants. It was the shortest path to the Enchanter's Tower, which made it the expedient choice. The reactions he saw from the male and female wizards he passed on the way gave him a great deal of satisfaction – if only he could park the wagon at their doorsteps to watch them squirm and endure the odor a bit longer.

Finally, the wagon rolled along a downhill street into the shadow of the tower. After circling the front, the fenced stable yard came into view. The wagon approached the open gate, where a guard in silver and black blocked their path.

The guard grimaced and approached the wagon. "Where do you think you are going?"

"My name is Jerrell Landish. My patron, Tyrell Lancomb entered a contract with Master Olberon last week. We have the delivery and are ready to fulfill the contract."

The guard grimaced at the pile of manure. "I highly doubt Olberon requested a wagon full of dung."

"Actually, the old coot demanded silver. A lot of silver."

Narrowing his eyes, the man said, "Don't tell me you think you can turn crap into silver."

Jerrell laughed. "That is exactly what I intend to do. Now, allow us into the yard where we will wait while you fetch Olberon and his entourage." He tilted his head. "Unless you wish to risk his wrath by turning away a wagon filled with silver."

An apparent inner struggle waged within the man, his eyes flicking from the wagon to the tower to Jerrell until he finally said, "Pull the wagon in but do not climb down until I return."

As the guard entered the tower, Lamond drove the wagon into a yard surrounded by ten-foot-tall walls. The tower loomed to one side and a single-story stone building with two stable doors stood beside it.

Minutes passed before the guard emerged with three men in black robes and another set of guards trailing behind. One of the enchanters was short with a wide body and brown hair combed over a bald spot. Another stood tall, his head completely bald, his face covered in a thick black beard. The third led the trio, his gray hair, gray beard, and bushy eyebrows marking his age.

Olberon strode up to the wagon, eyed the load with a frown, and turned to Jerrell. "Is this some sort of crude joke, Landish?"

Jerrell stood on the seat and said, "It was a wonderful joke, indeed, but you were not its target." He produced a pair of leather gloves. "The manure might be dry, but it is still nasty, and I prefer not to touch it," he explained before leaning forward and lifting a shovel from the wagon bed. "Watch."

He scooped a shovel full of dung and tossed it over the edge of the wagon. It landed in the gravel with a splat. A second scoop in the same location revealed nuggets that glittered in the sunlight. Once he emptied the shovel, Jerrell pointed with it. "What you see here is a ton of pure silver, straight from the mines of Souton. Since it is highly valued and there were others who wished to take it, I thought it best to use oxen manure to hide it. I mean...who would want to dig through a pile of crap?"

Olberon's scowl was replaced by a smile. "How clever." The man gestured. "Horsham. Go fetch the apprentices. I have a job for them."

The bald enchanter nodded. "As you wish, Master Olberon." He then turned and disappeared inside.

Olberon said, "Leave the wagon for the day. Return at noon tomorrow and you will find it emptied and cleaned."

"What of the gold I am owed?"

"If the load of silver is sufficient, you will receive that tomorrow as well."

Jerrell smiled. "Wonderful."

THE NEXT DAY, Jerrell, Haelynn, and Lamond returned to the tower. They were guided inside and brought to the fourth floor, where Olberon waited.

Jerrell entered the room to find a dozen men in black robes seated at the table. One held a ledger and was reciting numbers. A moment later, he finished, and all eyes turned toward Jerrell and his companions.

"Well, Mister Landish," Olberon said. "You've exceeded our expectations. I don't know how you came by the silver, nor do I care to know. It now resides safely in our tower, ensuring continuity in our ability to enchant. For that, I give you this."

When the old man gestured, a guard lifted a small chest from a stone table and carried it over. The guard held it out to Jerrell, who accepted it. The guard released his grip and the weight of the chest caused Jerrell to stumble and nearly drop the load. He strained to lift the chest and held it against his stomach.

Haelynn reached over, unlatched the chest, and raised the lid. Bright golden coins filled the interior. She gasped. "It is beautiful."

Jerrell's heart fluttered at the sight. "That it is."

"We are finished here," said Olberon. "Have a good day, Mister Landish. Should we ever again have need of your services, I will track you down or send a missive to your patron, Master Lancomb."

"Oh, I expect this will not be my last visit to your tower." Jerrell backed toward the door. "Have fun playing with your silver while I roll around in this gold."

Jerrell, Haelynn, and Lamond followed the guards out the door and down the stairs. Jerrell struggled to balance the heavy chest, but it was one burden he was happy to bear. They exited through the back door and into the stable yard where the wagon waited. The wagon bed was clean – neither a granule of silver nor a chunk of manure remained. Jerrell slid the chest onto the seat, climbed on, and was joined by Haelynn and Lamond.

Following Jerrell's directions, Lamond drove across the city and parked outside the Blue Hen. Once inside his apartment, Jerrell opened the chest and began to count the gold. He then dug out a canvas pack and dumped forty coins inside, which he gave to Lamond.

"As promised, this is for you and your family. We couldn't have done it without you."

Lamond grinned. "This more than makes up for our lost business. Better yet, we really stuck it to Razak and Roka."

"Yes, we did, but we are not done yet."

Haelynn said, "Not even close. Roka will get his, and when that happens, Razak will suffer as well."

Lamond headed toward the door. "Take care, you two. I must be heading back."

"You take care as well. Give Desmond and Marnie our best."

When the door closed, Jerrell turned to Haelynn. "I suppose you want your gold as well."

"Yes, and then I must be leaving."

Jerrell began counting coins. "Will I see you again?"

She smirked. "Will you miss me?"

He shrugged. "I will miss watching you bathe."

"With you in the tub with me."

"There is that as well."

Reaching out, she patted his cheek. "Do not worry, Jerrell. You've not seen the last of me."

Reaching a count of eighty, Jerrell dumped her coins into a sack and held it out to her. "Where will you go when you leave here?"

Haelynn moved close to him, cupped his cheek, and kissed him. Her soft lips meshed with his as his blood began to heat. She stepped back and smiled. "Until next time."

As she walked to the door, he asked, "Why are you so secretive?"

She opened the door and glanced back. "Caution has kept me alive this long. I suggest you learn a bit more caution yourself. If not, you may end up broke, dead, or worse."

"What is worse than being dead?"

"Be well, Jerrell. I'll see you soon."

The door closed, leaving him alone. He crossed the room, went into the kitchen, and dug out a sheet of parchment, a quill, and an inkwell. It had been a long time since he had written a letter, and this would be the first he'd ever written to a wizard lord. Still, the truth needed to be revealed, so justice could come to pass.

A FEW DAYS LATER, Jerrell returned to his office in the Bureau of Trading, expecting it to be unoccupied. He was wrong.

A beautiful blonde in a black dress sat on his sofa, her legs crossed, and her hands resting in her lap. When he walked in, she smiled, and the room brightened.

Hardly realizing it, he returned the smile. "I see you cannot stay away from me for long."

Haelynn shrugged, her movement oozing sensuality. "You interest me, Jerrell. You are unlike anyone I have ever met."

Despite an inner voice attempting to warn him, Jerrell's pride swelled. He sat in a chair across from her. "Are you here for business or pleasure?" He found himself praying for the latter.

"I have come across another opportunity and thought you might be interested."

He swallowed his disappointment. "I am listening."

"I know someone with a client who wishes to unload themselves of some troublesome goods."

Leaning forward, he asked in a hushed tone. "Stolen?"

"Yes."

"From whom?"

"The men who rule Cordium."

"Enchanters?"

"Of course."

"What, exactly, are we talking about here?"

"A ship that was bound from Cordium to the Great Bazaar in Balmor."

"A ship?"

"Yes. They stole the ship itself. It was loaded with magical objects."

"Where is this ship?"

"Moored in Shear Harbor."

"An entire shipload." Jerrell sat back and considered the possibility. He had earned over a hundred gold from selling just a few enchanted objects. An entire shipload. "Just how much would this cost?"

"The original asking price was excessive, but this individual has agreed to sell the entire load for a mere two hundred fifty gold pieces. After our success in Souton and calling in a few favors, I can muster half of that. I thought you might be willing to invest the other half."

Jerrell rubbed his jaw while considering the idea.

She added, "I visited the Enchanter's Tower this morning and met with Olberon. When I mentioned the stolen ship, the old man finally stopped attempting to bed me."

"What did he say?"

"He offered five hundred gold pieces if I could recover the goods and deliver them to him."

Jerrell considered the offer. "I suspect a load of that size would garner twice that amount."

"But at what risk? In this scenario, we double our money and all we need to do is see it delivered from Shear to Marquithe."

Although the use of one hundred twenty-five gold pieces would consume his savings, the opportunity to double his wealth was more than intriguing. Unable to find any flaws in her plan, he nodded. "All right. I am in."

She smiled. "I knew you could not dismiss the chance to earn easy gold." Rising to her feet, she stood over him. "I will arrange a carriage to take us to Shear. Meet me outside the Bureau in one hour. Don't forget the gold."

CHAPTER 25
A BILL OF GOODS

With the midday sun masked by a puffy white cloud, the carriage began the long, winding path down the cliffside above Shear Harbor. Jerrell felt relief to see the walls of Shear Castle fade behind him. While Terissa Wrenthal had promised she would not hold him accountable for what happened to her father, Jerrell worried that the high wizard blamed him for the loss of his eyesight and would hold a grudge. *I doubt the man could use his magic against me while blind. His guards are another matter.*

The carriage rolled along switchback after switchback, easing past hillside homes on its way down to the docks. Shortly after the ground finally leveled, the carriage drew to a stop.

Jerrell exited, extended a hand to Haelynn, and helped her down. She clutched his arm, and they walked together toward the docks. "Where are we to meet this contact?"

"Look for *Hassaka's Breath*. My contact and the cargo remain on the ship."

They slowed at the foot of the first pier while reading the names of the three ships moored there. None matched, so they marched past dockworkers and wagons before reaching the second pier. At the far end was a single ship. The red letters on the stern read *Hassaka's Breath*.

"There it is."

"Let's go meet him."

They headed down the long pier and passed a pair of dockworkers painting a thick mooring post. The pier was otherwise empty.

Jerrell said, "We will need to hire some wagons to haul the goods."

"I have arranged that. The three wagons at the foot of the pier are ours."

"How much did that cost?"

"Fifteen silvers for drivers to take a load from here to Marquithe."

Jerrell grunted. "It seems you have thought of everything."

She gripped his arm with her other hand and pulled him against her side. "I have learned from you, Jerrell." Leaning in, she kissed his cheek and whispered, "To celebrate, on the way back, we can take advantage of the privacy the carriage allows."

The ride to Shear had consumed the better part of two days. While the ride back was bound to take as long, it suddenly sounded far less boring.

A grin stretched across his face. "I like the sound of that."

As they drew near the ship, a man in dark clothing and a black cloak crossed the plank and met them on the dock. "Haelynn." The man pulled his hood back, revealing short black hair. His face was narrow, his build lean although he stood only a few inches taller than Jerrell. "I trust your trip was uneventful."

"Good afternoon, Arliss. Our trip went well enough, but I am unlikely to rest well until I am back in Marquithe."

The man turned his dark eyes on Jerrell. "Who is this?"

"My partner, Jerrell."

"Partner?" The man scowled.

"Two hundred fifty gold is a massive sum and too much for me to accumulate on my own. Jerrell can be trusted and, more importantly, has agreed to finance half of this deal."

Arliss glanced toward the ship and then back at Jerrell before turning to Haelynn. "You have the gold?"

"Yes. In the carriage."

Arliss turned toward the ship and waved. Two burly men crossed the plank and took a position to each side of him. Both men were armed, one with a scimitar, the other a longsword.

"What is this?" Jerrell asked.

"Protection." Arliss pointed toward land. "Let's go get it."

The five of them walked down the pier, passed the three parked wagons, and stopped outside the carriage. Jerrell opened the door and dug out the chest he had hidden beneath the bench. It was even heavier than when he had hauled it from the Enchanter's Tower to his apartment.

He walked over to the man, set the chest on the ground, and stepped back.

Arliss squatted, peered inside, and closed the lid. "Whitlock. Carry the chest to the ship."

One of the brawny sailors stepped forward, hefted the chest, and held it against his stomach.

"Pull your wagons up. I'll have the sailors open the hatch and begin unloading while I count the coins." Arliss and his guards headed back toward the pier.

Haelynn whistled and waved. The three wagons rolled down the dock, the horses clopping noisily on the wood surface. She and Jerrell followed close behind.

Jerrell spied a woman with a brimmed hat standing on the ship's quarterdeck, her black hair stirred by the wind. She wore a long brown coat over a white blouse and black corset. Her tight breeches and tall boots spoke to a lean and fit frame. Notably, a saber occupied the scabbard on her hip.

"Who is that?" he asked aloud.

Haelynn tugged his arm. "Never mind her. We have to see these wagons loaded." She leaned against him and whispered, "Remember the adventures waiting for you when we return to the carriage."

His pulse thumping, Jerrell smiled. "I'll not soon forget."

The hatch door opened, and a sailor slid a broad plank over to the pier. Another appeared from the shadows and carried a crate across.

Jerrell followed the man as he met the lead wagon. "Hold on. I want to see what is in one of these crates."

The sailor grimaced. "I don't know…"

"I either see what is in the crate, or this deal is off."

The man set the crate in the wagon. "Fine. Be quick with it. Captain Harlequin wants to set sail as soon as we are free of our cargo."

Jerrell pulled his dagger out and fit the tip beneath the crate lid. He forced the dagger in and then attempted to pry the lid open. The nails resisted but finally gave. He removed the lid and daylight revealed six objects packed in hay. He lifted an enchanted lantern, activated it, and smiled at the light. It alone could sell for two gold pieces.

The next object was a three-ended rod made of black lacquered wood with brass ends. The silver script of an enchantment marked the wood. With the object was a rolled sheet of parchment. Jerrell unrolled the scroll and read the text Dousing Rod. In the description, he found that the rod was used to find sources of water. A hexagonal brass object, a steel disk, a second enchanted lantern, and a wooden cross rounded out the objects in the crate. All included the silver script of enchantment.

Satisfied, Jerrell stuffed the items back in the crate and replaced the lid. By then, four sailors had begun placing crates of various shapes and sizes into the first wagon. One of the crates was the size of a coffin, requiring two men to carry it.

Over the next twenty minutes, sailors steadily emerged from the cargo hold with crates. The first wagon was soon full, then the second. Once the third wagon bed was stacked with crates, the sailors disappeared inside the ship, pulled the plank back into the hold, and closed the hatch.

Haelynn approached the first wagon driver. "You three are to follow our carriage. We will ride until sunset and then make camp. By tomorrow evening, we will be in Marquithe, and I will pay you the rest of what you are owed." She then turned to Jerrell. "Shall we? Our carriage is waiting."

He grinned. "It would be my pleasure." When she took his arm, he added. "It will be your pleasure as well. Twice by the time we reach the upper city."

～

WITH SUNSET FAST APPROACHING, the carriage and train of wagons rolled through the streets of Marquithe and approached the Enchanter's Tower. Although the journey had taken just as long as the initial drive to Shear, Jerrell found the return trip much more enjoyable. Haelynn had proven far more appreciative than he had anticipated, and by the time they had reached the city, he knew he would forever consider the ride among his favorite memories.

The carriage stopped outside the tower's front door, and Haelynn patted Jerrell's hand. "I am going inside to find Olberon and his cronies."

"I will come with you," he offered.

"No." She shook her head. "You remain with the carriage, so you can deal with the guard. He will recognize you, so you should have little trouble getting inside the stable yard."

Jerrell recalled the difficulty he had encountered the last time at the tower, although this load lacked the disgusting scent of the prior one. "I guess that makes sense."

"Of course it does." She leaned in, kissed his cheek, and opened the door. Once outside, she spoke with the driver and then entered the tower.

The carriage lurched into motion, rounded the tower, and stopped at the gate.

Jerrell jumped down and flashed the guard a smile. "Good evening."

The guard arched a brow. "You again?" He then looked toward the three wagons lined up behind the carriage. "Please tell me you don't have manure this time."

"Nothing of the sort. You'll find no oppressive odor, nor will you be forced to wield a shovel for this load."

"Olberon is expecting you?"

"He is. My partner just went into the tower to fetch him. We will wait in the stable yard."

The guard nodded. "Fine. Go on in. If you don't mind, I am still going to notify Master Olberon."

"That is your prerogative." Jerrell approached the carriage driver while the guard went inside. "You were paid to drive us to Shear and back. Well, we are here, so you may be on your way." He dug into his coin purse and pulled out seven silver coins. "This is for you. I included a couple extra silver pieces. You also might want to clean the carriage interior before you use it again."

The driver tipped his hat. "Thanks, Jerrell. From the sounds of it, you certainly had a good trip."

Jerrell beamed. "My favorite thus far."

The man laughed, snapped the reins, and turned his carriage around. The wagons followed Jerrell through the open gate and into the stable yard.

Minutes passed before the guard emerged from the tower with Olberon, two other enchanters, and two more guards. The old man wore the same, familiar grimace. "What is this about, Landish?"

Jerrell frowned. "Where is Haelynn?"

"Who?"

"My partner. The gorgeous blonde."

Olberon's scowl faded. "She is here?" He looked around. "I didn't see her."

"She went into the tower to find you, so we could complete our transaction."

"Transaction? What the blazes are you talking about?"

"The deal she struck with you to reclaim a ship full of stolen enchanted objects." He gestured toward the crates in the nearest wagon.

The old man's bushy eyebrows rose. "Someone stole a ship full of our magical items?"

"Yes. You agreed to pay five hundred gold for them."

"Five hundred gold?" Olberon snorted. "Are you daft?"

Jerrell stroked his stubble-covered chin, his discomfort increasing by the moment.

Olberon said, "Let's see these objects." He gestured toward the guards. "Derrick, go fetch us a couple of pry bars."

The first guard rushed into the stables and returned with a pry bar he used to begin opening crates. Jerrell and the three enchanters stood near the wagon while the driver watched in curiosity. The lid popped up and was lifted away to reveal straw.

Olberon leaned over the wagon and dug into the straw, his hands swishing through it, his brow furrowed. Finally, he looked up and said, "It is empty."

"What?" Jerrell reached in and felt around, finding nothing. "Open another one."

The men opened another crate, and another. They were empty as well. They moved to another wagon and opened six crates. All were empty. They tried the third and final wagon, this time opening four crates before giving up. All the while, a lump slid down Jerrell's throat before settling in his stomach.

The master enchanter scowled at Jerrell. "I am a busy man. I see no humor in this waste of time."

Jerrell did not reply, staring at the empty crates while his dread turned to anger. "She tricked me."

"Who?"

"Haelynn. She used me and robbed me of one hundred twenty-five gold in the process."

More than one man whistled.

Olberon patted Jerrell on the shoulder. "Women are nothing but trouble. It is why I remain unmarried after all these years." He grinned. "Besides, it frees me to chase anyone who tickles my fancy."

"There was one small crate with a few items in it," Jerrell said, grasping for a thread of hope.

"Which one?"

He identified the crate. The guard opened it to reveal the same objects Jerrell had examined in Shear.

Olberon dug through the crate and peered closely at each. After a few minutes, he turned to Jerrell. "You have two enchanted lanterns, each worth a couple gold pieces. The rest is junk."

"Junk?"

"Yes. The scribble on them is nonsense. They hold no magical properties."

Jerrell's shoulders slumped in defeat. He pulled the two lanterns from the crate, turned, and walked off, leaving the yard full of men, horses, and wagons behind.

CHAPTER 26
FAME

A bitter winter wind tugged at Jerrell's cloak, snaked around his neck, and sent a chill down the length of his spine. He crossed the square and headed inside the Bureau. Once inside, he pulled his hood down and headed up to his office on the second story terrace. He turned the corner and saw a thin man with a sharp face standing in his office doorway, hugging his clipboard while tapping his foot.

When he saw Jerrell, the man sighed. "It is about time, Landish."

Jerrell slipped past the man and removed his cloak before tossing it on the sofa. "To what do I owe this displeasure, Eggert?"

"Today is your anniversary. I have come to collect payment for another year."

Staring into space, Jerrell said, "It has been a year already?"

"Yes. Accordingly, I require a payment of twenty gold coins." The clerk held his hand out, waiting.

"I don't have it."

"I will wait while you go and—"

"No. I mean...I cannot afford to pay the fee."

A smile bloomed across the clerk's face. "So, the great Jerrell Landish is not so great after all."

"I am plenty great. Just ask any woman I have ever been with. But then what do you know about women?"

Eggert's lips tightened. "Gather your things, Landish. You are to be out by sunset. Don't bother returning." He spun on his heel and stomped off.

Now alone, Jerrell sat forward, put his elbows on his knees, and dropped his face into his hands.

His efforts to find another client had been wasted. The Whispering Man firmly controlled Marquithe's underbelly, which made things more than difficult for any thief, smuggler, whore, or beggar not under the man's thumb. Worse, the crime lord's bribes had paid off every clerk and official in the Bureau and beyond, ensuring all contracts came to him and leaving nothing for Jerrell or any independent agents seeking to ply their services.

"Hello, Jerrell," said a familiar female voice.

He raised his head to find a comely blonde standing in his doorway. "Haelynn." Her name came out as a growl.

"You are upset with me."

"You think?"

"I apologize for using you as I did, but I don't regret my actions." She waved at someone to come in. Another blonde, perhaps even prettier than Haelynn, stepped into the doorway and took her hand. "I told you about my sister. Rylynn, meet Jerrell. He is the best thief in the world and the bravest man I have ever met."

The woman smiled and Jerrell's heart skipped a beat. "Hello, Jerrell. I have heard much about you. From my sister's stories, I half expected you to be nothing but myth."

Haelynn walked into the office. "As you can see, Rylynn is returned to me, but it was not easy. Once I discovered her captivity in Sarmak, I found someone who could negotiate her release. Lord Sarazan agreed to release her, but at the cost of two hundred fifty gold."

Jerrell grimaced. "My gold."

"Half of it, yes. If another path had been available, I would have taken it, but you were the only person I knew who possessed the coin I needed. So, I arranged a shipment of empty crates, and...you know the rest." She slid an arm around her sister's shoulder, hugging her close. "If I had to, I would do it again. My only regret is the pain I caused you."

He pressed his lips together to hold back a snide comment. "You disappeared more than a season ago. In that time, I have had no clients." Gesturing toward his surroundings, he added, "I cannot even afford to retain this office."

She dropped to one knee and took his hand. "It is time you put your pride aside and agree to work for the Whispering Man."

"I have worked for a thieves guild before. It did not go well."

"This will be different. He wants you on his team and has already agreed to certain concessions."

"What do you know of him?"

Her eyes lowered to her hands. "I have been his agent for the past two years."

Realization clicked. "You manipulated me toward his ends."

"I did, starting with our evening together in Yor's Point."

That long ago? "So, it was all a lie."

Her hand touched his cheek. "Not all of it. You are a special man, Jerrell. Much of our time together was by my own choice, for my own desires."

He gripped her wrist and pulled her hand from his face. "I'll not allow you to use me again."

Her gaze dropped again. "I understand. You are hurt and I…"

"No. I must protect myself. Women are trouble. I should have known better than to let you get close."

Pain reflected in her eyes. "Not all women are like me, Jerrell. Don't close your heart forever, or you might miss out on finding a mate who makes life more than you believe is possible."

He glared at her in silence.

Haelynn continued, "While I hope you will one day forgive me, I know it will take time. I also thought it might help if you understood why I did what I did. Now that Rylynn is safe, I have no need to use you."

"Well, you won't get the chance either way."

She stood. "Be well, Jerrell. I wish you a prosperous future. Pay a visit to the Whispering Man. He is expecting you."

Haelynn and her sister walked off, leaving Jerrell alone with his troubled thoughts.

LATE AFTERNOON SUNLIGHT streamed through the Bureau windows by the time Jerrell left his office and made for the stairwell. Rather than descending, he headed up to the top floor and followed a dark corridor to a closed door bracketed by two tall, brawny men.

"I need to speak with him," Jerrell said.

"Do you have an appointment?"

"My name is Jerrell Landish. He is expecting me."

"Ah. Landish. Right." The man knocked on the door.

"Come in," came a voice from within.

The guard opened the door and moved aside. Jerrell swept past him, closed the door, and sat down. Similar to his prior visit, the room was dark – the only light emitted from a candle positioned behind the silhouette of the man in the chair.

"I am impressed," the man whispered. "I expected you to visit me long ago."

"I don't appreciate being manipulated."

"Yet, Haelynn wrapped you around her finger and waggled it until you were flung off."

"It was your doing. All of it."

"What do you mean?"

"Her offer to partner with me originated with you. When she came to me with a tip to spy on the meeting between Malvorian and the enchanters... that came from you. The sham of a stolen shipment of enchanted goods was your creation."

"Well deduced, Landish."

"This was all to twist my actions toward your own ends?"

"Not entirely, but I knew once you fully perceived the situation, you would come around. Sapping your savings and leaving you desperate for coin was part of my strategy as well."

"What do you want from me?"

"Your talent, Jerrell. I have access to contracts that require a skilled charlatan such as yourself. With your help, I can further my empire, and you will thrive as a result."

"Thrive? How so? What is in it for me?"

"I can give you something you desire."

"Tell me, what is it I desire?"

"Fame."

Jerrell leaned forward, suddenly interested. "Go on."

"Work for me, and I will see your name whispered across Farrowen and beyond. You will become the most famous thief in history. Your exploits will be talked about in taverns and courtrooms across the Eight Wizardoms."

Despite his prior reluctance, the offer suddenly became unexpectedly tantalizing. "What about coin?"

"You will be well compensated, I assure you. There is more than enough wealth to go around. The risks you are asked to accept will come with suitable rewards." The man reached over to the table at his side, picked up something that jingled, and tossed it.

Jerrell caught the sack. It held a good weight. "What is this?"

"A bonus for joining my ranks. Inside, you will find ten gold pieces. I recognize the weight of your recent loss, and it will do me no good to see you destitute."

The gold was a relief – Jerrell had been concerned about how he would pay his rent since his year was up soon.

"Let's say I agree to this arrangement. Now, what?"

"I will contact you when a suitable contract arises."

Sensing the conversation had drawn to an end, Jerrell stood.

"Before you go," the Whispering Man said. "I have another gift to offer, one that might provide a modicum of satisfaction." He leaned forward and extended a hand. A folded piece of paper rested between his outstretched fingers.

Jerrell took the paper and unfolded it. Golden light shone from inside. He read it with a furrowed brow. "This is an invitation to Marquithe Palace."

"It is."

"Who is Halvish?"

"He is the high wizard of Tangor."

"A Ghealdan?"

"Yes. The man is to visit Marquithe with his wife, Elana. Malvorian subsequently extended an offer for the couple to join him for dinner tomorrow evening. Of course, the real Halvish remains unaware."

"Why are you giving this to me?"

"You will want to be at that dinner, Jerrell. There, you will have a prime seat for a fine performance."

"I see. What does this Halvish look like?"

"He is but a few years older than you, with a brown goatee, his robes purple with an orange sash."

"What of his wife?"

"She is reported to be a beauty, blonde with blue eyes. I believe you know someone who matches that description."

Jerrell grimaced. "Haelynn."

"Very good." The man leaned back in his chair, his face nothing but shadows. "She is to meet you outside the palace an hour prior to sunset. Do not be late."

CHAPTER 27
SATISFACTION

Dressed in shimmering purple robes secured with an orange sash, Jerrell emerged from a busy street and strode across the square outside of Marquithe Palace. The fake goatee made his face itch and the round spectacles repeatedly slid down his nose, forcing him to push them back into place. As he crossed the busy square, he did not waver when others blocked his path, instead forcing them to avoid him. *I am a vaunted wizard. I am above you pathetic worms.* Holding tightly to the entitled attitude was an important aspect of his performance.

A tall blonde with a slim waist and enticing curves appeared from the crowd and walked at his side. She wore a lavender dress trimmed in white, the neckline deep enough to reveal a hint of cleavage. Her hair was piled atop her head and large, golden hoop earrings dangled from her ears.

The woman slid her arm around his. "I worried you might not show."

"My curiosity was too strong to deny."

A smirk appeared on her lips as they drew near the gate. "Admit it. You miss me."

"I want to stab you."

"With a dagger made of steel or flesh?"

"To tell you the truth, both."

She laughed. Despite his deep-seated ire toward her, he smiled as well.

As they approached the guards standing outside the palace gate, Jerrell reached inside his robes, withdrew his folded invitation, and held it out. "We are visiting from Tangor." His tone was haughty and left no room for argument. "Lord Malvorian has invited us for dinner. We are late, so you had better not dally before you escort us inside."

The guard opened the invitation. Golden light illuminated his face as he looked it over. The man then walked up to a tall, lean man in a midnight blue uniform and showed him the invite.

The man in the uniform strode over to Jerrell. "Welcome, Wizard Halvish. My name is Despaldi. I am captain of the Midnight Guard. I have been waiting for you." He took Haelynn's hand, bent, and kissed it before rising. "It is a pleasure to meet such a beauty, Wizardess Elana."

Haelynn beamed. "You flatter me, Captain. If I were not married, I might find myself smitten."

The man's smile faltered, his eyes flicking to Jerrell, who grimaced. "Yes. Well...too bad for me, I suppose. Please follow me. I will deliver you to the throne room."

The man spun on his heel and walked through the gate with Jerrell and Haelynn close behind. Jerrell took note of the man's interesting baldric, which carried a falchion with a jewel-encrusted hilt. His long-legged gait was purposeful, his chest thrust out. Stories of Despaldi were not uncommon in the streets and taprooms of Marquithe. The man was purported to be strict, stern, and displayed little patience for anything other than law and order – he was known to be harsh and cruel to anyone who strayed outside those lines.

They ascended the palace stairs and passed through the front door. Without pausing, Despaldi marched them across the entrance hall to a stairwell at the rear. There, they ascended four levels before entering a corridor. A pair of guards stood beside an open doorway. The two men nodded and moved aside as Despaldi entered the room with Jerrell and Haelynn strides behind him.

A sprawling room lay before them, an elaborate dining table occupying the heart of the chamber. The far wall was covered in windows made of diamond-shaped panes. Outside, the sun hovered above the mountains to the west, the glowing orb eclipsed by the silhouette of a tall, broad-shouldered man in midnight-blue trimmed silver robes. The wizard's size, bearing, and garb made him easy to identify. Malvorian. Another wizard in dark blue robes stood beside him. He had shoulder-length brown hair, a slim build, and stood a half a head shorter than the wizard lord. The two were talking softly until the smaller man bowed, turned, and crossed the room. His squinty eyes examined Jerrell and a smirk played with his lips, above which was a thin mustache.

The wizard did not say a word until he reached Despaldi's side, when he announced, "Your Majesty, you have guests."

With his hands clasped behind his back, Malvorian turned around to reveal a black beard, long, black hair, and dark, cold eyes. He appeared to be no older than fifty, yet he was rumored to be well over a hundred years old.

"Lord Malvorian," Despaldi dropped to one knee. "I bring your guests, High Wizard Halvish and his wife, Elana, from Tangor."

"Thank you, Captain," Malvorian's deep voice boomed. "You and Minister Thurvin are dismissed." When the wizard and uniformed man left, Malvorian crossed the room. He stopped before Jerrell and extended a hand. "Welcome to Marquithe."

Jerrell shook his hand. "It is an interesting city."

The wizard arched his brow. "I realize you hail from another wizardom, but I am unused to others omitting my title."

Oh crap. Jerrell suddenly recalled the wizard's anger when he found Jerrell spying on him. Lightning flashed before his eyes. He had narrowly avoided death in a daring escape. *What if he recognizes me?* The spectacles, robes, and beard made it unlikely. Yet, he stood before a wizard with unlimited power and realized he had best behave. He considered apologizing but could not bring himself to do so. "You are a man, as am I. Your station brings certain privileges and your ability to channel Farrow's magic makes my abilities pale when compared to yours, but at our core, we are still both men." When Malvorian grimaced, Jerrell hugged Haelynn against his side. "And, as men, we are slaves to the whims of beautiful women."

The wizard lord's gaze shifted from Jerrell to Haelynn and back. He burst out laughing and clapped Jerrell on the shoulder. "Too true, my friend. Too true." He turned and waved for Jerrell to follow. "Come. Let us sit and have a glass of wine while we wait for the others to arrive."

Others? Jerrell arched a brow at Haelynn, took her arm, and led her to the table. Malvorian flicked his fingers and a narrow cone of flames shot out from them, lighting the eight-candle candelabra. He then sat in the chair at the head of the table.

After circling the table, so he had a view of the door, Jerrell pulled out a chair and waited while Haelynn took a seat beside Malvorian. He then claimed the chair beside hers. "Thank you for inviting us to dine with you."

"It was Minister Thurvin's idea. He believes it is best that I get to know the leaders of the neighboring wizardoms."

Jerrell said, "You flatter me. While I govern a modest city on our western coast, Lord Taladain is the true leader of Ghealdor."

"Yes. Taladain sits upon the crystal throne of Gheald, which makes him the unquestioned leader so long as he lives."

Unsure of what Malvorian was inferring, Jerrell simply nodded.

"Just remember"—Malvorian smiled— "the man is over two hundred years old and not even we wizard lords live forever."

Despaldi appeared in the doorway. "Pardon me, Your Majesty, but your other two guests have just arrived from Souton."

Souton? Jerrell stiffened.

A robed wizard and a tall, swarthy man with a pointed black goatee entered the room. Jerrell recognized both men immediately. *Why are Roka and Razak here?* He then recalled Haelynn's attempt on Roka's life the last time she saw him. Jerrell gripped her hand, fearing she might do something rash.

She whispered, "Do not worry. I'll not attack Roka so long as you leave Razak alone as well."

Malvorian rose to his feet. "Roka. I feared you might not arrive in time for dinner."

The high wizard of Souton walked in. "When I received your summons, I came straightaway."

"This must be the trader I have heard so much about."

Razak frowned. Roka jerked back as if slapped, and fear flickered in his eyes.

Malvorian sneered. "What's wrong, Roka? Did you honestly believe I was unaware of your agreement with Sarazan?"

The wizard from Souton stammered. "I...I don't know of what you speak."

Malvorian roared. "Do not lie to me!"

Both Roka and Razak backed up a step. Razak turned toward the door, but Despaldi blocked his way with two guards behind him. All three drew their swords, and the sound of metal reverberated throughout the room.

"There is no escape," the wizard lord sneered. "The time has come for you to pay for your betrayal. But first, you will tell me why you did it."

Roka narrowed his eyes, pressed his lips together, and appeared unwilling to speak.

Malvorian raised a clenched fist, and the hair on Jerrell's arms stood on end. The tingle of magic was so intense, it was nearly unbearable. Roka's eyes widened and he stumbled back a step.

"Yes," the wizard lord crooned. "Now you better understand the breadth of my magic. How did you ever think you could challenge me?"

"I...I was promised an enchanted item – a hand chain of some sort. It was said to boost my magic three-fold."

The wizard lord arched a brow. "Such an item exists?"

"I don't know. I never received it."

Jerrell knew. He had seen such a capability in the bracelet he stole from Montague and later gave to Gurgan. *So, there* are *other items that augment magic.* Objects of such power were bound to be highly desired by wizards, offering the potential for added wealth but at what cost? The conundrum had led him to give the bracelet to Gurgan, a wizard he had come to respect.

The wizard lord said, "I now understand why you sent that young woman to Sarazan. Too bad for you, she has been returned to Marquithe and is safe from your schemes. I had wondered what Sarazan offered in exchange for the woman and what your motivation might be." He thrust a finger toward Roka, who flinched in response. "Backed by an army of your own, you thought to boost your magic, kill me, and place yourself in the position to gain the throne of Farrow."

Roka blinked. "How...how did you know?"

Malvorian smirked. "I learned this from a thief named Jerrell Landish."

Briefly forgetting his disguise, Jerrell smiled. *My letter.* His smile faded when he realized what the man had said. *But how does he know it was from me?*

Razak grunted. "A thief? How can you trust the word of a thief?"

"This man is no mere thief, Mister Razak. You see, he is the one who destroyed your ranch and the cache of weapons you had assembled, but not before he found proof of your own role in Roka's scheme." The wizard tilted his head while staring at Razak. "I know Roka awarded you with a contract to conduct all silver deliveries."

"I am a businessman and made a business deal. There is no harm in that."

"Those silver mines belong to Farrowen, as do the goods they produce. When they are shipped off to a foreign nation without Farrowen receiving any compensation, plenty of harm has been done. However, I hear you ran into trouble and lost a full wagon of silver a number of weeks ago."

Razak blinked. "What do you know about that?"

"Jerrell Landish, the same thief who destroyed your ranch, stole that load of silver and sold it to the enchanters here in Marquithe. Frankly, in doing so, he did me a favor. The enchanters were quite disgruntled and had they not found a source for silver, they might have become a problem for me."

Jerrell glanced at Haelynn and mouthed *How does he know*?

She shrugged, but Jerrell did not believe it. Other than Haelynn, only Desmond and Lamond knew about his role in the ranch fire and the silver theft.

Malvorian turned to Roka. "Your agreement to send silver deliveries to Sarazan is a betrayal of my trust. You intended to buy yourself a small army, along with the weapons needed to attack my palace, my home!" Malvorian's voice rose until he bellowed the last words.

Roka shook his head.

"Don't deny it, Roka. Lies will not save you."

Roka suddenly thrust his hands toward Malvorian. A magic-powered blast launched the wizard lord toward the table where Jerrell and Haelynn were seated. Jerrell dove sideways and wrapped his arm around the woman as their chairs toppled to the tile floor. Malvorian smacked into the candelabra, sending it spinning through the air. The wizard lord then crashed through the window, shattering it. In a shower of glass, he plummeted toward the ground, five stories below.

The room fell silent, everyone held in a state of shock. The curtains caught on fire, fed by the flames of the candelabra as Jerrell helped Haelynn to stand.

"I did it," Roka exclaimed. "I killed Malvorian!"

He turned toward Despaldi and the two guards still blocking the doorway. "Your wizard lord is dead. I claim the right to rule until the next Darkening, when I can be properly raised to wizard lord."

Despaldi scowled and lowered his falchion – the two guards behind him the same. The curtains burned hotter, forcing Jerrell and Haelynn to back from the windows.

Suddenly, a dark silhouette rose and eclipsed the setting sun outside the broken window. With arms spread wide and his torn robes fluttering in the breeze, Malvorian floated forward, past the growing fire, and landed on the table. Roka backed away, his eyes wide.

"You thought you could kill me?" A sinister smile lay nestled in Malvorian's beard. "You vastly underestimate the might of Farrow."

The wizard lord flicked his fingers and the burning curtains snuffed out, sending a puff of black smoke toward the high ceiling. Again, he flicked his fingers, this time launching Razak across the room. The man smashed into the stone fireplace with frightening force, surely breaking every bone in his body. His limp remains fell forward to the floor, the back of his crushed skull covered in blood and brain matter.

"Your turn, Roka."

Rather than flee, Roka chose to fight. He sent a blast of lightning at Malvorian, but the wizard lord waved his hands and sent the bolts arcing toward another window, which shattered. He then sliced downward with one hand. Roka's eyes bulged, his mouth gaped, and nothing else moved. At first, Jerrell wondered if Malvorian had somehow missed with his spell. Then, Roka collapsed, half of his body falling to the right, the other half to the left, his head and torso split clean down the center.

Malvorian floated down from the table and examined his torn robes. "I must apologize, Halvish. Dinner did not go quite as planned. The table is a mess, the dining room destroyed, and I must change into a fresh set of robes. Thus, we must postpone our meal for another time."

Jerrell closed his jaw and recovered enough to say. "Completely understandable, Your Majesty. My wife and I will eat at our inn."

"Perhaps you could join me tomorrow?"

"I am sorry, but tomorrow, we are bound for Lionne, where we are to meet with High Wizard Montague to negotiate this year's wine imports."

"Ah. That is a shame. I was hoping to get to know you better."

"We were as well."

The wizard lord gestured toward the two halves of Roka. "At least you now understand how I deal with those who defy my will."

Jerrell frowned. *Why would he say that to a high wizard from another wizardom?*

"Despaldi," Malvorian said. "Please escort my guests. Ensure they reach their inn without incident."

The captain of the Midnight Guard dipped his head. "As you wish, Your Majesty."

The wizard lord of Farrowen then stepped over his rival wizard and swept out of the room.

CHAPTER 28
NEW BEGINNINGS

A hood covered Jerrell's head. He kept his chin down and face cast in shadow as he walked in step with the other clerics. Like them, he wore loose white robes trimmed in midnight blue. Dressed in robes of gold and blue, High Priestess Sheuren led the group from the temple toward Marquithe Palace.

Jerrell's robes chafed at the shoulders, but the tight fit did not appear to catch anyone's notice. The young man he had stolen the robes from remained unconscious, bound, and gagged should he wake before Jerrell returned to free him. With Devotion over, night upon them, and the temple emptied, he was unlikely to be found until morning. By then, Jerrell's mission would be complete, and he would be long gone. *Until then, sleep well, young man.* After drugging the cleric, Jerrell had whispered an apology in his ear, but the unconscious man refused to accept such sentiments, which Jerrell considered inconsiderate.

They walked to the far end of a dark corridor, and then headed up two flights of stairs before traveling along another hallway and into a chamber furnished with two circular tables surrounded by chairs. The scent of baked bread wafted past Jerrell's nose, reminding him that he had yet to eat.

The priestess spun around, her black hair tied back in a bun, her dark eyes serious, her scowl ever-present. "Eat and get to bed. You've an early morning tomorrow. Anyone not in the temple at sunrise will be disciplined."

Sheuren turned and strode off. The clerics lowered their hoods and found seats at the tables. Jerrell hesitated, unwilling to expose himself. *Time to leave.* With his hood still raised, he turned toward the corridor.

"Alec. Where are you going?" one of the clerics asked.

Over his shoulder, Jerrell replied in a tight voice, as if straining. "The privy. It's an emergency."

The cleric chuckled. "I told you not to eat all of those sweetcakes at the reception."

"Yeah. Got to go."

He rushed off, turned the corner, and slowed to a casual walk. A guard waited at the end of the corridor, monitoring his approach.

When Jerrell attempted to pass through the door beside the guard, the man placed a meaty hand on Jerrell's chest and stopped him cold. "What business do you have in the palace?"

His face still shadowed by his hood, Jerrell looked down and fidgeted. When he spoke, it was in a higher tone than usual and lacking in confidence. "I am not supposed to say."

"Well, then I am not supposed to allow you past me."

"I am to visit...Chancellor Wexall."

"Does the chancellor know of this visit?"

"Yes. He invited me earlier, prior to Devotion."

"Invited you to what?"

"To dine with him and...more."

"More?"

Jerrell sighed, as if losing patience, which was true. "Surely, you must be aware of Wexall's preferences."

"Preferences?"

The guard's brow furrowed as a memory from a week earlier replayed in Jerrell's head.

~

RAUCOUS LAUGHTER RANG throughout the Storm Cell, the tavern packed with occupants still wearing armor of the city watch. Clean-shaven, his hair parted to the side to suit his persona as a puffed-up fop, Jerrell straightened the collar of his doublet and sauntered across the room. A brawny guard bumped into him, and Jerrell overtly stumbled before righting himself.

"Pardon me," he patted the man on the arm before giving his bicep a squeeze. "My, my, aren't you a muscular one."

The man growled, "Get your hands off me, or I'll break your fingers."

Jerrell urgently yanked his hand back and held it up, using his nasal tone. "Sorry."

"I think it best if you left. Your kind is not wanted around here."

The guard was not alone – three of his companions glared back with fire in their eyes.

Jerrell flipped his hand with flamboyance. "I would like nothing better, but I came looking for my friend. He is roughly my height with tan skin and black hair. He looks to be in his late teens and dresses in breeches one size too small. Have you seen him?"

"This is a guard taproom. Why would someone like that be here?"

Jerrell pressed his fists against his hips and tilted his head. "Because Ramon always eyes the brawny ones. It is no wonder he agreed to spend those nights with Wexall."

The guard frowned. "Chancellor Wexall?"

"That's the one."

"What would he have to do with the chancellor?"

"Ramon claims it was for the gold, but I have my doubts. Regardless, Wexall no longer calls on him. Apparently, the chancellor has found a new plaything among the palace temple clerics."

The four guards chuckled.

Jerrell craned his neck, searching the room. "Have you seen Ramon?"

Another guard answered, "You'll find nobody like that here. I suggest you go looking at the Fluffy Pillow. Your type frequents that establishment."

Scowling, Jerrell snapped, "Don't you think I looked there?"

The man blinked, taken aback. "I suppose you might have...but he is not here, so you had best move along."

"Fine." Jerrell spun on one heel and sashayed out the door.

The rumor had been planted and it would only take a day or two to reach the palace guards, well before his late-night visit.

PUSHING THE MEMORY ASIDE, Jerrell stared at the guard blocking his way and waited for the inference to process.

The man grunted. "Wexall? I thought that was only a rumor."

"You must be new here," Jerrell said.

"Well, I rarely work this door, so..."

Interrupting him, Jerrell pleaded, "Please, just let me through so I can get this over with."

"Over with?" The man's brow furrowed. "You don't enjoy his...attention?"

"I enjoy the gold he gives me for my...performance." An unsure shrug added to Jerrell's apparent indifference.

The guard grunted and stepped aside. "Go on. I've heard enough. When you return this way, please avoid sharing any details."

"Thank you." Jerrell slid past the man and entered the palace.

HOURS LATER, Jerrell slipped out of a fourth-story closet and crept down an empty corridor, still dressed as a cleric. He reached a closed door and tested it. Locked. Inside his robes, he found his lock picks. Moments later, the knob turned, and he eased into the dark chamber beyond.

A moonbeam streaming through the window gave shape to the room, revealing a divan and table to one side, beyond which was a desk and chair. A deep snore arose from a four-poster bed that dominated the other side of the room.

Jerrell reached into his robes again, dug out a vial, and removed the stopper, careful to hold both far from his face. Following the rumble of another snore, he crept to the side of the bed. The pale moonlight outlined the profile of a man with a trimmed beard, his face toward the ceiling. Jerrell recognized the wizard from his spying adventure above the palace throne room. *Chancellor Wexall.*

With care, Jerrell brought the vial to the sleeping wizard's chin and poured a drop of liquid into his open mouth. Wexall smacked his lips, swallowing the drug. Twice more, Jerrell repeated the process. With the third drop, the man stirred and blinked his eyes open. Jerrell yanked his hand back and froze.

The chancellor coughed, sat up, and rubbed his eyes, all the while grunting and groaning. The man's bare arms, shoulders, and chest were covered in muscle rarely seen on a wizard. He turned toward the window, his gaze sweeping the room until it landed on Jerrell.

Wexall jerked with a start. "What are you doing in my chamber?"

In a soft tone, Jerrell said, "I came as requested, Master Wexall."

"Requested?"

"Of course."

"I never..." The man wavered and put a hand to his forehead. "I don't feel so..." He collapsed with his head on the pillow and lay still.

Jerrell leaned close and felt Wexall's breath on his cheek, confirming the wizard was still alive. He shoved Wexall and gently slapped his cheek but got no response. Satisfied, he dug into his robes and removed a quill, an inkwell, and a waterskin filled with something other than water. He set those items down and picked up a flint, which he used to light the candle on the nightstand.

Beneath the flickering candlelight, Jerrell unfolded a parchment with two runes drawn on it. Studying the first carefully, he dipped the quill into the ink, bent over the unconscious wizard, and began drawing on the man's chest.

"Help!" Jerrell shrieked before yanking Wexall's chamber door open. He stumbled into the corridor and fell to his hands and knees. "Help!" he cried in a whimpering voice.

Footsteps stormed down the corridor. A pair of guards in silver plate appeared from the gloom, their midnight blue capes flapping behind them as they slowed.

A guard with a thick brown beard asked, "What happened?"

Still on the floor, Jerrell clutched his torn cleric robes to his chest and pointed toward the room. "It's Wexall. He sought to drain my blood for a ritual of dark magic!"

"What?"

"He said my sacrifice would help him rise to greatness."

The other guard, tall and lean with a thin mustache, snorted. "What sort of nonsense is—"

The first guard stopped the man by gripping his shoulder, his eyes on something in Wexall's room. "Look."

Dressed only in his smallclothes, the wizard lay on the floor at the foot of the bed. His head rested on his shoulder, the side of his head bloody. A small statue lay on the floor beside him, and a complex rune was visible on the man's chest.

"What did you do to him?" the tall guard asked.

"I was desperate," Jerrell whined. "When he came at me, I grabbed the only thing I could find and hit him on the head. I swear to Farrow, it was me or him."

The guards walked into the room, one squatting beside the incapacitated wizard, the other examining the eight-pointed star covering the floor — the shape drawn with the pig's blood from Jerrell's waterskin. A crimson circle ten feet in diameter encompassed the star.

"Have you ever seen something like this?" the bearded guard asked the other.

"No. Then again, what do I know of magic?"

The first guard walked over to the desk and picked up a parchment covered in script and runes. "And look at this."

Growing impatient for the two men to reach the obvious conclusion, Jerrell helped them along. "It is sorcery! Black magic, long forbidden! He was going to take my blood to augment his own magic. With it, he claimed he could defeat Malvorian and rule Farrowen."

One guard looked at the other. "Should we wake Malvorian?"

"I say we go to Despaldi first."

"Right." The guards stormed past Jerrell, one of them stopping in the corridor to look back at Jerrell. "Wait here. If Wexall wakes, don't let him leave."

"What? He is a wizard. How do I do that?"

"You hit him once. Do it again if you must. We will be right back."

The guards rushed down the corridor. When they faded from view, Jerrell turned and snuck down the hallway, heading back toward the temple.

JERRELL OPENED the door to an office on the top floor of the Bureau. He entered a dark room illuminated only by a flickering candle in the corner and sat across from the shadowy figure. "It is done."

"Yes." The Whispering Man nodded. "Malvorian interrogated Wexall this morning. It did not go well for the former chancellor."

"Former?"

"Wexall made the mistake of attempting to defend himself. As you are likely to surmise, his magic was insufficient against Malvorian's might. Malvorian's guards later hauled what remained of Wexall from the throne room and posted the corpse on a pike above the palace gate."

The wizard died because of me. Jerrell pushed his guilt aside. *It was a contract. If not me, someone else would have been paid to do the deed. Regardless, it wasn't me who ended his life.* "I'll take my gold now."

The Whispering Man tossed a pouch to Jerrell. "You will find twenty gold inside."

"Twenty?" Jerrell had been promised half that amount.

"You earned it, Jerrell. The extra gold is another reward of our arrangement, one I hope will continue for many years."

The weight of the bag satisfied Jerrell's hunger for wealth but left his curiosity wanting. "I need to know. Why Wexall?"

The man leaned back with his fingers tented before his shadowed face. After a silent beat, he said, "Wexall was in the way."

"Whose way?"

"Of the wizard who has been promoted to replace him."

"Who is that?"

"Thurvin Arnole."

Jerrell recalled the man from his meeting with Malvorian. He had seemed more a worm than a wizard. "Is he up to the task?"

"Oh, yes," the Whispering Man crooned. "While Thurvin is not a powerful wizard, he is highly intelligent and more than capable of excelling as Malvorian's most trusted advisor. His impact will be felt throughout Marquithe and beyond. With him at Malvorian's side, Farrowen will rise above other wizardoms."

Rise above? "Why do you care for Farrowen's welfare?"

"Think, Jerrell."

The answer was obvious. "Because your little kingdom will thrive so long as Malvorian's does."

The man chuckled. "How astute. Which brings up another aspect of our arrangement."

"What other aspect?"

"You've an ear to the streets, are smart enough to know when something is amiss, and are discerning enough to differentiate the wild rumors from those that are true."

"Your point?"

"If you come across information that affects Malvorian, Marquithe, or any other part of Farrowen, bring it to me. You will be compensated commensurate to the value of such information."

Jerrell frowned. "You want me to spy for you?"

"Consider it another source of income. After all, what do you have to lose by sharing rumors before they reach my ears by another route?"

"I will consider it."

"Good enough for now. I will send for you when I have need of your talents again. Until then, stay out of trouble."

Sensing he was being dismissed, Jerrell stood and turned to the door.

"One more thing," the Whispering Man said, "you will hear your name connected to Wexall's downfall, as has been whispered with the downfall of

High Wizard Roka. As promised, your fame will grow quickly. However, I suspect you will come to resent the notoriety you seek."

"Why do you say that?"

"Anonymity offers advantages of its own. To lose that…well, I think you will look back on it and see what I mean."

Jerrell left the room with the man's final words on his mind.

He had sought fame, and now that his exploits had begun to spread like fireside tales, his name would be widely known. The realization filled his chest with a satisfying warmth. *The world will finally acknowledge my skill.* Then, unwanted memories invaded – his failure in saving Everett Gurgan, Haelynn fleecing him out of a fortune in gold. The teen's death had haunted Jerrell, and Haelynn's betrayal had damaged him more than he would ever admit.

Others cannot be trusted, he told himself. *It is why I, Jerrell Landish, work alone. As the greatest thief in the Eight Wizardoms, I will rise until I can replace the Whispering Man himself.*

The End?

Jerrell then goes on to work for the Whispering Man…
Until he finds himself caught in the schemes of a wizard lord intent on world domination.
Join Jerrell and a compelling cast of characters in

Fate of Wizardoms

Note from the Author

You can read more about Jerrell in **Fate of Wizardoms** and **Fall of Wizardoms**, both fantasy series featuring a squad of misfit heroes caught in an epic struggle that will forever alter their world.

I hope you enjoyed Jerrell's solo adventures.

Another Wizardom Legends series releases in 2023.

If you would like to be among the first to know, join my author newsletter and NEVER miss a release, promotion, or giveaway. As a gift for joining, you will receive five Wizardoms companion novellas. If you are interested, proceed to www.JeffreyLKohanek.com.

Best Wishes,
Jeff

Follow me on:
Amazon
Bookbub
Facebook

ALSO BY JEFFREY L. KOHANEK

Fate of Wizardoms

Eye of Obscurance

Balance of Magic

Temple of the Oracle

Objects of Power

Rise of a Wizard Queen

A Contest of Gods

* * *

Fate of Wizardoms Boxed Set: Books 1-3

Fate of Wizardoms Box Set: Books 4-6

Fate of Wizardoms: The Complete Epic Series

Fall of Wizardoms

God King Rising

Legend of the Sky Sword

Curse of the Elf Queen

Shadow of a Dragon Priest

Advent of the Drow

A Sundered Realm

* * *

Fall of Wizardoms Box Set: Books 1-3

Fall of Wizardoms Box Set: Books 4-6

Wizardoms Legends:

The Outrageous Exploits of Jerrell Landish

Thief for Hire

Trickster for Hire

Charlatan for Hire

Runes of Issalia

The Buried Symbol

The Emblem Throne

An Empire in Runes

* * *

Runes of Issalia Bonus Box

Wardens of Issalia

A Warden's Purpose

The Arcane Ward:

An Imperial Gambit

A Kingdom Under Siege

* * *

Wardens of Issalia Boxed Set